MW01531166

Torn Asunder

Also by Donna Van Cleve

Grace Falling Like Rain

Mercy's Face

Torn Asunder

Donna Van Cleve

Two Story Publishing House
Hutto, Texas

Torn Asunder
Published by
Two Story Publishing House
P.O. Box 482
Hutto, Texas 78634

Copyright ©2008 by Donna Van Cleve
www.donnavancleve.com
Email: donna@donnavancleve.com

This book is a work of fiction. Names, characters, places and incidents are the products of the author's imagination or are used fictitiously.

Publisher's Cataloging-in-Publication Data

Van Cleve, Donna C.
Torn Asunder / Donna Van Cleve
269 p. cm.
ISBN 978-0-9787937-7-7 (pb)
1. Texas—Fiction. 2. Fence Cutters War— Texas—Fiction.
3. Brown County—Texas—Fiction. 4. Christian – Fiction.

2008901604

On the Cover:

Photo credits: Christy Roeder taken by Vanessa Roeder

For
Rick & Terri
&
Marsha & Bruce

In memory of their precious sons:

Cliff Beights
&
Brad Dockery

Acknowledgments

Thank you, *Sisterhood of the Comfy Socks*:
Vanessa, Audrie, Christy, & Susan
for your amazing support and encouragement.
My life is so much richer with you in it.

Thank you, CJ, for all your help—
several times over;
you're the best.

Thank you, *Texas State Historical Society*, for making available
The Handbook of Texas Online—
one of the best resources for Texas history.

Thank you, Dad & Mom & Jack, for all your tales & experiences,
many of which have found their way
into my stories.

Thank you, to the Great Physician
to whom we can go
whenever our lives & hearts
have been torn asunder

I also want to acknowledge
a good friend from my 4th - 6th grade years:
Annette Hill Snodgrass,
who could outrun every boy in elementary school
in Dell City, Texas

Chapter 1

Waco, Texas... November, 1883

J immy Taylor watched the burly man jerk on the reins of his horse, causing the grulla mare to back up and fling her head from one side to the other. Jimmy knew the horse was so confused she didn't know what she was supposed to do.

The man spurred her forward and jerked back on the reins again.

Jimmy exhaled loudly and looked away.

Julia glanced at her youngest son. His blue eyes burned pale against his dark skin when he was angry. She knew he couldn't stand to watch anyone mistreat a horse. But the Taylors weren't the only ones upset by the scene. Other folks on the street stopped to stare.

"Why is that man being mean to his horse, Daddy?" asked the little boy sitting between the two adults on the carriage seat.

"He's an idiot," said Jimmy, glaring at the man who seemed to be oblivious to the disturbance he was causing.

"What your father is trying to say, sweetheart, is that the man doesn't know how to properly handle a horse," Julia said to Jack, her five-year-old grandson.

"Little Jack knows more about handling a horse than that fool."

"He could stand to take some lessons from you."

"Good idea," said Jimmy, handing his mother the reins and climbing out of the carriage.

"Hold on, son! That's his horse—you can't do anything about that."

"I can at least try," he said over his shoulder as he walked across the street.

1

Julia watched her son approach the man and speak to him. She quickly looked around for anyone that might help if the conversation turned into a fight. But after more words, the man seemed taken aback for a moment. She held her breath as the man climbed off the horse and faced her son. She watched Jimmy offer the man his hand, and her mouth dropped open when the man shook it firmly. Then he turned and tied the horse to a hitching rail before walking over to stand beside several men outside an establishment known to encourage imbibing.

Several men in the street patted Jimmy on the shoulders as he walked back over to the carriage.

"What did you say to him?" asked Julia, shocked to see how easily Jimmy had changed the situation.

"I offered to buy the horse from him, and he agreed," he said.

"Good for you!"

"But at twice what she's worth."

"Oh!" Julia raised her eyes and smiled. "I hope you know you're not going to stay in the horse business for very long if you keep that up."

Jimmy grinned and nodded. "I'll make her worth my while eventually. But right now I need to go to the bank and withdraw some money. If Mercy comes back, tell her where I've gone. But I'm sure I'll be back before she finishes in the mercantile. You know my wife."

"Don't you fuss at her—she's just trying to find the best deal," Julia defended her daughter-in-law. "Mercy's become quite the money manager in your family. And you know she's not going to be happy about this horse deal."

"She won't mind when she finds out how he was abusing that mare. She feels the same as I do about horses."

"Don't forget to get a signed receipt from that man."

Jimmy waved a hand in agreement as he walked quickly down the street.

Julia looked down and smiled at her grandson. He had a good sprinkling of both of his parents—the olive-colored skin of his father, the blonde hair of his mother, and those piercing blue Taylor eyes.

Jack was looking across the street.

"What color is that horse, Meemaw?" he asked.

"It's called a grulla."

"It sounds like what Nah-kay calls you—Jew-ya—grew-ya."

"You're right!" Julia laughed. "How did you get so smart?"

He shrugged his shoulders.

"Well, I think the word *grulla* comes from a Spanish word meaning some kind of blue-gray bird," she explained.

Jack looked around at the sky. "Where did all the birds go, Meemaw?"

"When the weather starts to get cold, they pick up and fly south where it's warmer."

"How do they know how to do that?"

"I don't exactly know," said Julia. "God just put that instinct in them to go where it's warmer. That way they'll survive the cold months and come back so we can enjoy them."

"What's instinct?" He looked up at his grandmother.

"Hmmm." Julia smiled and thought for a moment. "I guess you can say instinct is a built-in knowledge. Birds build nests and fly south when they're supposed to without even thinking about it."

"Maybe some of them stayed later this time." Jack looked around.

"Maybe…"

"Do people have instincts?"

"I'm convinced your father has instincts when it comes to horses. And I know God puts things on our hearts at times, but I'm not sure if that's instinct or just God speaking to us."

"Have you really heard God speak?" Jack asked with wide eyes.

"Not out loud. Sometimes it's a strong feeling about someone or something we need to do."

"I think God's speaking to my tummy," he said.

"He is? What's He saying?"

"He's saying that I'm hungry."

Julia laughed and put her arm around Jack and squeezed him. "I think He's speaking to mine, too. Now where is your Momma?"

After a short while, Jimmy returned with an envelope and receipt and found the man where he left him. The man printed a simple scrawl of an initial and his last name, Hulsbam, on the receipt and took the money and slipped it inside his shirt. He turned around and picked up the saddle he had taken off the horse, and snickered as he ambled off. But Jimmy didn't care. He walked over to the mare as she tried to shy away from him.

"I know, girl," he said in a soothing voice, standing there for a moment to let her get used to him. "I'm not going to hurt you. Everything's going to be fine now."

He looked her over and noticed she was thin under a raggedy coat, but she had a good frame on her. Her brown eyes kept watching him warily. She had intelligent eyes.

"You're a smart girl, aren't you," he said softly. "You were trying to do what he wanted you to do, but he kept giving you mixed signals, didn't he."

He kept talking to her and slowly reached over to rub her neck. Her hide shuddered at the first touch, but eventually relaxed as he continued to rub her.

After a few minutes, Jimmy led her across the street and tied her to the back of the carriage.

"That horse doesn't know how fortunate she is," said Julia, "but most everyone else on this street does, don't they, Jack."

Jack nodded his head firmly in agreement with his grandmother.

Jimmy grinned at two of his biggest supporters in this world.

"Can I ride her, Daddy?"

Someone hollered angrily from across the street.

"Soon," he said, turning to see what the commotion was about.

He was surprised to see a young man stomping across the street towards them. He stopped in the middle of the street and yelled.

"Hey, you there!! Are you stealing my horse?"

Jimmy looked around to see who the man was yelling at.

"I'm talking to you, you damn thief!" the man said angrily.

"Now hold on—you're mistaken," Jimmy said as he started walking towards him. He looked down and pulled open his coat with his left hand and reached in the pocket for the receipt. "I just bought this—"

The sound of a gunshot interrupted him. Jimmy's head jerked up to see the man standing there with a gun drawn. He heard a cry from behind him and turned to see his mother slump against his son. A red stain blossomed across her shoulder.

He whirled around to face the man with the gun and screamed, "You just shot my mother!"

Jimmy saw the man's eyes widen as he pointed his gun at Jimmy again and fired, and this time he didn't miss.

Jimmy's head jerked back sharply before he crumpled to the ground.

Several men tackled the shooter and wrested the gun away from him.

"Somebody get the sheriff!"

"He was stealing my horse!" the man shouted. "And he was going for his gun!"

"You half-wit!! He was reaching for his receipt!" said one of the men as he pinned him to the ground.

"Don't you know who that is?" another man said. "Jimmy Taylor bought that horse fair and square."

"But I didn't sell him my horse!"

"Your *father* sold your horse, Carp! Not twenty minutes ago!"

Julia gripped the armrest of the carriage trying to stay upright. All she heard for a moment was a roaring in her head, and her peripheral vision clouded to the point that she thought she was looking down the barrel of a rifle. But even that started to go black, so she shook her head and took a deep breath as she tried to concentrate. What just happened? Was she having a bad dream? She shook her head again to try to clear it. Julia could see people running and shouting in the street, but the noise sounded muffled, like it was coming from far away. Her shoulder burned like fire. She looked down at her dress and saw a dark stain spreading. She touched it and pulled away a bloody hand.

The air was crisp—why did she notice that? The birds were gone. Horses and men ran back and forth in front of her, stirring up the dust. She could see some men wrestling on the ground. Another man lay unmoving in front of them.

She watched a little boy dodge through the big horses and run up to the motionless figure. Her heart caught in her throat to see him standing over his father crying.

She almost let her eyes close, feeling faint again, but some familiar memory flashed like lightning across her mind. Her eyes flew open with a start. She looked up at the cloudless sky and then back at the scene before her and remembered. Her heart almost stopped with the realization.

"No... no... no," she cried. "I need more time!"

Jimmy! She must get to Jimmy!

Several people stood beside the carriage blocking her way. They looked concerned. Had they said something to her? They reached for her when she started to climb down and half fell into their arms when her left arm refused to support her. She pushed her way through the crowd of people in the street and knelt by the little boy standing over his father.

"Daddy!" he cried. "Why won't he get up?"

Julia put her good arm around him to steady herself as much as to comfort him.

"I'm so sorry, Jimmy. You shouldn't be here, honey—you should never have seen this."

Someone reached down and plucked the little boy from beside her. "Mrs. Taylor, you're hurt."

"Give me a moment," she said to the man. "Where's Nah-kay? Can someone find her? I need to see her before we go. Is my husband here? Where's Matthew?"

The man just stood there staring at her. Julia didn't have the strength to repeat the words. She turned around and reached over to touch the motionless figure. She looked at his handsome face. Blood matted his hair on the side of his head where he'd been shot.

"I wasn't ready, Lord—I thought I'd have more time!"

A sob escaped her lips as she leaned over to lay her head down on his chest when someone screamed—screamed loud and very close. Julia looked up to see a beautiful, flaxen haired woman drop down opposite her. Her cheek was scarred. Nah-kay's cheek was scarred, but this wasn't Nah-kay. What was this woman doing here?

"Who are you?" Julia asked the woman, frowning at her. "This is not your place."

In the midst of her grief, the woman stopped wailing and stared, wide-eyed at her.

"Julia? What happened here? I don't understand what you're saying."

"Then listen to me! He told me this would happen."

"Julia, you're bleeding! You've been shot, too," the woman said. She looked up, beyond Julia. "She must be delirious, babbling on that way. Did someone send for a doctor?"

A voice from the crowd answered yes.

Julia watched the young woman put her hand on the lifeless chest and lean over to look at his face. She spoke softly to him.

"What are you doing? He can't hear you now," said Julia sadly.

The woman looked up at Julia. "What are you saying to me?" she asked, pleading.

The answer came in a whisper, but it wasn't from Julia. It came from the body lying on the ground.

"She's speaking my grandmother's language," said Jimmy, weakly. "She's speaking Apache."

Julia gasped as she stared at him.

"Nantan?" she whispered as the roaring filled her ears again. She turned to look for Jimmy. Where was Jimmy? She saw that the man still held her little boy behind her. He was safe.

Julia looked down again and noticed a white feather on the ground. She exhaled and her body relaxed as a ghost of a smile graced her lips at the reminder.

The darkness came for her again, and this time she let it take her.

Chapter 2

M atthew Taylor rode his horse past the fancy hitching rail and right up to the steps of the massive front porch of the Locke mansion. After Pate Janek came to tell them that Julia and Jimmy had both been shot in Waco, Matthew and his oldest son Matt had ridden hard and fast from their hometown of Grace—normally a ninety minute ride by buggy. Matthew didn't know how seriously injured they were—he was simply told to come.

Matt pulled up behind his father and told him he would take care of the horses. Matthew dropped the reins and ran up the steps. He didn't bother to knock before he threw open the door and rushed inside to look for his wife and son.

In the parlor to the left, Matthew saw Mercy's father Langston Locke on the floor with little Jack. He walked over to the boy and scooped him up and hugged him tight.

"Are you all right, Pony?" Matthew asked his grandson, using the nickname he had given him several years before.

The little boy nodded solemnly.

"Thank God." Matthew looked at Langston. "Where are they?"

"On down the hall, in the last room on the right," said Langston. "Mercy had us put them in the same room for now since the other bedrooms are upstairs."

Matthew told Jack that he would see him again in a little while and handed him to Langston.

He strode quickly down the hall and paused before the closed door. He had no idea what to expect, other than he knew they were both alive. He took a deep breath before stepping into the room.

Julia lay in the bed closer to the door. Matthew shuffled into the space between the bed and the wall and knelt down and grasped her right hand. Her left arm was in a sling, and he could see the bulge of bandages on her shoulder through the cotton nightgown.

"Julia?" he said, waiting for her to open her eyes. "Julia?"

She still didn't answer.

Mercy had been sitting in a chair between the two beds, but she stood when her father-in-law walked into the room.

He looked up and saw her.

"How bad is it?" he asked. "Why won't she wake up?"

"Dr. Smith said she's going to be fine, PaPa," said Mercy. "She's lost a lot of blood, so she's weak, but he said she should be all right. The doctor gave her something to ease the pain and help her rest."

"And Jimmy?" He looked across to the other bed.

Jimmy's head was bandaged, but he was awake.

Jimmy raised his hand. "I'm fine, Dad, other than a nasty headache."

"The doctor said the bullet probably cracked his skull, so he wants him to lie still for a while," said Mercy.

Matthew walked around the bed and across the room to take a closer look. He grasped his son's hand.

"I'm all right, Dad," Jimmy assured him again when he thought his father was going to break down.

Matthew nodded. "Thank God." He looked around the room. "Where's Fred? I need to talk to him."

"Dr. Smith left about thirty minutes ago, but he said he'd be back later," Mercy told him.

Matilda, the Locke's housekeeper and cook, came in with a pitcher of water.

"Hello, Mr. Taylor," she said quietly. "We're so glad you're here. Can I get you anything?"

"No, thank you, Matilda. On second thought, do you have any coffee?"

Matilda nodded and said she would bring him a cup.

"Matt's come with me, too, if you would let him in."

"Sure thing," she said as she left the room.

"Here," said Mercy, pulling up a chair. "Sit down before you fall down—you look exhausted."

"My horse is the tired one. I rode him hard to get here," he said as he sat down and rubbed his throbbing temple. "What in the world happened today? I see you all off this morning to go into town, and the next thing I know—

9

my wife and son have been shot." He turned to Jimmy. "What happened?"

"It looks now to be just an awful misunderstanding," Mercy spoke up. "Jimmy saw a man mistreating a horse downtown, and he offered to buy it from him."

"That sounds like you," said Matthew, looking at his son. "Who was the man?"

Jimmy started to answer him, and Mercy told him to hush. "I'll tell him, Jimmy—Dr. Smith said you need to rest quietly." She turned to Mr. Taylor. "Somebody by the name of Hulsbam. Do you know him?"

"I've heard of the name, but I've never met any of them."

"Well, after Jimmy bought the horse, he calmed her down and then tied her onto the back of our buggy," she continued, "but then his son came along and accused Jimmy of stealing his horse. When Jimmy tried to show him the receipt, the kid thought he was going for a gun and shot at him. The first bullet hit Julia, and the second grazed Jimmy's skull. And little Jack was sitting right beside Julia—they all could've been killed."

"Were there witnesses?" Matthew asked. "Did you see what happened?"

Mercy shook her head, no. "I was in the store, but there were plenty of folks around who saw what happened—before when Jimmy bought the horse from the father, and then later when his son started shooting."

"I hope he's not walking around free," said Matthew. "This is the 1880's—people can't get away with taking the law into their own hands anymore—especially if they're wrong."

"He's in jail—Ranger Williams saw to that."

Matthew scooted his chair closer to Julia's bed. He sat on her injured side now, so he reached over and put his hand on her leg, wanting to touch her, to let her know he was there.

"How long has she been asleep?" he asked.

Mercy glanced at the mantel clock. "It hasn't been quite three hours since the shooting," said Mercy. "We sent someone to Grace as soon as we could."

"We dropped everything as soon as Pate came running up to the barn shouting. I don't think we've ever made that trip so fast." He stared at his wife. "She's so pale. Are you sure she's going to be all right?"

"Dr. Smith assured us she would be," she said. "He said we needed to keep the wound clean, and that she would need to stay here for a few days. And Jimmy, too, for that matter, so that means I'll be here with them. Mother and Daddy don't mind at all. They're glad to help in any way."

"I appreciate them doing this, Mercy," he said.

"Will Vestal and Catherine mind keeping the girls while I stay here?"

"Of course they won't. Vestal considers herself as much their grandmother as Julia. And you know how Catherine fawns over those little girls since she and Matt only have boys. I'll send Matt back to Grace in a little while to let everyone know what's going on. The girls will be fine."

"But if it goes beyond a day or two, somebody's going to have to bring them to Waco," she said, looking at her husband. "Jimmy and I can't stand to be away from them for very long."

Jimmy opened his eyes and smiled at her, then shut them again.

"That can be arranged," said Matthew.

Julia stirred at the sound of voices.

"Julia!" Matthew said, reaching across her and grabbing her good hand. "Can you hear me? I'm right here, honey."

Julia's eyes felt too heavy to open, but she had the strength to squeeze his hand.

"You're going to be all right. You just rest as long as you need to, and I'll be here when you wake up."

Chapter 3

*J*ulia *dropped the firewood when she heard the gunshots. The sound came from the direction of the camp, so she ran as fast as she could back to where she had left Quiet Sky and Little Horse with Nah-kay and Nantan. She prayed that Justin was safe and would stay away from the camp. She stopped and hid in the brush nearby to see who was attacking them. Horses galloped through their camp—white men atop the horses! Her heart stopped when she saw Nantan running away from camp. He carried Little Horse, trying to shield him with his body.*

"Nantan!" she screamed.

His head turned at the sound of her voice, and he started running towards her. His eyes met hers just before a shot knocked him down. She saw the little boy pitch forward as his father fell. Little Horse stood up and tried to run through the horses to her, but then a horse blocked her view, and the gunshots continued.

Julia ran toward the men as she yelled for them to stop shooting. Several of them pulled up when they saw a white woman in their midst. She stopped when she saw Nantan lying on the ground. His lifeless arm draped over Little Horse, and Julia sank to the ground screaming when she thought she had lost them both.

Julia awoke with a start. It was dark—where was she? Someone was leaning over her, talking softly as she continued to weep.

"I'm here, Julia," Matthew said. "You're all right—the doctor said you're going to be just fine. Mercy, would you light a lamp?"

"Where's Jimmy?" she said as she remembered and panicked at the thought of losing him. "Is he all right?"

"Jimmy's fine—he's right here with us," said Matthew. "Mercy, move over so Julia can see him."

Mercy set the lamp on the table and stepped aside.

12

Julia looked across the room to see Nantan lying in the bed with a bandaged head. Where was her little boy? And what was Nantan doing in the same room with Matthew?

She looked back at Matthew, confused. "But where's..."

"Momma?"

Julia looked back at Nantan. She watched him slowly sit up and stand. The flaxen-haired woman helped him walk over to her. Julia glanced at Matthew, wondering why he seemed so calm right now. She looked wide-eyed back at Nantan standing beside her bed.

"Momma, it's me, Jimmy." He looked at Matthew. "What's happened to her? I don't think she knows me."

Julia saw worry in his blue eyes... blue eyes! It was Little Horse... no, Jimmy! But before she could force her mind to shut the door to the memories she had kept buried for so long, she realized anew that Nantan was lost to her. A well of sadness bubbled to the surface, and she began to weep again.

Fractured memories of the shooting that day suddenly surfaced along with the old memories, and Julia was even more confused. She tried to concentrate. Where was she? She looked around the room and came back to stare at a beautiful woman standing beside Jimmy. Mercy! Jimmy was married to Mercy. She looked back at her son.

"Jimmy! I'm so sorry," she said through her tears as she tried to hold out her arms to him, but only her right arm rose at will. Was she apologizing for the past or the present? She wasn't sure.

"I'm the one that's sorry, Momma," he said, leaning down to put his cheek against hers. He cringed at the pain it brought to his head. "I could've gotten you and Jack killed. Please don't cry."

"Try not to dwell on what happened today, Julia," said Matthew. "Think about the future—think about our children... and grandchildren." A peculiar sense that he had already had this same conversation with Julia washed over him.

Mercy handed him a handkerchief, and he gently wiped the tears from his wife's face.

Jimmy shut his eyes to the stabbing pain in his head and involuntarily put his hand to his forehead. Mercy took hold of his arm.

"You need to get back in bed, Jimmy." Mercy turned him around and walked him the few steps to his bed. She got him settled and turned around. "Is there anything I can get for you, Julia?"

"I'm thirsty," she said.

"I'll get it, Mercy," said Matthew. "You go on back to sleep. We'll be fine."

Mercy walked around the bed and slipped in under the covers beside Jimmy. She had first made a pallet on the floor beside the bed like Matthew had done so he wouldn't disturb Julia, but Jimmy told her either she would sleep beside him in the bed, or he would sleep with her on the floor.

She chose the bed.

Matthew poured a cup of water for his wife. She drank thirstily and asked for more.

Julia watched Jimmy and Mercy nestle together to ward off the chill in the room. She realized she felt cold, too. After she drank the second cup of water, she told Matthew she felt a chill.

"Let me find another blanket for you," he said, looking around.

"I don't want another blanket, Matthew," she said. "I want you to warm me."

"But I might accidentally touch your shoulder," he said. "I don't want to hurt you."

"You won't hurt me," she said, lowering her voice to a whisper, "unless you choose to sleep on the floor. I need you right now, Matthew. I need to feel you close to me."

Hearing the word 'need' was enough for Matthew to immediately do his wife's bidding. He scooted his pallet out of the way and leaned over and blew out the lamp. He felt for the bed and walked around to the other side—to her good side. He found the edge of the covers, pulled them back and tried to slip in beside her as gently as he could. The bed springs and frame creaked loudly as Julia struggled to move over and Matthew maneuvered awkwardly beside her.

"Could y'all hold it down over there?" Jimmy said, trying to lighten the mood. "Some of us are trying to sleep around here."

"We're not as young and agile as we used to be, son," said Matthew, "so have some consideration for us old folks."

There was only the briefest pause before a voice spoke in the darkness.

"Are you saying that was your bones making all that noise?"

Mercy snickered.

"You just wait, Jimmy Lawrence," said Matthew, smiling in the dark. "You're going to be old someday, too."

"Pleasant dreams," said Mercy.

" 'Night," said Matthew.

Julia prayed silently that the memories would not return to her dreams. She lived today, not in those memories of the years away from Matthew. She began to name her children: *Matt, Jenny, Justin, Jimmy, Faith;* next came her daughters and sons-in-law: *Catherine, Marcus, Allie, Mercy, and Ethan...* her grandchildren: *Tres, William, Michael, Robert, and Timbo, Josh, Luke, Maggie, and Clifford, Grace, Max, Bradley, and Mary J., Jack, Lilly Mae, and Biriney, Caitlin, Ella Vae, Cele and Sam,...*and then back to her children: *Matt, Jenny, Justin, Jimmy, Faith...*

Chapter 4

Matt brought his wife Catherine and his sister Jenny from Grace to the Locke mansion in Waco the following morning. The whole family wanted to come, but Matt had assured everyone that Julia and Jimmy would be all right, and that they needed as much rest as possible for now.

Mercy propped several pillows behind Julia to help her sit up. Jimmy insisted on sitting in a chair beside his mother's bed. Then Matthew and Mercy stepped out of the room while Jenny and Catherine came in. The looks they gave Julia were a mixture of worry and relief.

"Momma?" Jenny said tentatively.

"Hello, my sweet daughters." Julia smiled, looking from one to another. Jenny had her father's brown hair and his darker blue eyes. Catherine, blonde and willowy, looked more like Julia's daughter than Jenny did.

Afraid to touch her, the two women cautiously leaned down and kissed Julia's cheek in greeting. They gently hugged Jimmy as if he might break, too, and looked around for places to sit. Catherine pulled another chair up close. Julia patted the bed with her right hand, so Jenny walked around the bed and sat down and lightly grasped her mother's good hand.

"You two gave us quite a scare," said Catherine, shaking her head. "I can't believe something like this could happen right in the middle of Waco. What was wrong with that man?"

"We learned he's around my age, but he's a little on the slow side," said Jimmy. "His father had recently given him a gun to carry for snakes and such. He told Ranger Williams he had no idea his son would ever use it on another person."

"What are they going to do with him?" asked Jenny.

"Probably just take away his gun and send him home," said Jimmy. "He doesn't have sense enough to come in out of the rain."

"It's a wonder you both weren't killed!" said Catherine. "Does the boy even realize what he's done?"

"Dad said he's been bawling off and on since it happened, so he knows he did something bad."

"You both look so pale," said Jenny.

"Now, that's a first," said her brother, grinning. "I've been called a lot of things in my life, but pale was never one of them."

They all laughed, but Julia winced when it caused her to move her shoulder.

"No more jokes, brother," said Jenny. "We've been so worried about you both."

"We'll be just fine," said Julia. "We'll be home soon."

But that's all it took for Jenny to start crying, saying she thought she had lost her mother again. She lifted Julia's hand to her cheek.

"Please don't cry, honey," Julia said as she tried to brush the tears away. "We're all right, and I'm not going anywhere anytime soon."

Jenny nodded, but she couldn't hide the fear in her eyes.

Julia hadn't realized until that moment that Jenny still carried that fear with her all these years. Back in 1856, Julia and her youngest son, five-year-old Justin, had been taken by an Apache warrior, Nantan Lupan. During their time of captivity, she was away from Jenny and Matt for six years until Matthew finally found them and brought them home. It had been over twenty years since that had happened, but she could see that the wounds were still raw.

"Well, at least it wasn't my right shoulder that was hit, or I would've had two bum hands to deal with," said Julia, trying to lighten the conversation. "The doctor has my left arm cinched up so tight I can't even think about moving it. I can still use my right hand, but your father insisted on spoon-feeding me grits this morning. I think we put on a good show for your brother."

"Dad dripped half of it on her," said Jimmy. "I told Mercy we should never leave the girls in his care. And we appreciate you taking care of them, Catherine. How are they doing?"

"They're fine. Vestal and I will have them good and spoiled before y'all get back."

"Speaking of that, I need to get back to Grace real soon—I have too much to do."

Matt walked into the room at that moment. "Your horses are fine, Jimmy—we're taking care of everything. I know it's hard for you to be still for any length of time, and then to be cooped up with Mother on top of that, I really feel bad for you, brother."

"You just hush," said Julia, smiling at her eldest son.

"And I've never seen a prettier set of legs on a man," Matt continued, eyeing Jimmy's legs. "In fact, I don't recall ever seeing you in a nightgown before."

"It's a nightshirt, Matt, and it's borrowed," said Jimmy rising up too fast. He had to grab the chair to steady himself. "I don't even own one."

Catherine stood up and took him by the arm.

"I think it's time for you to get back in bed," she said. "Now, no arguing with me."

She helped him to his bed and tucked the blanket in around him.

"I'm twenty-six, Catherine," he reminded her.

"Sorry—old habit."

"Well, we need to let y'all rest," said Jenny. "Don't worry about a thing at Grace. Just come home soon."

They said their goodbyes, and Matt and Catherine walked out of the room.

Jenny paused at the door and said, "Thank the Lord y'all are all right. We just couldn't make it without you, Mom."

But before Julia could respond, Jenny told her brother that he did, indeed, have the most beautiful legs.

She giggled and shut the door just before a feather pillow hit it.

Matthew came back in the room and said he needed to return to Grace right after the noon meal to take care of some things, but would be back the following morning. Julia insisted that he take his time and do what needed to be done. She knew he had already gone to town after breakfast that morning to talk to the sheriff and Ranger Williams about the boy who had shot her and Jimmy. She also knew her husband well enough to see he was getting restless cooped up in that room and was looking for another excuse to get away.

"Are you sure you'll be all right without me for a while?"

"We have more than enough help here," Julia assured him.

"Well, then it may be closer to the afternoon before I get back. I'll bring Vestal, too. I'm sure she's chomping at the bit wanting to see you two."

"Tell her we're fine, and I'm sure the doctor will let us go home real soon. But if she insists on coming, we'd love to see her, too."

Matthew kissed his wife and squeezed Jimmy's shoulder before taking his leave.

Julia smiled at her husband. She didn't mind his leaving; she could rest more when he wasn't constantly asking if she needed anything.

"You know he doesn't have anything to do at home that Marcus and Matt and all their boys can't handle," said Jimmy.

Julia smiled wearily and nodded her head. "That's all right. Your father's feeling trapped in this sick room, and there's little he can do to help matters when what you and I need the most is to rest and give our bodies time to heal. And that's beyond his control."

"I guess you're right. I can't believe Vestal didn't insist on coming this morning. I bet she's fit to be tied right now."

"But somebody had to stay with your babies," she said, thinking about her dear friend.

Vestal was only two years older than Julia, but she looked much older. The Taylors had originally hired her when they lived in Illinois, and since she had no other relatives, she chose to come with them to Texas in 1852. Vestal was so much more than a housekeeper and cook to the Taylors. She had become an important part of the family.

Tall, big-boned, loud and loving—that was her description of herself. When Julia tried to encourage an interest in one of the few eligible men in the area not long after they arrived in Texas, Vestal quashed that notion immediately. She told Julia that she had only loved one man in her life, and he was lost to her. Vestal never said exactly what she meant by the word *lost*, and when Julia asked her, Vestal's eyes filled with tears, and she shook her head like she couldn't talk about it. Julia never asked her again.

After Nantan had taken Julia and Justin away from Grace four years after they came to Texas, Vestal became a surrogate mother to Matt and Jenny. At that time, the Taylors had recently completed their three-story home, and Matthew had big plans to build Grace into a thriving community. But those plans were put aside after his wife and youngest child were taken from him. Julia often wondered what kind of community Grace would have become if Matthew hadn't spent so much time and money looking for them those six years.

Julia's thoughts were abruptly brought back to the present when Mercy and Matilda came through the door with two trays. Matilda set Julia's tray on the table beside the bed and excused herself to go serve Mercy's parents.

19

"Go help Mother first," said Jimmy, when Mercy started to sit on the bed beside him.

"I'm sorry, Julia! Here, let me set this bed tray up for you. This is Mother's favorite—she used to use it regularly —especially when she had a case of the vapors." She lowered her voice to a whisper as she set the bed table across Julia's lap. "I learned that the vapors usually meant she was avoiding anything unpleasant or too stressful for her to face," she said, smiling. "But she doesn't use it much anymore. Would you like for me to feed you?"

"No, honey," said Julia. "I still have a good hand on me."

Jimmy looked at his mother's withered hand, barely visible at the edge of the sling. "I'm sorry Nantan crushed your other hand. He must have been a monster."

"Don't ever say that about him!" Julia said sternly. "You don't know what happened!"

When she saw the shock on Jimmy's face at her defense of the man who had kidnapped her, she apologized. "I'm sorry, Jimmy. I didn't mean to sound so harsh. I'm just not thinking clearly."

Mercy looked at Jimmy and raised her eyebrows, prompting him to speak.

"We were wondering something, Mother, if you don't mind us asking," he began.

"What?"

Mercy explained. "After you and Jimmy were shot and I found you both in the street, you talked to me, but I couldn't understand what you were saying."

"What do you mean?" Julia asked.

Jimmy continued. "You were speaking the Apache language, Mother."

Julia looked at her son questioningly. "Surely you didn't hear me right, Jimmy. Why would I do something so bizarre?"

"I don't know—maybe you were hallucinating?"

"Why don't we just eat our soup, Jimmy," said Julia, changing the conversation. "And then I think we both need to rest a bit."

Jimmy looked at Mercy, knowing his mother was skirting the subject, but he didn't know what to do about it.

"Are you having your own case of the vapors, Mother?"

"Eat your lunch," Mercy told him.

Julia ate a few bites of the soup before she asked Mercy to remove the bed table. She rolled over on her good shoulder to avoid facing Jimmy and eventually drifted off to sleep.

But sleep brought her no rest.

Julia found herself hanging on the edge of a precipice as the face of Dark Moon hovered above her. The edge of the woman's mouth turned up slightly as if she were smiling, but her eyes glinted sheer hatred. Her hands held a heavy rock, and she dropped it on Julia's hand to force her to fall from the cliff.

Julia screamed at the pain.

Chapter 5

Mercy hovered over the bed. "Julia! Wake up!"

Julia's eyes flashed open as she swung her right hand at the face in front of her. Mercy caught it in the cheek before she was able to subdue Julia's flailing right arm. Jimmy got out of bed to try to help.

"Mother! Wake up!" he shouted. "You're having a bad dream."

Recognition finally replaced fear in Julia's eyes, so she laid her head back down on the pillow and shut her eyes, breathing heavily. Her left shoulder throbbed from the exertion. After a few moments, she opened her eyes and saw the alarm in her children's faces, as well as a red welt on Mercy's face.

Did she hit her daughter-in-law?! What was happening to her? Was she losing her mind? Why were long-buried memories resurrecting themselves now? She felt as weak as a kitten, unable to be strong anymore. She shut her eyes tightly when the tears threatened to come, but they wormed their way out the corners and rolled down her cheeks unhindered.

"I'm so sorry, Mercy," she said. "Please forgive me."

Jimmy sat down in the chair beside his mother's bed.

"You need to get back in bed," said Mercy.

"I'm fine," he said, looking at his mother. "And I'm going to stay right here until she tells me what's going on."

Mercy handed Julia a hankie.

She sighed resignedly and looked sadly at her son.

"Some things are better left buried," she said, wiping her eyes and nose.

"I don't think you're going to get any peace about it until you get it all out," he said. "I've never seen you this way, Mother."

"I thought I had put all of this behind me years ago, but ever since yesterday, memories—good and bad—have filled my thoughts and dreams."

"Why did you defend Nantan earlier?" Jimmy asked.

She stared at his face for a moment before reaching out and touching it.

"You look a lot like him. But I think you have a good bit of us both. You got your eyes and your height from me, but you have his features and his way with horses."

"You didn't answer my question."

Mercy spoke up. "Would you like for me to leave, Julia?"

"No, honey… stay," she said, and then looked back at Jimmy. "You don't know what you're asking of me."

"Whatever it is, it's eating you up, Mother. Tell me what's haunting you."

Julia looked away for a while, fighting a battle within herself. She finally took a deep breath and looked back at Jimmy and Mercy. "I'll tell you, but anything I share with you should go no further than this room. Agreed?"

Jimmy and Mercy nodded their heads.

Julia looked down at her gnarled hand. "I guess this is as good a place to start as any."

"I already know what happened to your hand," said Jimmy. "Justin told me."

"Justin only knew what I had told him," she said. "He was young—only six years old when it happened. Time blurs facts and details. The story you heard had been repeated enough times that even I began to believe it years after it happened. But Nantan wasn't the one who crushed my hand."

"What!?"

"Well, maybe I should start at the beginning so you'll understand."

"Not before you tell me who hurt your hand," Jimmy insisted.

Julia paused again, looking down. A pained look crossed her face as she dredged up the memory. Jimmy started to speak again, but Mercy put her hand on his arm to stop him.

Julia finally answered. "A woman named Dark Moon shattered my hand, but you won't understand why unless I start from the beginning."

"But then why did you tell everyone Nantan did it?"

"He told me to."

Jimmy looked at her questioningly. "I don't understand."

"Sweetheart," said Mercy. "Shut up and let your mother talk."

Julia smiled at her daughter-in-law, and then looked away for a few moments to gather her thoughts.

"I said that time tends to blur our memories, and that's true, but when Justin and I were taken, I remember details of little things that particular day when I can't even recall the same kind of particulars from only a week ago."

23

She shut her eyes. "I remember how hot and still the air was, and Justin and I had walked down to the river to cool off."

"Is that where he took you?"

Julia shook her head, no. "But that's where he first saw us. He told me later that he would've passed on by our place if he hadn't seen us. He had no intentions of attacking our home—he was alone, separated from his group. He had just stopped to water his horse. But when he saw a young woman and a boy about the age of his own son when he was killed, all the anger and bitterness came to the surface and on a whim, he decided to exact his revenge by replacing what the white soldier had taken from him. A wife for a wife... a son for a son."

"Where was Dad?" Jimmy asked.

"In town, working on the building that he hoped would some day be a courthouse for our area. But it's remained only the school house all these years since Grace never became a county seat. The town site of Waco had only been laid out seven years before, and McLennan County was established in 1850. We came to Texas two years later and Matthew hoped to repeat what was happening in Waco. He'd named his new town Taylor at that time. But all those plans were put aside after Justin and I were taken."

"Where were Vestal and Matt and Jenny?"

"Jenny was helping Vestal in the wash house, and Matt was in town helping your father."

"Why wasn't he protecting his family? Weren't you afraid of getting attacked?"

Julia shook her head, no. "The Indians that had been living in the area had been moved to a reservation in Oklahoma a couple of years before. The wild frontier had been pushed more to the west and northwest of us. We rarely heard about any raids in our area."

"How did he take you?"

"He surprised us in the barn. He had a knife and grabbed Justin and motioned for me to be quiet or he would slit his throat. He made me saddle a horse for me to ride while he held Justin on his horse. I was so afraid for Justin's life, I did exactly what he wanted me to do."

"How did anyone know you were taken?"

"Vestal saw us leaving the barn. She hid Jenny in the wash house and ran to the big house to get a rifle, but by the time she returned, we had disappeared. She grabbed Jenny, and they ran to town to tell Matthew. He enlisted the help of several men, but most had to go get their saddle horses, and that took time. Matthew had been using a wagon that day and brought

Vestal and the children back to the house and then had to go to the barn to saddle his own horse. By the time the rest of the men came to the house, Nantan had a good forty-five minute lead on them. And he wasted no time getting us away from there. I'd never ridden so far or so fast on a horse before. Justin and I were exhausted after only a few hours, but Nantan seemed to be tireless on a horse. I didn't think I would survive the horseback ride, much less whatever he had in store for us later. Every so often he would walk the horses down a creek bed or over bedrock to hide our trail. We met up with six of his companions that evening. He seemed very proud to show us off in front of them."

"Did he hurt you?"

"No, although he slapped Justin when he started whimpering how tired he was. Justin didn't cry after that. We traveled until well after dark, slept a few hours, and then got up before sun-up and rode again. I just knew Matthew would find us quickly. These men weren't educated like my husband. I thought they were just ignorant savages. I had no idea how adept they were in living off the land and avoiding contact with people if they chose not to be seen. They had such an advantage over the white man when it came to those skills, but I didn't understand that for a while. And then when the days turned into weeks and the weeks turned into months, I began to realize that we wouldn't be found as quickly as I had originally thought."

Julia looked down at her gown, but she didn't see it. "I remember what I was wearing that first day—a pale blue blouse and light brown skirt. After a few days of dusty, sweaty riding, I remember being disgusted with myself at how dirty I had become, but after a while, we got used to being filthy, too. Justin didn't mind it nearly so much as I did."

"What was it like to live with the Indeh?"

"I think you got to experience a little of that with your grandmother."

"But she waited on me hand and foot—I was still recovering from my injuries."

"A woman's role in an Apache camp is much harder than a man's, but the life of the Indeh, as they called themselves, was so very hard, but that's all they knew and seemed to want. They took pride in the fact that they were tough—that they could endure the harshest living conditions. I remember when the warriors would train the young boys, they would make them take a dip in the river in the middle of winter just to toughen them up. I've seen children run around barefooted on the coldest days. I don't know how they conditioned their bodies to endure such discomfort. I'm so glad you didn't have to experience that type of thing, but we did experience hunger."

25

"I don't remember any of that, but I know Justin did," Jimmy said. "Just the little time that I stayed at Nah-kay's camp eight years ago made me realize I couldn't survive that kind of life."

He abruptly changed the subject. "Tell me about Dark Moon."

"We met up with a larger group of Indeh after several weeks. That's where I met your grandmother Nah-kay." Julia's face changed at the thought. "What an amazing woman she was and still is, for that matter. She taught me so much. I never would have survived that ordeal without her. And it wasn't until I had learned the language that I found out about Nantan's first wife and child. Not long after they had been killed several years before, he had taken another Apache wife—his sister-in-law actually, that already lived with them—"

"Dark Moon."

Julia nodded. "When he took his first wife, her sister also came to live with Nantan because they had no other family. So Dark Moon was already like a daughter to Nah-kay, and it seemed inevitable for Nantan to take Dark Moon as his wife. But she hadn't been able to conceive and give him a child, and Nantan's anger still burned hot inside of him because of his loss. Then he brought Justin and me to their camp, and Dark Moon became very jealous of me. I tried to make her understand that I already had a husband I loved, and he would find us and take us home some day. I tried to show that I was no threat to her, but Nantan messed that up when he began to..." she paused, trying to think of a tactful way to say what she needed to say, "... when he began to treat me as a wife."

Chapter 6

No one said anything for a moment.

Jimmy broke the silence. "And then I was conceived."

Julia nodded. "I thought Dark Moon would kill me right then and there when she found out. She believed *she* was the only one who should replace her sister and give Nantan another son, and I had usurped her role. She even incited some of the other women to catch me away from camp and beat me, hoping I would miscarry."

"What happened?"

"When the men were away hunting, some corn turned up missing from one of the women's belongings. I suspect now that Dark Moon had taken it, but she told them that I had taken it. A group of them caught me away from camp and began to accuse me and beat me with sticks. Nah-kay heard the yelling and knew something was wrong. She found us and defended me against them. Have you noticed the half-moon scar on her cheek?"

Jimmy nodded.

"She got that trying to protect me that day," Julia explained. "When Nah-kay learned that Dark Moon had provoked the fight by accusing me, she was very angry at her daughter. But Dark Moon convinced her that she had made a mistake and seemed very remorseful about it. That satisfied Nah-kay, but I knew Dark Moon would try to hurt me again, if not worse, and she probably would have succeeded eventually if she hadn't learned that she was with child, too.

"But when Nantan came back from hunting and found Nah-kay with a cut on her cheek and me with bruises and cuts, his mother had to tell him what had happened. He warned Dark Moon that he would banish her from the group if she ever tried to harm me again. So things were peaceful for a while.

"You were born in the spring of '57, and a month later, Dark Moon gave birth to a baby girl. At first she was livid when she learned that the best she could do after trying so long to give Nantan a son, was to give him a daughter.

"Nah-kay was thrilled to have a grandson and a granddaughter, and Dark Moon seemed to love her baby girl, so for a while I thought everything would be all right."

"Did Jimmy have an Indian name?" asked Mercy.

Julia nodded, yes.

"I had an Indeh name?" he asked. "Why didn't you tell me?"

"I had to look forward—we all had to look forward after your father found us. That life was behind us—I couldn't keep any reminders of it if I didn't want to lose my mind and possibly my marriage."

"But Dad wouldn't quit until he found you... us. Why would he give up on his marriage after that?"

"He never would have divorced me, but your father had his pride, and you were a constant reminder to him and the whole world that someone else had taken his wife, and for six years had replaced him in every way. After we returned to Grace, we slept in separate bedrooms for quite some time. But with God's help, we were eventually able to put it all behind us and heal our marriage."

"Can you tell me what you named me when I was born?"

"The Indeh didn't always name their babies at birth—they had to watch them to see what name would fit. Or if a baby was named early, their name might be changed to fit them when they were older. When you were about eight months old, Nantan gave you a name that meant *Little Horse* because you got so excited every time you were around the horses." She smiled at her son. "That ended up fitting you so well, didn't it? But in my heart, I had already named you Jimmy, after my father James. We added your middle name Lawrence after Matthew's grandfather when we returned to Grace. I thought that would give you and your father a connection, but we know that didn't resolve itself until after you and Justin brought Allie back to Grace in '75."

"Isn't it ironic that Matthew gave Jack the nickname *Pony*?" said Mercy.

Julia nodded. "I think I dropped a pan in the kitchen when he told me that. Jack is his father's son when it comes to horses, isn't he? But your father must never know about the coincidence of your names."

Jimmy nodded. "But what happened with Dark Moon?"

"She usually had little to do with me, even though we often worked side

28

by side. She spoke to me only when necessary. One of my tasks was to gather firewood, and I had walked quite a distance on this particular afternoon. We had been at this camp for a while because of the corn and—"

"The corn?"

"We moved around a lot during the year, but in several places we took the time to plant corn and would eventually work our way back to the fields around harvest time. And because we were there for a while, it didn't take long for the women to use up all the dry kindling near the camp, so I had to walk further out to find some. On that particular day Dark Moon joined me away from camp and told me she had found a lightning-split tree with plenty of dead wood, but she needed help to carry it back. I remember thinking that was odd, since she rarely gathered firewood—she usually left that task to me. But on the other hand, I was so pleased that she asked for my help. I thought that she was finally accepting me.

"This particular camp was nestled between some hills, and we were already some distance away. I set down the small bundle I had already gathered, and I followed her into the hills. We traveled a path—probably made by animals, and it became narrower and steeper as we walked along. When the drop beside the trail was probably sixty or seventy feet down, I stopped and told Dark Moon that I was scared of heights and wouldn't go any further. I couldn't see the tree ahead of us either, and by that time I began to doubt that there even was one. She pointed to a small tree growing out from the side of the cliff and said it looked like that kind of tree and wasn't much further. She broke off a dead branch and handed it to me, and when I reached for it, she grabbed my arm and jerked me toward the precipice. I fell towards the tree and caught myself, but she kicked and pushed me until I was hanging over the edge. I thought I was going to die at that moment.

"I screamed, and she started throwing rocks and dirt and anything she could get her hands on to make me fall. I clung to the narrow tree trunk with my right arm looped around it, and my left hand held onto a crack in a cleft in the edge of the cliff. She started stomping on my hand, but I was determined not to let go. She turned around for a moment, and I almost pulled myself up, but then she turned back with this heavy rock that she could barely hold herself. She smiled at me before she dropped it on my hand."

Julia looked down at her withered hand.

Mercy's hand went to her mouth.

"What happened, Momma?" asked Jimmy.

"The rock crushed my hand. The pain was unbearable, but then the rock did the opposite of what Dark Moon intended for it to do. Instead of forcing me to fall, it wedged in the cleft, keeping me from falling. And she couldn't budge it. When she realized what she'd done, she ran away. I thought she was going to leave me there to die trapped on the side of that cliff."

"What did you do? How did you survive?"

"I tried shouting, but I knew I was too far from camp for anyone to hear me. I've never been so scared in my life, but I knew I wasn't alone. I started to pray and ask God to give me the wisdom to save myself or to let somebody find me. I had found some toe-holds in the cliff face so my arms weren't holding my full weight. I tried jerking my hand loose, but the pain was so excruciating, I was afraid I might faint and lose my grip. So I worked my right leg until I was able to pull it over the tree trunk to help support my weight, and that helped take much of the load off of my arms.

"I don't know how long I hung there—maybe twenty or thirty minutes, before I heard someone coming up the trail. I thought God had answered my prayer, but I was devastated to see that it was Dark Moon returning. I began pleading with her to help me, and she stood there for a moment watching me. Then she pulled out a knife, and I was horrified when I realized she intended to sever my hand so I'd fall."

"Oh, Momma," said Jimmy, sick to his stomach. "What happened?"

Julia's face looked haggard and her voice sounded hollow as she relived that horrendous moment. "I remember her kneeling down above me, and she was smiling again so I knew something had gone terribly wrong in her mind. She leaned over with the knife, and I remember crying out to God. But then Dark Moon gasped, her eyes widened, and she tried to look behind her as she pitched forward over the cliff."

"Someone pushed her?" asked Mercy.

"No," said Julia, "but later I realized God had answered my prayer after all. No one knew Dark Moon and I were together, but we both had been gone a lot longer than usual. It was past time for us to nurse our babies, so Nah-kay was worried about us. She sent Nantan to look for us, and he found the small bundle of wood and the leather straps I used to bind them. He told me later that up until that point he saw only my tracks, but from there he recognized the tracks of two women and followed them toward the hills. He walked a ways, and from a distance he saw Dark Moon coming back towards the camp alone. She was watching the ground, and every few feet she knelt down and brushed the soil behind her. He realized she was covering her tracks. But she suddenly stopped and pulled a knife from her belt and looked at it for a moment. Then she sheathed it and turned around to run back the way from which she had come. Nantan knew then that something was wrong, and began to run after her. He caught up with her on the path just as she raised her knife. He told me he could hear me crying and knew Dark Moon was trying to kill me. He didn't even have time to think before he threw his own knife to stop her."

"He saved your life," said Jimmy. "But Dark Moon was the one who crushed your hand. Why did Nantan lead everyone to believe that he had done it? Even Nah-kay thinks that her own son crushed your hand."

"In saving my life, he killed the mother of his daughter," she said. "He couldn't bear to tell his own mother that he had killed someone she loved. I didn't want him to take the blame for my hand either, but he told me that if he had been able to stop Dark Moon without killing her, he would have had to banish her from the group for what she tried to do to me. And that would've been a torturous sentence for a woman alone in that land, if not worse."

"How old was her baby?" asked Mercy. "Did the baby have a name by then?"

Julia shook her head. "Eventually, she was called Quiet Sky, but at the time of her mother's death, she was only two months old. She has no idea what happened to her mother."

"I have a half-sister, and yet you and Nah-kay told me nothing about her. And you speak as if you know her still."

"Jimmy," said Julia softly, "you know her, too, honey."

"What?"

Julia reached over and grasped her son's hand as she answered him. "Dark Moon's baby was Faith."

Chapter 7

Jimmy was stunned. "Faith is my true half sister?"

Julia nodded.

He sat there frowning, trying to recall everything that he had been told about Faith.

"But I thought she had been orphaned when she was three years old—that she came and lived with us then," he said.

"I nursed both of you until you were around eighteen months old," said Julia. "I feel like she is my own daughter."

"Why did you lie to us about that? Faith should know about her father."

"I'm sorry, Jimmy, but I never wanted Faith to know she was Dark Moon's daughter because of what she did to me, and I never wanted Matthew to know she belonged to Nantan for fear that he would reject her, too. It took so long for him to accept you as his son." Julia sighed deeply and shook her head. "I never intended for any of this to be known. I just buried it after we came home to Grace. And it would've remained buried if you hadn't been shot yesterday."

"We need to tell Faith, Momma," said Jimmy. "She needs to know who her real father was."

"Matthew is her father, Jimmy. She knows no other father. I thought I was protecting her all these years—I don't know how she'll react to me not telling her the truth." Julia looked worried.

"Well, I think that's enough talking for now, Jimmy," said Mercy, coming to Julia's defense. "Your mother has eaten very little since this morning. We need to get some more food in her and let her rest."

Mercy led her husband back to bed, and then took Julia's bowl of cold soup out of the room to warm it.

"So what else have you not told me?" Jimmy asked.

32

Julia looked sadly at her son.

"Oh, no; you mean there's more? I intended to convince Mercy to let me go home today, but I think I need to stay around a while longer."

"I never intended to open up old wounds, but I realize now I never had time to heal."

"Are you talking about your hand?"

Julia shook her head. "No, son."

"Momma?" Jimmy stared at his mother. "Then what are you saying?"

Julia covered her eyes with her good hand.

"Are you telling me you had feelings for Nantan?"

Her head began to quiver as she tried to maintain control. A sob escaped, though, and it opened the gate for the flood of emotion she had so carefully hidden for more than twenty years.

Jimmy threw back the covers and hurried to his mother's side. He sat on the bed facing her and let her lean into him as he cautiously put his arm around her right shoulder. He had never seen his mother cry like this before. Part of him wanted to protect her and take away the hurt; another part was unnerved to see such a strong woman so vulnerable and devastated over something that had happened so long ago.

Mercy came in with Julia's soup, and seeing the look on Jimmy's face, she turned right around and walked out, shutting the door quietly behind her.

Jimmy held his mother until the shudders calmed.

"Are you going to be all right?" he asked.

Julia nodded and exhaled. "I'm spent, though. Can I rest a while before we talk some more?"

"Of course, and you don't have to say anything if you don't want to, but if you do, I'll be right here. Would you like to eat a bite first?"

Julia shook her head, no, so Jimmy removed a pillow and gently helped her settle back down onto the bed. He watched her shut her eyes, and noticed for the first time that his mother looked aged. Her hair had been white for as long as he could remember, but he had never thought she had ever looked elderly until that moment.

Julia slept hard for the next several hours, and afterwards, Mercy was finally able to get her to eat the entire bowl of soup and a bit of bread. Dr. Smith came by to check on Julia and Jimmy, and was satisfied with their progress. He said he would be back in the morning, and that he would probably allow Jimmy to go home at that time. But Julia's wound needed more time to heal before she was moved.

Jimmy slipped out of the room for a moment.

"You look rested, Julia," said Mercy. "Did you sleep well?"

Julia nodded. "No more nightmares this time. In fact, I feel like a huge weight has been lifted off my mind. But I'm sorry I had to burden you and Jimmy with my confession."

"It's no burden at all," said Mercy. "I can't believe you've been living with that all these years."

Jimmy came back into the room, minus the bandages around his head. He had also found his pants and slipped them on under his nightshirt.

"Now what did you go and do?" asked Mercy. "You weren't supposed to take off your bandage."

"I'll heal just fine without it." He pulled up a chair beside his mother's bed. "We need to do some more talking before I go home tomorrow."

"Would you like for me to step outside?" offered Mercy.

"No," said Julia. "I'd rather you stay. A husband and wife shouldn't have secrets between them." She paused. "But there are some times in life when revealing secrets can do much more harm than good, and what I've already told you and what I'm about to tell you can never get back to Matthew. It would cause him too much pain, and Lord knows he's suffered enough for one lifetime. I've never told anyone else what I'm about to tell you, and other than Faith, no one else need ever know. Do you understand?"

They both nodded. Mercy pulled up another chair beside Jimmy. She reached over and grasped his hand.

"I want you to know that Matthew Taylor is the love of my life, and that has never changed, nor will it ever change, even with what I'm about to tell you. But time has erased many of the details of those six years—especially the repetitive, mundane tasks I eventually learned to do daily without even thinking about them. Time has softened the hardships and misery we endured during periods of hunger and weary days of travel. I don't know if I can even remember the sequence of events correctly—many memories are lost to me, but the memories I've recalled so far have been connected to other memories like links in a chain, and when I pull one from my mind, another seems to follow."

"Tell me about Nantan."

Chapter 8

J ulia paused as she caught a reflection of herself in the mirror above the dressing table. Tears filled her eyes as the years slipped away until a beautiful young woman stared back at her.

"Nantan Lupan was a very strong and determined man, Little Horse. He came from a world I knew nothing about, other than the stories of savagery I'd heard while growing up. I'd always taken pride in the fact that I worked hard—even as a young woman, but the Apache or Indeh way of life was so much harder than the life I'd known.

"You already know the reason Nantan took Justin and me back in 1856. Several years before when he and the other warriors were away from their camp, white soldiers raided and killed many of the women and children, including Nantan's wife and five-year-old son. Nah-kay and Dark Moon were down by the river and hid from the soldiers. Nantan was grateful that he hadn't lost them, too, but losing his wife and child almost destroyed him, and from that experience he carried a hatred for the soldiers. Every chance he found to attack or steal from them, he would. And when our paths crossed all those years ago, taking Justin and me was simply one more act in an effort to appease his anger.

"I don't know why God allowed this to happen to me and Justin. God had blessed Matthew and me with three healthy children and a new life and home in Texas. Sometimes we think if we do everything right in honoring God, bad things won't happen to us. I learned that's not necessarily so. But what I also learned through the years is that no matter what difficulties we go through in life, God will always be there to give us the strength to endure.

"I'm not a brave woman. I'd heard stories about women who chose to end their lives rather than endure the hardships and humiliation of captivity with the Indians. But I wanted to live. And I wanted my son to live. I believed that Matthew would move heaven and earth to find us, and that my life wasn't finished with him. That didn't mean I didn't go through times of discouragement—that was a constant battle. But I learned to depend on God in ways that I had never experienced before.

"Nah-kay told me something not long after we were brought to their camp that helped me so much during those years. She said that water takes the shape of whatever vessel in which it is placed. I wasn't quite sure what she meant at first, but it finally dawned on me that she was saying that I needed to learn to adjust to whatever environment I found myself in. She had mastered that skill years ago because their group moved camp so often."

Jimmy nodded his head. "I was amazed at how fast she adjusted to living with us after we brought her back to Grace."

"I eventually learned to survive by becoming two people. Inside, I was still Julia Taylor, wife of Matthew, mother of Matt, Jenny, and Justin. In my heart I believe I stayed faithful to my husband, and I knew he would find me and reconcile our life together. But on the outside, I had been forced into a life I didn't choose for myself, and I did the best I could to survive with dignity intact. And in the process, I grew to love Nah-kay and eventually feel compassion for Nantan and his loss."

Julia stopped talking to try to think of something Jimmy and Mercy could relate to.

"Can you think of a place where you grasped hold of friendships you might not otherwise have chosen? Or have you at times gathered around you items that became symbols of security or survival? Or maybe you followed certain little routines that helped you get through a tough situation?" She paused, looking to see if Jimmy or Mercy understood what she was asking them.

Jimmy spoke first. "You used to sing *Amazing Grace* when you were scared."

Julia smiled in surprise. "How did you know about that?"

"Nah-kay picked up the tune from you, and she did the same thing when she was frightened. While we were there, she hummed it loudly during a thunderstorm, and she did it again when the soldiers came to take her from her home. It probably saved her life because the soldiers recognized it. Later, through Justin, she told us that she learned it from you—that it gave her courage."

"She did?" said Julia. "I'm glad to know that she learned something useful from me. But that was only one of the things I did to survive during that time. Have you ever done something of that sort?"

"Besides drinking coffee in the morning?" said Jimmy. He turned to his wife. "In fact, I think I could use a cup right now, honey."

Mercy frowned at him. She certainly didn't want to leave the room at that moment, but she submitted to her husband's request and asked Julia if she could bring her a cup.

Julia declined, and Mercy hurried out of the room.

"I didn't realize this was a survival skill, but there was a girl at that boarding school," said Jimmy.

"A girl in that all-boy school?"

"She didn't attend school with us," he explained, "but she lived there along with her sisters and her father. He was the headmaster. I spent a lot of time in the kitchen working off demerits, and one day she came in by herself. She didn't say much, but for the longest time after that, I felt like the day would be bearable if I just got to see her—through the fence, in a window."

"I never knew there was someone special to you at school."

"There never was a relationship. The headmaster's daughters were completely off limits to all of us, but there was definitely a rapport between us. I think she looked forward to those moments, too—like we could get on with our lives as long as we got a glimpse of each other during the day."

Mercy rushed into the room with a cup of coffee.

"Here." She handed Jimmy the cup and sat down. "What did I miss?"

"And the only friend I ever had at school other than Justin the few years he was there was this pitiful excuse for a male," said Jimmy, not missing a beat. "Nobody liked him, and everyone picked on him. He was five years older than me, but I found myself defending him since he was the only one who would have anything to do with me."

"Oh, honey," said Mercy. "That was so sweet of you."

"I would never have chosen him as a friend otherwise, but our common bond as outcasts brought us together," he continued. "Would you believe he would read your letters, Mother, and pretend they were from his own mother, in exchange for his helping me with my school work?"

"That is so sad," said Mercy. "Did he not have any parents?"

"He had parents, but they were too busy for him. He told me his father was always tied up with the family business and his mother was a socialite who spent most of her time either planning events or attending them."

"And he was your *only* friend at school?" asked Mercy.

Jimmy nodded, glancing at his mother.

"I'm so sorry you had to endure that, son," said Julia. "I never would've let it continue if I'd known how difficult it was for you."

"I didn't help matters much, either. They were glad to see me go, and I don't really blame them. I wasn't their best student."

"Did you really take that switch away from your teacher when he started to whip you?" Julia asked.

Mercy stared at Jimmy. "You did what?!"

Jimmy grinned sheepishly and nodded. "The man was an idiot, and I really *didn't* deserve the punishment that time. I was just tired of him using me as the whipping boy for the whole class. It didn't matter who broke the rule; he always blamed me."

"Well, that was the last straw for the school," said Julia, "so we brought you home."

"Whatever happened to your only friend?"

"Last I heard, he took over the family business when his father was killed in a hunting accident," said Jimmy. "He even ran for the Texas Congress last year and got elected. The kid no one paid attention to now has people fawning all over him. I'm sure no one at that school would ever have predicted that."

"Well, I'm glad you both survived that ordeal," said Julia. "Come to think of it, my time with the Indeh was about the same amount of time you were at boarding school. And I survived, too. I talked to God a lot during that time, and I learned to look for moments of joy or peace or beauty during each day."

"What do you mean?"

Julia was quiet for a moment. "I looked for things that reminded me of His presence. I told myself that if He was capable of creating this world and everything in it, He was surely capable of knowing what was going on in my life. Oftentimes I was encouraged by the simple beauty in the wildflowers, or watching the birds—especially the parents with their young. Sometimes it was a magnificent sunset in the evenings or finding a cool spring in the midst of a barren land that made me feel close to Him."

"Surely you weren't able to find one of those moments that day you were on the cliff?" asked Jimmy.

"But I did, son," said Julia. "What God showed me on the cliff that day reaffirmed that He was there with me—even in one of the worst moments of my life. After Dark Moon fell, I shut my eyes and clung to that tree even tighter. Nantan found a sturdy limb down the path that he brought back and wedged under the rock to pry it out of the cleft. My hand hurt terribly when Dark Moon dropped the rock on it, but it was agony when the rock was removed. I just froze there on the side of the cliff. I couldn't open my eyes; I couldn't move my hand; I couldn't unwrap myself from the tree.

"Nantan immediately tried to pull me up, but I couldn't let go. So he lay down on the trail with his face in front of mine. He started to rub my forehead and talk softly to me. He kept doing that until I was ready to open my eyes. The first thing I saw was his face. Then I looked over at the cleft in the rock, but I didn't see my bloody hand. All I saw was a white feather laying there in the crevice. I had seen no birds on the trail that day. But I knew then that God had placed it there for me. I remembered the Bible saying that God knows even when a sparrow falls, and I knew He was with me on that mountain. I was able to let go of the tree and let Nantan lift me back onto the trail. He held me as we sat there for a while. We said nothing—we were both heartsick over what had happened. Then he came up with the plan to tell Nah-kay and the others that he had punished me for trying to leave again."

"Again?"

Julia nodded. "I did try to leave with Justin not long after we were first brought to camp. But we didn't get very far. It didn't take Nantan long to find us, but he didn't hurt me for trying. He just told me that if he let us go, the land would devour us—that we didn't know enough to stay alive by ourselves. And he was right. I didn't try again because I wanted us to live. When we came back to camp, he made a big commotion about it for the others' sake, shouting at Justin and me, pushing us back toward his tipi.

"And when we came back to camp after he rescued me from the cliff, he made me walk ahead of him with my head down, and he put on the same show about how angry he was that I had tried to escape again. What nobody realized was that he had half-carried me down the mountain and hid me in a ravine. Then he took my moccasins and quickly created a new trail of us coming and going, but in a different direction than the mountain trail where Dark Moon had taken me. Then he paraded me through the camp. Nah-kay was beside herself when she saw my hand—she chewed on him for days about it. I don't think she ever forgave him for that."

"She actually believed that her son did that to you?"

"Nantan had never lied to his mother before—it would not enter her head that he hadn't been truthful with her. She doubted me, though, because she knew me well enough to know that I could not leave my children. So I told her that while I was out gathering firewood, I thought I saw smoke from a campfire in the distance and walked towards it to see if it was soldiers or someone who could rescue me. I told her that I'd gotten lost and that

Nantan had found me. I also told her that if I had been rescued, that I would have come back for my babies, and that explanation seemed to satisfy her. But she was also angry at me for days for what she thought I'd done."

"How did Nantan explain Dark Moon's death?"

"Nah-kay sent her son back out to search for Dark Moon because she hadn't returned to nurse her baby. You and Faith hadn't eaten in hours, so I had to nurse you both. It took everything in me to keep from crying while I held Faith, knowing what had happened to her mother. Nantan walked around the boundary of the camp until he supposedly came upon her tracks. He followed them into the hills, clearing any sign that I had walked the same trail. He came back with her body just before sundown, saying that she had somehow slipped and fallen off a steep trail and died."

"How did he explain the knife wound?"

"Her body was badly battered, and she had several deep wounds from branches impaling her. Nah-kay never suspected Dark Moon's death was anything other than what Nantan told her. The whole camp mourned for her, and Nah-kay told me that it was now my responsibility to take care of Nantan's daughter along with his son… you, Jimmy, and your sister Faith."

"Did you love him, Momma?" Jimmy asked.

Chapter 9

J ulia looked at her son. "I think it was a situation similar to your friend at school. I would never have chosen Nantan if I was free to do so, but in those surroundings and the situations where he saved my life on more than one occasion, I developed feelings for him. Matthew was so far away, and I wondered at times if I would ever see him again. Nantan was one of my means of survival during that time even though I regularly tried to talk him into letting us go home. But despite my circumstances, I eventually felt safe with him. And then after what happened to Dark Moon, he and I shared a secret that we thought no one else would ever know. He trusted me in that regard, although on the other hand he knew if I ever had the opportunity to go home with my children, I would take it. But I think he grew to respect me, too, if nothing else."

"When Justin found Allie and me with my grandmother and her group, we spent some time trying to communicate with Nah-kay—to get some questions answered," said Jimmy. "She told us that Nantan admired you because of your strength, and because you were able to do the hard work of a woman with only one hand. She said he felt regret for what he'd done to you."

"She told you that?" Julia smiled. "Nantan did feel regret for what happened, and he knew what a hardship the injury was to me, but he wasn't responsible. But then he and I were the only ones who knew that."

"I used to wonder why you weren't bitter towards him about your hand," said Jimmy. "Part of me hated him for doing that to you, although I would never admit that to anyone."

"I'm sorry you lived with that anger about Nantan," she said, looking at her withered hand. "I've lived with this for so long, I just quit thinking about it. And I've refused to dwell on the memories of that time on the mountain—they're just too painful."

41

"Were you ever angry at God for what happened to you?"

"No, although there were many times I questioned why He let all of that happen to us," said Julia. "But at the same time, I honestly don't think we would have made it through without our faith. It even helped your brother."

"How's that?"

"Justin started having nightmares, so each evening we began to ask God in our prayers to give Justin a restful night's sleep with no bad dreams. And God honored that for months, which was another reminder to me of His presence. But then one night Justin came to my side crying that he'd had a bad dream. I remember feeling so disappointed that God had let him down, but then Justin reminded me that we had forgotten to say our prayers before we went to sleep that night. So we said our prayers, and I started to get up to take my frightened little boy through the dark back to his bed in Nah-kay's tent since Nantan wouldn't let him sleep with us, but Justin shocked me when he said, 'That's all right, Momma, I can go by myself.' His fear had completely dissipated after we prayed. I've forgotten a lot of things during those years, but that memory stands out so clearly in my mind. It was such an encouragement to me and another affirmation that God answers prayers."

"I don't mean to sound disrespectful to God or you, but why do you think it took so long for Him to answer your prayers of being rescued?"

"I don't know, Jimmy," Julia said truthfully. "Maybe God placed us in that family so they could see His influence in my life. I think Nantan and Nah-kay both saw my faith and what it meant to me during those years."

"But Nantan was killed, Momma. Surely that wasn't God's will, was it?"

A sadness swept over Julia's face, and she started to speak when there was a quick knock on the door. Hazel and Matilda stepped into the room with supper trays.

Mercy's mother looked at their faces and said, "I'm sorry, are we interrupting anything?"

Julia shook her head. "No, of course not. You ladies are so sweet to do this for us. I feel so pampered in your home, Hazel."

"Well, I'm glad we're making you feel that way, although I'm sorry about the circumstances that brought you here." Hazel set the tray on the bed table Mercy quickly set up for Julia.

"Where's Pony?" asked Jimmy. "I tried to find him earlier."

"Langston took him to the bank with him after lunch, but they should be back any minute," said Hazel. "We sure have enjoyed having little Jack around for longer than an hour or so."

"I know, Momma," said Mercy. "We'll try to have more overnight visits with you. It's just hard to travel with the girls so young. I hope Catherine and Vestal are surviving."

"We're going home in the morning," said Jimmy. "They probably think we've abandoned them."

"Those babies are just fine, honey," said Julia. "They won't even realize you've been gone."

"I'm sure that's true, but it's actually Jimmy and I that can't stand to be away from *them* any length of time," said Mercy. "Do you think you'll be up to traveling in the morning?"

Jimmy nodded his head. "I could've gone home this evening. I feel fine, other than this sore noggin." He ran his fingers gingerly through his hair and looked down at the tray of food. "Ahhh, chicken and dumplings... and apple pie! My favorite, Matilda!"

Matilda laughed. "Now, I'm sure Vestal will be ready to spoil you, too, when you get home. Too bad you don't live in the big house anymore."

"Maybe we need to move in with Mom and Dad temporarily," said Jimmy.

"Now you know there's not any room over there since Matt and Catherine moved in with them," said Mercy, frowning. "And are you saying you're not happy with my cooking?"

Jimmy looked sheepish. "No, sweetheart—it's just that I know you're busy with the babies and all."

"Liar," said Mercy.

Julia smiled as she watched her youngest son and wife banter. In earlier years she had often wondered if Jimmy would ever make it to adulthood. He was such a lost, angry young man for so long; he didn't know where he belonged. He had even shut her out for a while, and from that point Julia had no idea how to help him, other than to pray for him. It had taken many years for that prayer to be answered, too, she realized.

She wondered why God chose to answer some prayers immediately, while others took so long. She knew a person's free will was involved, too, and figured stubbornness and selfishness were barriers. Maybe prayer helped sway free will in that God allowed people to find themselves in humbling or difficult situations where those barriers were more easily overcome. She knew God didn't force himself on anyone, except for maybe Saul on the road to Damascus, but he thought he was doing God's will in persecuting the Christians. He had no idea he was fighting against the God he claimed to be so committed to. Julia knew that after his conversion, much of the New Testament in the Bible was written by this man who started out so determined to stamp out the Christian belief in his lifetime. And most of his letters were written while he was imprisoned. God had placed him in a situation where there was plenty of time to pray and reflect and write. Maybe those letters wouldn't have been written otherwise.

Julia remembered asking God to give Jimmy a 'road to Damascus' encounter, if that's what it took to turn him around. Looking back, she realized God did just that when Jimmy took Allie from the riverbank that day. Throughout their ordeal, Allie showed him what grace was by her actions. Julia would never have chosen that difficult path for her son to take, but since then she had no doubt those circumstances and Allie were what led Jimmy to God and peace and reconciliation with his family and his heredity.

And now she prayed that the secrets she revealed to him would not bring back the bitterness and anger of his past.

Julia dipped her spoon into the dumplings and gravy and put it in her mouth. She shut her eyes as she savored the taste. Matilda was a wonderful cook.

"Are you going to eat your pie, Momma?" a voice broke into her thoughts.

Julia opened her eyes to see Jimmy beside her bed, fork in hand. She saw no trace of anger and resentment in his face, only a covetous look for her piece of apple pie.

She smiled and shook her head, no. "But I just want a taste first."

He waited until she had tasted a bite, then grabbed the dainty china plate and took it back to his bed.

"You impatient pig!" scolded Mercy. "That was your mother's piece of pie! I could've brought you another slice. Why do you turn back into a little boy around your mother at times?"

"I don't either!" said Jimmy, but his expression betrayed him.

And Julia couldn't have been more pleased.

Chapter 10

J ulia and Jimmy had no other uninterrupted moments to finish their talk before he and Mercy and Jack headed for home the next morning. His brother Matt had taken the new grulla mare back to Grace with him after his first visit so Jimmy wouldn't have to deal with that. Langston Locke had Matilda's husband Rune ready the Taylors' carriage while Jimmy and his family said goodbye to Julia and Mercy's parents.

"We're not finished talking, Mother," he said quietly as he leaned down to kiss her cheek.

"I know," she whispered.

"We'll see you soon, Julia," said Mercy as she kissed her goodbye and lifted up Jack to do the same. "You know Grace can't run without you."

"Bye, Meemaw," the little boy said.

"Bye, Pony. Y'all be careful, and don't let Daddy buy any more horses on the way home."

"I won't," Jack said solemnly.

Jimmy frowned at his mother. Mercy giggled as she steered Jack out the door.

"Sorry," said Julia, smiling apologetically. "That wasn't as funny as I thought it'd be. Kiss my baby girls for me. I've sure missed them."

That put a smile back on Jimmy's face as he nodded. He couldn't wait to see his daughters either. Mae was two and a half years old, and had black hair and blue eyes. Biriney was almost seven months and flaxen-haired like her mother. He already felt such a sense of protectiveness toward them. They were going to be beautiful like their mother, and he figured he would have to beat the boys off with a stick in the not too distant future.

He never realized how powerful love could be until he had his own children. He loved Mercy with a passion, but the love for his children was different—more overwhelming with the sense of responsibility and care. His mother had said that Nah-kay knew Julia couldn't leave her children, even if the opportunity presented itself. He understood what she meant. He understood why she couldn't leave him and Faith with the Indeh all those years ago when so many thought it would have been best for their sake. And as hard and difficult as raising children could be at times, he knew, too, that he could never abandon his own children.

Julia was surprised when he walked around the bed and hugged her again, this time whispering, "I love you, Momma."

Then he pulled back and looked her in the face and said, "And I never knew just how much you loved me until I had my own children. You never gave up on me. You always defended me. You always loved me, and I know you always did what you thought was best for me, even when I didn't understand it. And I'm so glad now that you made sure that Faith and I came back with you and Justin."

Julia's eyes filled with tears. "I could never leave you, Jimmy," she said, lowering her voice to a whisper, "even after Nantan told me when you were two years old that he would let me go home, but I had to leave my children. So there was no choice for me but to stay."

Jimmy shut his eyes, overwhelmed with his mother's admission of love. "I'm sorry I was such a pain in the—"

"Son—"

"—behind... all those years."

"You still are, dear," she smiled as she teased him. "But I love you anyway."

"I know," he said, grasping her hand. "I'll see you soon."

Matthew brought Vestal to see Julia that afternoon, and she insisted on staying and taking care of Julia until she was ready to come home. Julia stayed a full week with Langston and Hazel Locke until she finally convinced her husband that she could handle the carriage ride home without too much pain to her shoulder. She hated to admit it, but the injury was taking much longer to heal than she realized it would. But she needed to be home.

The carriage ride was difficult for her, and Julia tried to hide it, but her pale face and the dark circles under her eyes revealed the toll the bumpy ride had taken on her. Try as she might, she didn't have the strength to step down from the carriage. Matthew had to carry her inside, fussing every step of the way that they should have been more patient and given her more time to heal.

Julia tried to greet all of her family waiting to see her on the back porch, but Matthew marched right on past everyone and up the stairs to their bedroom, saying that Julia needed her rest. As soon as he gently sat her down on the side of the bed, she burst into tears.

"What's wrong?" asked Matthew, concerned that she had re-injured her shoulder. "Are you hurting? Dang it, Vestal. I knew we brought her home too soon. Can I get you anything, honey?"

Julia wiped her eyes and said, "I'm sorry I didn't handle that ride as well as I thought I would, Matthew, but home is *exactly* where I need to be right now. And I need to see my family. Right now. I refuse to get in this bed until I see my kids and my grandkids. You just plowed right on past everyone, and you ought to know that they're the best medicine I could ever have."

But before she had finished, Matthew was already out the bedroom door hollering for everyone to come upstairs.

Several more days passed until Jimmy had the opportunity to speak with his mother alone again. She sat in a chair on the front porch, built on the same level as the parlor and her bedroom on the second floor. Matt and Catherine and their five boys had taken over the third floor bedrooms. The house had become too big for just Matthew and Julia, so Matthew asked his firstborn and his family to move in with them since Matt would inherit the house and the land some day. Jimmy and Mercy moved into Matt and Catherine's house, which was a smaller, two-story version of the big house.

Jimmy had begun working with the new grulla mare, and had picked up the mail from his sister's store to take to his mother. He pulled up when he saw her wave at him from the front porch, and got down and tied the horse to one of the hitching rings.

He took the steps two at a time and greeted her with a kiss before handing her the mail and sitting down beside her.

"How are you feeling?"

"Like I've gone to seed. If I don't get up and start doing something soon, rigor mortis is going to set in."

Jimmy laughed. "You'll be running circles around us all in no time, Mother."

"It's hard," she said. "I feel pretty worthless."

"Just be patient. You got a letter from Faith in there."

Julia's face brightened, and she thumbed through the few pieces of mail until she found it. She started to tear open the envelope.

"We need to tell her, Momma. She's never going to forgive us for not telling her about the shooting."

"We're going to tell her, but at Christmas when they're coming anyway. If we tell her now, you know she'll want to come home immediately, and it's just too hard on them to travel with those babies. And then they wouldn't be able to come back in a few weeks for Christmas when Justin and Allie and Uncle John will be here."

"And they're all going to throw a fit, too, when they find out we neglected to tell them."

"Now if I was dying, then yes, we would've told everyone and they would've come. But I'm not dying, so we didn't need to tell them so everyone will get to come here for Christmas like we planned. I'll be much stronger by then and will enjoy the visit more."

"Well, we're all going to direct them to you when they start hollering about it."

"I can handle it." Julia unfolded the letter. "You want to hear what your sister has to say?"

"Sure, and then we're going to talk some more," he said, looking around, "if no one's within earshot."

Julia nodded and began reading.

"Dear Mom, Dad, & All,

Hope this finds you well…"

Jimmy snickered.

"Hush," said Julia as she continued to read.

"The little ones are asleep, Caitlin's doing chores in the barn, and I have only a few moments to myself to write you. I can't wait to see all of you at Christmas and catch up with everyone.

We finally bought that place I've been writing you about, and we moved out here three weeks ago. I'm sorry I haven't written sooner to tell you, but we've been so busy. I hope you'll be able to come see us soon. We were able to buy four sections of land about eleven miles southeast of town with the inheritance money. We've moved into the ranch house, but we also have a camp house, a barn, sturdy pens, a 40 acre horse trap, fifty-two momma cows and three happy bulls. As for water, we're fortunate that the place already has a windmill, and a well digger is almost finished drilling a second one right now, and Pecan Bayou also runs through our place.

More than half of the ranch is fenced, and Ethan plans to fence the rest of it as soon as he can. We've found the fences cut in several places in one of the pastures and are in dire need of repair before we run cattle on it. Ethan said he's heard there's been a lot of fighting over the fencing around here—that the cattlemen who prefer open range grazing are fighting farmers and ranchers who want to fence and protect their property. We've also heard that some people are fencing across public roads, and that makes it hard for folks to get around. Hopefully, they'll be able to resolve this soon. Ethan says he's not going to worry about it. I'll probably do enough worrying for both of us. (smile)

As for the children, I'm back to teaching Caitlin here at home since we're too far from town for her to go by herself to the community school. She is such a bright young lady—she only asks my help with her school work if she can't figure it out herself. And remember, she is a voracious reader, so there's a hint for Christmas. She's also her daddy's right-hand man—you should see her on a horse. She can out-ride me. She helps me so much with the little ones, too.

Ella Vae and Cele are such good company for each other and tend to stay out of trouble. Sam's another story, though. We have to watch him every minute or he'll be into something or on top of the table. Caitlin's trying to teach him to say the animal sounds. She asks him, "What does a horsie say?" He answers,

"Neigh!" "What does a cow say?" He answers, "Neigh!" and on and on. Neigh is his answer for every animal sound. He can make child-rearing so hard at times, but then he'll come lay his little head against my knee or hug me with such vigor that it just melts my heart. I don't know what I would do without these children. They are the best part of my life. And speaking of children, I hear a little boy stirring so I'll have to end this quickly.

Ethan and I are so grateful that we've been able to start building a good life for ourselves and our children. And we couldn't have done this without your help, Mom and Dad. I love you more than words can express.

I am always and sincerely your daughter,
Faith

"She sounds really happy, doesn't she?" said Julia. "I hate that I can't see those babies more than once or twice a year—and Justin's, too."

"We have to tell her, Momma," said Jimmy.

Chapter 11

Julia sighed and looked down the road leading into town.

"It all happened so long ago," she said, having second thoughts. "What good is it to dredge up the past? I've been questioning why I even told you now." She turned and looked at her son. "Has anything changed for you to know any of that?"

"Yes, it's changed my opinion of the man who gave me this skin," he said. "I need to know there was some good in him." He looked around. "Can you talk? Can you tell me some more about him?"

Julia looked around. "I think so, but let's be sparse in using his name, just in case."

Jimmy pulled his chair around to face his mother and the door. "Are you comfortable? Do you need a blanket?"

Julia shook her head. "The shawl is fine."

"Where's Vestal?"

"Her usual domain—either in the kitchen or the wash house," said Julia.

Vestal had the run of the first floor, part of which was below ground level. The kitchen, dining room, pantry, and Vestal's living quarters took up the entire area. Outside, the wash house was about twenty-five steps from the big house. Originally, the wash house was the first house the Taylors built when they came to Texas until they eventually built their three-story red brick house. Now Vestal used it primarily as a work area for laundry, storage, and a summer kitchen. Everyone else used it for baths in the big claw-footed tub.

"She rarely climbs those stairs anymore—her knees just can't take it," said Julia. "Catherine does most everything up here now, or will until I get back on my feet. She and Robert and Timbo are upstairs," she paused and listened. "No—it's too quiet. They must be down at the barn with Matt. And your father went to Waco with Marcus." Her eyes drifted to the horse pulling up the grass around the hitching post.

"What was he like, Momma?"

"How's your mare working out?"

"She'll make a good horse," said Jimmy, glancing at the grulla mare that had been the reason for the shooting. "But you're dodging the question. Tell me about Nantan."

Julia continued to watch the horse, but her thoughts were elsewhere. "He knew he was going to die."

"What?"

"He told me that he wouldn't live to see you become a man," she said. "I don't know how he knew that. Maybe God put it in his heart."

"Did you want him to die?"

"No, of course not. Nantan was a fierce warrior against his adversaries, and I'm sure he did some reprehensible acts toward the white man, but within his life… his ways… and with his people, he was an honorable, hard-working man who loved and provided for and protected his family with just as fierce a determination."

"That sounds like Nah-kay."

Julia smiled and nodded. "He and his mother were very much alike. It didn't take long for me to learn that Nah-kay was a treasure—I learned so much from her."

"You said that he was willing to let you leave, but you couldn't take your children."

Julia nodded. "He knew I wouldn't leave without them, but after I was there a while, I think it was important for him to think that I was staying of my own free will."

"Were you?"

"No, although I didn't feel like a prisoner after we were there only a few weeks. I think a part of me was glad that the children kept me from making that choice."

"Why?"

"Because I felt like I wasn't being unfaithful to my husband as long as I was there against my will, and the children forced me to stay."

"I need to ask you something," said Jimmy, "and I understand if you won't tell me. Justin told me years ago that Father didn't kill Nantan, but Justin wasn't there when it happened. I was, but I don't remember. And I won't be angry about it—I spent enough years being angry about something I understood so little of. Now that I have a wife and children, I know how

51

I'd feel if someone took them from me. But you were there. You saw what happened. Was Justin telling me the truth, or were you trying to protect me from what really happened?"

Julia's eyes filled with tears at the memory. "Your father didn't kill Nantan. And I'm telling you the truth, son. I am so grateful that Matthew wasn't the one who fired the shots. It would have been even more difficult for me to cope with that. Nantan was holding you—running with you toward me. He was trying to protect you, knowing you would be safe in my arms. But he didn't make it, and by the time I reached him, you were lying beside him with his arm draped over you. I thought you both had been killed, and that was the worst moment of my life—it's what I saw again in Waco when Jack ran up to you lying motionless on the street. It all came back to me so vividly—the shock and the horror of that day."

"I'm so sorry, Mother. If I'd only known what buying that horse—"

"No, honey," Julia interrupted him. "That wasn't your fault. What happened happened, so please don't let guilt eat you up. For weeks after Nantan died, I wrestled with the 'what ifs' until it just about drove me mad. I thought I could've saved Nantan's life if I had waited only ten minutes before leaving... if I had been in camp at that moment instead of out in the corn field..."

She paused with the memory. "The corn harvest was the best time of the year for us—a time of abundant food and celebration. But it was also a time of greatest vulnerability for us because the corn tied us to those areas for certain times of the year. If our enemies found our corn fields, they knew we would eventually return to them. And that's how your father finally found us. Someone he had hired had found our corn field among several others in this particular area. The stalks were about knee high, so he had time to travel to get word back to your father about the fields."

"How did he know that corn field belonged to the group you were with?"

"He didn't, but that wasn't his job. He was hired to scout for either Apache bands with a yellow-haired woman among them or corn fields that meant a band would be coming back there eventually. That wasn't the first time they had found and watched the corn. Someone had told Matthew to look for seemingly abandoned corn fields—that the Apaches had planted them and moved on, but would eventually return. This was the third planting season that Matthew had been finding and watching corn fields his scouts had located."

"You said yellow-haired woman."

"My hair wasn't always white," said Julia. "It used to be as yellow as corn silk when I was taken."

"Like Mercy's?"

Julia nodded. "By the time Matthew found us, though, it had turned completely white. My father's hair was the same way, although I was younger when mine turned."

"I've always liked your hair. It never made you look old to me—maybe regal, but not old."

Julia smiled. "You sure know how to make an old woman feel good."

Jimmy chuckled.

Julia's face became solemn. "In telling you these things about our past, I don't want to make you angry or sad or bitter."

"It won't, Mother," said Jimmy. "I know you were forced into a situation you had no control over. I know Nantan used you and Justin to try to right a terrible wrong that happened in his life. But that still didn't justify what he did to you. In a strange way, though, it's comforting for me to know that your life during that time, the time that brought me into the world, wasn't all bad—that my birth wasn't a mistake—"

An involuntary gasp from Julia interrupted him. "Did you think that all these years?"

"I tried not to dwell on it, but yes, that was always in the back of my mind."

Julia's face crinkled up, and the tears came again.

"I'm sorry, Momma," Jimmy said, concerned. "I didn't mean to upset you."

She shook her head and tried to gain her composure. "I'm the one who should be sorry. I had no idea you thought that. Don't ever think you were a mistake, Jimmy Taylor. You brought such joy to my life—to Nantan and Nah-kay's lives—even your brother Justin loved you so. And you know what you mean to Faith. But I want you to know that your coming replaced the sorrow and deep anger in your father's life."

"You called him 'my father.' I don't remember you ever doing that before."

"Well, he *was* your father, but after we came back to Grace we just didn't talk about him. We couldn't. We had to put that life behind us if we wanted to get on with our lives as Taylors. And you are a Taylor now, Jimmy."

"I know, Momma. But I'm glad you told me about Nantan. I'm glad to know he was an honorable man among his own people. I'm so glad to know he wasn't the one who hurt you, and I'm especially thankful that he saved your life and took good care of you... of us."

"Me, too."

"Can we tell Faith when she comes at Christmas?"

Julia nodded. "But until then, we mustn't speak of it again for your father's sake. Agreed?"

"Agreed."

Two weeks before Christmas, Julia received a short letter from Faith saying that she and the children would arrive by stage on Christmas Eve. She wrote that Ethan would have to stay and watch the fence lines—that they had found more cuts in the fences and a written warning nailed to a post. She said Ethan had assured her they were just empty threats, and repaired the fences anyway.

Julia was disappointed that Ethan wouldn't be able to make it, and she was worried about the fence-cutting. "It sounds like the situation is getting more dangerous for them."

"I think some of us need to go back with Faith to help Ethan for a little while," said Matthew. "There's no reason a man can't protect his property with a fence."

"Maybe Justin can help, too, when he gets here," said Julia. "I'm sure John will allow him a little more time off when he finds out what's happening."

"Who are these people cutting the fences?" asked Matt.

"From what I've read," said Matthew, "the trouble started with people fencing property that blocked access to public land, and that affected the landless cattlemen who depend on the open range to graze their cattle. And some people fenced across public roads and blocked access to schools and churches, too. So the fencers haven't been entirely innocent in this conflict. But now the fence-cutting has spread to legally owned ranches like Faith and Ethan's. The drought this year hasn't helped matters, either. Cattlemen are getting desperate for water, and Ethan and Faith have it."

"Sounds like it's getting completely out of hand," said Matt.

"And their ranch in Brown County is right in the thick of it."

Chapter 12

Brownwood, Texas

George Samuel spooned some honey onto his plate and asked Ethan to pass him the biscuits.

"What's the sheriff going to do about the fence-cutters, Ethan?" he asked. "Did you see him at church this morning?"

"The dinner table's not the place to discuss this, George," said France. "The children…"

"We're not babies anymore," said Mac, ten years old and the youngest of the Samuel children.

"We already know about it, Mother," said Finn, a mature fourteen-year-old. "Everybody's been talking about it at school for weeks now."

"The sheriff wasn't there," said Ethan. "I heard the fence-cutters are hitting just about every place around here, and our lawmen are stretched really thin."

"I thought you were going to get into it with Mr. Tyrrell after church," said K. James. "Your face was pretty red."

"K. James!" said France. "Mind your manners."

"Well, he said the wrong thing within earshot of me, and everyone knows he sympathizes with the fence-cutters," said Ethan. "I have a feeling he knows some of the people doing the fence-cutting in our area, if he's not one of them."

Ever since Faith and Ethan had moved out to the ranch they still attended church on Sundays in Brownwood, and had made it a practice to eat Sunday dinner with the Samuels. If a dance or church social was scheduled on Saturday night, they would come in to town on Saturday afternoon and stay with the Samuels. The ranch was a good hour and a half from town by wagon or buggy. A loping horse could travel it in half the time.

Faith Taylor had moved to Brownwood to work for the Samuels over six years before. She was a full-blooded Apache, but the community had accepted her because the Samuels had accepted her. George and France had no children of their own, but had adopted eleven children over a short period of two years. They had hired Faith to tutor the younger children and help France with the household chores. Faith's brother Jimmy had known the Samuels for several years and had recommended his sister for the job. During that time she met and married Ethan Murray after working eight months for the Samuels. That was five and a half years ago, and Faith continued to help the Samuels until her first child, Ella Vae—now four, was born. Lucille, 'Cele' for short, came along eleven months later, and Sam—Samuel, named in honor of the Samuels, was born two years after that.

The Samuels were currently down to only eight children under their roof since Katherine and Lorelle had married local boys and moved out, and eighteen-year-old Joseph was in his second year at Baylor University, an all male school in Waco.

France lifted up her hands in resignation at the direction the conversation had headed. "Well, maybe it's time for me to get the coffee and cake then. Faith, would you like to help? Jenna can hold Sam, and Annie, would you help the girls finish their dinner?"

Faith handed a wiggling Sam to Jenna and excused herself from the table to follow France into the kitchen.

"He's a handful, isn't he?" said France. "But he's cute as a bug."

"He's been wearing me out since he started walking at nine months," said Faith. "Neither of the girls started walking until they were around a year old so I thought I'd have at least three more months of relative calm before he started getting into everything. The girls were never this rambunctious."

France pulled a large tea towel off a big rectangle-shaped pan holding the cake and set it on the table. She grabbed a knife and started cutting squares.

"That smells good," said Faith. "Nutmeg?"

France nodded. "And more—it's a spice cake. Can you get a stack of saucers and some cups down from the cupboard for me? I think Ethan and George and my three oldest boys are the only ones that want coffee, or do you?"

Faith shook her head, no. "On second thought, I think I can use a cup so I won't doze off and fall out of the buggy going home."

"You ought to stay and take a nap before you leave. George and I take our day of rest very seriously around here—it's the only day I allow myself to take a nap anymore. The kids know not to be loud in the house after dinner, and Emma and Zane would love to have Caitlin for a bit longer. They've sure missed seeing her at school every day."

"That sounds so tempting," said Faith as she picked up some crumbs from the pan and tasted them. "Mmmm. I just haven't had the time to fix many sweets lately. It's too hard with Sam right now."

France lowered her voice. "I imagine Finn would've been a lot like Sam when he was a baby, but fortunately, we got him when he was eight. And you know what? My stubborn little boy is turning out to be the most loyal and hardest-working one of the bunch. So if you can just have the resolve and energy to keep Sam on the right track, I imagine he's going to turn out to be an outstanding young man."

"That's encouraging to hear," said Faith, smiling. "How's Joseph doing at school this year?"

"His last letter was a far cry from the first one he sent us when he went off to college last year. Sounded like he was going to fail that first term—he said the courses were much harder than his schooling here at home. But by the second term, he was figuring out how to study better and keep up with his readings instead of waiting until the last minute, which he always did before. He met some friends that have helped tutor him as well, so he's doing very well this year. He'll be home on Tuesday for the Christmas break."

"I thought he was working."

France nodded as she spooned a sweet, white sauce on the cake slices. "He is, but his job is with the school, and they close during the time off, too."

"Here," Faith reached for the sauce spoon. "I can do that—you can keep cutting."

"His working is part of our agreement with Joseph. We'll help him through school if he'll pass his courses and help support himself. George believes his education will mean more to him if he's invested something in it. And he's gaining some work experience along with his book knowledge."

"I think Ethan wants to talk to George about hiring him during the weekdays over his holiday. He really needs the help, France. Caitlin works as hard as any man alongside her daddy, but she's just not strong enough to dig very many postholes at a time and pull fence wire tight enough, and the job's too big for Ethan by himself. In fact, he could use R. James and K. James, too, if George can spare them."

"Is it dangerous," asked France, "you know, with the fence-cutting going on out there?"

"Ethan said they do their dirty work at night, and it hasn't happened that often, so he doesn't seem to be too worried about putting up new fence or repairing old fence during the day. Nobody's ever dared confront Ethan during the daytime. He'd put some fear into them if they did."

"Well, my boys will eat you out of house and home. Have you noticed how tall they've grown?"

Faith smiled and nodded her head as she carried the tray of cake slices to the table.

France followed with the tray of coffee and cups.

"… and it's just during the week, if you need them to work on the weekends for you," Ethan was saying to George.

"Well, I was counting on Joseph and K. James to take a third freight wagon with Max and make a trip to Fort Worth while they're out of school. That'll take up most of their break."

"I can go in Joseph's place, Father!" said R. James. "I'm fifteen years old. Joseph's been doing it since he was thirteen. And you know he'd rather work at the ranch with Ethan."

The freight hauling trips had become a sort of rite of passage into manhood for the males in the Samuel household. Hauling freight was actually George Samuel's first job when he and France moved to Brownwood years before. But he eventually built a store with the profits and sold the freight business to a friend, Max Roeder, who continued the work to this day.

Joseph had started traveling with Ethan during the summers and a few other times during the year after Ethan returned to Brownwood. He had come back to try to make a home for Caitlin, his five year old daughter. He had left her with the Samuels after his wife had died because he wasn't able to work and take care of her since his job with the railroad laying track meant long hours and constant relocating. After the Samuel's barn burned and Ethan thought for a terrifying few moments that he had lost Caitlin, he resolved never to leave her again. He found work at a local sawmill for a while, but ended up quitting in order to haul freight full time with Max Roeder. After Joseph left for college, K. James started hauling with Ethan and Mr. Roeder.

When Faith turned twenty-five, she came into her trust money set up by her father. The oldest Taylor child, Matt, would inherit the family home and land at Grace, so the other four children would receive monetary bequests.

Jenny and her husband Marcus used her inheritance to build a general store in Grace. Justin would inherit his Uncle John's land and cattle near Dalton in South Texas, so he still retained most of his money other than using some of it to build onto his house for his growing family. Jimmy started his horse breeding and training business in Grace, and Faith and Ethan purchased a ranch in Brown County after spending almost a year waiting and looking for the right place to buy. As soon as they signed the papers, Ethan retired from the freight-hauling business and began ranching full time.

"I can help Ethan, Pa," said Finn. "I'm as strong as Joseph."

"I wouldn't go saying that around your brother," said George, grinning. "He's liable to whip you."

"He can try," said Finn with a smirk. "I know how to work cattle. That's all I did last summer. I can help him with those fences."

"You were a line rider, son," said George. "You were guarding an invisible boundary. You've never worked with barbed wire."

"The horse trap was fenced in—I've been around fences."

"I don't think you know what you're getting into."

"I can learn," said Finn. "I'm a quick learner."

"And I'll pay them a fair amount, George," said Ethan.

"If Finn goes, then who'll milk Clara?" asked Zane.

"It's about time Mac learned," said Finn. "Me and R. James have done it long enough."

"R. James and I," corrected Zane.

"I can milk Clara," said Emma. "Why can't a girl do it?"

"Yeah, why can't a girl do it?" said Mac. "That sounds like a good idea to me."

"Then you'll have to wash the dishes, Mac," said Zane.

"Nuh-uh! Boys don't do girl's work!"

"Turn about is fair play," said Emma.

"*I* do boys' work, Mac," said Caitlin, siding with Emma. "I help my father build fence and work cattle. Girls aren't helpless, you know."

Mac couldn't think of a good retort, so he just frowned at them.

George looked at France. "What do you think?"

"About who milks Clara?" she teased.

"No, about Joseph and Finn helping Ethan the next few weeks."

"If Ethan can promise me they won't be in any danger, then it's fine with me."

"I wouldn't be asking if I thought it was dangerous," said Ethan. "It'll just be long days and hard work."

"I can do this, Father," said Finn. "And I'd like to earn a little money before Christmas."

"Finn needs money to buy something pretty for a girl," said Emma, and then sang, "Finn's got a sweetheart."

"I do not!!" he said adamantly, but the red creeping up his cheeks said otherwise.

"Well, France probably won't let Joseph loose until Wednesday so she'll have ample time to interrogate him about school," said George, which earned him a playful slap on the arm from his wife. "But I don't see any reason why Finn can't go back with you this afternoon."

"Great! I'll need to buy some more gloves, and I've got plenty of wire and steeples, but I'll need another pick and shovel—can I make a list and leave it with you for Joseph to bring?"

"And we're going to need some more groceries," said Faith, glancing at France.

"Why don't we just go down to the store right now before you leave so you can pick up what you need," said George. "I'll make a note of everything and you can take care of it next weekend."

"You're too generous, George." Ethan looked at Faith and France and added, "I've always said it pays to have a store-owner as a best friend."

"Hey, you don't know what it's going to cost you to feed my boys over the next couple of weeks," said George, grinning. "I just hope we're still speaking by then."

Chapter 13

C aitlin rubbed her eyes as she trudged into the kitchen early Monday morning. Daylight came late this time of year, so it was still dark outside. She plopped down in a chair and set the brush and ribbon on the table before she crossed her arms and laid her head down on top of them. Her long blonde hair fell across her shoulders.

Faith took the skillet off the hot stove and walked over and picked up the brush and began brushing her hair.

"Good morning, glory," she said.

Caitlin groaned a reply. She worked hard for her daddy, but it always took her a while to wake up and get going in the mornings.

"Daddy and Finn are already out in the barn loading the wagon, sleepy head."

Caitlin's head shot up. "Finn's awake?"

"I think he's already done most of your chores for you, too," said Faith. "He's even milked Birdie. It's going to be hard for you to keep up with that boy."

"Well, why didn't you wake me up earlier?"

"This is when you always get up."

"Well, he can't just come out here and take over everything like I'm not even here," she fussed.

"He's doing you a favor, sweetie. And he's just trying to impress your father. I'm sure he'll slow down before too long."

"Especially after a day of posthole digging," said Caitlin, smugly. "He doesn't know what he's in for."

She sat there quietly for a moment while her mother worked on her hair.

"Could you hurry it up? I need to get out there."

"Not before you eat some breakfast." Her fingers moved deftly through Caitlin's hair to make a single braid down her back. "Hand me the ribbon."

"I'll just take something with me."

Faith wove the ribbon into the last half of the braid before tying it into a bow and then firmly double-knotting it. "Maybe that'll stay until lunch. I don't know what you do out there to loosen that hair."

"I work hard, Momma," said Caitlin, jumping up to grab her coat and gloves.

"I know you do." Faith wrapped a thick piece of bacon in a pancake for her. "Here, drink some milk before you go."

Caitlin downed a cup of milk, and wiped her mouth before giving Faith a kiss and heading toward the door. She grabbed a beat-up old felt hat off a hook and started for the door.

"Wait! Don't forget your lunch," said Faith as she grabbed the wire handle of a covered bucket and handed it to her.

Caitlin almost let it drop since it was much heavier than usual.

"What'd you put in here? Rocks?" asked Caitlin before she remembered. "Oh yeah, Finn's eating with us now."

"I don't know how much that boy eats, so I probably put in more than I should have."

"I'm sure he'll eat every bit of it," she said, opening the door. "He's a Samuel, remember?" Then she waved her hand and said, "Love you!"

"Love you more!" said Faith.

Faith smiled at Caitlin's usual parting words. It didn't matter if she was going to town with her father or going to the outhouse, she always said, 'love you,' before parting.

Faith recalled memories of Caitlin when she first came to live with the Samuels. She threw tantrums and screaming fits over the least little thing. France helped Faith understand that Caitlin was reacting that way because of all the loss in her life—her mother had died and then her father had to leave her in an unfamiliar home. She said the little girl was trying to cope the only way she knew how, but her behavior made life miserable for everyone in the Samuel household those first few weeks until Mercy came to live with them for a while. Caitlin latched onto Mercy, and her behavior improved considerably when she didn't want to disappoint her. France said that Mercy may have reminded Caitlin of her mother—their hair color was the same.

Whatever it was, though, Caitlin's demeanor changed significantly for the better. But she never let go of the fear of losing someone she loved. Faith thought that might be why she began to say, 'love you,' in place of 'goodbye' not long after the barn burned down. Faith realized Caitlin's choice of words didn't sever a moment or period of time when she was apart from her loved ones. For Caitlin, saying *I love you* instead of goodbye meant the words continued; they sustained until they were together again.

Caitlin also used to hide from everyone. Sometimes it was to get out of a chore, or when she was upset about something or if she simply wanted to go play by herself. It never bothered Caitlin to be alone at times—she seemed to need moments to herself. And that continued to this day. But after a few big scares when she disappeared for several hours and no one knew where she had gone, Faith finally made her understand how important it was to let someone know where she was at all times.

Faith smiled to herself to see how far Caitlin had come. She was almost twelve years old and had grown into such a beautiful young lady. But since moving to the ranch, Caitlin had become very comfortable wearing bibbed dungarees and sturdy cotton shirts to work in. No one from Brownwood ever saw her in pants, though, and she easily turned back into a young lady when they went to town on Saturdays and Sundays, so Faith wasn't worried about her gaining a tomboy reputation.

Caitlin stepped out on the porch and looked up at the moon in the western sky. For the past several months, every stage of the moon was blue, whether it was a sliver or half or the almost full moon like this morning. Her daddy told her the newspaper said the moon looked blue because a big volcano named Krakatoa had erupted on the other side of the world sometime this past year. She didn't understand how that would turn the moon blue. The color made it seem sad to her somehow.

The moonlight and gray promise of daylight approaching in the eastern sky lit Caitlin's path as she walked across the yard. Each step stirred up a puff of dry powder. Her daddy said that the drought started as soon as he signed the papers for the ranch, but she knew better. She had heard the old-timers say that 1883 had been the driest year in decades, and that wasn't good for a new rancher. But she had also heard that was the reason they were able to buy this place at such a good price. They were fortunate to have water for the cattle, but they needed rain for the grass to grow or the cattle would have to be sold off. The ranch could hold a lot more cows if they just had the grass to feed them. She sent up another prayer for rain.

Caitlin sauntered into the barn, and Finn took one look at her and dropped a claw hammer on his foot.

"Ow!" he said before he caught himself.

Caitlin snickered as she picked up one of the barn cats. "You're going to need sturdier shoes to work in if you felt that."

"Girls aren't supposed to wear pants!" he said.

"You sound just like Mac. But I'm not about to work on a fence wearing a dress. My skirt would get tangled up in that barbed wire in no time flat."

Finn frowned disapprovingly, but he realized she did have a point.

"I bet your girlfriend doesn't wear pants," she teased him.

"No, she doesn't." He turned away from her to face Ethan.

That surprised Caitlin. He actually admitted he had a girlfriend.

"Stop picking on him, Katie," said her father. "I don't want you to run off my help on his first day."

Caitlin rolled her eyes and grinned. She loved teasing the Samuel boys.

Her father continued. "Have you come up with a brand for us yet? I need it before you go to Grace. I'm going to take it to the smithy right after Christmas so we'll have it when you get back. We have some calves that need working."

"What about a heart with an M in the middle of it?" asked Caitlin. "I think that'd make a good brand."

Finn snorted.

Ethan smiled, but shook his head, no. "I just can't see my bulls and steers wearing hearts on their rear ends—the cows, maybe, but we can't have two different brands. What about something like a 'rocking M' or '6 bar M' or something along those lines?"

Caitlin looked disappointed.

"Why'd you come up with a heart?" asked Finn. "Nobody uses a heart for a brand. Can you honestly see a tough cowboy flitting around like a pixie branding everything with a heart?"

"I just thought a heart would make us look friendly," she said, sulking. She set the cat down on the ground and petted another one that had walked up to rub against her legs. "And how would rustlers be able to change that brand easily?"

"Well, that's true, but you need to come up with something else," said Ethan. "I was just showing Finn what tools we use to build fence, although all you'll need this week is a pick ax and shovel and..."

"A strong, thick-headed boy to dig the postholes," added Caitlin. "Are you strong enough, Finn?" She reached over to grab his arm.

Finn tightened his arm muscle quickly before she touched it.

Caitlin's eyes widened before she pulled her hand away. His arm was rock hard.

"What have you been doing?" she asked.

"Would you leave the poor boy be, Katie?!" said Ethan.

"I still haul hay for Mr. Watson," he said, knowing he had impressed her.

"And you'll need string and a measuring stick," Ethan said as he held up the lantern and looked around. "And where's that tamping tool?"

"Here it is." Caitlin picked up a heavy iron bar leaning against the wall. It was chiseled on one end and blunt on the other.

"I'll take that for you," said Finn, feeling confident at that moment. "And I've won my fair share of wrestling matches."

"Yeah, with your little sisters," she couldn't help but say under her breath. The look on Finn's face told her she had taken the teasing too far, but she was stubborn.

"I can carry it myself," said Caitlin, walking to the wagon and setting it beside the stack of cedar posts.

"And *I'll* need some wire and the claw hammer and pliers and steeples— where's that can of steeples?"

"It's already on the wagon, Daddy."

"I'll just need a few to take with me, and we can leave the rest here for today. And posts—we've got a wagonload of posts. Could y'all bring up the horses and start hitching them to the wagon? I'm going to ride Crazy Ears, Katie, so can you bring him in, too? I'll get you two started on the fence around the new south windmill, and I'll use Crazy to ride the fence in the west pasture and make any repairs. We haven't had any problems in this front pasture, and I hope it stays that way. Now get going. We're burning daylight," Ethan said and then paused. "But I need to go to the house for a little bit."

They watched him walk out of the barn.

"His daily constitution," explained Caitlin, sighing impatiently. "You can set your clock by it."

Finn's face turned beet red.

"And if I didn't find everything for him, it'd be mid-morning by the time we got away from the barn. Did you see that blue moon?"

"Couldn't miss it," Finn muttered as he looked down kicking the dirt.

"Well, come on." Caitlin walked over to the wall to pull three bridles off some hooks and turned and handed them to him. Then she strode over to the corn bin and scooped up some kernels in a bucket and walked over to a door that led outside to a covered alley and several small pens attached to the barn. They stepped in one of the pens, and Caitlin shut the gate behind them.

"Just wait here; I'll bring them in this pen where we can put the bridles on them."

She walked across the pen and opened another gate, leaving it open this time. She stepped out into the horse trap and began whistling and shaking the bucket of corn so the horses could hear it.

"Jimmy taught you to do that, didn't he?" said Finn.

Caitlin turned and nodded. Three horses came trotting across the pasture towards the familiar sound. They flattened their ears and bit at each other, vying to be the first one to dip their head in the bucket. Finn thought they would trample Caitlin before she turned around and hurried back into the pen to dump the corn in a trough. The horses came running into the pen and up to the trough, and Caitlin slipped around them and shut the gate.

She turned around and motioned for Finn to come in so they could bridle the horses.

He handed her one and hung the extra one on the fence before walking over to put the headstall on the nearest horse.

"Don't mess with him yet," said Caitlin.

"Why?"

"I'll have to show you how to put a bridle on *him*."

"I already know how to do that," said Finn. "I'm not stupid."

"I didn't say you were, but that's Crazy Ears. You can't put a headstall on him the regular way or he'll go berserk."

Finn stared at the horse. "What's wrong with him?"

She worked while she explained. "Before he belonged to us, a chicken got in his stall one day and kept squawking and fluttering around his head. He went plumb crazy and kicked the fence down to get away from that bird. And from then on, he wouldn't let anyone touch his ears. Daddy bought the horse for next to nothing because everyone thought he was ruined. But Daddy figured out how he could unbuckle the headstall and bring the straps up from both sides of the neck to secure it without going over his ears."

"He doesn't look crazy to me," said Finn warily, reaching out to pat his neck.

"He's fine just as long as you don't touch his ears, but if you do, he's liable to kick you to kingdom come."

Finn backed slowly away from the horse and gave him a wide berth to get to the other horse at the end of the trough.

Chapter 14

Ethan and his small crew rode up to the new windmill in the pasture southeast of the house. The rock tank was about half full of water, so Ethan released the brake which started the blades turning. Finn hurried over to watch the water come out of the pipe perched above the tank. But nothing happened. He looked up to see the windmill blades turning and listened to the swooshing sound of it pumping, but only heard a hollow sound in the pipe. In a minute or so, though, he began to hear the sound of water gurgling up before it spilled out of the pipe into the tank. He couldn't help but smile as he held his hand under the clear, cold water splashing onto his fingers.

Ethan walked about a hundred yards southeast of the windmill to find the boundary post marking the property line. Finn followed him and asked him why he was pumping water in the tank when there weren't any cattle in the pasture yet.

"The tank's new, and I need to make sure it'll hold water," Ethan said as he began unrolling a ball of string.

Finn looked at the post. "That looks like it's been here a while."

"Ever since they surveyed the original property twenty years ago."

"This is the property line?"

"Yeah, and it may even be the county line some day. I've been hearing talk that they're going to carve out another county from Brown, Comanche, Hamilton, and Lampasas counties. I just hope it doesn't cut our property in half. I don't want to be taxed twice on the same cattle that happen to eat grass on both sides of the line."

Ethan took the end of the roll of string and tied it low on the post. He began unrolling it and walking away at an odd angle.

"This post doesn't mark a square corner," Finn told Ethan.

"You're right. It's far from being a right angle," he said. "The surveyors said it was a hundred-forty degree angle—which is harder to brace, but I'll figure out a way to do it. I want this pasture to follow the property line all the way up to the main road. The surveyors marked the perimeter of the ranch where it's unfenced, so we have something to follow."

"You said this post has been here for twenty years? That's older than Joseph," said Finn. "What kind of wood is that? Shouldn't it be rotten by now?"

"It's made from bois d'arc."

"Boydark? Never heard of it."

"That's French for 'wood of the ark' or something like that. It's also called gopherwood—like Noah's ark was made out of in the Bible. But I think most people around here know it as Osage orange wood. It's impervious to rot and insects," he said. "I plan to use it on all my corner posts and every fifth post. The rest of the fence posts are cedar. I don't want to have to come back in a few years and do this all over again."

"Sounds like you've put a lot of thought into this," said Finn.

"Yep—taking the time to learn what you can and think things through is important. And I had plenty of time to read and think when I was hauling freight all those years."

He walked up to a stake in the ground about fifty yards from the boundary post and tied the string.

"When you get here, untie the string and walk off another fifty yards to the second marker and tie the string again." Ethan went to the wagon and came back to hand Finn a six foot measuring stick and told him that the postholes needed to be about twelve feet apart. Caitlin followed him this time.

"You're going to make some people mad, Daddy," she said. "This part of the ranch has never been fenced before."

"Well, there's not enough grass to go around, and we're going to need every bit of it this year if we want to keep our cows," he explained. "We're past the days of letting free range cattle graze wherever they choose. I want to keep this ranch for you and your sisters and brother. I want to make it even bigger so you all can live off of it if you choose. But right now we don't have a choice if we want to be able to make a living on this place. We have to protect what's ours. Do you understand what I'm saying?"

Caitlin nodded her head, but she still looked concerned.

"I'm not trying to be mean, honey. I'm just looking out for my family."

"I know, Daddy. I just don't want you to get hurt."

"Nobody's going to hurt me, Katie. Now, do you think you can show Finn how to dig a decent hole?"

Caitlin grinned and nodded her head again. She walked back towards the wagon.

Finn looked to the west of the boundary post. "Why are we starting here in the middle? Why aren't we starting from the west pasture fence corner?"

"Mr. Johnson's going to help us with that stretch of fence since it borders his property, but he won't be able to start until after the first of the year. He has a couple of sons that'll come help him then. So we just have to concentrate on this line of fence to the main road and half a mile to connect it to the existing fence near the front gate."

"Why do you have to build this part of the fence by yourself?" asked Finn nodding towards the east. "Won't that property owner go halves with you?"

"That's public property for now, and free grazers use it. Their cattle come through this part of the ranch to water on a short stretch of Pecan Bayou that isn't fenced in… yet. That's why they're upset about this fence."

They started walking back toward the windmill.

"Can't you talk to them?"

"I've tried, but it almost comes to blows," he said quietly so Caitlin couldn't hear. "I think they've hired some men of questionable repute to do their dirty work for them, so most of the free grazers claim they're innocent—that it's cattle rustlers cutting the fences. I don't know what we're going to do about it, but I know I'm going to protect what's mine. I'm going to head over to the west pasture now and ride the fence line to see if there's been any more damage."

Finn spoke up. "Aren't you going to show me how to build the fence?"

"The holes are going to take you and Katie quite a while. She'll show you how deep they need to be. And if you get this stretch dug, take the string and tie it to the next marker."

Finn looked back at the line of string toward the corner post and nodded his head. "Will do," he said firmly. He refused to look the other direction where the rest of the pasture seemed to head toward infinity. He would concentrate on one section at a time.

"I'll be back around noon to see how y'all are doing," said Ethan as he mounted Crazy Ears. "And go easy on him, Katie."

"Yes, sir," she said, grinning mischievously as she walked up beside Finn. "Love you, Dad."

"Love you more!" he said as he turned Crazy and started trotting away.

Finn thought that was an odd way of saying 'bye.' He loved his parents, too, but he never said it aloud to them… except for last summer before he left for three months working as a line rider on the Weathers ranch north of town. He felt like he might never see his parents again and didn't want to leave this earth without letting them know how he felt about them. But then he came back in September, and life carried on as usual.

Finn's first lesson on fence building was left up to Caitlin, and it didn't take long. She told him he would start by digging holes… a lot of holes.

"All right, Mr. Finn," she said. "I'm going to get some rocks to mark where the holes should be. Let's start measuring from the boundary post— that'll be how many holes to that first marker? Let me see…" Caitlin squinted her eyes and looked up toward the sky while she tried to figure the answer.

"About twelve holes," said Finn.

"I'm not very good with my numbers."

"I am—I could help you sometime."

"Really?"

Finn nodded. "But we'll save time if we just measure as we dig each post—otherwise we're walking this fence line twice. Let's get to digging—I want to get as many done as we can before your father gets back."

Caitlin stood there thinking as she watched Finn get a shovel out of the back of the wagon and head towards the fence line. What he said made a lot of sense. Why hadn't she thought of that? She hadn't realized Finn was so smart. And here she had admitted she wasn't very good with her numbers, and now she showed she had little common sense, too. She hoped he didn't think she was completely daft.

"Come on!" he yelled impatiently over his shoulder.

She grabbed a shovel and hurried to catch up with him.

"How deep?" asked Finn.

"At least two feet," she said. "There's a mark on the measuring stick."

He laid the measuring stick down twice and started to dig on the windmill side of the string. The top layer of the ground was dry and hard. Finn threw down the shovel and ran back to the wagon to get the pickax. He came back and raised the pickax over his shoulder time and time again, chopping away at the hard ground with a vengeance. Then he set the ax down and picked up the shovel to move the dirt and rocks.

"Slow down, Finn," said Caitlin. "You're going to wear yourself out in no time."

"We've got a lot of fence to build and less than three weeks to do it," said Finn, shoveling while he talked. He stopped and wiped the sweat off his brow—and the air was cool. He had no idea one hole would take so long.

"Daddy said this stretch of fence is only half a mile to the road, and we'll get it done eventually, whether you've gone back to school or not," said Caitlin. "They're not all going to be this tough—we've just hit a rocky patch along here. We may have to get a bunch of holes started, and then pour water in them to help soften up the soil for us."

Caitlin ran back to the wagon and grabbed a couple of tin buckets while Finn used the pickax to start several holes. She went to the windmill tank and filled them and walked back to the boundary post.

"What if we work together on these holes?" she suggested. "You loosen up the soil, and I'll dig it out."

And she didn't say aloud, 'And we can both rest a bit while the other is working,' but she sure was thinking it. She knew Finn's pride would force him to turn down her offer if he thought she was making it easier for him.

"Sounds good to me," he said.

After the hole became too deep for the pickax, Finn found he had to use the tamping tool to break up the soil. Caitlin stayed on her hands and knees and reached down into the hole with a tin can to scoop out the loose dirt.

On the fifth hole, they hit an area where the ground was much easier to dig, but neither of them suggested working separately. They took a break for water.

"We make a good team," said Finn. "You handle that shovel and tin can pretty good for a girl."

"Hope it doesn't get back to your girlfriend. She might get jealous."

"What she doesn't know won't hurt her, unless you're planning on telling someone about this… partnership we have?"

"It'll be our secret."

"Come on, let's get back to work," he said.

They had just started on the ninth hole when Ethan came back. Finn was disappointed that they hadn't reached the first marker yet, but Ethan seemed pleased that they had made it that far. Caitlin set the lunch pail on the back of the wagon, and they helped themselves to biscuits, slices of roasted beef, and molasses cookies.

"I didn't find any more damage to the fences—maybe they'll leave us be for a while," said Ethan. "I heard the folks in Austin are trying to write some laws that'll punish fence-cutters. The governor even called for a special session a couple of months ago for that very purpose."

"But how will they catch them if the fence-cutters do most of their work at night?" asked Caitlin. "And unless they catch them actually cutting the wire, how can they prove they're guilty? It's not like stealing cattle and the sheriff finds them with the stolen livestock."

"I don't know, but I heard they might even go so far as charging someone with suspicion of fence-cutting if they catch him with a pair of pincers or wire-cutters in his pocket," said Ethan. "But ranchers like me carry that kind of tool to work on the fences, so I don't know how they're going to figure that out. I know our sheriff's worn ragged trying to curtail all the problems this is causing."

"You said that's probably why you and Momma were able to buy this ranch at a good price," said Caitlin.

"Yeah, I didn't know we were buying a battleground, but I think it'll run its course before too long. Most people aren't used to fences on such a large scale, but that's the way everything's headed. It's the folks that are fencing public property they don't even own, or blocking free grazing cattle from public lands that's making it bad for the rest of us. And as long as this drought continues, it's liable to get worse."

"You think you'll ever run out of water, Ethan?" asked Finn, glancing at the windmill still pumping.

"Not unless we have a drought of biblical proportions," he said. "I'd heard some windmills are going dry in our area because they weren't drilled deep enough, so I had the driller go twice as deep on this well. They're going to come back and re-drill the other well deeper to prevent that from happening. Land is pretty useless to raise cattle if you don't have water."

"This fence is going to block cattle from getting to Pecan Bayou, too," said Caitlin.

"The river runs right through the middle of our ranch, Katie—we can't help that."

"Well, what are the free range cattlemen going to do now?"

"They can sell me their cattle and go into another line of work if they can't provide land and water for their own livestock. This ranch can run three times the amount of cattle than what we have now. But I'm not about to buy any more until it's all fenced in. Now let's get back to work. Y'all keep digging those holes, and I'm going to start setting posts behind you. Now where'd you put that tamping tool, Katie?"

Chapter 15

Caitlin was so tired Monday night that she could hardly keep her eyes open at the dinner table. She had never done that much work before in one day, and Finn was the reason for that. She was perturbed that he didn't seem to know when to quit. Every muscle in her body ached from digging all day long. She finished eating before everyone else and got up from the table, washed her plate and headed toward her bedroom.

"I know you're tired, Katie," said Faith, "but I need you to take that bedding stacked by the door over to the camp house and fix Finn's bed." She looked at Finn. "I cleaned it out for you and Joseph today, but I just couldn't get back over there to get your beds made."

"I'm sleeping in the camp house tonight?" asked Finn, feeling quite grown up to be treated like a true hired hand.

"I thought you'd be more comfortable in a place to yourself," said Faith.

Caitlin turned to walk over to the door and pick up the bedding.

Finn could see how tuckered out she was and quickly spoke up. "I can do it myself, Faith. Caitlin doesn't have to make my bed for me."

"Are you sure?" asked Faith.

Finn nodded. "I'll see you in the morning, Katie."

Caitlin smiled appreciatively and nodded wearily and said, "Love you," as she trudged upstairs.

"Love you more," said Faith and Ethan.

"Love you, too!" echoed four-year-old Ella Vae.

As Caitlin's head touched her feather pillow a little while later, the last thought that went through her mind was that she would wake up before Finn in the morning.

But that didn't happen.

Faith had to rouse her out of bed later than usual. Caitlin was so stiff and sore she could hardly move. She dressed at the speed of an arthritic tortoise and plodded slowly downstairs. She sat at the table and assumed her usual position of placing her head on her folded arms to rest for just a few more minutes.

Faith smiled when she began to hear a light snoring in less than a minute. She saw that Caitlin's fingers held her hair ribbon, but she had forgotten to bring her brush downstairs. Faith slipped out of the house and asked Ethan and Finn to go on without Caitlin—that she needed her help for a little while. She said she would send her on Crazy Ears later if they would leave him saddled for her.

Caitlin showed up in the south pasture an hour later. She carried the lunch pail and told Finn that she had to wait for the gingerbread to finish cooking so Faith could put it in their lunch.

"Thanks for doing my chores… again," she said. "But Momma needed my help this morning."

Ethan turned to hide his smile. He saw his daughter sawing logs at the breakfast table when he came back through the big house on his way to the little house earlier.

"You missed the blue moon this morning," said Finn, grabbing the pail and setting it in the wagon. "You sleep good?"

Caitlin nodded. "You?" She counted two new holes already.

"Like a baby," he said. "You sore?"

"Naw," she said, but she stifled a groan and her eyes crossed when she stepped out of the saddle. "I'm ready to dig some more holes. Where's my gloves?"

Finn and Caitlin worked silently side by side for a while, both more tired than they cared to admit. By noontime, though, they had dug six holes in addition to the two that Finn had dug earlier. But between yesterday afternoon and that morning, Ethan had already set eighteen posts.

"He's gaining on us," said Finn, watching Ethan finish tamping down the soil around the last post before he joined them for lunch at the wagon.

"But that's an easy job compared to what we're doing."

"Look how far we've come, though," he said. "We're almost to the third marker."

Caitlin smiled as she looked back. The boundary post looked small indeed. Ethan came walking up to the wagon.

"We're making good progress, kids," he said. "I hadn't thought about it until now, but one advantage of building a fence during a drought is that we

74

haven't had to clear much undergrowth around the fence line. The ground's almost swept clean."

"But it's awfully hard to dig in places, Pa," said Caitlin, looking at her blisters.

"If they can drill a hole for water, why can't we drill a hole for a fence post?" said Finn. "There's got to be a better way than what we're doing. I bet Joseph can come up with something."

"Or maybe he's heard of a tool we can use," said Ethan. "I've never had to build fence on this large a scale before."

"I wonder what the big ranches are doing," said Finn.

"Probably hiring a lot more help than I've been able to," said Ethan. "But I've got some pretty good hands here."

Caitlin smiled at her father's compliment.

"And look out when Joseph comes," said Finn. "There'll be no stopping us."

The next morning, they found some stray cattle drinking at the windmill tank. Ethan ran them off, to Caitlin's dismay.

"But they're thirsty, Daddy!"

"I don't want them to get in the habit of using this tank when it'll be fenced off before too long. It's not helping livestock to let them get used to coming here for water and then cutting them off. They'll just stand by the fence and die of thirst."

When they stopped the wagon at the new fence line, they found a number of posts had been pulled out and scattered. A ragged piece of paper was tacked to one of the posts left standing. Ethan jerked it off and read it to himself.

The river belongs to all of us—don't fence it off if you know what's good for you.

"Who do they think they are—telling me what I can and can't do with my own property?!" he said angrily. "And I guess the grass belongs to all of us, too. Their cattle would graze all the way to the river and back, leaving nothing for my livestock. But according to this note I shouldn't be bothered about that."

"I told you this fence would make them mad," said Caitlin.

"Well, they've made me mad, too. I'm coming back out here tonight."

"No, you're not, Daddy!" said Caitlin, alarmed to see her father so angry. "It might be dangerous."

"I'm not going to allow y'all to come out here and work your fingers to the bone just to let some riffraff destroy all our hard work, Katie. There comes a time when you have to stand up and defend what's yours. You can't let people run over you."

"But I don't want you to get hurt!" she said, almost on the verge of tears.

"I'm not going to get hurt, honey—I'll stay out of sight, but if I hear something milling around our fence line, I'll just spray the area with buckshot."

"You're going to shoot your gun? What if they shoot back?"

"I won't be out in the open. But I'm going to protect what's ours. If I don't, we'll eventually lose it."

"And I can come with you and help," said Finn, determinedly. "I know how to shoot a gun."

"You're not going anywhere but your bed tonight," said Ethan. "Your mother would kill me on sight if I put you in any kind of danger."

"You said you weren't in any danger, but it's sounding more dangerous all the time," said Caitlin.

"I promise I'm not going to let myself get hurt, Katie. How could y'all run this ranch without me? Now let's get this mess cleaned up and repair the damage."

Chapter 16

J oseph Samuel showed up an hour later. After an enthusiastic reunion with his younger brother since he hadn't seen him in four months, Ethan had Joseph help him gather up the rest of the fence posts that had been pulled out and re-set them.

"We're the ones that need the most help," mumbled Finn, perturbed that Joseph was getting off so easy.

Caitlin told him that her daddy was probably catching him up on the situation. She was right. Ethan told Joseph about the fence-cutting problems that had been going on in the area. He also shared what he planned to do that night, and Joseph insisted on coming with him, but Ethan wouldn't hear of it.

"I promised your mother that you and Finn would be in no danger working on this fence, and I wouldn't be able to live with myself if something happened to either of you."

When Joseph tried to argue, Ethan stopped him and said that he and Finn were not allowed to leave the perimeter of the ranch headquarters after dark either. When Joseph balked, Ethan said he would send him and his brother home right then and there if he didn't give his word. Joseph finally gave in, but he wasn't happy about it.

The two had become good friends hauling freight together, and Joseph felt that if someone was picking on his friend, he was picking on him, too. But Ethan steered him away from the subject by asking what all was going on in the world outside of the ranch. Joseph had a lot to report.

"The State's opened up another college in Austin this term, but I'm thinking about pulling out of Baylor and transferring to Texas A.M.C. in Bryan."

"Really? Isn't that a military school?" asked Ethan. "Is that what the 'M' stands for? Or does it mean 'All Male College'?"

Joseph laughed. "Yeah—I'm not too happy about going to another school without girls, but maybe I'll pay more attention to the professors and actually learn something while I'm there. A.M.C. stands for 'Agricultural and Mechanical College,' which is what I'm most interested in, but they also require every student to join the Corps of Cadets."

"What do you want to do when you get out?"

"I'm not sure, but I know I like to build things. I've always liked to take things apart and see what makes them work."

"Maybe you can invent something that will speed up this fence-building process," said Ethan. "Finn said he thought you could—he said if they can drill a hole for water, why can't they drill holes for fence posts?"

"He came up with that?" said Joseph, glancing at his younger brother. "That's a good idea. I'll have to give it some thought."

He looked toward Caitlin and Finn down the line. They already looked tired. He told Ethan he would go over and relieve them for a while.

"Here he comes," said Caitlin, "unless Daddy isn't finished visiting and calls him back. And if that's the case, they're going to catch up with us quick."

"I did some figuring last night," said Finn, "The markers are fifty yards apart. So if we have a mile to fence this pasture in, that's one-thousand, seven hundred sixty yards, or thirty-five markers. It takes twelve holes for every marker, so that's twelve times thirty-five, or four-hundred and twenty holes that we have to dig, right?"

Caitlin just stared at him wide-eyed. "I haven't the slightest idea how you came up with that, but I think I'd rather not know how many holes we have to dig. It sounds impossible now."

"Well, with Joseph's help, I think we might be able to make it."

"Let's just keep digging and not think about those four hundred and twenty holes ahead of us," she said.

"Actually, it's only three hundred and eighty-four holes left."

Caitlin frowned at him. "Oh! Thanks, Finn. That makes me feel *sooo* much better." She laid the measuring stick down twice and stepped on the shovel to start the next hole. "I'm going to have blisters on top of my blisters," she mumbled to herself.

Joseph walked up to her. "Here, Katie—give me that shovel. Why don't you go help your father for a little while?"

Caitlin gladly handed her shovel over to him and stepped back.

"Ethan told me your idea about a posthole boring tool," he said as he watched Finn loosen the ground with a pickax. "I think we can come up with something that'll help save time *and* our backs. Let's draw something on paper and go see the smithy on Saturday."

"Really?" asked Finn. "You think it will work?"

"Never know until we try," he said. "Now back up and let me shovel awhile."

After supper on Wednesday night, Ethan took a bedroll and his shotgun and started out the door. Faith didn't say much about it earlier at the dinner table when Ethan told her his plans. But after she put the little ones to bed, she was ready to talk. Joseph and Finn had already left for the camp house. Caitlin had gone upstairs to bed, but she could still hear their voices.

"You're not going out there by yourself, Ethan," said Faith, following him out the door. "What if you get shot?"

"They're not going to see me," he said. "And I'm not going to play this seesaw game of us working hard to put this fence up just for them to tear it down and us have to turn around and put it back up for them to tear down again. It's got to stop."

"Are you going to shoot them?"

"If somebody comes around, I'll just fire some warning shots in the air to let them know somebody's watching. That ought to scare them off."

"How do you know that? What if they shoot back at you?"

"I'll be hiding behind something. I'm not going to take any chances, Faith."

"Well, how do you know where they'll strike?"

"I don't, but I'm going to watch along where we've been working. Sounds carry a long way at night."

"I don't like this, Ethan," said Faith. "I don't like this one bit."

"I'll be all right," he assured her. "And Crazy and I will come running home if there's bigger trouble."

"What if you can't get home?" asked Faith, close to tears. "I'm scared for you, Ethan."

"I promise I'll be home before breakfast," he said, setting his gun against the house. He leaned down and kissed his wife and hugged her tight. Then he picked up his shotgun and headed toward the barn.

The sound of a window sash sliding open above the porch broke the silence.

"Love you, Daddy!" Caitlin hollered.

"Love you more!" he hollered back.

Faith stood on the porch and watched him mount Crazy Ears and wave at her before she turned around and went back inside the house. She walked across the room and into her bedroom and shut the door before she allowed herself to cry. She undressed and slipped her nightgown over her head and crawled into bed. It seemed so big without Ethan in it. She wiped away another round of tears and asked God to protect him. Then she tossed and turned in the bed for hours before finally going to sleep.

Just before daylight she woke with a start and felt the bed next to her.

Still empty.

She had to go find him. She jumped up, dashed through the dark house bare-footed, threw open the door, and ran right into the arms of her husband.

She let out a startled yelp. "Ethan?"

"Who else were you expecting?" he said, teasing her.

Her arms wrapped around his neck so tight, he thought she was going to choke him.

"I told you I'd be here before—," he tried to say, but her kiss cut him off.

Faith was kissing him like there was no tomorrow, so he dropped his bedroll on the porch, and tried to lean the shotgun against the wall before he dropped it, too. He picked her up and carried her into the house and ran into the table trying to get to the bedroom.

After a minute or so, Ethan came running back out on the porch in his long johns and quickly kicked his bedroll inside and grabbed his shotgun to put up safely out of the way of little hands.

Across the yard in the shadow of the camp house porch, Joseph chuckled before heading back inside. He paused to look at the moon, which seemed to bathe everything in a mournful shade of blue.

Chapter 17

Breakfast came a little late Thursday morning. Out of the clear blue, Joseph commented that sounds do carry farther during the night. Ethan waited for him to expound on the statement, but Joseph responded only with silence and a smirk.

"I didn't hear or see a thing last night," said Ethan. "I ended up getting a pretty good night's sleep out there under the stars. And when that blue moon rose, I had to put my hat over my head to shut out the light."

"Well, I'm glad *somebody* got some sleep around here," said Faith.

Her eyes were swollen and bloodshot. And she had a full day ahead of her washing clothes and packing for the trip she and the children would be taking to her parents' home in Grace early Saturday morning.

She was disappointed that Ethan couldn't go, and even told him earlier that they would stay home with him. But he knew this was the only time during the year she would get to see all of her family together, so he insisted that she and the children go. Matt and Jenny and their families lived in Grace, but Justin and his wife Allie and their four children would be traveling from Dalton in South Texas along with their mother's brother, John Stockton. They had made it a tradition to come every Christmas and stay several weeks. The only time that didn't happen was when Allie was too close to delivering her third child, Blake, four years ago.

The Brownwood stage normally left around noon on Saturdays, and the trip to Waco took three days, arriving at noon on Tuesdays. But since Christmas fell on a Tuesday this year, the stage line re-scheduled the trip to start at daybreak on Saturday in order to get to Waco Monday evening so their drivers could spend Christmas Day with their families.

Ethan had arranged to meet the stage coach at ten minutes to eight at the gate to their ranch for them to pick up his family. The house was about a mile off the main road, and the trip to town was another ten miles, so that cut twenty miles off their trip.

Faith planned to have their Christmas dinner Friday evening with Ethan and the Samuel brothers. They would exchange a few small gifts at that time.

The fence crew made good progress that Thursday. Ethan worked on the braces of the original property post, and then planned to brace a post every hundred feet or so for support when they would stretch the wire. But that wouldn't happen until all the posts were set. Ethan said they didn't have to worry about any fence-cutting along there since the wire wasn't up yet, but they knew now that it wasn't only the wire that was tampered with. He planned to stay out there again that night and make sure no one bothered the fence posts.

After they came back to the house, Ethan said he needed to check some of the old fence line before he went back to the new pasture. Instead of sitting down to dinner, he tore off some bread and wrapped some meat in it and told Faith he would be back before breakfast Friday. He leaned over and kissed her cheek.

"Will you be waiting at the door for me, sweetheart?" Ethan asked with a hint of a smile and anticipation in his eyes.

Joseph guffawed in the middle of a bite of food. Faith's mouth dropped open in shock as she stared at Joseph. Then she glared at her husband.

"What?" he asked innocently.

"In answer to your question—no, I won't be waiting at the door. I'm sure I'll be sound asleep when you come in," Faith said coolly.

Ethan looked at the faces around the room for a clue to what he had said to upset his wife. Caitlin shrugged her shoulders.

"Love you, Daddy," she said, smiling.

"Love y'all, too," he said as he turned toward the door.

Joseph set his fork down and followed him out the door.

"I'm sorry, Ethan," he said, walking alongside him to the barn.

"Sorry for what?"

"Faith thinks you've been talking to me," he said.

"Talking to you? What's wrong with that?"

"I heard a noise early this morning and got up to check on it," explained Joseph. "But all I saw was you and Faith on the porch."

Ethan thought for a moment and finally put two and two together. "Oh!" He couldn't help but grin at first, but it disappeared just as quickly. "So she's mad now because she thinks I've been talking to you about our private matters?"

"I reckon so."

"Well, you tell her I haven't been talking to you."

"I'm not about to tell her that—it's not my place," argued Joseph. "That'll make her even more uncomfortable." He turned around to head back to the house. "You tell her when you get back. And be careful out there tonight."

"I was kind of hoping to have another welcome home greeting like that tomorrow morning."

"I didn't hear that," said Joseph, walking away.

"But I guess that's out of the question now," Ethan mumbled to himself.

He climbed on Crazy Ears and headed toward the west pasture. After riding a mile or so and seeing that part of the fence was intact, he turned and rode alongside Pecan Bayou toward the south to get over to the new pasture so he could get settled in before dark. He could hear a calf bawling incessantly and a mother cow answering and figured they had gotten separated, so he rode towards the sound. He came upon a dry slough where water had washed out and exposed the roots of a tree. He got off his horse and walked to the edge and saw that a calf was tangled in the roots. It looked like it had slipped down the embankment and the momma cow couldn't get to it. She sounded mighty unhappy.

"Hang on, Momma," he said, climbing down towards the calf. "I'll get your baby loose in no time."

Ethan was able to un-wedge the front legs and the calf struggled to get away from him, but some smaller roots were frayed and twisted around a back foot. Ethan pulled out his knife from its leather sheath and started sawing on them.

"You're a pretty little heifer," he said. "And feisty, too. I just might have to name you Katie."

He sawed through the last of the gnarled roots and the hoof came free. The calf gave Ethan one swift kick for good measure before scrambling away.

"Well, you ungrateful hussy!"

Ethan felt a burning in his left leg and looked down. The hand holding the knife had taken the full force of the kick, and it had jabbed the four inch blade full into his thigh. Ethan suddenly felt light-headed just looking at it. Watching the bloodstain crawl down his pants leg made him nauseated.

"Dadgummit," he said as he sat back on the roots. "Faith's going to be mad if I ruin these pants."

He took a couple of deep breaths and looked away. A thought passed through his head that it might help to holler when he pulled the knife out, so he hollered as he jerked it out. Blood squirted from the slit in his pants, so he untied his kerchief from around his neck and tied it over the wound. He wiped the bloody blade on his pants leg and sheathed it, and then turned quickly and leaned over and lost what little supper he had eaten.

He sat there for a moment, breathing deeply before chancing a look at the wound again. How big could a knife wound be? He decided he would let Faith take a look at it instead of him. He tried to stand on his leg, and the thought of hurting actually bothered him more than the pain did. But it did hurt when he started to climb up the embankment, so he growled to mask the pain. Then he half hopped and limped over to his horse. Crazy wasn't quite sure what was coming towards him and shied away until Ethan spoke to him.

"Calm down, Crazy. It's just me."

He always mounted a horse from his left side, left foot in the stirrup. But he didn't think he could step up into the saddle with his left leg so he limped around to the right side of the horse. When he put all of his weight on his left leg in order to lift his right, the pain worsened, and it took everything he had to keep from yelling aloud so he wouldn't spook Crazy. The horse was already confused and started side-stepping with Ethan mounting him on the wrong side, but he was still able to pull himself into the saddle. It felt like his heart was beating in his thigh, and he knew the wound was still bleeding. He untied one wrap of the kerchief knot and tightened it as hard as he could and secured it.

"Faith will get this fixed up," he said to his horse. "Let's go home, Crazy."

He turned the horse and cut across the pasture instead of going back to follow the fence line. After about ten minutes of riding, he came to the wire gap only a hundred yards from the barn, but still out of sight from the house and bunk house. He couldn't open the gate without getting off his horse, and he felt dizzy again. And he knew if he got off his horse, he wouldn't be able to get back on. He didn't think he could walk that far either. He thought about firing one of his guns, but he had never fired a shot so close to Crazy and didn't know how he would react. He looked down at his leg and realized he had to chance it. He figured if Crazy pitched him off, at least someone would come looking. The pistol wouldn't be as loud as the shotgun, so he removed the rawhide thong from the hammer and pulled it out of its holster.

"Easy, boy," he said, patting Crazy's neck.

He lifted the pistol and pointed it up and away from the house and fired. Crazy jumped sideways and tried to take off running, but Ethan held tight to the reins and let him circle around a couple of times before he pulled up.

"Good boy," he said. "That wasn't so bad now, was it?"

He watched the barn for any signs of life, and after a few minutes, he smiled slightly when he saw the edge of a head peek slowly around the corner to look his way. It had to have been one of the boys. Ethan waved and hollered, and Joseph stepped out from behind the barn. Finn came through one of the pens connected to the barn, and they continued to walk warily towards him, looking around to see where the shot had come from.

"I need your help, boys," Ethan hollered. "Don't tarry."

The boys started to trot towards him until they got to the gate.

"What's the matter?" asked Joseph.

"Who fired the shot?" asked Finn.

"I did because I needed someone to open the gate," said Ethan as he turned his horse a bit to the right. "I did something stupid and wouldn't be able to get back on my horse without help."

Joseph and Finn looked at the red kerchief tied around his leg. Then they realized it was red because it was soaked in blood. Their eyes widened.

"What happened?" asked Joseph as he raised the top wire loop to loosen the wire gate and stepped on the bottom wire loop as he lifted the post and drug it aside.

Finn stepped back as Ethan walked Crazy through the gap.

"A calf kicked me after I got her loose from a tangle of roots near the river," he explained. "I jabbed myself with my own knife. Danged inconsiderate of that little heifer after what I did for her."

Joseph dropped the wire gate. "Close the gate, Finn. I'll take him to the house."

Faith and Caitlin stood on the porch waiting for the boys to come back. She saw Ethan coming around the barn and Joseph running alongside him. She stepped off the porch to meet him. Ethan's face looked white as a sheet, and she knew something was wrong.

"Ethan?" she said as he pulled up.

Joseph reached up and helped him off his horse, and Faith saw the bloody leg.

"Oh, dear Lord," she said. "The fence-cutters shot you."

She ran up to support his other arm.

"Yep, honey," Ethan said to his wife as he winked at Caitlin, "I fought 'em off as long as I could, but there were just too many."

"Joseph, you go get the sheriff right now," said Faith. "This is the last straw—"

"Stop it, Daddy!" said Caitlin, knowing he was teasing. "What really happened?"

"Sorry, girls, I just couldn't resist that. I wasn't shot by any fence-cutter. Nah, I did this to myself."

They half-carried him to a chair, and Caitlin helped strip him of his coat, hat, gun belt, and knife while Faith fetched a bowl and poured some water in it. She grabbed a towel and carried the bowl to the table. She knelt down in front of Ethan and tried to untie the kerchief tied around his thigh, but the knot was too tight and too wet with blood.

"You're going to have to cut it off," he said.

Faith glared at him with a mixture of anger and concern as Caitlin handed her his knife. She started sawing through the bloody kerchief. "What happened, Ethan?"

"I stabbed myself. I had to use my knife to get a calf untangled from some tree roots, and as soon as I did, she kicked my hand and I ran the knife into my leg. A clumsy accident, I know. And I'm sorry about the pants."

"I don't care about the pants," she said, pulling one boot off, then the other. "Take them off."

Ethan looked at her and glanced around. "I can't do that in here."

"It's just family—nobody cares that you'll be sitting around in your long johns," said Faith.

"I've seen you in your under drawers, Daddy," said Caitlin.

"Yeah, we've all seen you in your under drawers, Ethan," said Joseph.

"I haven't!" said Finn.

"Well, just be glad it's cool weather or you all would see a lot more than his under drawers," said Faith.

Everyone laughed except for Ethan. He pulled his suspenders off his shoulders and unbuttoned the flap across the front of his trousers. He half-stood and leaned on the table to support himself while Faith pulled his pants down past his hips.

"Here I am, mortally wounded, and all y'all can do is make fun of me and my under drawers," Ethan said. "That hurts!"

"So you can tease us, but we can't tease you back?" asked Faith.

"No, I'm saying that hurts my leg when you jerk on my pants that way," he said, stepping out of them.

"Oh, sorry!" Faith threw the pants aside and cut off the bloody leg of his long johns above the tear and pulled it off his leg.

"Daddy, that looks awful," said Caitlin, staring with disgust at the wound.

"It looks like the knife twisted after it went in," said Finn.

Ethan looked down at the ragged, oozing hole in the middle of his bloodstained, hairy thigh and pitched forward in a dead faint.

Chapter 18

Joseph and Caitlin caught him before he fell out of the chair.

"Momma? What's wrong with him?" asked Caitlin, afraid that the wound was more serious than she realized.

"He just fainted, honey." Faith patted his face. "Ethan, wake up! Are you all right?"

She dampened a corner of the towel and began to rub his face.

Ethan's head came up and his eyes opened as if nothing had happened. But the look on everyone's faces told him otherwise.

"Did I just pass out?"

"Like a girl," said Joseph.

"Joseph!" said Faith sternly.

"I was hoping I'd outgrown that," he said. "I tend to faint at the sight of blood."

"But you helped when Sam was born and did just fine," said Faith. "And most men would be terrified at that."

"Seeing other people's blood doesn't bother me—seeing mine does, though."

He took a deep breath and shut his eyes.

"You're not going to faint again, are you, Daddy?" Caitlin asked, still holding onto his shoulder.

He shook his head. "But could you hurry and get that patched up and let me rest a bit?" he said. "I'm feeling awfully tired all of a sudden."

"You lost a lot of blood," said Faith, cleaning the wound as gently as she could. "I'm so glad you didn't faint and fall in the river."

"I wasn't by the river," he said. "It was a dry slough."

Faith took a good look at the cut. "It's deep, and it needs stitching," she said. "Caitlin, could you go get my sewing box?"

"Oh, crap," said Ethan under his breath.

Faith frowned at him. "I'm so glad the little ones are in bed, or that would be Sam's favorite new word."

"Sorry," said Ethan, looking more nauseated by the second.

Joseph took pity on him this time and motioned for Finn to stand behind Ethan and hold him if need be. Then he walked around the table and pulled out a chair at the corner of the table so he could face Ethan.

"I think Finn and I have come up with a pretty good design for a boring tool to help speed up your fence building," he said.

Ethan's eyebrows rose. "Really? What do you have in mind?"

"Miners and water well drillers use something called an auger to dig holes. I don't know why we can't rig up something like that to dig postholes."

Caitlin handed the sewing box to her mother.

"Sounds promising," said Ethan, glancing at Faith pulling out a needle and thread. "Is it like a wood auger?"

"Yeah, but much larger. Caitlin, do you have something I can draw on?" asked Joseph. "If we could figure out how to stand an auger up—maybe with a tripod, then run a bar across the top where two men can turn it to bore a hole into the ground."

"Like a giant screw," said Ethan.

"Right!"

Caitlin handed Joseph a slate board and a piece of chalk. He started sketching.

"You're talking about a simple machine here," said Ethan.

Joseph nodded and showed Ethan the sketch. "The boring shaft is the screw. Me and Finn would be the wheel to turn it, and the inclined plane wrapped around the shaft forces it to go up or down."

"But you'd need to weight it," said Ethan. "Otherwise you'd just be turning circles on that hard ground."

"Good point."

"And your tripod should be attached between the turning bar and the auger blades," suggested Ethan. "Maybe in a ring where we can keep it greased so it can turn freely?"

"That's a great idea," said Joseph.

"You think four legs would work better?" asked Finn.

"That would make it more stable," said Ethan, "but the added weight might be a problem."

"Maybe we could make some smaller versions to see what works best," said Joseph.

"How did you boys get so smart?" Ethan asked.

"All done!" said Faith.

Ethan looked down in surprise to see eight neat stitches across the ragged cut. "I thought you were still cleaning it!"

Faith smiled at him and then looked at the Samuel brothers. "I'm wondering, too, how you boys got so smart."

Joseph just grinned.

Ethan's leg began to hurt even more after he went to bed, so he didn't get much sleep that night. Faith took his breakfast to him in bed so he wouldn't have to stand on his leg. He called the boys and Caitlin into his bedroom and asked Joseph to ride the fence line in the west and southwest pastures first to make any repairs if need be. Caitlin and Finn would take the wagon and keep digging holes.

Faith handed them their lunch pail, and they walked solemnly out of the house.

"Ethan looks awful," said Finn.

"He just didn't get much rest last night," said Joseph.

"I've never seen my father stay in bed for breakfast before," said Caitlin, "even when he was sick. He'd get up, get dressed, eat breakfast, and then sometimes go back to bed, but at least he got up. How could something so small hurt him that much?"

"The wound was deep and ragged," said Joseph. "It might have done more damage inside."

Faith set the ingredients for the pumpkin pies on the table and stared at them for a moment while she thought. She knew she couldn't leave Ethan right now to go to Grace, so she would just postpone their Christmas dinner until Christmas Eve. She decided to go ahead and make the pies and not worry about telling Ethan yet because she knew he would argue with her. She and the children could make the trip after Christmas and still get to see her family and Justin and Allie and Uncle John before they left for South Texas.

She spooned the pumpkin into the bowl and started stirring in the other ingredients.

Her family... None of them were blood kin to her, but they were all she had ever known and loved. She felt closest to Jimmy because he was half-

Indeh. She was full-blood Indeh, just like her grandmother Nah-kay, although she wasn't her real grandmother either. Once in a great while she wondered about her mother and father. Which one did she look like? Were they kind and wise or were they savage and ignorant? Maybe she would get up the courage to ask her mother or Nah-kay about them when she went back to Grace this time. Maybe enough time had passed that it wouldn't hurt her father or make him angry to ask about her past. Or maybe he didn't even need to know about any questions she had.

She remembered her father's reaction the one time she did ask him about the Indians. She was around seven years old at the time. He asked her why she needed to know, and she told him that someone at school had called her a dirty Indian. She told her father that she walked right up to that boy and told him that she was a Taylor and she took baths, and that he needed to look at his own rusty hands and ankles—that *he* was the one who was dirty. Her father smiled at first, and picked her up and hugged her and said she was absolutely right. But when she told him that the boy spit on her after that, her father became very angry and told her that she was not an Indian—that she was *his* daughter and that they would never mention the word *Indian* again. Then he marched into the school the next morning and threatened to close it down if anyone disrespected or mistreated his daughter in any way. And no one did after that, or at least not to her face.

She smiled as she thought about how protective her family had been towards her in her growing up years. And people learned to accept her, but for the most part they were lonely years for her, especially after Justin and Jimmy were sent to a boarding school when she was six. She had seen Jimmy and Justin get into fights at school that first year after they came to live at Grace and at times during their summer visits through the years, but she didn't understand why they had fought. And up until the day the boy spit on her, she never realized she was any different than any other child in Grace or Waco.

In the middle of kneading the dough for the pie crusts, she realized she needed to write a letter to let her family know why she wouldn't be on the stage Christmas Eve, so she wiped her hands on a towel and sat down and wrote a quick note. She would ask Finn to meet the stage in the morning and send the letter on in their place.

Ethan tried to get up for the noon meal, but decided he wasn't that hungry and lay back down on the bed. Faith checked on the stitches and noticed the area around the cut looked swollen and inflamed. She dampened a towel in hot water and put it on the leg. She even cut an aloe vera leaf and smeared it on the cut before wrapping it again. Ethan groaned every time she touched his leg. It put an ache in her, too, to see him hurting. She put her hand on his forehead and felt her own, and it felt about the same as hers, so she was relieved he didn't seem to be running a fever, but the wound itself looked feverish.

Dinner time was somber after Faith announced that Ethan needed to see the doctor. She asked Joseph if he would help her take Ethan to Brownwood in the morning.

Joseph assured her he would and that he could tie his horse to the back of the wagon so he would have a way to come back to the ranch later.

Faith turned to Finn. "I need you to meet the stage at eight in the morning and give them a letter for my parents to let them know we won't be able to make the trip to Grace right now."

Caitlin was disappointed to hear that, but her concern for her father was uppermost in her mind.

"I'm sorry, honey, but we'll still get to go before too long. And I know this is asking a lot of you, but I need you and Finn to stay here with your sisters and take care of the animals," said Faith.

"What about Sam?"

"I'll take Sam with me," she said. "I'm sure France and the girls can keep him while I tend to your father. I'd take Ella Vae and Cele, but the ride to town would be too hard for me to deal with all three little ones and still be able to help your father, too."

"Is he going to be all right?"

Faith smiled and nodded her head, masking her own concern for her husband. She had heard of people losing limbs after an infection set in, and hoped and prayed the doctor would be able to get rid of the infection before it got too bad.

"He's going to be fine," she said, trying to assure herself as much as her daughter.

Chapter 19

But Ethan wasn't fine. Faith woke Caitlin at half-past five, saying she couldn't wait until sun-up to take Ethan to town. She lit the lamp beside the bed and sat there for a moment to make sure Caitlin was awake and understood what she had just said. But Caitlin was wide awake this time, wide awake and scared. Scared for her father and a little scared to stay in the house with only her little sisters.

"Are you going to be all right?" she asked Caitlin.

Caitlin nodded. Her mother caught the look of apprehension in her eyes.

"Finn's going to stay here in the house with you," said Faith. "I told him to sleep in our room until we get back."

Caitlin was visibly relieved to know she wouldn't be alone in the house taking care of her little sisters. "But what about the fence?"

"Don't worry about the fence," said Faith. "It'll just have to wait. I've asked Finn to ride the fence line tomorrow over in the west pasture to make sure there's no place where the cattle can get out. You'll need to saddle Crazy Ears for him, though. Can you handle him?"

Caitlin nodded again.

"Why don't you put on some beans in a little while—that's simple enough to cook. And there's biscuits and bread from yesterday you can spread butter and honey on for breakfast."

"I can cook Finn some eggs, too, and then make cornbread later," said Caitlin. "The girls love cornbread and milk."

"That's a good idea," said Faith.

"But I won't know when the oven's ready. You always tell me when to put it in."

"Don't put so much milk in the batter and cook it in the skillet like pancakes," said Faith. "And open any canned food you feel like eating."

93

They heard the door open downstairs.

"Joseph's brought the wagon up, so we have to go," said Faith as she leaned down and kissed Caitlin's cheek. "I love you."

"I love you, too, and I need to go tell Daddy."

"Come on, then." She pulled the covers back and Caitlin stepped onto the floor in her bare feet.

"Is he going to be all right?" asked Caitlin. "Why can't you wait to take him later this morning?"

"I'm afraid the wound's infected, and it can spread if we don't get it stopped. I need the doctor to tell me what else I can do to help him get better."

"Meemaw's going to be worried why we didn't come," said Caitlin.

"I've asked Finn to take a letter for Meemaw to the stage this morning. It explains about your father's injury. You and Finn watch that clock and then you send him down there early so he won't miss the stage. We'll all be in hot water if they don't get that letter."

They walked down the stairs together.

"What else do you need me to do around here, Momma?"

"I did all the washing on Thursday since we thought we were leaving today, so you don't have to worry about that. Why don't you ask Finn to cut a small tree to put up in the house, and you and the girls can decorate it since we'll be here for Christmas after all," said Faith. "That'll put a smile on your father's face when I bring him home."

Caitlin smiled at the thought, but it disappeared when she saw her father sitting on the side of the bed. He looked haggard. How could someone so strong and full of vigor become so sick and feeble in such a short amount of time?

Joseph leaned over and Ethan put his right arm around his shoulder to help him stand up without putting any weight on his left leg. Faith supported him on the other side.

Faith told Caitlin to grab the satchel and follow them to the wagon. They half carried Ethan through the house and outside to where Faith had put some blankets in the wagon for him to lie on. Finn stood by, holding Joseph's horse, but handed the reins to Caitlin so he could help lift Ethan onto the wagon bed. Then Joseph tied his horse to the back of it while Faith went inside to fetch her sleeping son.

The night air was cold, and Caitlin shivered before she realized she was standing there in her flannel nightgown. She hugged her arms to herself as she watched her father sitting quietly in the middle of the wagon bed.

"We'll be ready to get back on that fence when you come back, Daddy. You just get better."

He nodded and half-smiled.

"Don't you worry about a thing here," she said. "Finn and I will take care of everything."

"I know you will," he said hoarsely, clearing his throat.

Faith walked out of the house and handed Finn a sleeping bundle of Sam. She climbed up in the back of the wagon beside Ethan and spread a blanket over him. Finn handed her the little boy and she covered him with another blanket. Joseph walked around and climbed up on the wagon seat.

"Joseph or somebody will come back later to help, kids," said Faith.

"We'll be fine, Momma. Don't worry about us."

The wagon started to roll.

"I love you, Daddy!"

"Love you more," he said.

Finn and Caitlin stood side by side, watching them disappear into the darkness. They listened until they could no longer hear the horses' footsteps, the wheels rumbling over the ground, and the creaking of the wagon.

"Aren't you cold?" he asked.

But Caitlin just stood there staring at the dark.

"What if I never see him again, Finn?"

"Don't say that! Your daddy will be fine."

"How do you know? Momma's awfully worried about him."

"She's just being cautious. Now come inside so you don't catch a chill."

Finn grabbed the lantern off the hook, and they walked back in the house.

"Do you want to go back to bed and sleep awhile longer?" he asked her. "I'll stay down here."

"Momma said we'd better keep an eye on the clock so we don't miss the stage. I have to bring up Crazy and saddle him for you, and that may take me a while."

"I can do that," he said.

"Well, I guess I can put some beans on," she said.

"Are you going to do that in your nightgown?"

Caitlin looked down and snorted. Then she turned and ran toward the stairs. "I'll be right back."

In a few minutes she came back downstairs in her bibbed pants, but this time she had a pretty blue calico blouse on under it. Her hair was brushed and down, but she had tied a blue ribbon from the back of her neck to the top of her hair to keep it out of her face.

Finn thought she looked mighty pretty for wearing pants.

"What would you like for breakfast?" asked Caitlin.

"Your mother fed me and Joseph before we hitched up the wagon," he said, looking at the stove. "But I wouldn't mind another cup of coffee." He grabbed a cup on the table and handed it to her. "This was my cup."

Caitlin brushed her fingers across his hand as she took hold of his cup. She glanced at him and saw something raw in his eyes that made her look away. She walked over to the stove and grabbed a towel to cover the hot handle before she poured him a cup. She came back to the table and handed it to him.

"Thanks."

She sat down across from him and looked around the room. The house felt so different knowing her mother and father weren't around. It made her feel grown-up and more responsible in a way, knowing that her parents had left her in charge of taking care of the place. And she would do her best to make them proud. She glanced at Finn and a thought flitted through her mind. Was this how it felt to be married and have a place of one's own?

"What?" he asked, noticing the look she was giving him.

"Nothing."

He watched her for a moment. He liked the way her hair looked when it was down. Her eyes looked even bluer in the lamplight.

"Do you think the fence-cutters will come up to the house?"

"Nah," he said, shaking his head. "From what Ethan says, they do their work where no one can see them. Kind of like skunks and coons that only come out at night."

Caitlin giggled. He made her feel better about the fence-cutters. Finn seemed to be more grown-up than she realized.

"What are we going to do today?" he asked her.

"The chores first."

"I'd be glad to milk Birdie again for you," he said. "You can let the chickens out and get the eggs if you want."

"I'll wait and let Ella and Cele do that with me. They love to gather eggs." She stood up and walked over to a bucket under the dry sink. "There's not much in the slop bucket—we'll have to feed the hogs some corn, too." She looked at the dirty dishes. "I guess I can start washing these dishes."

"Are you going to eat breakfast?"

"I'll eat when the girls get up," she said.

"I guess I can go see Miss Birdie," he said, standing up.

96

Caitlin glanced at the clock on the mantel. "She won't come up to the barn for another hour."

"Well, I'm sure there's something I can do out there, even if it's just straightening up." He stood and stretched, yawning as he reached for his hat.

"You need to leave by 7:30 to meet the stage," said Caitlin, "so that's an hour and a half from now."

"I don't need to leave at 7:30—it won't take thirty minutes to get to the front gate. I'd have to sit there for twenty-five minutes," he said, frowning.

"Actually, the stage is supposed to be there at 8:10, but I don't want you to miss it in case it comes early."

Finn stood there looking at her. "I can't stand waiting around with nothing to do."

"All right, you can leave by 7:40, but no later," she said firmly. She grabbed a book off the mantel and handed it to him. "Here—that'll give you something to do while you're waiting. Read the pages where it's bookmarked. Then we can talk about it later."

Finn read the title and raised his eyebrows. He couldn't turn this book down without sounding like a heathen, so he tucked it under his arm and walked out the door.

Caitlin smiled to herself as she poured water into a large wash bowl.

By 7:15 she had dressed her little sisters and sat them at the table while she poured some honey onto a dollop of butter sitting on a plate. She smashed it and stirred it good with a fork and smeared some onto biscuit halves for the girls. She told them she had to go to the barn and help Finn, and to not get out of their chairs until she came back. She grabbed a biscuit for herself and smeared honey butter on it.

"And don't get honey all over your clothes," she said, taking a bite as she walked out the door.

Ella Vae looked at Cele and then got up on her knees so she could lean over the plate to eat her biscuit. Three year old Cele followed suit, but instead of picking up her biscuit, she just dropped her face down to the biscuit to lick the honey butter off of it.

Caitlin walked into the barn to see Crazy already saddled. She looked around at a much neater barn, too. Finn had been busy. She walked out the side door and into the alley and found him shoveling manure from Birdie's pen. He had taken off his shirt and hung it on the fence as he worked in his cotton undershirt with his sleeves pushed up off his forearms. She smiled and watched him for a moment. Finn wasn't hurt-your-eyes fine-looking like her uncles Jimmy and Justin, but he had a strong face and a determination about him like he knew where he was going in life. And there was something very attractive about a hard-working man who didn't have to wait to be told to do something when he saw work to be done.

"You don't have to do that, Finn!" she finally said. "Daddy just leaves it."

He looked up at her and smiled. He walked into the alley and propped the shovel against the wall.

At that moment they heard a loud, heavy splattering coming from Birdie's direction. Finn and Caitlin looked at the cow and then at each other.

"It's a lost cause," said Caitlin, laughing.

"Well, it gave me something to do while I was waiting," said Finn, grinning back. He pulled his undershirt sleeves down and grabbed his shirt and put it on as they walked back inside the barn.

"And you saddled Crazy—I figured I'd have to come help you."

"You told me how your father put his bridle on him, so I unbuckled it and slipped it on like you said. He was just fine since I was careful not to touch his ears."

"You learn things quick," said Caitlin. "I'm going to get the girls so we can gather eggs. Did you leave some milk out for the cats?"

Finn nodded. "Why don't y'all get a dog? They're good to watch the place."

"We plan to, but we want to get a couple of puppies we can raise around the cats so they won't try to kill them," she said as she reached down to scratch a gray cat. "We've had you a long time, haven't we, Lincoln."

"He survived the barn fire six years ago, didn't he."

Caitlin met his eyes and nodded.

"Do you remember much about that day?"

"Not really—just a few things, but mostly I remember how I felt."

"How's that?"

She looked away. "I remember being afraid when that man came in the barn. I remember the shock of watching him beat Mercy and I felt so helpless—I didn't know what to do." She shuddered at the memory.

"I didn't mean to upset you. I'm sorry I brought it up."

"I don't mind. I wouldn't be here if it hadn't been for Mercy saving my life. I guess it's made me appreciate everyone I love."

"I've noticed that about you. You sure don't mind telling them how you feel."

Caitlin nodded her head. "I don't think most people learn that until they're a lot older or until it's too late. I don't want to have any regrets if I lose someone close to me."

"What do you mean?"

"Remember Mr. Totten's funeral last year and all the wonderful things his family and friends said about him?"

Finn nodded.

"I remember thinking, what a shame that everybody heard how much they loved and appreciated Mr. Totten—everyone heard but Mr. Totten himself. I thought how sad that they didn't bother to tell him all those things when he was alive. Why do we wait until someone dies before we say how much they mean to us?"

Finn watched her face—she was an open book he'd been reading for some time, and he liked her story. He felt like she had stripped away every bit of armor he had so carefully put on to protect himself. And his eyes began to say things his voice hadn't the courage to express.

Caitlin's heart started pounding, but she didn't look away as he stepped up directly in front her.

"Has anyone ever told you how special you are?" he said, leaning towards her.

She shook her head slowly wondering what Finn was doing.

She felt his breath on her face as he lightly kissed her cheek. Then he whispered in her ear. "Well, you are."

He turned and loosed the reins from the hitching rail, mounted Crazy and walked him out of the barn.

Caitlin stood there touching her cheek for a moment. Then she ran out and watched Finn walk down the lane.

"What's your girlfriend going to say?" she yelled.

Finn turned around and answered that his girlfriend would never mind him kissing a baby.

"I'm almost twelve!" she hollered indignantly. "And I've been told I'm very mature for my age!!"

He just grinned at her before spurring Crazy to a trot.

Chapter 20

After delivering the letter to the stage driver, Finn rode the fence line in the west pasture and found no more cuts in the wire. Then later he rode over to the new fence line and found more posts pulled up and scattered along with another threatening note. He came back to the barn and wrapped some tools in canvas and strapped it behind the saddle and headed back over to the windmill pasture to fix what had been torn down. He dug a few more holes just for good measure and cut down a small cedar tree before heading back to the house before supper.

Joseph brought the Samuels' buggy back with him Saturday evening so he could take Finn and the rest of the Murrays to church the next morning. He also brought a smoked ham and several cans of peaches from his mother's kitchen. That, along with the beans and cornbread Caitlin had made earlier, ended up making a bountiful meal for supper.

Caitlin had set the table nice and had even put on a dress, but Finn acted like he took no notice of her efforts when Joseph was around. She didn't know what to think, so she turned her attention to fixing the girls' plates.

"How's Daddy doing?" she asked Joseph.

"The doctor said there's not a whole lot he could do with infections. He said it was a waiting game—that the body is the best healer of itself."

"Well, if that's all there is to it, Daddy could've done his waiting out here just as easily as he could've in town."

"I think he was putting some kind of salve on it to try to draw out the infection, and was giving him something for the pain. Ethan's leg was swole up like a watermelon."

"I love watermelon," said Ella Vae.

Finn glared at his brother, so Joseph backtracked when he noticed the look on Caitlin's face.

"But I'm sure he's going to be fine," he said. "And you need to pack up some clothes for Ella and Cele because Mother's insisted on taking care of them while your parents are decomposed."

"The word's *indisposed*, brother," said Finn. "You're in college, for Pete's sake! Why don't you just shut your mouth and chew on your food for a while?"

"Sorry, Caitlin," said Joseph. "But I was supposed to tell you that. We'll all go into town tomorrow for church, but only us three will come back and take care of things."

"I thought my parents would be back home by then."

"Are we going to see Momma?" asked Ella Vae.

"And Aunt France and Uncle George, too!" said Caitlin.

Ella Vae giggled and clapped her hands with the excitement of going to town. Cele followed suit, but she wasn't sure what they were excited about.

Caitlin turned to Finn. "And without you-know-who here on Monday, I can help you and Joseph put in a good day's work on the fence before we go back Christmas morning."

"But we always open gifts on Christmas Eve," said Finn.

"The family won't mind waiting," said Joseph. "And this way we can take care of the livestock Monday night and Tuesday morning before heading into town. Then we can stay all day and come back that evening."

Joseph told Finn that he had spent most of the day at the smithy's working on a posthole auger design. He said Mr. Beights was really excited about the idea and thought he might be able to come up with something workable in three or four days.

They finished supper, and the boys went out to the barn to feed while Caitlin bathed her sisters in the tub by the warm stove and then dressed them for bed. She took them upstairs to their bed and listened to their nightly prayers and tucked them in. She gathered up some clothes to pack for the trip to the Samuels' house, turned the lamp down low and went back downstairs.

The brothers came back inside, and Joseph said he preferred not to sleep with his little brother and would be in the camp house if they needed anything.

"See you two in the morning," he said as he shut the door.

Caitlin spoke up as soon as Joseph was beyond earshot.

"I have a plan to get the fence-cutters off our backs while Daddy's away," she told Finn, "but I don't know if Joseph will go along with it. I wanted to ask you about it first."

"What do you have in mind?"

"I think we ought to put a wire gate directly in sight of the windmill—even before the wire is strung," she said. "Maybe they'll see our intentions that we're willing to share the water, and they'll leave us alone."

Finn thought about it for a moment and decided that the idea was worth considering.

"You know your dad will run the wire right over it, though."

"Well, maybe he'll get used to the idea by the time we stretch the wire and would be willing to share the water," she said. "That's just being neighborly. But until then, maybe this gate will allow us to finish the fence."

"Yeah, I'm tired of re-doing the same work all over again," he said. "And I think Joseph would go along with it."

"And did you get a chance to read what I asked you to read this morning?" Caitlin asked.

Finn nodded.

"What'd you think?"

"I'm familiar with Moses parting the Red Sea," said Finn. "Everybody knows that's how God saved the Israelites from the Egyptians."

"That's where I got my idea for saving the fence."

"I don't understand."

"But in our case, we're parting the fence to save it—to save all the work we keep putting into it, and the fence-cutters keep destroying."

Finn wrinkled up his forehead trying to figure out how all of that fit together. "I like your idea about putting a gate in the fence, but I don't know how in the world you came up with that idea after reading about Moses parting the Red Sea. That makes no sense to me."

"Well, maybe God just gave me the idea of sharing the water," she said. "But it came to me after I read that story."

"I just thought of a problem, though, with your gate," said Finn. "How are the cattle going to reach the water without someone there to open it for them? The free grazers don't stay with their cattle all the time— after the roundups they sort them out for the trail drives. And a cow can't open the gate. And if they get in, they don't know to go back out the gate. They just might choose to stay on your ranch. And your father surely won't go for that idea."

Caitlin looked crestfallen. "What are we going to do? How can the cattle get to the water without coming into our ranch?"

Finn thought for a moment. "I think you're onto something there. Where's that slate board?"

Caitlin fetched it and handed it to Finn sitting at the table. He drew a circle and said that was the windmill tank. Then he drew a long U where the bottom of the U sat across a third of the tank.

"We can fence in a U-shaped alley off of the main fence that's about fifty feet to the windmill tank—that's only about ten postholes we'll need to dig. We can make the alley a little wider than the tank so if there's a bunch of cattle coming in and out, they won't get too crowded. We can stretch a couple of wires across the tank so the cattle can't cross it into your ranch." He looked up at her. "What do you think about that idea?"

Caitlin's eyes grew wide. "I know Daddy will have a fit, but I think it's brilliant. And if we get it done before he gets back, maybe he'll see the sense in having it. The fence-cutters won't have a reason to tear down our fence if their cattle can get to water."

"Right!" Finn looked down at the drawing. "You know, maybe this is a different way of parting the water to save something."

Caitlin smiled.

"But I still don't see the connection to Moses here," he admitted.

"I guess that sounds kind of stupid, huh."

"Well, if that story's what gave you the idea to save the fence and bring some peace around here, then it's not stupid at all."

"I guess we'd better go to bed or you're going to sleep through church." Caitlin stood and walked toward the stairs.

"Wait," he said, pulling something out of his pocket. "I made something for you today. It's a similar version of your brand."

He walked over to her and handed her a piece of wood where he had carved a heart and the initials *KT* in the middle of it.

"K T," she slowly read aloud, and then read it again a little faster, "KT… Katie! Oh, how clever!"

"I didn't think you'd ever get to see a heart brand on a cow's rump around here, so I thought I'd carve it for you."

She turned it over to find an *FN* carved on the back. "F N, effin?"

"No, it's just 'fin' when you put f and n together," he said.

"Wait 'til I find out who your girlfriend is," she said, grinning mischievously. "I bet you haven't carved anything for her."

"Yes, I have," he said defensively. "But this is our secret, remember? You won't show this to Emma or Zane, will you?"

"No," she admitted. "And I have a special box where I keep my most valuable possessions that few people have ever seen. So your secret gift is safe with me. Thanks." She started walking up the stairs.

" 'Night, Katie," he said.

"Like you," she said as she turned around to look at him, daring him to respond.

He took the challenge. "Like you, too."

She smiled at him and continued up the stairs.

Caitlin woke up before dawn and pulled on a long-sleeved shirt and stepped into her bibbed pants before heading downstairs to work on breakfast. She put on the coffee and made skillet bread, eggs, and fried ham. She was none too quiet, either, hoping Finn would wake up soon, but all she did was wake up Ella Vae who came downstairs rubbing her eyes.

"Good morning, Ella. Are you ready for some breakfast?"

Caitlin walked over and picked her up off the bottom step and carried her to the table. She looked at her parents' bedroom door and had just about decided to go over and knock on it when the front door opened. Finn walked in carrying a bucket of milk, and Joseph was right behind him.

"I didn't know y'all were up yet," she said.

"Why wouldn't we be?"

"Ahhh... coffee!" said Joseph, sniffing the air. "And breakfast, too? I'm impressed, Caitlin."

She spooned a little bit of egg, forked a small piece of ham and put a piece of buttered bread onto a plate and set it in front of Ella. Then she grabbed a cup and poured her some fresh milk.

"The cups and plates are here by the stove—y'all come help yourselves while I go wake up Cele."

The brothers piled their plates high and poured themselves some coffee and sat down at the table with Ella. Joseph took a swig of coffee and made an awful face.

"That's stout," he said. "You might want to water it down, Finn." He reached over and poured some of Ella's milk into his coffee.

"It can't be that bad," said Finn, but after a taste, he grabbed Ella's milk and poured some into his cup, too.

Caitlin came downstairs with a sleepy little girl and sat her beside her sister.

"Somebody had better bless this food we're about to eat," she said as she looked at their plates. "And all the food we've eaten. Joseph, would you?"

"Sure," he said with a mouthful of food.

"And don't forget to pray for daddy's leg and rain," she added, "and that the fence-cutters won't bother us any more."

Joseph obliged and said the blessing.

When Caitlin opened her eyes, she noticed Ella's half empty cup of milk. "You must've been thirsty, sis," she said. "You want some more milk?"

Ella nodded, so Caitlin carried her cup to the milk bucket. Ella started to tell on the boys, but Joseph smiled and held his finger to his lips to shush her. Ella just giggled.

Chapter 21

The Samuel boys and Murray girls arrived at church during the congregational singing of the first hymn. They made their way to sit behind George and France and the rest of their children. Emma and Zane slipped out of their seats to sit with Caitlin. Ella moved to the row in front to sit between the sixteen year olds, Jenna and Annie, and France turned and leaned over the pew to pick up Cele to sit on her lap after everyone was seated. Caitlin leaned over to France.

"Where's Momma?" she asked.

"With your daddy at Dr. Hood's place," she whispered back.

"How's he doing?"

"He'll be off that leg a while," said France, not wanting to tell her during the church service how sick he was. "We'll go see him after dinner."

Caitlin nodded and sat back against the pew. Pastor Sluder announced their second hymn, *Sweet Hour of Prayer*, and called for people to pause in a moment of silence to pray for rain.

"What did she say?" whispered Finn.

"We're going to go see Daddy after dinner," she whispered back.

"Tonight?"

"No, after lunch."

"Lunch and dinner's always confused me," he said. "Which one's which?"

"Lunch is always at noon, and I think dinner can be either the noon or the evening meal, as long as it's the bigger meal."

"Ssshhh!" said George over his shoulder.

Pastor Sluder's voice broke the silence. "And I want to remind you to also remember in prayer, Brother Ethan Murray, who might lose his leg due

106

to an injury."

"What?!" Caitlin blurted out. "Daddy might lose his leg?"

France turned around and tried to allay her fears, but Caitlin had already stood and was stumbling over Finn and Joseph to get to the end of the pew. She ran down the aisle and out of the church.

France handed Cele to George and slipped out of the pew, but not before glaring at the preacher before she turned and walked quickly down the aisle to the back of the church.

"I'm so sorry," the preacher said from the pulpit. "I thought everyone knew. Let's remember the entire Murray family at this time as we sing *Sweet Hour of Prayer*."

Emma and Zane started to follow, but Finn stopped them, whispering that Caitlin could outrun them both. He said he would go help his mother deal with Caitlin.

Finn walked quickly out of the sanctuary during the singing and grabbed his hat from the vestibule before hurrying outside. France stood in front of the church looking around. There was no sign of Caitlin.

"She's gone to her daddy," said Finn. "I'll go get her."

"Poor baby," said France as Finn started to walk away. "Bring her back to the house, honey. And hey, I haven't seen you all week."

She stood there with open arms so Finn came back and gave her a hug and a peck on the cheek. Then he turned and started trotting away from her, but not before he said, "Love you!" over his shoulder.

France's mouth dropped open, wondering who that child was since it certainly could not have been her stoic Finn.

Finn saw Caitlin walking along about two blocks from Dr. Hood's house. He could see that she was still crying, so he called out to her. She glanced over her shoulder and started running again, but he caught her by the end of the block. He grabbed her arm, and she tried to jerk away from him. He wouldn't let go so she started pushing at him, crying even harder and yelling at him to let her go. He grabbed her in a bear hug until she stopped fighting him.

"I have to see my daddy," she sobbed.

"I know, Katie, but you can't go in there all hysterical-like," he said. "That's not going to help your father at all; in fact, it'll probably make him feel worse to see you so upset like this. You need to go in there with a smile on your face and give him some hope. He'll think he's dying by the way you're acting right now."

Caitlin looked up at Finn and knew he was telling the truth, but she couldn't stop crying. She dropped her forehead on his chest.

Finn looked around and led her to the nearest porch stoop to sit down.

"All right," he said. "Get it all out."

"Widow Turner won't appreciate us sitting on her steps," she cried, glancing at the door behind them.

"Well, she'll never know since she's at church right now."

"How can I face my daddy with a smile after what I just heard? I don't think I can act like everything's all right."

"Well, then maybe you ought not to see him right now."

"But I have to."

"Are you thinking of him or are you thinking of you?"

Caitlin sat there quietly for a moment. "I guess I'm thinking of me. But what if he dies, Finn? And what if I don't get to see him?"

"Didn't you tell me that you never leave things unsaid to the people you love in case something happens to them?"

She nodded her head.

"He knows you love him—how could he not when you tell him every time he turns around."

She sniffed, and she knew he was right.

"So that's what you need to think about when you see him—that you've never held anything back from him."

She nodded and took a deep breath and shuddered when she let it out.

They sat there in silence for a while.

Then Caitlin finally spoke up. "I'm ready to see him now."

They walked to the next block and up to the two-storied white clapboard house that was home and office for Dr. Hood. Two bay windows adorned the front and two more could be seen on the side of the house, and more dormer windows upstairs than Caitlin had ever taken the time to count. They stopped at the front door, and Finn rang the bronze bell mounted to the door frame.

"I've always loved this house," she said, looking at the stained glass transom window above the door.

They peeked through the oval glass into the foyer and hallway and saw Faith step out from a door on the right.

Caitlin didn't wait for her to come to the door. She opened it and ran to her mother and held her tightly. Faith leaned back to look at her face. She knew Caitlin had been crying.

"What's the matter?" she asked.

Caitlin pasted on a smile and shook her head.

Finn stepped into the parlor on the left and motioned for them to follow him.

He spoke in hushed tones since the house was so quiet. "The preacher asked folks to pray for Ethan so he wouldn't lose his leg."

"He worded it like that?"

"I didn't know Daddy was so bad off," said Caitlin.

"He's real sick, honey, and there's always the chance of losing a limb when infection sets in, but Dr. Hood's doing everything he can to prevent that from happening," said Faith. "He's tried a number of different treatments and early this morning he started using a poultice made from some herbs and honey, and this one seems to be helping."

"Really? So you think he's not going to lose his leg?"

"That's what I've continued to believe and to ask God in my prayers," said Faith. "I'm sorry the talk around town has said otherwise, but folks aren't being mean; they're just concerned. I'm glad to know our church is praying for your father."

"Can I see him?" asked Caitlin.

Faith nodded. "The doctor's been giving him something for the pain, so he's in and out. But he'll know you're here. Don't be shocked when you see him, though. He looks pretty rough."

She took Caitlin by the arm and led her down the hall to the first door on the right.

"Where do the Hoods live?" she whispered, looking around.

"The children's bedrooms are upstairs, and Dr. and Mrs. Hood's room is the door at the end of the hall. But they're all at church right now."

Faith opened the door to let them in and realized Finn hadn't followed. She turned around and saw him standing in the doorway to the parlor, hat in hand.

"Come on, Finn," she said, gesturing with her hand. "You can see him, too, if you'd like."

Finn walked quickly down the hall. "Are you sure it's all right?"

Faith nodded. "You're family. He'd want to see you, too."

Caitlin walked into the room. Three tall, narrow windows created another bay window behind the bed. Thick curtains covered the windows, and the air had a sick smell to it. Caitlin turned up her nose and looked at her mother. She was with the two people she knew best, but it felt so strange and foreign to step into that room.

"Come on," said Faith, leading her to Ethan's bedside.

The shadows in the room and strain on Ethan's face gave him a look of unfamiliarity, but it was comforting somehow to hear him breathing heavily. Caitlin stood beside the bed and looked at her father. Several days without shaving darkened his skin. His eyes looked sunken in dark sockets. She saw lines on his face she had never seen before. It unnerved her to see him so weak and vulnerable when she had never seen her father as anything but strong.

Faith leaned over the bed. "Ethan, Katie and Finn are here."

"Where?" he asked with his eyes still closed.

Faith smiled. "Right here, honey. You need to open your eyes."

His heavy eyelids blinked a couple of times and he saw his wife. He looked beyond her and smiled when he saw Caitlin.

"Hi, Katie," he said in a raspy voice. "How's my girl?"

"Fine," she said, and not sure what else to say, she rattled on. "And everything at home is fine, too. We've been feeding the livestock, and they're fine, and Finn rode the fence line for you, and it's fine, and we'll have a surprise for you when you get back."

"What is it? You know I don't like surprises."

"Well, Finn and I—"

"Got a tree and decorated it for you," said Finn, looking at Caitlin and shaking his head slightly.

"Hello, Finn. I appreciate you helping Katie," he said, shutting his eyes again. "I want you to…"

They waited for him to finish the sentence, but he started to breathe heavily again.

"Momma? What's wrong with him?" Caitlin whispered.

"The medicine makes him sleepy," she said.

"Think we should go?"

"That's up to you," said Faith. "But if you stay, this is what you'd see most of the time."

"Are you getting any sleep yourself?"

Faith nodded. "I have a cot right over there, and I've had plenty of time to rest."

But Caitlin could see the fatigue and strain on her face, too.

"Can we bring you anything?"

"No, honey. I'm fine. I'll probably go over to the Samuels to see the girls and Sam after their naps this afternoon. What time are y'all heading back to the ranch?"

Caitlin looked at Finn. "Probably around four so we can do the chores before it gets dark."

"You sound so grown-up, Katie," said Ethan, with his eyes still shut.

They all turned and looked at him.

"Are you awake?"

"Yeah."

"We're going over to the Samuels for Sunday dinner, but we'll stop by again before we head home."

"I'll be right here," he said, "unless the doc lets me go with you."

"Only when you're better," said Faith. "And you're getting better. I'm going to walk the kids out, Ethan."

"Love you, Daddy," Caitlin said, leaning down to kiss his forehead.

"Love you more," he whispered.

"See you, Ethan," said Finn.

"Take care of my Katie."

"Yes, sir."

Faith walked them to the front porch. "If your daddy continues to improve, the doctor said we could move him to the Samuels' house. I'm hoping we'll be there by Christmas Day."

"We'll be coming into town that morning," said Caitlin.

Faith nodded. "I hope we'll all be together then."

She hugged her daughter and patted Finn on the shoulder. "I'll see y'all at the house before you go."

"Don't you worry about a thing," said Caitlin.

Chapter 22

After Sunday dinner, Finn asked his father if he could run down to the store for something.

"Why can't you wait until tomorrow?" asked George.

"We won't be back until Christmas morning, remember?"

"He has to buy his girlfriend her Christmas present," teased Emma.

Finn denied it, but his red face gave him away again. His father went to his desk in the parlor to give him the key, and Finn almost ran out the front door.

The girls headed upstairs to talk.

"You really need to stop teasing him about his girlfriend, Emma," said Caitlin. "That's so sweet of him to get something for her. You know Finn; I'm sure it's not easy for him."

"Yeah, romancing a girl doesn't come natural to him," said Zane.

"And you're not helping matters either."

"We're not supposed to," said Emma, flopping down on the bed. "He's our brother."

"Has he told you who she is?" asked Zane.

Caitlin shook her head. "No, other than he definitely has a girlfriend. He talks about her all the time," she said, stretching the truth a bit.

"Really? What has he said about her?" asked Emma.

"Promise you won't say a word if I tell you?"

Both girls nodded their heads.

"Let me see your fingers," said Caitlin.

The sisters held up their hands. Two of Emma's fingers were crossed.

"I'm not going to tell you a thing if you're going to go blabbing to everyone... especially Finn."

She uncrossed her fingers. "All right, I swear."

"Well, she seems to be quite a lady with manners and everything," said Caitlin.

"He told you that?"

"Not in so many words, but he seemed shocked when he saw me in my workpants and said his girlfriend didn't wear pants."

"A real lady…" said Zane, trying to think of who that might be in town. "What about Molly Franklin? I can't imagine her ever wearing pants."

"I don't think she would give him the time of day," said Emma. "What else did he tell you about her?"

"That he carved something for her," said Caitlin, racking her brain to think of anything else Finn might have hinted about his girlfriend.

"Carved what?"

"Their initials on something—maybe a tree somewhere around here or in town?" suggested Caitlin.

"We'll have to check every tree we pass by," said Emma. "And if we find *his* initials anywhere, we'll find her initials, and then we'll know who she is. What else did he say?"

Caitlin was plumb out of the truth, but she liked how it felt to sound so knowledgeable on a subject, so she added just a few things that she figured were probably true.

"He said that she was pretty and smart and very nice."

"Well, it sounded like Molly until you said the word *nice*."

The girls snickered.

"I know why he might like *her*, though," said Emma.

"Why?"

"She's already fourteen and well-blossomed," said Emma, looking down to smooth her dress over her twelve-year-old chest. It was as flat as a pancake.

Zane and Caitlin did the same, with only slightly better results.

"Mine look like mosquito bites," said Zane, sighing. "I think you've got us beat, Caitlin, and you're younger than us."

"Only by a few weeks," she said, admiring her little mounds. "Momma says I'm mature for my age."

They could hear their older sister Jenna yell at their younger brother Mac and then holler up the stairs that Faith had come, so the three girls headed back downstairs. Caitlin was relieved she didn't have to make up anything else about Finn's mysterious girlfriend.

Finn came back from the store, and everyone went outside to see them off. While Finn shook his father's hand, Emma patted his back to distract him while she slipped a folded piece of paper out of his back pocket. She motioned for Zane and Caitlin to follow her as she stepped behind her parents to see what he had bought for his girlfriend. She quickly unwrapped the paper to find a necklace with a heart locket.

Emma's eyebrows rose as she looked at her sister. "He must be smitten," she whispered. "This is pretty."

"I've got to go," said Caitlin, hugging her friends. "I'll see you Tuesday."

Emma and Zane stepped up beside Finn, smiling at their brother.

"What? No smart remark before I go?" He looked at them suspiciously. "What have y'all been up to?"

Emma held up the necklace for all to see.

Finn felt his empty back pocket. "Give me that!" he grabbed the necklace and the paper and stuffed them into his front pocket this time.

"Girls!" said France, coming to Finn's defense. "Is that all you do—sit around and figure out ways to pick on your brother?"

Mac answered for them. "No, they sit around trying to blossom, too," he said as he placed his hands on his chest just before he took off running to the barn with Emma and Zane screaming after him.

Everybody laughed. Caitlin acted like she didn't know what in the world Mac was talking about, but inside she was horror-struck that anyone might actually think that they had been upstairs talking about their bosoms. With a flushed face, she hugged her mother one more time before climbing in their wagon, since they were leaving the Samuels' buggy in town this time. She didn't dare look Finn's way for fear he would guess that they had also been talking about his girlfriend.

Caitlin and the Samuel brothers stopped by Dr. Hood's again before they left town. This time the drapes were pulled back and several windows opened to bring in the light and fresh air. Caitlin thought it looked like hope had moved in, too, and that made a smile come easier to her face.

Ethan seemed to be more lucid this time. He asked the boys if they had found any more fence damage. Joseph answered, saying that everything was fine. Finn looked questioningly at his brother.

"Maybe they've given up and decided to leave us be," said Ethan. "Free grazers are going to have to get used to fences. Everybody's putting up fences around their property now."

Joseph told him that the smithy was building a posthole-boring tool for them to try out this week. Ethan was very pleased to hear that.

"We just might be able to finish that mile of fence before I have to go back to school," said Joseph.

Dr. Hood came in to check on Ethan's wound. Everyone stepped back away from the bed, but they could still see the swollen, oozing gash.

"Your leg still looks awful, Daddy!" said Caitlin.

"The poultice doesn't help the looks of it either," said Dr. Hood, "but the swelling seems to have gone down a bit, and his color's looking better. If he keeps this up, I may let your mother take him to the Samuels on Christmas Eve or Christmas morning."

"That's great news!!" said Caitlin.

Ten minutes later they were in the wagon on their way back to the ranch.

"Why did you tell Ethan that nobody's bothered the fence posts?" asked Finn.

"He doesn't need anything else to fret about right now," said Joseph. "He's got enough on his plate to deal with."

"Tell him about our idea, Finn," said Caitlin.

Finn told Joseph about their plan for a fenced-in alley leading up to the windmill tank. He described it in detail, even to the number of posts it would take.

Joseph sat there for a good minute without saying a word, other than clicking his tongue at the horses, but then he looked at Finn.

"I know Ethan's going to hate it," he said, "but that's a great idea. I think it might be the only way to keep that fence intact."

"It was Caitlin's idea," said Finn.

"Really? This little squirt came up with that?"

Caitlin elbowed him. "I'm almost twelve, Joseph. But my idea was just putting a gate in the fence. It was Finn that figured out a way to keep our cattle in and their cattle out, but both would still be able to get to the water."

"Between the three of us, we ought to be able to get the holes dug and the fence posts set tomorrow before we have to go back into town Christmas morning," said Joseph, "and if it's already done, I don't think Ethan will ask us to tear it down."

Chapter 23

Monday started early for Caitlin and the boys, and they were able to dig all ten holes and set the posts for the alley by mid-afternoon. They used Osage orange posts on each side of the tank in case water pooled around them. The fence would leave one third of the rock tank rim open for the free-range cattle to gather around to drink the water.

Joseph left a little earlier on his horse to check the fence line in the west pasture, leaving Finn and Caitlin to load up the wagon and head back to the house to do the chores. They felt a sense of satisfaction with the work they had done that day, and right before they left, they stepped back and looked at the alley. It was four measuring sticks across, or twenty-four feet wide, and a little over eight measuring sticks from the fence to the tank, or around fifty feet, according to Finn.

"Do you think they'll recognize it for what it is?" asked Caitlin.

"I think so, especially since we've taken out that fence post in the middle of the original fence," said Finn. "Surely they'll know we won't string wire across a twenty-four foot gap in the fence. But if they don't figure it out, we can put up a big sign saying, 'Help yourself to the water' or 'Water Alley,' or something like that."

Caitlin nodded. "I think we need to post a sign before we go to town. Daddy has some white wash in the barn—I can paint something quick, and we can bring it back and put it up before supper if that's all right with you."

"Good idea."

"Now let's go home so we can come back before it gets too dark," she said. "Can you believe it's already Christmas Eve? Tomorrow's my favorite day of the year, and I haven't even had time to think about it."

They headed back to the house, and Finn told her he would feed all the animals if she wanted to work on the sign.

Caitlin climbed up the ladder to the hayloft and rummaged around a pile of scrap wood to find a two-foot long board. She chunked it off the ledge to the dirt floor below.

"Be careful up there!"

"You sound like Daddy," she said as she climbed down the ladder.

She found the paint tin, but had to ask Finn to come open it for her. She found a stick to stir it first, and then used it to print **Free water** along with some accidental drips.

"It's done!" she said. "Let's go put it up."

Finn walked over to her and put the lid back on the paint.

"I think that's about as clear as you can get," he said, grinning. "But it's not dry yet—it's going to run if we turn it sideways."

"Well, let's finish the chores and maybe by the time we get back over there, it'll be dry enough to keep from running," she said.

The sun was down, but they could still see to nail the sign to one of the posts beside the entrance to the water alley.

Caitlin stood there admiring her work in the fading light. She looked up at Finn. He was staring beyond her, and a look of concern and even fear crossed his face. He looked down at Caitlin.

"Stay calm, Katie," he said quietly, "and don't look around."

"What is it?" she whispered, fighting the urge to turn around.

"Just act normal. We're going to walk over to the wagon and load up. Come on." He took her by the arm and led her to the wagon and helped her up on the seat. "Just look at the windmill or something."

While Finn walked around the wagon, she turned her head toward the windmill, but cut her eyes back toward the fence and the sign and beyond where Finn had been facing. She didn't see anything.

Finn started the horses walking and turned them around to head back to the barn.

"What is it, Finn?" she said more adamantly.

"Riders," he said. "Don't look around! I don't want them to know we saw them."

"I didn't see anything."

"There were two of them," he said. "I just saw their hats behind some brush. They were watching us."

"What do we do?"

"Nothing. We go back to the house."

They rode in silence for a while. Caitlin watched his face in the fading

117

light. He looked at her and turned around to see how far they had come from the windmill. Then he pulled the horses to a stop and started to climb down.

"Stay here," he said.

"Where are you going?"

"I just want to see if they see the sign."

"I'm coming, too!" She started to climb down.

"No, you're not—your daddy will kill me if something happens to you."

"I'm not staying here by myself, Finn," she said. "What could happen to me? You're not going to do anything stupid, are you?"

"No, I'll stay hidden," he said. "Dadgummit." He grabbed her around the waist and set her on the ground.

"But we need to hurry, and we have to be quiet," he said, taking her hand as they started running back towards the windmill.

They slowed down before they came in sight of the windmill, and Finn worked his way through the trees and brush until they had a good line of sight of the water alley. It was getting dark, but they could still see two horses walking along the fence line.

Caitlin could hardly breathe; her heart was thumping in her throat. "Fence-cutters," she barely whispered. She could see Finn nod his head.

They watched the silhouettes of the two riders reach the gap and heard a murmur of them talking. One of them climbed off his horse to take a closer look at the sign. He even lit a match and held it up to it. Finn saw the man's face, but he didn't recognize him.

"Well, I'll be damned," the man said, his voice carrying clearly in the evening air.

The man mounted his horse and they started to walk slowly out of sight.

Finn and Caitlin heard them mumble more words, and one of them even laughed.

"It worked!" said Caitlin.

"Not so loud—sound carries, remember?" said Finn. "Come on, Joseph is probably wondering where we are. And I'm starving."

Joseph was at the wagon by the time they got there.

"Where've you two been?" he asked. "I didn't know what to think when I found this wagon without you in it."

Finn explained what they had done with the sign and what had happened with the fence-cutters, but Joseph was angry that they had gone back to the windmill. Finn tried to state his case, but his brother cut him off, telling him they would have a talk when they got back to the house.

Finn dropped Caitlin off at the house to start supper while they took care of the horses.

"They never knew we were there," Finn argued. "I know better than to confront men that are up to no good."

"But what about Caitlin?"

"She insisted on going with me, Joseph," he said. "I didn't have a choice about that. She would've followed me anyway. I just wanted to see if our sign worked. And it did—they read it and rode away. They didn't touch the fence posts."

"Well, I saw some riders, too, on the west side," said Joseph, "but they weren't looking at the fence."

"What do you mean?"

"They were looking beyond the fence," said Joseph. "I think they were looking at Ethan's cattle. I've heard that rustlers are taking advantage of this fence war to steal livestock, and the fence cutters are getting blamed for it. And I imagine everybody in the area knows by now that Ethan's sick and away from his ranch."

"Did you let them see you?"

Joseph shook his head, no. "I'm thinking now that I should have, though. I'd hate for Ethan to come back home to find all of his cattle stolen. But these men had guns. I didn't want to confront them by myself. But I probably should have let them know that somebody was still around."

"You did the right thing, Joseph," said Finn. "No telling who they were. They could've shot you on sight. And what's even worse, you'd have to face Momma if she found out you had confronted some cattle rustlers by yourself."

Joseph snickered and nodded.

They finished feeding the horses and let them out into the trap before heading to the house.

Chapter 24

Caitlin had cooked a meal of fried eggs, something they had plenty of, along with fried potatoes flavored with bacon and onion. The boys devoured it like it was the best meal they had ever tasted. Caitlin knew they were just hungry after a hard day's work, but then it tasted pretty good to her, too. She made a mental note to pack up the extra eggs and milk to take them into town in the morning for France to use.

Joseph took his plate to the dry sink and said his goodnights to Finn and Caitlin. Finn tarried a bit, watching Caitlin clean up the dishes.

"That was a good supper," he said. "You're a pretty good cook."

Caitlin was happy that she had pleased him. "I still have a lot to learn," she said modestly.

Her mother had told her when she turned twelve, she would get a hope chest to start filling with items she would need to set up a house of her own. Caitlin already knew how to sew a few basic stitches, but she would also learn to sew clothes, linens, tea towels, and quilts. Her mother would teach her how to crochet doilies. She already knew how to cook simple meals, churn butter, and basic household chores. She hadn't learned everything yet, but cooking these few meals for Finn and Joseph the past few days made her feel grown up and confident that she could run a good home of her own someday. She wondered who would cook for Finn some day.

She decided to do some digging for information. "Does Molly cook?"

That took Finn by surprise. "Molly?"

"Yeah, Molly Franklin. She's real pretty, Finn."

"What does that have to do with anything?"

"I was just wondering if she was your girlfriend."

"Did Emma put you up to this?"

"No, of course not," said Caitlin, a little too fast.

Finn almost smiled, knowing that he and Molly must have been a recent topic of conversation between Caitlin and his sisters.

"What if I said, yes?" said Finn, watching her face. "She *has* blossomed quite a bit, you know."

Caitlin's mouth dropped open, and her face turned red. "Is that all you silly boys think about?"

"Well, as a matter of fact, yes," said Finn, still teasing her.

She growled and threw the cup towel at him and started toward the stairs. He grabbed her arm. "I'm just teasing, Katie. I didn't mean that. And Molly Franklin isn't my girlfriend, although I'm sure you discussed that thoroughly with my sisters."

Caitlin still frowned at him, but inside she was relieved to hear that. "We'd narrowed it down to her."

"She's a little too uppity for my tastes".

"Then who'd you get the necklace for?"

Finn paused for a moment. "If I tell you, will you promise not to tell anyone else—especially my sisters?"

"I promise," said Caitlin.

"And you can't even tell your mother or father until it's out in the open."

"I promise."

"I'll be right back." He disappeared into the bedroom, and came back holding the necklace. "I wanted to do this tomorrow, but now's as good a time as any… maybe better."

Caitlin looked at him questioningly.

"It's yours, Katie, if you want it."

Caitlin's eyes widened, and she couldn't say anything for a moment.

"Are you teasing me again?" she asked suspiciously.

"No."

"You're giving it to me?" she asked softly.

"Yeah."

"Does this mean I'm your girlfriend?"

Finn nodded his head. "If you want to be."

Caitlin smiled shyly and looked at the necklace. She turned around and let him put it around her neck.

She looked down and touched the locket. "It's pretty, Finn, but why me?"

"I've liked you for some time, but you're always with Emma and Zane."

She turned around and faced him.

"I liked you, too, but I thought you only saw me as a baby."

"You're still young, Katie. That's why you can't tell anybody for a while. Your daddy sure won't let me come within a mile of you if he knew how I felt about you. And can you imagine what everyone in town would say with you being out here by yourself with me and Joseph if they knew we liked each other? Everybody figures we all think of each other as brothers and sisters since you lived with us for a while, but it's been a long time since I've thought of you as a sister. I don't want you to get a bad reputation because of me."

She looked down at the necklace again. "I'll wear it under my clothes so nobody will know but us."

"Merry Christmas."

"Merry Christmas, Finn."

"Now go on to bed. This is our secret, right?"

Caitlin nodded. "Love you," she whispered, raising her chin and shutting her eyes for their first kiss.

Finn leaned down and kissed her on the cheek. "Love you, too."

She opened her eyes and watched him walk across the room to her parents' bedroom. He turned and smiled at her before shutting the door. She smiled back and reached up to touch the heart locket, amazed at what had just taken place. Her life had gone from utter despair the day before when she thought she was losing her father, to sheer bliss tonight with the thought that Finn had chosen her as his sweetheart. It suddenly felt like a moth was fluttering back and forth between her tummy and her heart. She wondered if that was what love felt like.

She blew out the lamps and floated upstairs to her bedroom. Her thoughts went every which direction exploring this wonderful feeling that someone wanted her. She already knew what it was like to have someone like her—Jake Donovan told her he loved her last summer. She was very flattered since he was considered quite a catch, but once she got over the giddiness that some boy liked her, she realized the feeling wasn't mutual. But with Finn, she knew she liked him, too. She had yet to have her first kiss, though, and was a little disappointed that it didn't happen tonight, but she was convinced it would happen soon.

Caitlin couldn't go to sleep, so she slipped downstairs and lit a lamp and began to gather up the family Christmas gifts that sat under the tree. She had wrapped most of them herself in pages of the *Brownwood Bulletin* and tied them with string. She piled them beside the door to take with them to town in the morning. Her mother had told her that the ranch was the family's biggest present that year, so gifts would be sparse. Caitlin had wrapped up her miniature porcelain tea set for her sisters since she had long outgrown it. She bought her mother a hair comb and her father a kerchief at the Samuels' store several weeks before. She didn't exchange gifts with anyone outside her family except for Emma and Zane, her closest friends in the world. She had discreetly acquired several more cedar cigar boxes from Mr. Samuel and decorated them with buttons and ribbon so both sisters would have chests in which to collect their treasures.

She touched her hand to her chest where the heart locket lay under her gown. She felt so full of happiness, she thought she would burst. It was going to be so hard to not say anything to anyone, but she had promised Finn, and she knew he was right. Her father would throw a fit if he found out that Finn thought of Caitlin as anything other than a little sister. They had to put some distance between this time together by themselves on the ranch and the time they would announce they had feelings for each other. But she loved that Finn was already protecting her.

She suddenly realized she didn't have anything to give Finn for Christmas. She couldn't ask her mother for any money to buy him something because she would have to confess whom the gift was for. She ran upstairs and looked around her room. She owned three books given to her from her grandmother, but Finn couldn't hide those easily and everyone would know where they came from. And she wanted something more personal to give him. She opened her chiffarobe and tip-toed in order to reach the top shelf for the cigar box that contained her most precious belongings. She carried it over to the bed and turned it over and spread everything out. She sat there running her fingers through the items: a dozen rocks of various colors— some with flecks of crystal in them, a pretty feather, a melted headstall buckle from the barn fire six years before, several ribbons from spelling bees at school, secret notes from Emma and Zane, a brooch that had belonged to her real mother, letters from her grandmother tied in a bundle, a first place medal she earned for being the fastest kid in school when she was in the sixth grade the year before, and last of all, the piece of wood that Finn had carved for her. She picked it up, wondering why she hadn't seen it for what it was when he first gave it to her. But he had led her to believe he had a girlfriend. She just didn't know it was her until tonight.

She smiled at the thought.

What could she give him? Of all her keepsakes, her mother's brooch meant the most to her, but she couldn't part with that, even for Finn, who wouldn't want it anyway. Her second most valuable keepsake was the medal—a tin winged foot attached to a ribbon. She picked it up, remembering how it felt to outrun every student in their primary school— even the boys. They didn't like it one bit that a girl could outrun them, but everyone still admired her for it. She realized this would mean something to Finn, especially since he had done something no one else had been able to do.

He had caught her.

Chapter 25

Waco, Christmas Eve

Matthew Taylor and his son Jimmy stood on the porch of the hotel watching the stagecoach pull up in a cloud of dust as they waited to pick up Faith and her children. It was Christmas Eve and much later in the evening than the stagecoach usually arrived since they had changed the schedule to allow for the holiday.

Two men climbed out of the stage, and Jimmy walked up to the coach steps to greet his sister. He looked inside.

The coach was empty.

"They're not here," he said to his father.

"What?!"

"Do you think they missed the stage?"

"Let's find out."

They followed one of the stage drivers into the hotel. The man set a bag of mail on the counter.

"Excuse me," said Matthew. "My daughter and her four children were supposed to have been on that stage. Do you know Faith Murray of Brownwood?"

"I know of her," he said, rummaging through the mail pouch. "A boy met us at the gate to their ranch Saturday morning to tell us Mrs. Murray wouldn't be able to make the stage. He handed us a letter to give to you." He found the letter and read the name to himself. "You must be Mr. Taylor."

Matthew nodded, took the letter from him, and thanked him. He ripped open the envelope and read the short letter from Faith that explained Ethan's injury and that they would have to visit Grace later. She apologized for inconveniencing them in a wasted trip to Waco, but that Ethan's injury was more serious than she first realized.

"They need some help," said Jimmy. "Who's able to watch the fence lines while Ethan's down? His cattle could be halfway to Mexico by now."

"I think you're right," said Matthew, walking out to the buggy. "I'm going to talk to your mother tonight and the rest of the family tomorrow. I think you and your brothers and I need to pay a visit to Brownwood and help your sister for a few days. We can get that fence up and make any repairs and lay down the law for anybody that's been giving them trouble. Then I'll find Ethan some help so we can bring your sister back for a visit. Momma's not going to be happy with us bringing home an empty buggy tonight."

Matthew was right. Julia was disappointed to learn that Faith and the children weren't with them. Matthew shared his plan with the family—that he and Jimmy were going to Brownwood to help Faith. Matt and Justin agreed to go, too. Julia's brother, John Stockton, said he would be glad to stay in Grace until they returned. He had left his ranch in good hands and would send word to Dalton that his trip would be extended. Jenny's husband Marcus wanted to help, too, but Matthew told him they couldn't take all the men away from Grace.

"You're needed here, Marcus," said Matthew. "We can handle everything in Brownwood."

They planned to leave right after the noon meal on Christmas Day.

Later in their bedroom, Julia shared her apprehension with her husband. "Something's wrong, Matthew," she said. "I don't know what it is, but I'm scared for Faith."

Matthew took her in his arms to comfort her. "I know. I feel it, too. I don't know what we'll be facing when we get there; I just know we need to go."

Chapter 26

Christmas Day in the Samuel household was even more joyful because almost all of the Samuel children were present—with the exception of R. James and K. James who were hauling freight, but the entire Murray family was there, too. The doctor had released Ethan to his wife's care that morning, although he cautioned her to wait a couple of days before returning to the ranch. He said it was just too far and too difficult a trip for Ethan in case the leg took a turn for the worse.

That meant Caitlin, Finn, and Joseph would have to continue running the ranch themselves for the next few days. After Christmas dinner Joseph asked his father to go out to the barn with him—that he had something he needed to tell him. When they were out of earshot of the house, Joseph told him about the men he saw looking over Ethan's cattle.

"Are you sure they weren't Mr. Johnson's sons?"

"Yes, I'm sure. I've never seen these men before."

"Well, I don't want you to confront anybody on that fence line," said George. "If it looks like trouble, back off and get Finn and Caitlin and y'all come to town. Then we'll go talk to the sheriff."

"But what if they take Ethan's cattle?"

"The sheriff can track them down. They can't hide that many tracks."

"You know the sheriff and his deputies are stretched thin right now," said Joseph. "They may not even be in town if we need them. Cattle thieves could easily have a huge lead on the law, and there's a good likelihood they won't get caught."

"I'm not going to let you kids go back out there, Joseph, unless you promise me that you will not confront anybody on those fence lines," said George sternly. "That's not your job."

"You're starting to sound like Mother," said Joseph, jokingly.

"I'm serious, son," he said. "Those kinds of situations can be very dangerous—you don't know what those men are capable of doing. I've heard that there have already been three killings over fences somewhere around here, and I don't want any of you to get hurt."

"I think Caitlin and Finn solved the fence-cutting problem," said Joseph. He told his father how they had built an alley leading to the windmill that would allow outside cattle to reach the water tank without them getting into the rest of the pasture, and that Ethan's cattle could still water and not get out. He told him they posted a sign that said 'free water' last night. He couldn't help but mention the riders that stopped and read it and walked away without tearing up the fence posts.

"When did you see them?"

Joseph covered for his brother by saying that *he* was the one who hid in the brush and watched the riders come up to the fence instead of Finn and Caitlin. He was sure his father would refuse to let them go back out there if he knew Finn and Caitlin had been out after sunset.

"Does Ethan know about this water alley you've set posts for?"

"No, and I also didn't tell him that the fence cutters were still damaging his fences," said Joseph. "But I don't think they're going to bother the new fence anymore since they've seen that their cattle can still get to water."

"I think that was a good idea, but you ought to tell Ethan soon."

"When he's better, Pops, we'll tell him."

"All right, and I still haven't heard a promise out of you."

"I promise I won't do anything that will put me or Finn or Caitlin in danger," he said. "Satisfied?"

George nodded and put his hand on his son's shoulder.

"Do you need me to help you with anything before we leave?"

"Not that I can think of," said George. "Oh, and Albert told me yesterday to tell you that he has that posthole boring tool ready, or at least the first attempt at it. He said he wanted you to come by the house and try it out before you leave this evening. Then if you have any more ideas on how to improve the design, he could keep working on it until he saw you next."

Joseph immediately went to find Finn and tell him what his father said. They agreed to slip out of the opposite sides of the house after a few minutes to meet down the street and go talk to the smithy.

Finn met up with Joseph in front of the neighbor's house and they quickly walked the three blocks to Albert Beights' home. They knocked on the door, assuming he would be in his house on Christmas Day. A boy about Mac's age answered it, but before they could say anything, the boy said he'd be right back with his father. Albert came to the door and hollered over his shoulder that he was going outside for a smoke and stepped forward to greet the Samuel boys.

"Come on, Bugs," he said to the boy. "You can help us."

"We're sorry for interrupting your holiday, Albert," said Joseph, shaking his hand. "I hope we're not getting you in trouble with the missus."

"Nah, don't worry about it. I was hoping you'd come by today—I think you're going to like what you see."

The boys followed him to his blacksmith shop out back. Finn noticed holes of varying depths in the pen beside the building. Albert pulled open the door wide so they would have plenty of light to see. He walked over to what looked like an oversized iron screw with a tray sitting on top and a bar attached just below the tray. It stood in a tripod attached to a ring that held the boring shaft. He asked the boys to carry it outside. Joseph and Finn took hold of each side of the bar and lifted it.

"This is heavy," grunted Finn.

"Yeah, I thought that might be a problem," said Albert. "Go through that gate into the pen and find a spot and try it out."

The boys carried it into the pen, riddled with shallow holes.

"Looks like you've been practicing around here," said Joseph. "Is that as deep as it would go?"

"No, but Bugs is going to have to fill in all these holes, so we didn't take it as far as it's capable. And it was just he and I working with it—no one else knows about this tool," he said. "You never know who might steal your idea."

They set the tripod in place and lifted up the heavy auger about a foot and dropped it, forcing the point into the ground. They started walking around, turning it, which worked fine in the loose dirt of the pen.

"It's working fine," said Joseph, "and the hole is nice and narrow— unlike digging a hole with a shovel. But you're right about the weight, Albert. It's going to be awfully hard to carry this contraption for any distance."

"If it was lighter and the bar across the top shorter than this one, I think one person ought to be able to handle it," said Finn.

"Hard ground might be a problem—think of how much pressure it takes to bore a hole in wood," said Joseph. "What if we shortened it a bit so we can lean on it to put our weight on it, if need be. The screw blade doesn't need to come up this high—the bottom part does all the work."

"Or we could just set Katie on that shelf," said Finn.

Albert repeated the adjustments back to Joseph and Finn to make sure he heard them correctly. They carried the tool back into Albert's shop.

"I think we can sell a bunch of these things if we get it to working like you planned, Joseph," said Albert. "We can partner on this if you want—I can build them and you can sell them."

"I think we can make it work," said Joseph, shaking his hand. "I'm going to write the patent office for an application. By the time I get it back, we should have a patentable tool."

"But you'll be back in Waco by the time that application gets here," said Finn.

"I'll have them mail it to me at school," he said. "Now let's get back to the house before Mother realizes we've disappeared."

"Come by Saturday or Sunday," said Albert. "I'll have it modified by then."

The boys could hardly contain their excitement about the posthole tool.

"This is going to revolutionize fence building," said Joseph. "No telling how much time this is going to save in putting up a fence."

"We're going to be rich!" said Finn.

"I don't know about that, but I do know this is the type of work I'd like to do as a career."

"Building fences?"

"No, inventing things that help people, especially farmers and ranchers. That's why I want to transfer to Texas A.M.C.—that's the kind of stuff they teach you there."

"You'll probably be out before I get there," said Finn, "but I'd like to work with you someday."

"I think we'd make a good team, brother."

Chapter 27

J oseph and Finn slipped in the back porch door that led to the bedrooms. Emma, Caitlin, and Zane were coming down the stairs. Caitlin looked upset.

"Momma's been looking for y'all," said Zane.

"I told you she'd find out we'd left," said Joseph, elbowing his brother before he walked on into the parlor.

"What's the matter?" Finn asked Caitlin.

"Nothing."

But he knew better. Finn looked at his sisters. "Have y'all been talking about me and Molly Franklin again?"

"No, Finn," said Emma. "We know *she's* not your girlfriend."

Finn looked back at Caitlin, thinking she might have said something. She shook her head almost imperceptibly and walked on past him and out on the back porch.

"What did you say to her?" Finn asked angrily.

"We found where you carved your initials in a heart—yours and J.C.'s," she said.

"What are you talking about?"

"Out in the barn—up in the hay loft," said Zane. "R. James told us about it."

"The only J.C. we know around your age is Johanna Casey," said Emma. "Did you already give her the necklace?"

"She's not my girlfriend, so just shut up about it!" said Finn, watching Caitlin walking to the barn out of the corner of his eye.

He turned and walked into the parlor where the men and boys had gathered around Ethan to visit. He stood and listened for a while trying to figure out a way to get to Caitlin without raising any suspicion. He slipped

131

out the front door and walked around the house towards the barn, but stopped when he heard his sisters giggling. They had followed Caitlin outside.

He found no opportunity to talk to her alone for the rest of the afternoon. Later, they rode back to the ranch in silence.

"Would y'all let me get a word in edgewise?" Joseph teased them. "Are you all talked out? What's wrong with you two?"

"Nothing, Joseph," said Caitlin. "I'm just tired."

"Me, too," said Finn, looking away.

"Well, Mother sent plenty of food—you won't have to fix anything for supper, Caitlin, and I don't know about y'all, but I'm eating pie for breakfast."

"That's good," she said. "I think I'll just turn in early."

The boys dropped her off at the house with the box of food, and then took the wagon to the barn and unhitched the horses. Joseph started feeding while Finn got the bucket out of the back of the wagon to go milk Birdie. By the time they got back to the house, Caitlin had set some of the food out for supper, but had already gone upstairs. They ate a quick supper, and Joseph talked about his plans for the auger.

"And while you're doing chores, think about ways you can do things better," he said. "So many of us just do what's always been done before without ever questioning anything. I was talking to the librarian at Baylor one day about this very thing, and he had recently changed the library hours after fifteen years. He said the schedule was different every day. The library was closed some mornings, and it was always closed for an hour and a half at noon. Few people could remember the odd schedule, which seemed to cause a lot of frustration. The librarian I was visiting with had been there for a year before he questioned why the hours were so inconsistent and impractical. He finally learned from one of the older professors that the original part-time librarian had set up the library schedule around his whist playing. This went on for about five years, and when the university found out about his card playing, he was let go. But for the next ten years, nobody ever questioned the odd library hours. They just followed them as if they couldn't be changed."

"Interesting," said Finn, but he could hardly hear what his brother was saying for worrying about Caitlin.

"Get in the habit of questioning why things are done the way they're done," he said. "Don't assume it's always the best way."

Finn nodded his head and said he was going to turn in, hoping Joseph would take the hint. He did, and pinched off some more bread before he left the house.

"See you in the morning."

" 'Night," said Finn.

He waited to give his brother time to get out of earshot before he ran up the steps. There were two doors, and one was open and empty, so Finn went to the other one and knocked lightly.

"Katie, we need to talk."

Silence greeted him.

"All right," he said. "I'll talk right here. I don't know what my sisters said, but Johanna isn't my girlfriend. I swear."

"I saw the heart, Finn." Caitlin had walked over to the door. "It was in the hay loft. You can't deny that."

"I'd forgotten it was even there, but I didn't carve it!" he said. "K. James did it a couple of years ago to tease me."

"You promise?"

"I promise."

Caitlin opened the door and stood there looking at him. Then she smiled.

"This has been the best and worst Christmas I've ever had," she said. "My dad was with us, but then when your sisters showed me that heart, I thought I'd lost you before I even had you."

Finn shook his head. "I thought you'd told them at first."

"No, I promised you I wouldn't tell." She stepped closer to him.

"I'm sorry it took so long for me to get to explain everything to you," he said.

He looked down and noticed Caitlin was still dressed.

"I thought you were going to bed."

Caitlin smiled. "I was hoping you'd come talk to me."

"Well, are you going to be ready to dig some more postholes tomorrow?"

Caitlin nodded.

"Then we'd better get some sleep." He leaned over and kissed Caitlin on the forehead.

"Why don't you really kiss me?" she asked. "Don't you want to?"

"More than you know. But I want to be able to tell your father that I've been nothing but a gentleman around you."

"When are you ever going to kiss me then?" said Caitlin, a little disappointed.

"When we're ready for everyone to know about us," he said. "Good night."

"Wait! I almost forgot." Caitlin reached into her pocket and pulled out her medal. "I wasn't able to buy you anything for Christmas, but I wanted to give you something." She held out her hand.

Finn took the medal and held it up to look at it. He smiled, recognizing what it was. "I saw you running that day."

"You did?"

Finn nodded. "Some of us older students were helping with the games. I remember you had such a look of determination on your face when you came across the finish line. We couldn't believe a girl could outrun all the boys."

Caitlin smiled.

"But I can't take it from you, Katie."

Her face fell. "Why not?"

"I know this is really special to you," he said as he looked at it. "You earned it."

"It *is* special to me, and that's why I want you to have it. Please take it— I want to know you have something of mine when we're away from each other, just like I have the necklace you gave me."

"Are you sure?"

Caitlin nodded.

"Then I'd be proud to have it. Did you know I earned a couple of these medals myself?"

"You did?"

"Yep, so you're not the only fast runner in Brown County."

"I may have to race you some day," she said. "Are you worried I might outrun you?"

Finn grinned and shook his head, no.

"Oh yeah, you caught up to me in front of Widow Turner's house on Sunday," Caitlin remembered.

He nodded.

Caitlin smiled as she touched the locket under her dress.

"Now go to bed," he said as he kissed her cheek and turned to go downstairs.

"Love you, Finn."

"Love you, too."

Chapter 28

O n Wednesday, Finn and Caitlin continued to dig holes and set the posts on the new fence line while Joseph patrolled the property line in the west pasture. He had promised his father he wouldn't confront anyone on the fence line, but he walked his horse up and down the property line about fifty yards away from the fence. He was determined to do what he could to protect Ethan's cattle... within his capabilities and the bounds of his promise.

On Thursday evening after completing the chores, the boys walked out of the barn to see four horsemen riding brazenly towards them from the direction of the main gate. Joseph, fearing the worst, stepped in front of his brother and held his rifle up in plain sight. Finn set the bucket of milk down and stepped up next to his brother.

"Stay behind me!" Joseph ordered.

"I'll stand beside you," said Finn. "Maybe they'll think I'm armed, too."

"Ethan?" one of the riders called out in the fading light.

"Hold it right there! What do you want?" Joseph yelled in his sternest voice.

But Finn could hear a tremor in his brother's voice and knew he was scared.

"Joseph?! It's me, Jimmy!"

"Jimmy?!" Joseph lowered his gun and exhaled audibly.

"Yeah, and my father and brothers," Jimmy said. "We've come to help Ethan."

"Thank God," he said, walking over to the Taylor men as they dismounted their horses. He grabbed Jimmy in a bear hug. "You don't know how glad I am to see a familiar face right now."

"Good to see you, Joseph," said Jimmy. "You remember my brothers, Matt and Justin? And my father?"

"Yes, sir," he said, shaking each of their hands. "How you doin'? I'm so glad to see all of you here. How'd you know we needed help?"

"Faith sent them a letter telling them that Ethan hurt his leg," said Finn, then he turned to Jimmy. "But I thought she just told you why they weren't able to come for Christmas."

"That's what her letter said, but we all felt like we needed to come," said Matthew Taylor. "What's been happening around here? How's Ethan? Is he inside?"

Joseph explained that he and Faith had taken Ethan into town on Saturday with an infected leg, and that he had stayed at the doctor's house until Christmas Day.

"He seems to be on the mend, but he'll be off that leg for a while," said Joseph. "We've been taking care of the place in his absence, but we've had to contend with folks tearing up the work we've done on the new fence. Everybody knows Ethan's been sick, too, and I'm afraid rustlers may take advantage of him and steal his cattle before he comes home."

Joseph told them about seeing the riders watching Ethan's cattle a few days before, and that he had been patrolling the fence line to discourage any potential livestock theft.

"You might be setting yourself up as a target doing that," said Jimmy. "You don't need to go anywhere by yourself from now on."

"We're here to help in whatever way we can," said Justin.

"We're going to get that fence up, and nobody's going to steal Ethan and Faith's cattle while we're around," said Matt.

"So everyone's in town?" asked Matthew.

"Except for Caitlin," said Finn. "She's inside fixing supper."

"Caitlin's here?" said Jimmy. "She shouldn't be out here by herself."

"We've been with her the whole time," said Finn defensively.

"This sounds too dangerous a situation for her to even be out here," said Matthew. "Whose idea was that?"

"Her parents'," said Joseph. "But we've been careful and have made sure we're back at the house before dark. The fence tampering has taken place at night, but I think we solved the fence problem on the east side."

He explained how they designed a U-shaped gap in the fence and posted a sign, and that the fence cutters hadn't touched it since.

"But sharing the water won't change a thing if cattle thieves are involved," Jimmy added.

Finn picked up the bucket of milk and said he needed to get it in the house.

"Let's get these horses taken care of," said Matthew. "We've ridden them pretty hard the past couple of days. And then I need to see my granddaughter."

Matt and Justin told their father and brother to go on ahead—that they would take care of their horses, so Matthew and Jimmy followed the Samuel boys to the house. Caitlin opened the door at the sound of the voices, and when she saw her Uncle Jimmy, she ran and hugged him. Then she squealed with delight when she saw her grandfather and hugged him just as hard.

"Something sure smells good in here," said Jimmy. "Don't tell me our little Caitlin's actually cooking?"

Her smile filled her face, and then she realized she needed to set some more plates at the table heat up some more food.

"She's done a good job," said Joseph.

"Most of this is from Christmas dinner," she admitted, "straight from France's kitchen."

"Matt and Justin are here, too," Jimmy told her as he watched her set two more plates at the table.

"Momma's going to have a cow when she sees all of you," she said. "I'm so glad you're here. We were disappointed that we didn't get to go to Grace for Christmas. How's Meemaw and everyone?"

"They're all fine, and Julia's fine—other than being a little worried about your daddy," said Matthew. "How's he doing?"

"Everybody thought he was going to lose his leg for a while there," she said, "but he's doing better. He got to move to the Samuel's house on Christmas Day, and we're hoping they're coming home real soon."

"I didn't tell Ethan about the riders on the west side," said Joseph. "I didn't want him to worry, but I told my father and he wouldn't let us come back out here until I promised him that we would avoid any confrontation. But I've been worried Ethan and Faith might be coming home to a ranch with no cattle."

"You can take us around the fence lines tomorrow, Joseph, and then we'll take it from there and you can get back to work on your fence-building," said Matthew. "Once we've gotten the word out that cattle thieves and even trespassers will be dealt with severely, I think their cattle will be safe."

"You may have to post some signs, too," said Caitlin. "Did Joseph tell you about our sign at the water alley?"

Jimmy nodded. "That was a smart thing to do, and mighty generous on your father's part."

Caitlin glanced at Finn before admitting that her father didn't know about it yet.

Jimmy laughed. "I didn't think that sounded like Ethan. It'll be interesting to see his reaction to it, but I think we can convince him that it'll prevent further grief from the free-grazers."

"We'll help you finish the fence before we leave, too," said Justin.

Matt nodded in agreement.

Caitlin smiled at her uncles and sighed with relief. It felt like a huge burden had been lifted off her shoulders.

The next morning Joseph took the Taylors around the west pasture. This time they rode right beside the fence and soon came across cut wires. Dead brush had been piled against the fence to hide it. Joseph was upset.

"I haven't been riding close enough to the fence to spot it," he said. "I promised my father I'd stay away from any confrontations. Should we go after them?"

Jimmy and Justin climbed off their horses and walked around looking at the tracks.

"It looks like they got no more than eight or ten head, including some calves," said Justin, "as recent as yesterday."

"Since they went to the trouble of hiding the gap in the fence, I'd say they're probably coming back for more."

"Let's cover our tracks and back off for a while to see if anybody shows up today," said Matthew, looking around. "Justin, why don't you go on and check for any more cuts in the fence around this pasture. Make a wide swing when you get back over here and meet us in that stand of trees yonder."

Justin nodded and mounted his horse and rode a little ways from the fence before he turned to follow along parallel so his tracks wouldn't be so noticeable to potential trespassers.

Matthew told Joseph to go meet Finn and Caitlin and continue to work on the fence. "Rustlers won't bother you over there since you're working in an empty pasture. This is where the cattle are. But if you hear any gunfire, take Finn and Caitlin back to the house and wait for us there. And if no one comes through that gap today, we'll go looking for them tomorrow."

Joseph was reluctant to go, but he knew they needed to get that fence up and finished for Ethan. With the Taylors here, he was convinced they could get it done. And if anybody could find the stolen cattle, Jimmy and Justin could. They were known for their tracking skills.

Jimmy climbed off his horse and handed the reins to Matt. He and Matthew led the horses away from the fence while Jimmy started covering their tracks.

Justin came back after a while to report that the fence was intact except for the gap they had been watching. The Taylor men waited in a stand of trees until late afternoon before deciding that no one was coming back that day for more cattle.

"We'll pick up their trail in the morning and go after them," said Matthew.

They rode back to the ranch house, tired and hungry.

"The kids won't be back yet," said Matt as they neared the barn. "I guess we're going to have to cook something for ourselves."

They came through the wire gap, and when they rounded the corner in sight of the house, they noticed a buggy with the horses still hitched to it sitting out front.

"I think that's the Samuel's buggy," said Jimmy, spurring his horse forward.

At that moment, the door opened partway and Faith peeked outside, shielding her eyes from the western sun. She saw the riders and noticed one break away from the group to head towards her, so she stepped out on the porch to get a better look. When she realized who it was, she knew immediately who the other riders were. They had come to help.

Her brothers had come to help.

She dropped her face in her hands and burst into tears.

Chapter 29

J immy scrambled off his horse, dropped the reins, and took the three steps to the porch in one bound. He wrapped Faith in his arms, keenly aware of the blood kinship they shared.

He held his sister, his true sister.

Jimmy had always felt protective of Faith, but the feeling was magnified now after what his mother had told him. He so badly wanted to tell her, but he knew that the time wasn't right.

"Everything's going to be fine now," he whispered.

She wept even harder and laid her head against his chest, needing to feel his strength. For days now, she had been the strong one for Ethan, but it had taken its toll. She was exhausted.

Faith had planned to wait a few more days before coming back to the ranch, but George had told Ethan about the riders Joseph had seen and shared his suspicions that they were cattle rustlers. Ethan had insisted on coming home that very afternoon. She knew he was capable of doing little or nothing to protect their cattle from rustlers because of the fragile shape he was in, but she couldn't convince him otherwise.

France knew how difficult the next few days would be for Faith, so she offered to keep the little ones for a while longer. She was upset with George for letting their sons and Caitlin go back to the ranch after hearing about the suspicious riders. But George assured her that Joseph had promised to not put himself or Finn or Caitlin in any kind of danger.

Matt and Justin walked up to the porch, and Faith smiled and hugged them, and tearfully thanked them for coming. She assumed Marcus was the fourth rider, and her eyes widened when she saw her father standing there with open arms.

"Daddy?" she cried. "You came, too?"

She ran into his arms.

"Hello, sweetheart," he said, hugging her tight. "How's my girl?"

"How'd you know?" She looked up at him and then turned around and looked at her brothers. "How'd you know?" she asked without finishing the question with *we needed help*, knowing Ethan was within earshot.

"We got your letter, but your mother and I both felt like it was much more serious than you let on," said Matthew. "We just had an uneasy feeling about it."

"We all felt that way, sis," said Justin.

"Mr. Taylor?" said Ethan from inside the house. "Is that you?"

Matthew and Faith led everyone inside so they could greet Ethan. He sat in the rocking chair by the fireplace. His leg was propped up on a pillow atop a chair.

"Where's Katie?" he asked.

"She's with Finn and Joseph working on the fence," said Jimmy.

"Thank God you've come, Mr. Taylor," said Ethan, shaking Matthew's hand.

"We're way beyond you having to call me Mr. Taylor, Ethan," said Matthew. "It's either Dad or Matthew."

"I know," said Ethan, grinning. "It's out of respect, sir."

"And probably some healthy fear, too," said Jimmy. "But you know I still expect you to call me *Mr. Taylor* and *sir*, though."

"Yes, ma'am," Ethan said irreverently to Jimmy. "I'm really glad you're here, brother."

"Where are my grandkids?" asked Matthew, looking around.

"France offered to keep them a few more days for us," said Faith. "She has plenty of good help with her four girls. I was hoping to stay in town a while longer, too, but Ethan wouldn't hear of it."

"I'm afraid we're going to lose our cattle," he said.

"You've already lost some," said Justin. "But we'll get them back for you."

They told Ethan and Faith about the cut fence and the tracks they found, and that they had waited most of the day to see if the rustlers returned for more. He said they would leave first thing in the morning to track down the stolen cattle.

The sound of footsteps thumping on the porch preceded the door bursting open and Caitlin running into the room.

"You're home already?!" she yelled out, looking through the faces to find her parents. Her long, blonde hair was in disarray and her face and clothes were smudged, but nobody noticed them for the expression on her face. Her blue eyes sparkled and her smile lit up the room. She ran and hugged her mother first, then tentatively leaned over to gently hug her father. He grabbed her roughly in a bear hug.

"Dad! Be careful... your leg!" she scolded him.

"I'm fine. And look at you—working as hard as any man. I'm so proud of you and how you and Finn and Joseph have taken care of things around here." He looked beyond her. "Where are the boys?"

"Doing their chores and putting the horses up," she said. "I have 'em well-trained."

"I bet you do."

The Taylor brothers excused themselves to join the Samuel brothers. Jimmy told Faith that they would take care of the buggy and their horses, too. Faith admitted that she had already forgotten about them.

"That's always been my job, Faith," said Ethan. "I'm sorry I haven't been able to help you."

"You'll be up and around in no time."

Jimmy stuck his head back in the doorway to tell her he was starving—that they hadn't eaten since breakfast.

Mother and daughter scurried around the kitchen to heat up some of the dishes of food Faith had brought from the Samuels. She blessed France again for coming to her rescue—first with taking care of her children, and now feeding her family. And France knew
nothing about the Taylors coming. She just figured Finn and Joseph had to have been eating them into the poor house. Faith told Caitlin that in return they needed to do something special for France real soon.

After supper, Finn headed out to the camp house with Joseph since he'd moved back out there the night before after the Taylors came. Faith put Caitlin on a pallet in her room, and the Taylor men took over the second floor bedrooms.

Matthew rose well before sun-up and treaded lightly down the stairs. He put some wood and kindling in the stove and stirred the embers to start a blaze. Then he rummaged around the kitchen as quietly as he could, trying to find the makings for coffee. Faith heard him, though, and slipped in the kitchen to help.

"Good morning," she whispered.

"Sorry, sweetheart," he whispered back. "I didn't want to wake you."

"That's all right." She smiled and hugged him. "I still can't believe you're here."

"How'd you sleep?"

"Better than I have in some time," she said, taking over the coffee fixing. "What would you like for breakfast?"

"Don't go to any trouble—we're going to get an early start."

"It's no trouble at all; in fact, you'd be doing me a favor if you let me cook you some eggs. We have eggs running out our ears."

"Then fry me a couple of eggs. Got any meat?"

"Ham or bacon?"

"Bacon."

She lit another lamp and sent him through the door under the stairs that led down to the cellar to get a slab of bacon.

Matthew brought it back to the table and pulled out his knife to cut some slices off of it.

"I'll start some biscuits and make them small so they won't take as long to bake."

"That's a nice cellar you have down there," he said. "I see you have it stocked good, too."

"Most of it's from our garden in town. Our old cellar was away from the house, but I like that this one's inside and easy to get to. Would you believe you can even hide the stairs down to the cellar by pushing the shelves up against the door once you're inside the closet? Then it looks like it's just a pantry under the stairwell."

"Really? That's clever."

"I heard that the family built it for protection against the Indians. Don't think we're ever going to need it for that reason, but it'll be good protection from bad storms."

She picked up the bacon pieces Matthew had cut and dropped them in a hot skillet.

"Now sit there and talk to me while I'm cookin' this. You said everybody was fine last night, but how's Momma really doing?"

"She's much better now that she can lift her arm," said Matthew without thinking.

Faith turned around and stared at him. The look on her face reminded him that she knew nothing about the shooting.

He tried to cover it by saying, "She's doing just fine—she can't wait to see you and the babies."

"What are you talking about? What happened to Mother's arm?"

"You'd better watch that bacon."

"Daddy?!" she said sternly.

"We were going to tell you when you came home. We didn't want to worry you."

"This is my home now. What were you going to tell me after I got to Grace? You didn't want me to worry about what?"

Matthew took a deep breath. "About three weeks ago your mother and Jimmy were shot in Waco."

"What?!"

Chapter 30

Faith dropped the fork she was using and left the bacon frying to walk over and face her father.

"But they're fine now," he said.

"This happened three weeks ago? Why didn't you send word immediately?"

"Your mother was afraid you'd come right then and not get to come back for Christmas. And she didn't want you to miss seeing Justin and Allie."

"But Daddy—"

"Was she right? Would you have dropped everything to come to Grace then?"

Faith had to admit she would have. "Tell me what happened."

"Don't you burn that bacon. I'll pull my chair up closer."

Faith went back to the stove, and Matthew told her what had led up to the shooting and about the young man who had shot them. He told her where her mother and brother had been shot, pointing to his shoulder and to his head.

Jimmy awakened to the sound of voices and dressed and started to come downstairs when he heard his father telling Faith about the shooting. He paused on the stairwell.

"They were taken to Mercy's parents' home, and that's where Matt and I found them. I haven't mentioned this to your mother, but I was told that she was speaking gibberish right after it happened."

"What do you mean?"

"Pate Janek told me it sounded like she was speaking Indian—like she had lost her mind for a moment. A number of people heard her and didn't understand a word she was saying. I'm sure she was in shock with what had happened, though. I think she thought Jimmy had been killed."

145

Faith shook her head. "Why would Momma speak Apache in public after all these years?"

"I don't know, honey, but she's back to her old self now, and she's hoping we can bring y'all back for a visit. She misses you terribly."

"Same here, and I've missed you, too, Daddy." She leaned over and squeezed his hand. "I don't know what I'd do without you. This means the world to me that you all came."

"You're my daughter. I couldn't do anything less knowing you needed my help."

She smiled at her father, feeling such a sense of security in his presence. She turned back to fork the bacon out of the frying pan onto a plate. "That is so odd about her speaking Apache in front of all those people. I wonder what prompted that?"

Jimmy figured that would be a good spot to interrupt the conversation. He walked on down the stairs, and when Faith saw him, she handed the fork to her father and rushed over to hug him.

"Hey, what's all this about?" he said, teasing her. "I already told you hello last night."

"Shut up," she said as she led him to a chair and forced him to sit down so she could take a look at his head. She gently brushed his hair back from the side of his head to find the still-red scar. She exhaled loudly and shook the thought out of her head that he had come so close to dying.

"Why didn't you tell me?"

"When could I have told you? We just got here."

"Last night—as soon as you saw me."

"I didn't even think about it. We had more important matters to tend to—like your stolen cattle, for instance. How 'bout pouring me some coffee."

"You and Momma could have been killed. Thank God you weren't."

"We're fine, so don't worry about us."

Matthew broke some eggs into the hot grease. "You'd better go rouse Justin and Matt. We need to get an early start. No tellin' how far those cattle have been driven."

"The calves will slow them down some," said Jimmy, standing. "And I think they intended to come back for more since they went to the trouble to take the slack out of the fence and hide the cut."

Matthew nodded. "How many eggs you want?"

"A bunch if we're going to skip lunch again," he said walking toward the stairs.

"I'll pack you something to eat," said Faith.

Justin and Matt saved Jimmy the trouble of rousting them out of bed when they came walking down the stairs. Faith noticed their guns were already strapped on and realized anew the danger they would be facing.

"Maybe we ought to just let the cattle go," she said, pouring each of them a cup of coffee. "It wasn't that many head, was it? They're not worth putting y'all in danger."

"We can't let them get away with it, Faith," said Justin. "They'll for sure be back for more if nobody stands up to them."

"They're not worth any of you getting hurt," she said, "or worse."

"Have a little faith in us, sis," said Jimmy. "We're not a bunch of greenhorns."

"I know… I just wish the sheriff could take care of this."

"He's strapped too thin, honey, and you know it," said Ethan, leaning against the doorway to the bedroom.

"What are you doing out of bed?" said Faith, rushing over to help him get to the rocker. "Take the biscuits out of the oven, Daddy."

"Yes, ma'am."

"I wish I was going with y'all," said Ethan. "I need to be defending my own ranch and taking care of things around here."

"Everybody needs help at one time or another, Ethan," said Matthew. "You'd do the same for us if we needed it."

Matthew set the pan of biscuits on the table, and then brought the plate of bacon and platter of fried eggs to sit beside it.

"I didn't know you could cook," said Matt, grinning. "This doesn't look half bad."

"Well, between your mother and Vestal, I haven't had very many opportunities, but I could keep myself from starving if I had to," he said. "Your sister gets credit for the biscuits, though. Eat up so we can get going."

Faith had to fix another pan of biscuits and start frying some more bacon and eggs for Finn and Joseph, who had come in about the time the Taylor men were leaving the house. Caitlin came out of the bedroom earlier than usual, too, since the voices that had long ceased to be quiet woke her. She took over the skillet-cooking while Faith packed up some food for her father and brothers to take on the trail.

Faith walked out to the barn to find them saddling their horses.

"Please be careful, Daddy." She set down her lantern and handed him the bundle.

Matthew tied it to the back of his saddle.

"We will, honey. Don't you worry."

Faith hugged him before he mounted his horse.

Jimmy watched his father and sister. He knew his father loved Faith as if she were his own flesh and blood. He wondered what effect it might have on their relationship for Faith to know that Nantan Lupan was her actual father, not some unnamed Apache brave. Would she feel any different about Matthew Taylor when she realized that he had been responsible for killing the man who had brought her into this world?

Did he want to risk damaging his sister's relationship with the only father she had ever known? Jimmy realized he needed to pray long and hard about this. As much as he wanted Faith to know that they were blood kin, he knew it wasn't as simple a revelation as he first thought. Maybe his mother was right; maybe this secret should stay buried.

Faith caught him staring at her, lost in thought. She walked over to him and repeated the admonition she had given her father.

"Don't do anything foolish, brother," she said, glancing at the side of his head where the new scar was. "And be sure to duck if the situation calls for it."

She hugged Jimmy and her other two brothers before they mounted their horses. She carried her lantern and walked on ahead of them to open the wire gate to the west pasture for them. As they passed her by, she looked at each of their faces, burning them in her memory along with the sight of her father and brothers riding off together. She tried to recall the last time she saw the Taylor men like that, and realized she was witnessing a first. She had never seen them so unified before. They made an impressive sight, and she felt so proud to be a Taylor.

A chill ran through her, though, and she knew it was more than the crisp morning air. She lifted up a prayer for their protection and watched until the gray shadows swallowed them. She walked back to the house to get the fence-builders on their way, the opposite direction from the Taylors.

The sun was just peeking over the eastern horizon when Matthew suggested they come from behind the same grove of trees they had waited among yesterday before heading to the gap. It was about a hundred yards from the cut in the fence and would hide their approach temporarily. They walked through the trees and were almost out into the open when Justin suddenly put up a hand of warning, and everyone pulled up. He stared intently towards the brush across the property line for a moment.

148

No one saw anything for a moment, but Jimmy watched his horse and his reaction told him something was out there. Everyone sat unmoving in their saddles—even the creaking of the leather would carry a good distance in the quiet morning.

Justin looked over at his father and brothers and nodded toward the gap. Their timing had been wrong about the rustlers yesterday, but their assumption was dead right.

The thieves had returned.

Chapter 31

Caitlin held her hand under the water flowing from the windmill pipe. It was cold and clear, unlike the thick, murky water of a river suffering through a drought. She looked up at the sky and lifted up another prayer for rain. Then she looked down the alley they had built leading up to the tank. The posts stood as sentries guarding entry to the rest of the pasture. She hoped her father would agree to keep it.

"These holes won't dig themselves," said Joseph, sitting in the wagon seat.

"Come on, Katie," said Finn, climbing on the back of the wagon. There was only a little more than a foot of sitting space between the ends of the cedar posts and the edge of the wagon bed. "We'll come back and shut it off after a while."

She cupped her hands under the water to catch some and ran up to the back of the wagon and threw the little bit that was left on Finn before she started to climb on the wagon bed.

"Hey! You can just walk," he said as he grabbed her arms to keep her from hopping on the wagon as it started forward.

She giggled and clinched his arm like a vice grip to pull him off, so Finn gave up and pulled her up beside him. He put his finger to his lips and glanced back at Joseph before hopping off the wagon and jogging along acting like he was running in slow motion before he jumped back on again. Caitlin snickered and jumped off and skipped along behind before Finn helped pull her back on again. They repeated the act, each performing a new routine before jumping back on the wagon. Then they both hopped off and started dancing along together, laughing as quietly as they could. This time Joseph turned and saw them, and he prompted the horses to speed up, leaving them hollering in the dust behind him. Finn and Caitlin had to run the rest of the short way to get to the fence line where they had left off working the day before.

They didn't realize they were still holding hands as they ran up to the wagon, but Finn dropped Caitlin's hand when Joseph saw them. She glanced at Finn, but still continued to laugh as she tried to catch her breath.

"You turkey," said Finn to his brother. "Why'd you run off and leave us?"

"I didn't know you weren't on the wagon anymore," said Joseph innocently. "Did you two fall off?"

"Yeah, when you sped up," said Finn, grabbing a shovel and a pick ax. "Come on, Katie."

Caitlin grabbed the tamping tool and tin can and followed Finn.

Joseph watched the two walk off together. Something was different today. "And no more dancing on the job!" he hollered.

Caitlin's head turned and grinned at Joseph before looking adoringly up at Finn.

Immediately, Joseph knew what it was. And he knew he would have to have a talk with Finn later.

The Taylors watched the three riders come up to the fence where the wire had been cut. One of the men dismounted and pulled the dead brush aside, opening the gap. He walked into the pasture and looked around at the ground, and Jimmy held his breath, hoping he had covered their tracks well enough from the day before. He breathed a sigh of relief when the man walked back to his horse and mounted, leading the others into the pasture.

Matthew whispered to his sons. "Let them get inside a good ways before we swing around behind them to block their way out. Don't get in each others' line of fire. We need to take them alive, if possible, but you defend yourselves first. These men have no scruples and won't hesitate to kill you. And none of us will go off by ourselves—let's partner up."

"Justin, you go with Jimmy," said Matt. "I'll go with Dad."

"Why don't you two stay at the gap," said Justin. "That's the first place they'll head when they know someone's after them. If they get by us, they'll come right back to you. And we'll know where you are if the shooting starts."

"But stay low anyway," added Jimmy.

"Good plan," whispered Matthew, nodding his head. And without shutting his eyes, he said a quick prayer. "Lord, we're asking your help and your protection at this time. Give us wisdom, quick judgment, and justice in handling these men who have wronged Faith and Ethan. Amen."

"Let's go get 'em," said Justin.

Joseph was still working on his first hole, and Finn and Caitlin had just started digging their second one when they heard gunshots in the distance. All three heads shot up in unison as they looked to the west. Then they looked at each other.

"Oh, my gosh," said Caitlin. Her heart started to pound when she realized what the gunfire meant. "The rustlers came back."

"Get to the wagon," said Joseph. "We need to go back to the house right now. Come on!"

They ran to the wagon and threw their tools in the bed.

"Get in the back, and hunker down," said Joseph as he climbed up on the wagon seat and started the horses forward. "No telling where they might scatter, and it won't take long to get across your ranch running at full tilt. We need to get back and help your mother."

Faith stood beside one of the front windows holding a shotgun, watching toward the west. Ethan sat at a second window, propping a rifle on the sill. The window sash was lifted about halfway up. A pistol and a box of shells lay on a small table next to him. They could hear intermittent gunfire.

"Do you think the kids heard?" asked Faith, trying to keep her composure. "Do you think they're on the way home?"

Ethan nodded, although his eyes never left the window. "They'll be here soon. Joseph won't waste any time getting them home."

"Lord, please keep my family safe," she said under her breath.

Ethan saw a rider coming in fast across the pasture toward the back of the barn.

"Look beyond the barn," he said to Faith. "Can you tell who that is?"

Faith squinted her eyes and then walked over and opened the door to get a better look. "I can't tell."

"Well, he's not heading toward the wire gate behind the barn—so it must not be anyone we know. You'd better get back inside."

Ethan could see the man looking behind him as he came running through the brush, and he didn't see the fence until he was right on top of it. The horse saw it, though, and pulled up fast, throwing the rider clean over the barbed wire fence. He lay on the ground unmoving while his horse trotted off towards the south along the fence line away from the barn.

"Did you see that!?" said Ethan, standing to get a better look.

Faith had just gotten back to her post at the window and looked outside. "See what?"

"Dang it," he said, limping towards the door. "If I could just run out there and set my sights on him."

"What are you doing?" Faith leaned her shotgun against the wall and hurried over to help him walk.

"A horse just threw his rider, and he's lying out there on this side of the fence."

"You can't go out there!"

Ethan opened the door. "He's not moving. If I can just get close enough to him, I can keep him from going anywhere until your father or brothers show up."

They walked out on the porch, and Faith could see the man about fifty yards away. But by this time the man was on his hands and knees like he was trying to catch his breath.

"He's getting up," said Ethan. "Hurry!"

"Are you sure about this, Ethan?"

He was trying to walk faster, but he could hardly put any weight on his leg. Faith was struggling under the load.

About that time the man looked up and saw the couple hobbling towards him. He stood shakily and looked around for his horse and couldn't see him, so he started to stagger towards the barn. The man was big, but he could move.

"Hold it right there!" Ethan hollered at the top of his lungs as they kept walking towards him.

The man ran even faster.

"Stop, Faith!" said Ethan, trying to get his gun up. "Let go of me!"

Faith couldn't get untangled fast enough, and when she finally did and stepped away, Ethan couldn't keep the gun barrel still enough trying to balance on one leg. They watched the man run into the barn.

"He's going to get away!" said Faith.

Ethan looked at the big pen behind the barn and could only see one horse. The Samuels' other horses were in the trap beyond.

"No, he won't. Help me to the barn."

"What if he has a gun?"

"He'll be busy for a little while," he said. "That'll give us time to get over there."

They limped back toward the house and walked up to the barn from the

153

east side, out of sight from the door on the south side. They both leaned against the side of the barn, breathing heavily.

"I should've brought my pistol," he said under his breath. He leaned over and whispered to Faith, "I want you to go back to the house and stay."

"I'm not leaving you here."

"I'll be fine," he said. "If Crazy's the only horse in there for him to saddle, he's not going anywhere. Now go!"

Faith shook her head, no.

"Then go watch for the kids on the road and keep them away from here—but take my pistol so you'll be armed."

She had forgotten about Joseph, Finn, and Caitlin coming, and she realized she needed to warn them. But she froze when she heard a horse scream and a man's voice curse from inside the barn.

"Go!" said Ethan, pushing her towards the house.

Faith ran back to the house and found Ethan's pistol in the chair where he had left it. She started out the door, but paused when she saw Crazy Ears come squealing and running out of the barn. The man had successfully put the halter and lead rope on the horse, but he must have touched the horse's ears trying to put the bridle on him. The man was hanging onto the lead rope and trying to set back on his heels, but Crazy jerked him off his feet and dragged him halfway across the yard before the man let go.

Ethan stepped away from the barn and started to raise his rifle when Joseph and the wagon came racing up to the barn, blocking his sight. Neither Faith nor Ethan had seen it approaching with all the commotion Crazy Ears was causing.

As Joseph stopped the horses, he was surprised to see Ethan out of the house by himself and couldn't understand why he was hollering and waving his arm at him. Faith screamed his name at that moment and Joseph turned to see a man running towards him—towards the wagon. He flicked the reins as hard and as quickly as he could and the horses lurched forward, but it was too late. The man lunged for the side of the wagon and pulled himself up. He pounced on Joseph and grabbed him in a bear hug to throw him violently off the side of the wagon and climbed into the seat to take the reins.

He never saw Finn and Caitlin wide-eyed and hunkered down in the bed of the wagon.

Ethan couldn't believe what had just happened. Joseph lay sprawled on the ground. The rustler had turned the wagon to head down the road leading to the front gate of the ranch. Ethan couldn't let him get away, but he was afraid to shoot for fear of hitting Finn or Caitlin still on the wagon. But then he couldn't let him take his children either. He had to chance it. Ethan raised his rifle, only to lower it when he couldn't keep the barrel still.

He screamed in frustration as the runaway wagon disappeared from sight around a curve in the road. And before he realized it, his wife was running down the road after them.

Chapter 32

Finn braced his arms against the side of the wagon bed above Caitlin and pressed his back against the fence posts to keep them from battering them as the wagon jolted brutally down the road. He looked at Caitlin's face six inches from his own. Tears streamed down the sides of her eyes as she lay on her back, but she kept quiet. He knew she was terrified. He was scared, too, but he had to do something before the stranger realized they were in the wagon with him. He looked over his shoulder and saw one of the shovels within reach.

He turned back to Caitlin and put his lips next to her ear and said, "Brace yourself against the posts for me."

He pushed himself up to a crouch above Caitlin, holding onto the side of the wagon. She pulled her legs up to wedge against the posts as best as she could so they wouldn't knock Finn off his feet.

Finn reached over and grabbed the shovel and stood up the rest of the way. The man in front of him was big—he had thrown Joseph off the wagon as if he were a rag doll. Finn reared back with the shovel and swung it around as hard as he could to whack the rustler on the side of his head. The man never knew what hit him as he fell off the wagon. Finn leaned over the seat to grab the reins, but they dropped to the ground.

"Finn! I can't hold them anymore!" cried Caitlin as some of the posts tumbled over on her.

He turned around and threw some of the posts off the wagon and grabbed her arm to lift her up to stand beside him. They held onto the back of the wagon seat as it continued to rumble down the road.

"Hold on!" he shouted. "I can't reach the reins! We're just going to have to let them run for a while!"

"Will the horses turn when we get to the front gate?"

"I don't know!" he yelled.

"What if they run over the gate or turn too sharp—either way the wagon's going to wreck," she shouted. "I can reach the reins if you'll hold me."

"It's too dangerous—you might fall!"

"We're running out of time, Finn!" she said, looking down the road. She could see the main gate to the ranch up ahead.

Finn didn't have to be told twice. He climbed over the seat and helped Caitlin over. The reins were threaded through rings above the flanks of each horse, so Finn realized she could reach forward to grab them on the rumps of the horses rather than the ends that flopped around down by the horses' hooves. He put her in between his legs and braced against the foot rest while he wrapped his left arm around her waist and his right hand held on tight to the waistband of her pants. She leaned out over the backs of the running horses to retrieve each rein. He jerked her back in his lap and grabbed hold of the reins and leaned back and pulled as hard as he could. The gate was coming up fast and the horses slowed some, but Finn knew he couldn't get them stopped in time. He saw a gap in the scrubby trees to the right and turned the horses in a wide arc away from the gate. The horses finally came to a stop about fifty yards off the road.

"You did it!" she said, going limp against him.

"No, we did it," he said, feeling his arms shaking from the strain and the fear of the situation.

"I can't believe you knocked that man off the wagon," said Caitlin over her shoulder, giggling.

"I can't either," he said. "My arms were shaking so bad, it's a wonder I was able to pick up the shovel, much less whack him with it." He looked back toward the road. "I want to get back and see how Joseph is, but I don't know if I hit that buzzard hard enough to put him out of commission. And I sure don't want to meet him back there on the road since we're not armed."

"What if he sees us and shoots at us?" said Caitlin. She began to realize anew the danger they had been in and could still be facing. "I don't know if we ought to go back just yet."

Finn could feel her trembling.

"Let's just sit here for a while and watch the road," he suggested, unsure himself of what they should do next. He slid her off his lap to sit beside him.

A tear spilled over and down her cheek when it started to sink in what had just happened. "We could've died back there, Finn," she said quietly.

"I won't let anybody hurt you, Katie," he said. "I promise."

A gunshot pierced the air, and they both jumped.

That's all it took for Caitlin to start wailing. Finn put one arm around her to comfort her and the other hand over her mouth to quiet her.

"Shshsh! That wasn't real close," he said, "but we don't want anyone to know where we are just yet... at least until we know it's safe."

"Do you think it was him?" she asked quietly.

"I don't know."

"I hope Momma and Daddy are all right."

He nodded his head and paused for a moment. He hated sitting there—doing nothing. But he sure didn't want to take Caitlin back into a dangerous situation. He knew he was fortunate to have caught the big man off guard; otherwise, he wouldn't have had a chance against him. But that man could be coming down the road heading straight for them, and Finn had no way of protecting himself and Caitlin.

"Why don't we go get the sheriff?" he said. "And we'll be heading away from any trouble. The sheriff's going to have to deal with these rustlers anyway. It'll save your family some time."

"But Mom and Dad will be worried about us if they don't know where we've gone."

"We can leave them a message near the gate," he said, looking back in the wagon bed.

"I hope Joseph's all right," said Caitlin. "But if he's not, how will they get him to town?"

"Your mother brought Ethan home in our buggy, remember?"

"That's right," she said, looking back towards the ranch. "Then let's go. That rustler might be coming this way."

Finn started the horses forward.

Faith stood in the middle of the road, pointing her pistol at the big man sitting on the ground. His hand covered his busted ear, which had bled down the side of his neck and onto his shirt. He had tried to get up once, but Faith fired a shot in the ground next to him with a warning to not move.

"You gonna stand there all day?" the man asked sourly.

"For as long as it takes," she said firmly. "My husband will be here shortly."

"Didn't look like he's much help to you."

"My father and brothers will come, too. And they don't have as much patience and self-control as I do."

"So that's who ambushed us."

"I don't think *ambushed* is the right word when you were encroaching on our property with the intent to steal our cattle."

"We just took a wrong turn, and your family attacked us," he argued.

"Well, you can save your story for the sheriff and the judge and see if they believe you."

The man looked her up and down. "Are you an Injun?"

Faith said nothing.

"You don't sound like an Injun, but you look like one. What are you doing owning a ranch and cattle?"

She just stared at him.

"It ain't right," he said. "I've busted my butt all my life and don't have a damn thing to show for it. And here you are, a redskin with your own ranch. You belong on a reservation with your own kind—not out here with the white folks."

He waited for her to react to his words, to catch her off guard, but she just stood there silently.

"Cat got your tongue?" he goaded her. "Well, I don't plan to be sent to jail on the word of some Injun. Who'd believe you?"

He started to get up again. A bullet hit the ground in front of him, and he fell back. He looked up at her, but he knew she hadn't fired her gun this time.

Faith smiled, but she never took her eyes off of him.

The rustler looked past her where the shot came from. Two men rode their horses towards them. He recognized one of them as the woman's husband, and he was riding that crazy horse bareback. The other man was almost as dark as the woman.

They pulled up behind Faith.

"You all right?" Ethan asked.

"I'm fine," she said without turning her head.

"What happened? Where's Finn and Katie?" he asked, looking around, and then came back to glare at the man on the ground. "What'd you do with our kids?"

"That was a kid that hit me?" the man said, still holding the side of his head.

"Finn knocked him off the wagon with a shovel," said Faith. "They're down the road somewhere. How's Joseph? I wanted to go check on him, but I couldn't let this man get away with the kids in the wagon with him."

"I think something on his shoulder's broken," said Jimmy. "I got him to

159

the house, but we'll need to take him to town."

Faith looked at her brother. "We need to go find the kids, Jimmy, and then I'll be back to help Joseph. And then Ethan's going straight to bed."

Jimmy ordered the rustler to get up and start walking back to the house. The man took a wide berth around Crazy Ears, mumbling something about a devil horse.

Faith handed Ethan her pistol, and he put his arm down to pull her up behind him.

"Where's Daddy and Justin and Matt?" she asked Jimmy.

"They'll meet us back at the barn."

"Did they catch them all?"

"You got the last one, sis," said Jimmy. "I'll see y'all back at the house."

They turned Crazy Ears and headed toward the main gate.

"Was anybody hurt?" she asked Ethan.

He nodded his head, yes. "But none of your family. Two of the rustlers have bullet wounds. We'll need to take them to town in the wagon."

About forty yards from the gate, they could see the wagon tracks heading off to the right.

"Where were they going?"

"The last I saw of them, the horses were running awfully fast," said Faith.

"Maybe they couldn't stop them," said Ethan as he spurred the horse on to follow the wagon tracks off the road.

They found where the wagon had stopped and pulled around and headed parallel to the fence line back towards the gate. When they reached the gate, they found a pile of fence posts dumped off to the side. The wagon tracks had gone through the gate and turned toward town.

"What happened here?" said Faith, suddenly worried. "Why didn't they come back to the house? Are you sure they got all the rustlers?"

"Looks like they lightened their load," said Ethan. "And look at those fence posts away from the pile. They're pointing like an arrow."

Faith slipped off the horse and walked over to the tip of the arrow. Scratched in the dry ground were the words, *Gone to get sheriff* in large letters, and in smaller ones, *Afraid to go back.*

She read it aloud and looked at Ethan. "Well, at least we know they're all right."

"I hope the sheriff's in town," he said.

"You know they'll go to George first, and he'll know what to do."

"Then let's go home," said Ethan, offering her his arm again.

She hooked her arm around his and let him pull her up behind him again. "I wish you could've seen Finn swing that shovel, Ethan," she said, chuckling. "You would've been so proud of him."

"I just might have to hire that boy full time."

Chapter 33

Jimmy and Matthew Taylor stood guard over the three rustlers tied up in the barn while Matt and Justin headed out to retrieve the stolen cattle. Jimmy wanted to *persuade* one of the injured thieves to tell them where they were holding the cattle, but Justin told him not to bother—that he could track them down.

Justin and Matt found the livestock in a fenced-off arroyo about five miles away from the ranch.

"They must be greenhorns," said Matt. "Ignorant greenhorns that don't know a thing about livestock."

"Or they just plain don't care," said Justin.

They found not only the Murray's cattle, but five horses, two mules, and a donkey along with a dozen other cattle—some branded, some not. They all were drawn up like empty tow sacks from lack of food and water.

"They could've at least taken care of them after they'd stolen them," said Matt, angrily. "They must've been planning to take them soon—otherwise they wouldn't have anything to sell if they waited much longer."

"I don't know how they could drive them for any long distance in the shape they're in," said Justin, dismayed at what he saw.

One of the calves was so weak Justin had to carry it across his lap. He and Matt had no problem with the livestock straying as slow as they were moving. They drove them back to the ranch and through the gap in the fence. Once inside, the Murray livestock led the rest of them to the river. Matt stayed to repair the fence while Justin headed back with the calf.

He looked down and brushed his hand across the back of the little heifer. Justin figured Caitlin would get the job of taking care of it. He looked up at the clear blue sky and prayed for rain. The sun and his stomach told him it was well past noon. He hoped they could get Ethan back on his feet soon so they could return to Grace and he could take his family on home to Dalton in South Texas. He already missed his wife and children something fierce. But he was glad, too, that they had come. The rustlers would have easily cleaned out Ethan and Faith if they hadn't been here to stop them. And now that the rustling had been taken care of, they should be able to focus on getting the rest of the east fence completed in a few days. And by then the rancher south of them would be able to help Ethan build the rest of the fence to tie in to the west pasture.

Back at the house, Faith had wrapped Joseph's arm to his chest to keep it as still as possible. Then she went to the barn to bandage the two rustlers' gunshot wounds as best as she could. She even cleaned the blood off the big man's ear and face, to his surprise. Jimmy had tied his hands behind his back to a post in the barn, so he was little threat to her. Faith took an aloe vera leaf and cut it open and reached over to wipe the oozing sap across the man's cut ear, but he pulled back.

"Are you trying to poison me?" he asked suspiciously.

"Why would I have gone to the trouble to clean you up if I wanted to poison you? It's medicine—it'll help your ear heal."

"Yeah, so you'll look pretty before they hang you," said Jimmy, trying to fix a broken stirrup on the saddle of one of the rustlers.

"Jimmy!" said Faith sternly.

The man stared at her. "Why are you helping me?" he asked, remembering how rude he had acted towards her on the road.

"I learned this from my mother," she said, averting the question.

"Is she Indian, too?"

Faith shook her head, no, and glanced at her father standing in the doorway watching for Matt and Justin. "She and my father adopted me after my parents died. They're the only family I know. What's your name?" she asked in a flat tone.

The man hesitated.

"What's your first name then?" she asked.

"Faith, stop talking to him," said Jimmy. "He's not your friend."

"Is he your brother?" the man asked, nodding his head toward Jimmy.

Faith nodded. "He's a bit protective of me. Well, all of the men in my family are."

"I don't have any family," the man said. "I've been on my own since I was eleven. I was always big for my age, though, so people didn't give me much grief. It's Bear."

Faith looked questioningly at him.

"Everyone calls me Bear," he said. "But that's not my real name. Nobody knows my real name."

"What made you start stealing cattle?"

"Everybody takes cattle around here. Before the fences came, an unbranded cow or calf here or there was free for the taking and nobody knew any better. Most of the big herds in Texas are built that way—first by gathering up wild cattle that nobody really owned, or by changing the brands."

"But we bought our cattle," said Faith. "We owned our cattle, Bear, and you cut our fence to steal them."

Jimmy walked over to them. "Why are you still talking to him, Faith? He stole your cattle."

"I want to know why. Now leave us be."

Jimmy stomped off.

"He's got blue eyes," said Bear. "How can an Indian have blue eyes?"

"He's my mother's son," said Faith quietly. "It's a long story."

"So he's not your real brother?"

Faith shook her head, no.

"You favor him," he said.

Jimmy came stomping back over to them. "What are you doing, Faith?" He grabbed her arm and pulled her away from Bear. "Just go to the house. You don't need to be telling this man anything about our family. And I *am* your brother, so don't you go telling anybody otherwise."

"I'm sorry!" said Faith, exasperatedly. She turned back to Bear. "You need to straighten your life up, Bear. You're young—maybe you'll still have time to do some honest work when you get out of jail. And you ought to be a better example to your two friends here."

Jimmy started pulling her away from him. "This ain't missionary work, sis. These are dangerous men."

Faith looked at the men she had bandaged. The two that had been shot looked only a little older than Finn. And Bear probably wasn't as old as she was.

"They're just boys," she said.

"What's *your* name?" Bear called out.

"Don't you dare tell him," Jimmy warned her as he led her toward the barn door.

"Thanks for doctorin' my ear!" Bear hollered.

Jimmy pushed her toward the house. "Don't you come out here again," he warned her. "We'll take care of 'em from now on."

Faith stormed out of the barn. She stopped when she saw her father leaning up against the wall outside. She walked over to him.

"I'm sorry, Dad," she said. "I shouldn't have been so forward with that man."

He put out his arm and she stepped into it. "Let me walk you to the house. And if it makes you feel any better, your mother would be doing the same thing—trying to set those boys on the straight and narrow."

Faith smiled.

"It's been years since I've been reminded of you and Jimmy's heritage. I don't see that in you. I just see my daughter and son."

"I know, Daddy. I have to remind myself at times because I feel like a Taylor."

"Are people around here treating you right?"

She nodded. "The people who know me are, and I don't pay any mind to those that don't. They usually just stare at me like I'm a fish out of water. I just smile and go on."

"Well, Jimmy gets mad enough for both of you," he said. "And I don't blame him. I don't like to see you hurt either."

They stopped at the front porch, and Faith hugged him tightly before going inside.

"Thank you again for coming, Daddy," she said, knowing full well they had prevented a catastrophe. "I don't know what we would've done without you."

"We're family, Faith. We Taylors stand by each other," he said. "And we Taylors are getting mighty hungry. I don't know what happened to that bundle of food you packed for us. It must've fallen off in the pasture somewhere."

"Oh, my goodness!!" she said, realizing she hadn't thought a thing about fixing the noon meal. "Why didn't you tell me sooner!"

She turned and ran into the house. Matthew walked back to the barn to the sound of pots clanging and glass clinking.

Just like your mother, he thought as he smiled to himself.

Chapter 34

Caitlin and Finn could see the taller buildings of Brownwood in the distance. They had made good time, but Finn had slowed the horses down the last couple of miles. They weren't used to this much running, and both had worked up a lather under their collars and straps from the effort.

The sky was a vivid blue with not a cloud in sight. It was the end of December, and the nights and mornings were chilly, but a person could still break a sweat most afternoons doing the least amount of work. They'd had several cold, dry northers that brought frosts with them, but so far this winter had been mild.

"What's today?" asked Caitlin over the rumble of the wagon.

"Saturday, I think," said Finn.

"I can't believe it's only been four days since Christmas—it seems like it was a month ago."

"A lot's happened since then, hasn't it?"

Caitlin nodded.

"We're almost there," he said. "Are you all right?"

Caitlin nodded again. "Did we do the right thing, Finn? Are you sure Mom and Dad will find the message we left them?"

"Yeah. Nobody except a blind person could miss that big arrow you insisted that I make with those posts pointing to your message. And even then, a blind person would trip over it for sure."

Caitlin giggled.

"We'll go by the store first and tell my father," he said. "I just wish I had news about Joseph. Surely he's all right—he's a tough guy. I couldn't see him after he was thrown from the wagon. But Mom's still going to kill us both."

"Me, too?"

"No, just me and Joseph for getting ourselves in a dangerous situation."

"But you couldn't help that."

"That won't matter at all with Mother. And don't tell her we were in the wagon with that rustler or that I hit him with a shovel. She'll never let me leave the house ever again—especially to go work for your father."

Caitlin laughed. "I'll never forget the sight of you swinging that shovel for as long as I live. Wherever that man is, I bet he still has a nasty headache. Do you think they caught him?"

Finn nodded. "Between your grandpa and uncles, I'm sure of it. Those Taylors can be fearsome."

"You know they're not my real grandpa and uncles, don't you?"

"Just like George and France aren't my real parents?"

Caitlin nodded, recognizing another connection she had with Finn. "Can you remember your mother and father?"

"Some, although it's getting harder to remember what they looked like," he said. "Can you remember your mother?"

"Not really," she said. "Every time I try to imagine her, I just see Aunt Mercy. But at least you still have your sister Zane."

"I don't know who gives me more grief—she or Emma."

"I'd say Emma," said Caitlin. "She's convinced that I know who your sweetheart is."

Finn turned and looked her. "Well, you do."

"I mean, she won't stop pestering me about it. I don't know why she feels like she has to tease you like she does. I think if y'all didn't live under the same roof, she'd be sweet on you."

Finn made a face. "But she's my sister!"

"But not blood-kin, remember."

"Well, after you turn twelve tomorrow, we can tell everybody. Maybe that'll put an end to her shenanigans."

"You remembered my birthday was tomorrow?"

"You used to always fuss about your birthday being so close to Christmas—that all your celebrating was done around the same time of year, and you'd rather have it spread out so you wouldn't have to wait a whole year between celebrations."

"I can't believe you even listened to me, much less remembered," said Caitlin. "I can't wait until everyone knows."

She slipped her hand around his arm.

"You know your daddy's not going to let us hang around by ourselves anymore after he finds out."

167

Caitlin looked at Finn in surprise. "Why not?!"

"Because it wouldn't be proper."

"Proper!? You've been nothing but proper towards me. You haven't even kissed me."

"You're still too young to be kissed, Katie. I don't want to get on your father's bad side either. I want to be able to look him in the eye and tell him the truth about us, and that he can trust me with you. But I'm afraid he might decide we can't see each other for a while."

"Well, Rosie Bickle got married when she was thirteen. That's just a year older than me."

"She *had* to get married, remember?"

"Oh, yeah."

"She's only a year older than me now, and she's already got three kids," said Finn. "That's one reason a father tends to worry about his daughter having a beau."

"Why?"

"They don't want their young daughters becoming women too soon."

"That won't happen to me," said Caitlin confidently, wondering what exactly it was that turned a girl into a woman.

She dropped her hand from his arm. In her mind, she began to sort through the girl talks she'd had recently with Emma and Zane. She glanced down at her chest, trying to remember if that was the key to becoming a woman.

"What won't happen to you?" asked Finn, wondering if Caitlin even knew what she was talking about.

"Becoming a woman any time soon."

"Do you know what it means to become a woman?"

"Of course!" said Caitlin, not wanting to sound ignorant.

He looked at her, waiting for an explanation, so she took a shot at it.

"Emma said it has something to do with the tongue when you kiss, so I plan to keep my mouth shut when and if you ever kiss me."

Her cheeks had turned a rosy pink during the conversation, but she held her chin exceptionally high as if she were an expert on the subject of becoming a woman.

He looked away for a moment. It took every ounce of self-control for Finn to not burst out laughing. But at the same time he loved her innocence, and he planned to be the one to teach her some day what it meant to be a woman. He had heard men talking about it, and some of his friends bragged about it, but he himself had some learning to do before then, too.

They had come to the houses on the edge of town, so Finn scooted over to put some space between them. Before he reached the town square, he turned the horses down the alley that led to the back of his father's store and pulled them to a stop. He climbed off the wagon and secured the team before he helped Caitlin down, and they ran up the steps and into the back of the store.

Finn could see his father talking to a couple of women near the bolts of cloth and sewing notions. His sisters Annie and Jenna were behind the front counter. He caught his father's eye and waved at him. George escorted the ladies to the front counter before walking back to his office to meet Finn and Caitlin. George was surprised to see them.

"Finn? Caitlin? What are you two doing here? I thought we wouldn't see you until church tomorrow. Is everything all right?"

"Cattle rustlers hit the ranch this morning, and we need to get the sheriff, Dad."

"What?! Where's Joseph?"

"He's back at the ranch with Ethan and Faith," said Finn. "But we're pretty sure they caught 'em, so we need to get the sheriff."

"I told your brother to steer clear of any trouble."

"We were working on the new fence on the east side of the ranch," explained Finn. "Faith's brothers and father rode in night before last to help, and they came upon the rustlers this morning."

"What happened?"

"Yesterday they'd found where the fence had been cut in the west pasture and saw tracks that showed some of the livestock had been stolen. The gap in the fence had been hidden, so they figured the thieves planned to come back to get the rest. The Taylors watched and waited most of Friday, but no one showed up, so they planned to track them this morning. They ended up meeting the thieves coming back through the gap in the fence."

"Is everyone all right?"

Finn nodded. "We just thought it'd save time if we high-tailed it to town to get the sheriff."

"And y'all were working on the fence?"

"Yes, sir, but Ethan told us if we heard any gunshots to come straight back to the house, so that's what we did," he said, choosing his words carefully.

"So Joseph's all right?"

"He stayed at the house to help Ethan and Faith, and we came on to town."

George exhaled loudly. "Good for him, and thank God the Taylors came. I've felt so bad about Ethan going back to the ranch in the shape he was in—all because of me."

"What do you mean?" Caitlin spoke up for the first time.

"If I hadn't have told him about the riders Joseph saw, he wouldn't have insisted on going home when he did. But then I didn't want y'all out there by yourselves either."

"Me and Katie are fine, Dad. And Joseph was real careful to do the right thing. You didn't need to worry about us."

Caitlin looked at Finn, trying to figure out if leaving out important details was the same as lying or not. She figured the preacher's sermon tomorrow would probably cover that very topic, along with a good sprinkling of hell-fire and damnation. She swallowed hard and nodded her head, determined she would stand alongside Finn and face the devil if she had to.

Chapter 35

George put his hand on Finn's shoulder. "Well, I don't know if the sheriff's around, but let me tell the girls where we'll be and to lock up the store if I don't make it back in time. Then we'll drop Caitlin by the house before we go on down to the jail."

Caitlin sat on the back of the wagon so Mr. Samuel could sit with his son. Finn walked the horses out the other end of the alley and turned toward the town square, and then left again at the furniture store to head toward the Samuels' house.

Caitlin swung her legs back and forth as she faced the empty square. Only trees remained around the center of it since Brownwood's courthouse had burned down three years before. But she had heard there were plans to build a new courthouse that would be much larger and more stately-looking than the old one. She hoped they would start building it soon. The town square looked so empty without it.

Finn pulled the wagon to a stop to let Caitlin off in front of the Samuel's house. He told her if he didn't see her later that night that he would see her at church in the morning. She mouthed the words, *love you,* and watched him smile before he turned back to the horses. Then she looked down at her dusty bibbed pants and realized she didn't have any clothes for church in the morning.

The front door opened and Emma walked out carrying Sam. Zane followed with Cele and Ella Vae yelling, "Katie! Katie!" Caitlin hadn't seen them in four days and didn't realize until that moment how much she had missed her sisters and baby brother. She kneeled down to hug and kiss her young sisters. Then she stood and took Sam from Emma's arms and hugged him tight. Sam put his arms around her neck and laid his head on her shoulder. Caitlin could feel his little hands patting her back. She smoothed his loose cotton dress and felt of his bare feet and what her mother called his *cankles* where a seam seemed to connect his calves and ankles. She squeezed his chubby thighs and rubbed his back. She sniffed his hair and kissed his head and cheek when he lifted his face to look at her. It felt so good to hold him.

"Ka-dee, Sis-see!" he said, emphasizing the second syllable.

"I've missed you so much, Sam," she said, and then looked down at her sisters. "And gathering eggs hasn't been the same without you two."

"I wanna go home, Katie," said Ella. "I want Mommy."

Cele just stood there quietly beside her sister, but she looked like she was ready to cry at the mention of her mother.

"We're going to see her tomorrow, Ella. And tomorrow will be here before you know it. And can you guess who else is at the ranch?"

That caught her attention. "Who?"

"Uncle Jimmy and PaPa Taylor! And do you remember Uncle Justin and Uncle Matt? They've come to visit, too!"

Ella's big brown eyes lit up as she nodded her head and clapped her hands. Cele followed suit.

"Let's go back in the house, girls," said Emma.

"What are you doing here so early?" asked Zane. "Y'all weren't supposed to come in until tomorrow."

"Finn and I came to town to get the sheriff."

"What for?"

"Don't answer just yet," said Emma, "or you'll have to tell it all over again to Mother. Come on—she'll want to know everything. She's out back doing laundry."

"I'm supposed to be helping her while Emma watches Sam and the girls, but then Emma saw you through the window and hollered at me."

They found France struggling with an armful of wet sheets.

"Here, Mrs. Samuel," said Caitlin, handing Sam back to Emma. "Let me help you with that. I love to hang sheets."

Caitlin took half of the pile and Zane took the other.

"Thank you, Caitlin!" she said, following them to the clothes line. "Look at you in boys' pants!"

"I can't dig postholes in a dress."

"How'd you get to town?" France asked. "I thought we wouldn't be seeing you 'til tomorrow. Is your momma with you? Is your father all right?"

"Yes, ma'am, he's fine, and Mother's not with me. Finn brought me."

France looked beyond her, hoping to see her son.

"He left with Mr. Samuel to go find the sheriff."

"Finn's with George? What's wrong?" she asked. "Is Joseph all right?"

Caitlin nodded as she continued to hang the sheets and avoid looking Mrs. Samuel in the eye. "Cattle rustlers hit our place this morning, and my grandfather and uncles were tracking them down when we left."

"Oh, my! Cattle rustlers? Is everyone all right?"

"As far as I know. Finn and I left to get the sheriff before everyone had come back to the house."

"You said your uncles... Jimmy and Justin are here?"

"And Uncle Matt and PaPa Taylor from Grace," she said. "They came in Thursday night, thank heavens, or I don't know what we would've done to keep from losing all our cattle. The thieves had already stolen some. I hope they can get them back."

"How'd the Taylors know y'all were having trouble?" asked France.

"Momma had Finn meet the early stage last Saturday to take a letter to my grandparents explaining what happened to Daddy's leg and why we wouldn't be on the stage. PaPa told us after they got the letter that they all felt like we needed their help, so they came."

"They must've left Christmas Day to get here so quickly," said France. "How fortunate for your parents."

Caitlin nodded and changed the subject. "I hope Sam hasn't given you too much trouble."

France smiled and looked over at him playing on the porch beside Emma.

"That little boy stole my heart some time ago," she said.

"He's got a mind of his own, and if something's dangerous, he'll find it."

"I know, and we've all kept an eye on him. Finn was eight years old when he came to live with us, but I have a feeling he was a lot like Sam when he was little. And look how Finn is turning out—he's one of the hardest-working and most dependable young men around. But he still has a stubborn streak and danger still tends to find him at times."

The thought of Finn swinging that shovel against that big rustler came to Caitlin's mind, and she nodded her head and couldn't help but smile at the mention of Finn's name.

"We've turned out to be a pretty good post-hole digging team," she said. "But I know what you mean about his determination. I can hardly keep up with him."

"That's Finn."

"Have you found out who our brother's sparkin'?" asked Emma from the porch.

Caitlin shook her head and felt the guilt pile higher on her shoulders for lying.

"Was it Johanna Casey like we thought?" asked Zane.

"He told me that R. James carved those initials in the barn just to tease him," she said. "He'd forgotten that it was even there until you had mentioned it."

"Would you girls leave that boy alone?" said France. "You're torturing him about his girlfriend. He'll make it known when he's good and ready and not one minute before."

Caitlin changed the subject again. "Could I borrow a dress for church tomorrow? We left so quickly I didn't have a chance to pack one."

"Sure—come on in the house and you and Zane can help me finish the ironing, too," said France. "Emma, would you mind watching the little ones for a while longer?"

Emma quickly nodded, thinking she had the better end of that deal.

France and the girls stopped half-way through the ironing to fix the noon meal, and it didn't take long afterwards to finish all the laundry chores with the extra help Caitlin provided.

France walked outside to gather up her laundry items, and Caitlin and Zane followed to get the last of the bed sheets off the line. France picked up the washboard beside the tub, and realized she had forgotten the children's naps.

"Emma, can you take Sam and the girls inside to put them down for their naps?"

But Emma didn't respond. Her face held an odd expression as she stared at the kitchen door. France turned around to see a beautiful blonde-headed woman step out onto the porch. Two more comely women followed her—the one in the middle was older with white hair, but still very attractive... and familiar for some reason. France met her eyes—those piercing blue eyes—and immediately recognized who she was although she had never met her in person.

But she knew her children.

Chapter 36

France looked back at the blonde-headed woman and smiled as tears filled her eyes and laughter filled her throat. But her feet were rooted to the ground from the shock of seeing her.

"Mercy? Is it really you?" She dropped the washboard and opened her arms to her.

Mercy stepped off the porch and ran to her friend's embrace. They both cried and laughed as they hugged each other.

"MeeMaw?" said Caitlin, running to her grandmother.

"How's my girl?" said Julia Taylor, hugging her granddaughter tightly. Then she leaned back to take a look at her. "And in pants, of all things! Why am I not surprised?" She kept her arm around Caitlin and turned her to face the third woman. "You don't see her but once a year, but you remember your Aunt Allie, don't you?"

"Of course!" said Caitlin, hugging her aunt. "Did y'all bring any of my cousins?"

Allie shook her head, saying they had to leave them at Grace—that they just didn't have room in the stage coach for them all.

"Allie!?" said France. "Justin's Allie?"

Mercy nodded her head and walked France back to the porch and up the steps to the pretty, dark-headed young woman.

"It's been eight years since Justin and Jimmy brought you through our town and to our home," said France, "but I've never forgotten you."

Allie folded her arms around the petite woman and shed more tears at the reunion.

"I'll never forget the kindness and hospitality you showed us that day," said Allie. She turned to Julia. "We were complete strangers to this woman, and not only that, we were frightful-looking after all we'd been through, and this woman took us home with her and fed us and let us spend the night here." She turned back to France. "I'll never forget how welcome you made us feel."

"And I feel as though I know you because of what you've done for my children," said Julia. "I'm so glad to finally make your acquaintance, France."

"Oh! I'm sorry!" said Mercy. "I forgot to introduce you two."

"I feel like I've known you for years," said France, holding out her hand to Julia.

"Hi, Mercy!" said Caitlin.

Mercy grabbed Caitlin and hugged her. "Ah, Caitlin, honey. We have quite a history here, don't we? I remember the first time I saw Caitlin," she told the others. "I was standing right here on this porch watching a ragtag little towhead throwing a screaming fit in what used to be the garden right over there."

"I'm sorry I was such a brat," said Caitlin, embarrassed that Mercy had brought up something so unbecoming about her.

"You were just trying to cope the best way you knew how," said Mercy. "And then you came in the kitchen and crawled up on my lap and went to sleep that day. I think that was the moment my heart started working like a heart should. And you saved my life, too, remember? Right over there."

"The fire," said Caitlin, looking towards the barn. "I still remember that."

Emma brought Sam and the girls up to the women. Caitlin introduced them to everyone.

"Emma and Zane are my best friends."

"Is this my Sam?!" Julia took him from Emma.

"Careful with your shoulder," said Mercy.

"I'm fine," said Julia, holding Sam with her good arm.

"And Ella and Cele, too," said Caitlin, bringing the little girls into the middle of the women. Mercy and Allie each picked up a girl.

"I can't believe we're getting to see Faith's children already," said Julia, stepping back to sit down in a rocker on the porch. "I thought we were going to have to wait hours until we got to the ranch." She sat Sam in her lap and just looked at him for a moment.

"I'm your MeeMaw, Sam. Look at those blue eyes! You are such a handsome boy." She looked around. "Pull up some chairs, girls. I need to see my grandbabies."

Mercy and Faith each gathered a chair close to Julia and sat down. Caitlin sat at Mercy's feet.

"Ella, do you remember MeeMaw?" Caitlin asked. "You remember Momma talking about MeeMaw and PaPa, right?"

Ella nodded her head.

"Me, too!" Cele nodded her head, and everyone laughed.

"Ella looks like Faith," said Julia, "and Sam looks like Ethan, and Cele's a good mix of them both. They're beautiful." She kissed Sam's face and he reached up to touch her hair. She blew on his neck, and he giggled.

"Would y'all like something to drink or eat?" asked France.

"I would love a cup of tea," said Mercy.

Allie nodded her head, too.

"I'll bring a tray," said France. "I have some pumpkin bread, too, we can slice. Emma and Zane, can you give me a hand?"

Sam put his head on Julia's shoulder, and she shut her eyes for a moment, basking in the feel of him.

"He's sleepy," said Caitlin. "Emma said he hasn't napped yet."

"Caitlin, you're looking so grown-up and pretty," said Mercy. "Why are you wearing pants, though?"

"I've been digging postholes at the ranch with Finn and Joseph," she said. "Oh, yeah, y'all don't know what's been happening out there."

Julia opened her eyes in alarm. "What's been happening? Is Ethan all right?"

"Daddy's still on the mend, but we've had cattle rustlers to deal with."

Julia glanced at Mercy and Allie. "Cattle rustlers? When did your PaPa and uncles arrive?"

"Thursday night," she said. "They'd come to help us build the fence, but then on Friday, they found a place in the west pasture where the fence had been cut and some of our cattle had been taken. They thought the rustlers might come back because they'd gone to the trouble of hiding the cut in the fence, so they waited around most all day yesterday to see if they'd come back, but they didn't."

"That's a relief," said Mercy.

"But they came back this morning," said Caitlin, "and me and Finn and Joseph were over in the east pasture digging postholes when we heard gunshots."

Julia's face paled. Allie reached over and patted her arm.

France stuck her head out the door. "Gunshots? You didn't mention gunshots earlier, Caitlin."

Caitlin swallowed, trying to remember exactly what she had said before to France and what she had left out.

"I didn't?" she said, feigning ignorance. "Well, Dad told Joseph if he heard any gunshots from the west pasture that he was to bring me and Finn back to the house immediately, and that's what he did. And then he stayed with Mom and Dad while Finn and I came to town."

France exhaled in relief and stepped back in the kitchen.

"Is everyone all right?" Julia asked in a strained voice.

"I don't know," she answered honestly. "We didn't see anybody before we came to town. We came straight to Mr. Samuel's store, and then he and Finn dropped me off here and went to find the sheriff."

"I'm sure they're fine, Julia," said Mercy. "Can you imagine facing four angry Taylor men? Those rustlers didn't have a chance."

"You know how they feel about Faith," said Allie. "I'm sure Mercy's right. They'll get their cattle back and have those thieves behind bars in no time."

Julia smiled and nodded, not wanting to worry Caitlin.

"Tell me what you've been up to, Caitlin," she said.

"Did Momma write you that I won a medal for outrunning everyone in the primary school last May?"

"She most certainly did."

"You even beat the boys?" asked Allie.

"Of course!"

Julia laughed. "You'll have to show me your medal."

Caitlin nodded proudly, and then remembered with a start that she didn't have it anymore. She hoped that MeeMaw would forget about it later.

France stuck her head out the door and asked the ladies to come inside to sit around the dining room table. Julia carried in a sleeping Sam, and France offered to take him and put him down. Julia wanted to continue to hold him, but her shoulder was aching and she knew she shouldn't overdo it. France laid him on one of the cushioned sofas in the parlor and covered him with a shawl. She placed a couple of chairs against the sofa to keep him from rolling off.

Emma brought some cups and saucers to the table and Zane came out of the kitchen with a plate of sliced pumpkin bread. France brought the tray holding the teapot and condiments.

"I'm still in shock that you're actually here," said France, pouring tea for the ladies. "I can't tell you how often I've dreamed of seeing you two girls again. I was so afraid it would never happen."

"I'm sorry it's taken so long to get back here," said Mercy. "But I'm so glad we've continued to keep in touch through letters."

"And Mercy's kept us informed about you and George and the children," said Allie.

"And vice versa," said France. "I hear you have four children now, Allie."

Allie smiled and nodded. "I don't know how Julia keeps up with her grandchildren."

"I have twenty—do you want me to name them?" she said proudly.

"No, we believe you!" said Allie, laughing.

"I didn't find out that your husbands were at the ranch until Caitlin told me a little while ago," said France. "In fact, we didn't know about the rustlers either. This has all been so sudden. Joseph told his father on Christmas Day that he'd seen some riders watching Ethan's cattle from across the western fence line and was worried that they might be planning a raid."

"Did they see Joseph?" asked Mercy.

"No, he stayed out of sight, thank heavens," said France. "And the only reason George let them go back to the ranch by themselves was that he promised not to confront any potential cattle thieves. They were to only work on the new fence."

"And we solved the problem of the fence cutters tearing it up," said Caitlin. She told them about the water alley they had set the posts for that led up to the new windmill.

"I can't believe you're doing a man's work, Caitlin," said Emma. "Boys won't take a second look at you if you keep dressing in pants and digging postholes and..."

"Especially outrunning them," teased Mercy. "I speak with experience in saying that some day you'll meet the right boy, and that's when you'll have to let him catch you."

"I can be a lady when I'm supposed to," said Caitlin, smiling at the thought that Finn loved her just the way she was. She couldn't wait until everyone knew, but in the meantime she didn't want to chance losing time spent alone, albeit innocently, with Finn. She knew her father would put the quietus to that once he found out they no longer thought of each other like a brother and sister.

"How did you get here?" France asked the women.

"We took the stage the day after Christmas," said Mercy.

"No, I meant from the stage office after you got here."

"We walked," said Allie.

"Where's your luggage?"

"We left it at the hotel," said Mercy.

"How do you plan to get to the ranch?"

Mercy looked at Julia.

"We hadn't thought that far ahead," said Julia. "But Mercy and Allie thought maybe we could borrow your buggy?"

"Girls," France spoke to her daughters. "Could you put Ella and Cele down for their naps in the front bedroom? And why don't you take Caitlin upstairs and help her pick out something for church tomorrow."

Julia leaned down to kiss the little ones before they left the room.

France spoke again. "I'm so overjoyed to see you, Mercy and Allie, and I'm so honored to finally meet you, Julia, but at the same time, I'm wondering why you came when no one seems to know that you were coming. Am I right about this? Or were your husbands expecting you?"

Mercy shook her head and looked at Julia. "I told you she has an uncanny way of getting to the heart of the matter."

"Then why are you here?" France asked, looking at each of their faces. "Do you know something that I don't know?"

Chapter 37

J ulia confessed. "It's my fault, France. Ever since we received Faith's letter on Christmas Eve, I've had an uneasy feeling in my spirit. My husband Matthew felt the same way. We both felt that there was more to Faith and Ethan's problems than she let on. Matthew announced on Christmas Day he was coming over here, and Matt, Justin, and Jimmy also wanted to help their sister."

"Marcus and Uncle John would have come, too," said Allie, "but some of the men needed to stay at Grace."

Julia nodded. "And even though I know Matthew and the boys are extremely capable and could do whatever needs to be done over here to help Faith and Ethan, the uneasy feeling in my spirit hasn't let up. Something's wrong, and I don't know what it is, but I had to come. We'd heard about the fence-cutters, but we didn't know anything about the cattle rustlers until Caitlin told us a while ago. I just hope and pray everyone's all right out at the ranch."

"And we couldn't let Julia come all this way by herself," said Mercy. "Allie and I decided it was a good time to visit Faith and Ethan and their new ranch, and you and George…"

"And my grandkids," said Julia.

"And our husbands, of course," said Allie. "I don't know how long they plan to stay or how long that fence is going to take, but we decided we could help, too. Uncle John is anxious to get back to South Texas, and Justin can't stay away indefinitely."

"Who's Uncle John?" asked France.

"My brother," explained Julia. "Justin and Allie manage his ranch outside of Dalton."

"Well, the idea of digging postholes doesn't appeal to me in the least, but I can haul water and help with the meals," said Mercy.

"I've dug postholes, myself," said Allie. "Justin sometimes likes my company when he's working, so I've gotten to do more man's work than I care to admit. But I enjoy being with him, no matter what we're doing. I'm so glad my mother lives close by or I would never get to leave the house. And Mercy and I couldn't have come on this trip if Vestal and Catherine and Jenny hadn't offered to keep our children."

France smiled at Julia. "I hope my children are half as loyal to their family as yours are. Faith is so fortunate to be a Taylor."

"We're the ones blessed to have her," said Julia. "I'd like to go out to the ranch this evening if we can. Is there any way we could borrow your buggy?"

"I wouldn't mind at all, but the buggy's already at the ranch," France said apologetically. "Faith took Ethan home in it on Thursday, and we figured the boys would bring it back for church tomorrow. Finn and Caitlin came to town in the wagon today, but that's not the best way for ladies to travel." She paused for a moment. "Well, we have Mercy's wagon, but Boomer can't pull it by himself. But you know, I could ask the Fugates next door. I'm sure they wouldn't mind you using theirs if it's available, and especially if I promise to have it back before church tomorrow morning. Do you think that's possible?"

Julia assured her that somebody would bring the buggy back early in the morning.

"It gets dark early, so you only have a few more hours of daylight to get out there. I'll run over there and ask Inez right now."

France excused herself and hurried out the back door.

"I don't know how much room Faith has in her new house," said Julia. "We might be sleeping on the floor."

"As long as I can sleep with Justin, I don't mind," said Allie.

"As long as I can sleep with Jimmy… and a blanket and a pillow, I don't mind," said Mercy with a wry grin.

"One of my bags is just quilts and pillows," said Julia, "so I think we'll be all right."

"You and Matthew will get a bed," said Allie.

Julia didn't argue with her. "I'm glad old age is good for something."

"I hope we get to go out there tonight since we only have until Tuesday to do what we can to help Faith," said Allie. "We have to be on the next stage out of here."

"Well, Matthew and I can always stay longer if we need to," said Julia. She stood up and began to look at France's furniture and the personal touches in the dining room and parlor. She smiled to see all of the items that were obviously handmade by the children in their younger years proudly displayed at every turn.

Mercy and Allie followed her into the parlor.

"Would you like to see where they've added onto the house," Mercy whispered to Allie, "and where Faith and I stayed upstairs?"

Allie nodded, and Julia said she would stay with Sam, sleeping soundly on the sofa.

She sat down at his feet and sighed, completely content watching the little boy breathe. Sam had grown so since she had seen him last. She couldn't help but lean over and run her fingers lightly through his brown hair. The ends lifted up with a hint of a curl.

After a few more minutes, France came running up the back porch steps and into the house. She found Julia in the parlor and said that Mr. Fugate would meet them at the barn behind their house—that he was already on his way out there to hitch up the horses.

"It's a two-seater like ours," she said quietly, "so you'll have plenty of room for your bags."

"I hope we get to visit with you more," Julia said. "Maybe you and Mr. Samuel could come out to the ranch for Sunday dinner?"

"I'll ask him. We see Ethan and Faith just about every Sunday when they come in for church, but I've yet to make the trip out there and see the ranch. Time just gets away from us."

"I know what you mean, and the older we get, the faster time passes, doesn't it. I don't want to waste one minute while I'm here. And speaking of that, would it be all right if I took my grandchildren with me to the ranch? Faith will have plenty of help the next few days."

"Of course!" said France.

France quickly packed up the children's things and rounded up everyone to head over to the neighbors'. They saw Mr. Fugate leading his horses and buggy out of the barn.

"Thank you again for everything you've done for my family, and especially Faith," said Julia, stepping forward to hug France. "I hope you know how special you are to all of them."

France shook her head and smiled, but her eyes fought back the tears. "No more than they are to me. I've always wanted to meet the woman who raised these extraordinary children. I had hoped to come to Faith's wedding, but it was just impossible to get away."

Caitlin asked her grandmother if she could stay in town with the Samuels that night and go back to the ranch after church tomorrow.

"I've been at the ranch all week, and I know Momma won't mind."

"I'm sure this little gal needs a break," said France. "She's been digging postholes and taking care of the ranch and cooking for Finn and Joseph all week."

"Are you sure it's all right?" asked Julia.

"Of course! Caitlin's family. Zane and Emma have missed her so much since she moved to the ranch."

Julia asked Caitlin to give them directions, so she told them what to watch for and described the entrance gate. She hugged her grandmother and aunts and said she would see them tomorrow. Mr. Fugate finished giving Allie instructions about the buggy and the horses and to make sure Boots, the one-eyed gelding with the white stockinged feet, did his fair share of the pulling. Mercy sat in the back seat to help Julia with Sam and Cele. Ella sat in the front with Allie. They waved goodbye to everyone and started heading back to the hotel to retrieve their bags.

"Love you!" Caitlin hollered as the buggy pulled away from the Fugate's barn.

"We love you, too, honey," said Julia. "See you tomorrow!"

Two blocks away, people stopped and stared at the troop of men entering the town square. Matthew drove the Samuels' buggy, which carried the two wounded cattle rustlers in the back seat and Joseph sat in the front, cradling his arm. Justin rode alongside them. Bear's arms were tied behind him as he rode his horse between Jimmy and Matt Taylor as they followed the buggy.

The townspeople recognized Joseph Samuel, and some even remembered Jimmy Taylor. Everyone knew something serious had taken place noticing the injured and captive men. Joseph gave Matthew directions to Dr. Hood's house, so the entourage headed north. Matt and Jimmy would take Bear to the jail after they made sure the others arrived safely at the doctor's office.

When the women entered the town square only a moment later, they noticed that people had gathered in groups buzzing with talk. A number of folks stopped to stare at the buggy of beautiful women passing by. Several recognized Mercy and waved at her, which started another flurry of talk.

"You must have made quite an impression when you were here, Mercy," said Allie.

"Well, I *was* a pretty good sales clerk. Or maybe they're remembering the fire." She involuntarily pulled at the netting that covered her forehead and the side of her face as she continued to look around. "No, something else is going on."

At the hotel, Mercy and Allie hurried inside to get their bags.

Julia watched the men standing under the trees near the middle of the square. Several men stopped talking to tip their hats toward her. She nodded her head in acknowledgment and looked away, hoping she hadn't appeared too forward with her gazing. People had noticed them earlier when they had walked through and had greeted them politely. But the atmosphere of the square had changed considerably since then.

Something *had* happened during the time they were at the Samuels house.

Chapter 38

D r. Hood stood in the foyer of his home and said, "I have to say, Joseph, that between the Murrays and the Samuels, y'all have kept me quite busy lately. I'd rather work on you first, son, but the gunshot wounds take precedence. Have a seat in the parlor and I'll see you as soon as I can."

Joseph nodded and let the doctor's eldest daughter Jamie lead him to a divan. He noticed she had grown up and filled out since he had left home. She smiled demurely at him as she gently placed a pillow under his arm and offered to get him some water. He found himself staring at her walking gracefully across the parlor.

The doctor noticed the odd look on Joseph's face. "Will you be all right, Joseph? Is anything else hurting besides your shoulder?"

Joseph shut his open mouth and looked at Jamie's father. He began rubbing his chest. "My scrotum sure has been bothering me, too, Doc. I think I must've done something to it in the fall."

Dr. Hood's eyes widened and his face turned red, but Matthew and Justin snickered.

"What's so funny?!" asked Joseph.

"There's absolutely nothing funny about it," said Dr. Hood, glancing at the door his daughter had just walked through.

"I think he meant sternum, Dr. Hood," said Justin.

Joseph's mouth fell open again when he realized what he had said in front of Jamie... and her father, too. His face turned every shade of red.

"I'm so sorry, Dr. Hood. I don't know how it came out that way."

"Well, I'll take a look at your *chest*, too, in a little while. Mr. Taylor, if you and your son will follow me and bring those men to the first room on your right, I'll work on both of them there."

Justin half-carried the groaning man to the room and sat him on a hard examining table. Matthew led the other young man to a chair.

"Cattle rustlers, you say? Has the sheriff been notified?" the doctor asked Matthew as he took off the young man's hat and dropped it on the floor behind him.

"My other two sons are taking care of that," he said. "There was a third man involved that has some cuts and bruises, but I wouldn't want you to examine him outside of a jail cell. He gave us some problems."

"Lay down, son," said the doctor, looking more closely at the young man's face. "Oh, dear Lord. Is that you, Tanner? Didn't your parents teach you better than this? Why in the world are you stealing cattle?"

"I'm sorry, Doc," said the boy as he started to cry. "Bear said nobody'd ever know. It hurts, Doc."

"It oughta hurt," he said, taking off the young man's shirt and looking at the bullet wound in his side.

"Am I gonna die?"

"I doubt it, but your father may kill you. And it's going to break your mother's heart to find out what you did." The doctor looked up at the other boy more closely, but he didn't recognize him. "Who are you?" he asked.

The boy stared sullenly at him, saying nothing.

Tanner spoke from the table. "His name's Bowen. He and Bear are from Coleman County."

"Shut up, Tanner," the boy said irritably. "Don't you speak for me."

"Who's Bear?"

"He's the one my brothers took straight to jail," said Justin. "He was a little hard to handle."

"Will they need to stay here or should we take them to the sheriff after you patch them up?" asked Matthew.

"You'll need to take them," said Dr. Hood. "I'll go check on them at the jail. My family lives here, and I'm not about to put them in danger."

"I would never hurt you or your family, Doc. You know that."

"I'm not talking about you, Tanner," he said, glancing at Bowen. "But then I never would've thought you'd lower yourself to stealing cattle either."

"I'm so sorry," he said as he started to cry again.

"You weak, blubbering son of a..." Bowen started to say when Justin got in his face.

"I'd shut up right now, if I were you. At least he's showing some semblance of a conscience. I think you're just mad you got caught."

Bowen tried to stare him down, but he couldn't. Not with those eyes.

After the doctor had treated the boys' wounds, Matthew said they would take them on to the jail house while the doctor worked on Joseph's shoulder. They escorted the boys into the foyer and paused to talk to Joseph.

"We'll be back in a little while to take you home," said Justin.

"Momma's gonna kill me for getting hurt," said Joseph, when it dawned on him that he still had to face her.

"We'll tell her it wasn't your fault," said Matthew. "You stayed away from trouble, but it ended up finding you."

"And could you make sure Finn and Caitlin got to town all right?" he asked.

Matthew nodded. "I think my granddaughter was in pretty good hands, though. Be sure and tell the doc what your brother did to Bear."

Jimmy and Matt recognized the Murrays' wagon and team in front of the jail house. They pulled up and dismounted, tying their horses to the hitching rail before helping Bear get off his horse. The trip to town was uncomfortable for him since his hands were tied behind his back. They hadn't intended for him to ride like that, but earlier when his hands were tied in front he had caught Matt under the chin and knocked him down. He managed to get on a horse and away from him before the others realized what had happened. Matthew and Justin were loading the injured onto the buggy when Bear came high tailing it out of the barn past them. Jimmy mounted Brave and gave chase. Nobody was better on horseback than Jimmy, though, and he quickly caught Bear and brought him back, this time with a couple of extra knots on his head from Jimmy's pistol. He hadn't given them any more trouble since then.

Inside the jail, George and Finn saw the Taylors ride up and came out to meet them.

"Looks like you've been busy, Jim," said George, extending his hand to Jimmy. "Friend, it sure is good to see you."

"How are you doing, George?" said Jimmy. "This is my oldest brother, Matt. And this is George Samuel, who we've been telling you about for years."

"And this is Bear," said Matt, "who's gotten himself in some serious trouble. Is the sheriff around?"

George shook his head. "We were told he'd be here soon, but we've been waiting for hours. One of his deputies is tracking him down. The jailer's here, though, if you need to lock him up."

They walked Bear inside and had the jailer escort him to a cell.

"Weren't there more rustlers than this?" asked Finn.

"Yeah, Justin and our father took two more to Dr. Hood's to get patched up, along with Joseph," said Jimmy. "I'm sure they'll be along shortly."

"What happened to Joseph?" asked George.

Jimmy missed Finn shaking his head at him from behind his father.

"Bear threw him off the wagon, and we think the fall broke his collarbone," Jimmy continued. "Bear had no idea he was getting away with Finn and Caitlin in the back, but..." he stopped when he saw Finn running his finger across his throat telling him to shut up.

"But what?" asked George, turning around to look at his son. "Finn neglected to tell me this part of it. What happened, Finn?"

Finn stood there, unsure of what to say next. "We didn't know Joseph got hurt. He told us to lay down in the wagon."

"How'd you get away from Bear?"

"Well..." he started, then stopped. He wasn't quite sure how to tell his father he waylaid a rustler.

"I'll tell him, Finn," said Jimmy. "He didn't do a thing wrong, George; in fact, you'd have been proud of him. The kids had come back to the ranch house like they were supposed to if they heard gunshots, but they didn't know one of the rustlers—Bear—had run his horse towards the house and barn. He didn't see the fence coming up, and his horse ended up throwing him over it and took off. Bear saw the barn and more horses so he ran inside and tried to saddle Crazy Ears—"

"Crazy Ears?" said George, grinning at that point. "I would've loved to have seen that show."

"Well, Crazy pitched and dragged him all over the yard before Bear gave up and let go. 'Bout that time the kids came up to the barn in the wagon, and Bear saw another chance to get away. I was still a little ways from the barn, but I saw Bear jump on the wagon and throw Joseph off the seat before he knew what hit him. Bear took off down the road, not realizing Caitlin and Finn were still in the back. We didn't see it, but Faith ran down the road after the wagon and said she saw Finn stand up in the bed holding a shovel and rear back and knock Bear upside the head. He went flying off the wagon, and the kids ended up coming on to town to get the sheriff."

"We didn't go back, Pa," said Finn. "We heard another gunshot, and we were afraid that man might shoot us to get the wagon back. So we came on to town to get help."

"They didn't know Faith had caught up to him and had her pistol trained on him," said Matt. "She was the one that had fired that shot to let Bear know she was serious about him not moving."

George looked at Finn. "So you really knocked that big man off the wagon yourself?"

"Well, me and my shovel," said Finn, unsure if he was in trouble or not.

George chuckled. "I would've liked to have seen that, too."

"Really?" asked Finn.

"You may have saved yours and Caitlin's lives," he said.

"I wouldn't a shot no girl," yelled Bear from inside the jail cell. "But I'd like to have another go at that kid with the shovel. My ear still hurts."

Finn's eyes widened.

"Shut up, Bear!" said Jimmy towards the hall, and then turned back and lowered his voice. "Sorry, I forgot he was within earshot."

"Let's go outside and wait for the sheriff there," said George.

Chapter 39

The sheriff showed up an hour later, and the Taylors and Samuel boys explained why the jail had three new prisoners. A deputy recorded their statements and said they would be notified by mail when the circuit judge would be in town. Matthew Taylor said he could come back to testify if they needed him.

The sun was getting low on the horizon when the men pulled up at the Samuel house.

"Y'all come eat supper with us," said George. "You can't leave town without seeing France."

"I'm starving," said Justin.

"We have to go in and see France before we leave," said Jimmy. "You haven't seen her in how long?"

"Eight years," said Justin. "She probably won't remember me."

"Yeah, you're an old man now," said Matt.

"She remembers you, brother," said Jimmy.

"Well, I remember her apple pie," said Justin.

"Let's go around to the barn and y'all can water and feed your horses and then come feed yourselves," said George.

"And we need to get Caitlin and take her back with us," said Matthew. "I'm sure Faith's worried about her."

"Momma won't be nearly so upset with me and Finn if y'all are at the dinner table," said Joseph.

"She's not really mad," said George. "That's just how it comes across when she's scared. She just worries about you."

"But I'm a man now, Dad." Joseph said as he sat in the buggy with his arm in a sling.

"All she'll see is her little bird with a broken wing."

Joseph groaned. "I left the nest over a year ago, Pops."

"Well, you won't have to dig postholes any more," said Finn.

"I can at least oversee that post-hole digger," said Joseph. He explained to the others about their hole-boring tool they designed. Finn said he could take it back to the ranch tomorrow and try it out.

France looked out of the kitchen window to see a passel of men in their buggy, the Murray's wagon, and atop three horses pulling up at the barn. She smiled, knowing she would have company around the dinner table this evening. She quickly counted heads.

"Set four more plates, girls," she said, scurrying around to finish supper. "We have some hungry men to feed."

George brought Joseph to the house first while the others took care of the horses. France only yelled once when she saw Joseph. Then George explained what had happened. Then France shed a few tears. And then she hugged Joseph a little too tightly, but he wasn't about to yelp out loud at the pain for fear his mother would start crying again. By the time Finn and the Taylors came to the house, France was her old self again. She told the girls not to say anything about their earlier visitors—that she would break the news when they were well into the meal.

It didn't take the men and boys very long to clean their plates and reach for seconds.

"I'm so glad to have the pleasure of your company, gentlemen, and now that you have some food in you, I have some good news," she said, looking around the table. "And I apologize for not telling you immediately. But I didn't want them to have to go to the trouble of feeding you at bed time, because after you hear this news, I feel sure you'll cut this meal short."

Matthew smiled and looked questioningly at France.

She looked at Caitlin and said, "Would you like to tell them, honey?"

Caitlin looked as though she was about to burst. "Meemaw's here!"

"What!?"

"And Aunt Mercy and Aunt Allie!" she said, giggling.

The men didn't believe her, but they couldn't help but look around for their wives.

"I mean—they were here earlier, but they've gone to the ranch," she explained. "They came on the stage this afternoon."

"How'd they get to the ranch?" asked George. "The buggy wasn't here."

"They borrowed Mr. Fugate's, and we promised him that someone would bring it back before church. But since our buggy's here now, the Fugates can use ours, and we can take Mercy's wagon to the ranch tomorrow for Sunday dinner after church."

Jimmy wiped his mouth and excused himself from the table. He walked around and kissed France on the cheek and thanked her for the meal, and said that he had to go. Justin stuffed the last few bites in his mouth, and excused himself as well.

"Hold on, boys!" Matthew said. "I guess Caitlin and I have to take the wagon."

"I'm staying here tonight, PaPa," said Caitlin. "Meemaw and France said it was all right. I'll come home tomorrow."

He looked at France, who nodded her head and smiled. He stood and thanked his host for their hospitality and meal.

"They're not going to wait for us," he said, grabbing his hat.

"I'll ride along with you, Dad," said Matt. "I don't have any reason to hurry back."

"Then maybe you ought to take the wagon and let me have your horse," he said, anxious to leave, too.

Matt laughed. "All right, but somebody had better wait up for me to make sure I get there all right."

France and George walked them out to the porch and waved at Jimmy and Justin leaving the barn post-haste.

A minute or so later, Matthew Taylor followed on Matt's horse.

"Oh! I forgot," said France, running back into the house. She came out with something wrapped in a dishtowel, and she and her husband walked her over to Matt getting ready to leave in the wagon.

"You know my brothers well, Mrs. Samuel," he said, "to not tell them about their wives before they'd eaten."

"I was being selfish," she said, "and call me France. I knew they wouldn't stay, but I knew y'all were hungry, too, and needed to eat something. Here, since y'all didn't stay for dessert."

She handed him the package.

"What's this?" he asked, feeling the warmth and lifting it up to his nose. "Don't tell me—apple pie. I heard them talking about your apple pie, France."

"There's a fork in there, too, so eat all you want on the way home. I'll bring a couple more pies for Sunday dinner tomorrow."

"But you don't have to tell your brothers that," added George. "You ought to hand them a pan of crumbs for running off and leaving you."

He laughed out loud. "Good idea," he said. "And thanks for supper, France."

"It was my pleasure, Matt. And we're so glad to have met you."

"Same here—I've heard about y'all for years now. It's about time I got to meet George and France Samuel in person," he said, tipping his hat to them. "Good night."

"See you tomorrow, Matt."

Caitlin had been careful to not pay Finn too much attention during dinner. But then she must have carried that act a bit too far because Emma asked if she was mad at her brother. Caitlin tried to recall how it was to be normal around him, but she had a tough time remembering what that was like. Things had changed drastically between them, and she found it hard to keep her feelings bottled up inside. She didn't know Finn was struggling with the same thing himself.

Emma asked Caitlin to keep her company while she milked Miss Clara, and Caitlin was glad to get out of the house to take her mind off of Finn. But he ended up coming out to the barn to feed the livestock with Mac. Caitlin couldn't help but frown when she saw him.

"Are you sure you're not mad at Finn?" Emma asked her.

"No, of course not," she said, trying to adjust her expression to normal again, whatever that was. "You heard my uncles at dinner. Your brother saved my life today."

"Did you remember to thank him?"

"Well, no. I hadn't thought about that."

"The way you've been acting, he probably thinks you don't appreciate it."

"You think so?" She glanced at Finn carrying hay to the horses outside. "I hope I haven't hurt his feelings."

"Then go talk to him while I finish milking."

Caitlin walked out the barn door and up to Finn throwing hay over the fence.

"What are you doing?" he whispered, looking around.

"You know, we can still talk to each other occasionally without anyone becoming suspicious."

"You're right," he said, exhaling. "What do you want to talk about?"

"Emma said I needed to come out here and thank you for saving my life today," she said quietly. "I do appreciate it, and I hope I didn't hurt your feelings by not telling you before now."

Finn snickered. "You don't have to thank me."

"Well, I should have, and I didn't. You're my hero, though, and I want to shout it to the world. But I can't even think straight anymore, and it's all your fault."

"You're having that problem, too? Well, let's stop this foolishness and tell everybody tomorrow."

"But then Daddy probably won't let us work on the fence together at all, much less by ourselves anymore. I know my birthday's tomorrow, but let's wait to tell everybody after you go back to school. That'll give us another week together."

Finn nodded his head. "You're right. By then I won't get to see you until Sundays anyway. I don't want to cut our time short before then."

"Oh, and I need to borrow my pin back just for tomorrow," said Caitlin. "Meemaw wants to see it."

"Sure."

"Do you think I've taken long enough to thank you without Emma becoming suspicious?"

"Probably."

"And as much as I love your sisters, I'd rather stand out here and talk to you the rest of the evening," she said. "But I guess I'd better get back in there."

"Yep."

"Love you, Finn," she whispered, and then said loudly, "And thanks again for saving my life!"

"Any time!" he said just as loud, and then whispered, "I'll be thinking about you tonight."

Chapter 40

The Taylors rode fast for the first several miles since they could still see by the fading remnants of the sunset. The darker it got, though, the more they slowed down, but the stars were so bright in the moonless sky they could still see the road stretched out like a pale ribbon leading the way to the ranch.

Matthew couldn't help but quote a verse. "The heavens declare the glory of the Lord, and the sky above proclaims his handiwork."

That prompted a couple of amens from his sons.

Jimmy was the first to arrive at the Murrays' barn. He had ridden with Justin and his father until they reached the front gate, but once inside, he didn't see the need to tarry on their behalf.

Several lamps were lit inside the barn and out, and he knew she was waiting for him. He walked Brave into the barn and dismounted, tying his reins.

"I know you're here," he said, looking around.

Mercy came from the shadows at a run and he caught her and picked her up to swing her around. She threw her head back and laughed; her long, blonde hair cascaded down her back. But the laugh was muffled by a lingering kiss.

"I knew you'd get here first," she finally said, trying to catch her breath. "I've missed you."

He kissed her again and held her tight. "I don't know why y'all came, but I sure am glad to see you. This has been the longest four days."

"Is everyone all right?"

"Yeah, other than Joseph's broken collarbone, and Matt has a bruised

196

chin, but the swelling makes him look more masculine. Catherine's going to swoon over it."

Mercy giggled as she looked him over. "Any place I need to kiss and make better?"

He held up a fist. But the little finger on his left hand stood at attention. It was swollen and too stiff to bend.

"Ohhh, you poor thing," she said, kissing it. "And how did you obtain this life-threatening injury?"

"It got between a cattle rustler's hard head and the butt of my pistol," he said, enjoying the medical treatment.

Mercy stopped and stared at him. "You mean you hit your own finger with your own gun?"

"He'd gotten away from us, and we were on horseback running full tilt," he said, defending himself. "I didn't want to shoot him, but I had to slow him down somehow to bring him back. I just knocked a little sense into him."

"It's a wonder you didn't shoot yourself."

Matthew and Justin rode into the barn and dismounted. Mercy walked over to hug them and asked where Matt was. Justin told her he was bringing the wagon home and hoped he would get there by morning.

"Don't believe a word he says," said Jimmy. "Well, the part about the wagon is true, but Matt will be here before too long."

"If he doesn't get lost in the dark," Justin added.

Allie came running into the barn to greet Justin, and Matthew met Julia walking from the house. She said they had been waiting on the porch for them to return. She tried to see his face—to read his expression, but she could barely see from the dim porch lamp.

Matthew took her in his arms.

"Are you all right?" she asked apprehensively. "Is everyone all right? I only saw three horses."

"Yes, I'm fine—we're all fine. Matt's coming home in the wagon," he said. "We were just too impatient to wait on him."

"You sound tired."

"It's been a long day. I'm glad you're here, Julia, but you shouldn't have traveled all that way. Your shoulder—"

"My shoulder's fine."

"Why'd you come?"

"The uneasiness hasn't let up—I just felt like something was terribly wrong here," she explained, "and I knew I had to come. Allie and Mercy

197

insisted on coming with me, too, but they'll be going back on Tuesday. I can stay longer if Faith needs the help."

"We can stay as long as it takes. I'm sorry you were worried about us."

"We didn't know about the cattle rustling until today. Maybe that's what's causing this heaviness I'm feeling."

"They were only kids—the oldest one looked to be about Jimmy's age or younger. The other two probably weren't any older than Joseph and Finn."

"Did they have guns? Did they shoot at you?"

"Well, yes."

"Then it didn't matter how old they were—you were still in danger."

They turned and walked back to the barn for Julia to greet her sons. Jimmy told his parents to go on to the house and go to bed—that they would take care of his horse. So Matthew and Julia said their goodnights and walked back to the house.

"How's Ethan?" asked Justin.

"Tired and sore," said Allie. "He and Faith went to bed with the little ones right after sundown. We must've just missed y'all coming into town this afternoon. But by the way everyone was acting around the square, we knew something unusual had just happened."

"I bet y'all were something to see—you Taylor men riding into town like you'd just come in from a battle," said Mercy.

"I guess it created a big stir since it involved fence-cutting and cattle rustling," said Jimmy. "And since Finn and Joseph aren't here, dibs on the camp house tonight."

"The camp house?" said Mercy. "Why do *we* have to stay in the ol' camp house?"

Jimmy just looked at her and raised his eyebrows before throwing his saddle over the board fence.

"Then we'll take it," Justin said, leading his horse into a stall.

"No, no, that's all right," said Mercy. "You can have Ella and Cele's room—right next to your parents."

"And above Faith and Ethan," added Jimmy, grinning wickedly.

"Would y'all just hush?!" said Allie, blushing.

"We'll manage just fine," Justin said to his brother. "You know how quiet I can be sneaking up on someone, unlike you."

"Well, we all know who got to the barn first," said Jimmy.

"That has nothin' to do with what we're talking about," said Justin. "Unless *getting to the barn first* has another meaning, and that's nothing to brag about."

Mercy squealed with laughter.

Jimmy frowned at her before telling his brother, "That's not what I meant, and you know it."

"I wouldn't know a thing about it."

"You ought to be ashamed of yourselves talking that way!" said Allie. "And why does everything turn into a competition between you two?"

Justin grinned. "We're brothers."

"We can't help it," added Jimmy, grinning back. "And we have to get in a whole year's worth of railing each other during your annual visit."

"When are *y'all* going to come down and see *us*?" asked Allie.

"One of these years, I promise," said Mercy. "Maybe when Biriney's a little older."

The two women walked over to a chest and sat down to wait for their husbands to finish taking care of the horses.

"I love that name," said Allie, wrapping her coat more tightly around her. "I've never heard of it before, though. Where did you come up with that?"

"I heard it somewhere—I can't even remember, but I loved the sound of it," said Mercy. "Beer'-a-nee," she pronounced it slower. "Wouldn't it be awful, though, if we found out it actually means *fish gutter* or *toothless woman* in some other language?"

Allie laughed.

"I've even had nightmares about it," said Mercy.

The brothers finished tending to the horses and each grabbed a lantern in one hand and a wife in the other to head to their respective sleeping quarters.

"You'd think they would've had all their visiting done on the long trip over here," said Justin.

"Yeah, Justin and I got all our talking out of our system about ten miles outside of Grace," said Jimmy.

"I think it was closer to five," argued Justin.

"Here we go again," said Allie, rolling her eyes. "Pleasant dreams, Mercy."

Chapter 41

Jimmy and Mercy rose up early Sunday morning to make the trip back to Brownwood again even though France had said they didn't have to bring the Fugates' buggy back to town before the church service. But they had made friends in the community six years before and thought church would be the best time to see most everyone. They would ride back to the ranch with the Samuels in Mercy's wagon, the name France had given a funeral hearse that Mercy had arrived in when she came to live with and work for the Samuels six years before.

Jimmy had bought the hearse to take Mercy, or Florine Locke as she was known at that time, back to Waco after she had run off with a gambler. The man had abandoned her in Fort Worth, and Jimmy had found her and brought her home in the only thing he could find to leave town in after they had missed the stage. But when her father threatened to send her East because of her scandalous condition, Florine ran away from Waco in the funeral hearse to live with the Samuels in Brownwood. Florine changed her name and her life during that time, and gave the hearse to the Samuels so they would have a big enough wagon to haul their large family around.

Back then George and France had eleven adopted children and one foster child—Caitlin living with them by the time Faith and Mercy came along. The funeral wagon proved to be perfect for hauling the family everywhere, and the school even borrowed it occasionally to carry groups of children when needed. No one except strangers thought of Mercy's wagon as a hearse anymore.

Faith was up before everyone else and fixed Jimmy and Mercy a quick breakfast of pancakes and coffee. She sent them on their way to town before the rest of the Taylors had come down for breakfast.

Matthew had decided they would have their own worship service there at the ranch instead of going into town. After breakfast, he asked Julia to lead them in singing a hymn.

"We don't let a Sunday go by without singing *Amazing Grace*," she said, "because we're so thankful for God's grace in our lives. And I'm thankful for his protection of our men yesterday, and for Ethan's continued recovery from his injury, and for this new home and ranch, and of course, my precious grandchildren."

She began singing the words by heart, and everyone joined in.

> *"Amazing grace! (how sweet the sound)*
> *That sav'd a wretch like me!*
> *I once was lost, but now am found,*
> *Was blind, but now I see.*
>
> *'Twas grace that taught my heart to fear,*
> *And grace my fears reliev'd;*
> *How precious did that grace appear,*
> *The hour I first believ'd!*
>
> *Thro' many dangers, toils, and snares,*
> *I have already come;*
> *'Tis grace has brought me safe thus far,*
> *And grace will lead me home.*
>
> *The Lord has promis'd good to me,*
> *His word my hope secures;*
> *He will my shield and portion be,*
> *As long as life endures.*
>
> *Yes, when this flesh and heart shall fail,*
> *And mortal life shall cease;*
> *I shall possess, within the veil,*
> *A life of joy and peace.*

The earth shall soon dissolve like snow,
The sun forbear to shine;
But God who call'd me here below,
Will be forever mine.

Matthew stood at the head of the table, holding Ethan and Faith's Bible open to the book of Psalms.

"I was talking to Joseph yesterday at the doctor's office—he was worried that his mother would be angry at him for getting hurt. I told him that it wasn't his fault—that he hadn't done anything wrong. But there are times in life when we've done everything right and have done the best we can, and still difficulties come our way. Look at Job and what he went through. I don't know that I would've been as strong as he if I'd lost what he lost. But God tells us in Psalm 46:1 that 'He is our refuge and strength, a very present help in trouble.' And Faith and Ethan have experienced trouble these past ten days. They didn't do anything to deserve it. They didn't ask for it, but difficulties came. God never said that life would be easy, and it hasn't been easy for any of us. But when trouble comes, we need to remember we have each other—we're family, and we need to remember to lean on God— He can bear the load when we can't."

Matthew bowed his head and prayed. When he opened his eyes, Faith was standing beside him.

"Thank you, Daddy," she said, and then turned to everyone. "Ethan and I are so grateful for your help and support. You don't know what this means to us."

Ethan spoke up. "Before I married into this family, the few memories I had of family were bad ones. I've been on my own from the time I was Katie's age. And then after my first wife died, I didn't even know if I would get to raise my own daughter since I had no one to help me. But I know now if something was to ever happen to me, Faith and our children would be taken care of. And that's taken such a load of worry off my mind. Y'all have done so much for us, and I really appreciate it, but I don't want to keep you from your work and your homes any longer. We can take it from here."

"Well, the stage doesn't come until Tuesday, and we can still get a lot done between now and then," said Matthew. "And I know it's the Sabbath, but under the circumstances, I think the Lord will forgive us for getting the ox out of the ditch today."

"What do you mean?" asked Faith.

"Your fence needs finishing," said Matt. "I think we can get a good four hours of work in before the Samuels get here for dinner."

"Then let's go," said Justin.

"I'll come help you this evening and tomorrow," Allie said to Justin. "But this morning I need to help in the kitchen."

"We're going to have a small army to feed, and we women have a lot to do before dinnertime, so you boys go on and get out of our hair," Julia said sweetly.

The men left obediently as if she had cracked a whip at them.

"Now, if I had said those exact same words," said Mercy, "Jimmy would pout the rest of the day."

"Where do we start?" asked Allie.

Julia glanced at the clock on the mantel for the tenth time in the past five minutes. The big hand was straight up two o'clock now. They had fed the little ones an hour before, and they were down for their naps.

"What's taking them so long?" said Faith. "Everything's getting cold."

"Maybe the preacher went long this morning," said Mercy.

The men had returned around one o'clock, and Julia had them scrounge around the barn to find something to use as make-shift tables out in the yard.

"It's such a pretty day," she said. "We might as well eat outside."

Faith put the finishing touches of icing on a cake to celebrate Caitlin's birthday.

"I can't believe she's twelve years old now," said Mercy. "It seems like only last week we were throwing tantrums together."

The women laughed, and Faith looked at Mercy from across the table. So much had changed in their lives since they had lived together with the Samuels. Mercy or Florine, as Faith had known her in their growing-up years, was the most pampered and spoiled girl she had ever met. Pride-shattering circumstances and the loss of her baby had brought Mercy to her knees, but through it all she emerged with a new name and a new heart. Still beautiful even with a scarred face from the barn fire, Mercy was one of her closest friends. And now she was her sister-in-law.

Faith covered the cake and glanced out the window to see Jimmy carrying a couple of stumps to set up as seats around the table. It was still hard to believe he and so many of her family were actually here. She thanked God again for them.

"Oh, dear," said Julia, as she pulled off the apron Faith had loaned her. A big, greasy stain had soaked through the apron and onto her bodice.

"Well, look at that," she said. "I knew I was getting a little wild with that gravy. I'm going to go change out of this before everyone gets here."

Julia walked up the stairs and into Caitlin's room. She slipped out of her dress and draped it on the iron footboard. She opened the door to the chiffarobe, and a box started to topple off the top shelf. She reached up and caught it, recognizing that it was a wooden cigar box. It felt heavy—she wondered what Caitlin was doing with a cigar box. She lifted the lid and smiled when she saw the bundle of letters she had written to her granddaughter. She stepped back and sat down on the bed and lifted up the letters to see ribbons and a number of pretty rocks—some were probably gathered at Grace. She picked up a slice of cedar wood and held it to her nose to sniff, taking in the fresh-cut scent. She saw the initials FN carved on it, and turned it over to see a heart with the letters KT inside of it.

She turned it back over and looked at the FN again and decided Caitlin must be keeping a friend's secret for her. She looked around for Caitlin's racing medal and started to lift up another small bundle of paper when Faith yelled up the stairs.

"They're coming, Momma!"

Julia left the box on the bed and grabbed the first dress her hand touched in the chiffarobe and pulled a black silk dress over her head before hurrying out of the room. She reached the bottom of the stairs and caught Allie walking out the door.

"Can you button me?" she asked.

"You look so elegant," said Allie. "What's the occasion?"

"No occasion—I just soiled my other one," said Julia.

She hooked the last of the buttons at Julia's neck when they heard the children screaming.

Chapter 42

Allie and Julia rushed out the front door to see a horde of young people climbing out of a white funeral hearse with Jimmy and Mercy in the driver's seat. George and France followed in their buggy, along with Jenna and Annie holding dishes of food.

"Sorry we're so late!" said George, helping his wife down. "It took us some time to load all the food France prepared."

"I didn't bring that much," she said. "We were late getting home from church."

"Hi MeeMaw! What do you think of our ranch?" said Caitlin, rushing by with Emma and Zane to show them her room upstairs.

Julia started to answer, but the girls had already passed by. She stepped back in the kitchen to help haul the food to the tables outside, but Mercy told her to go sit down and rest—that they could get everything ready. So she turned and walked back outside to sit on one of the rockers on the porch, and found Matthew there. He pulled the chair up close beside him and patted it.

"They ran me out of the kitchen. I'm not as helpless as they think I am."

"Your sons did the same to me," he said. "They're just giving us a break. We might as well sit back and enjoy it."

Julia nodded and looked around at the mass of people milling about the place. At first glance it seemed like noisy chaos, but she watched the petite France directing her army with a combination of quiet commands and loud accolades and laughter. Julia silently thanked God for the influence this woman had on her family through the years. She reached over and grasped her husband's hand.

"We're so blessed, aren't we," she said.

Matthew nodded and squeezed her hand. They watched Joseph coaching Finn and Mac as they unloaded an odd looking iron object from the wagon.

"What is that contraption?" she asked.

"Joseph and Finn have designed a posthole digging tool," answered Matthew. "Ethan was telling me about it. They're hoping it will speed up the fence building."

"How interesting. Do you think it'll work?"

Matthew nodded his head. "It's a good design. Joseph's applying for a patent on it soon."

"How long do you think it's going to take to finish the fence?"

"Sooner than Ethan expects," said Matthew. "I asked Jimmy to put out a call for helpers at church today. He told me ten men agreed to come out tomorrow. They'll be working the half mile along the stage road."

"How nice of them to volunteer."

"Well, we actually hired them," he admitted. "That's why we have a good number coming. Everybody's strapped for cash at the end of the year."

Julia smiled, patting his hand. "Patience has never been one of your virtues, Matthew, but then you know how to get a job done. Thank you for doing this for Faith and Ethan."

"Ethan doesn't know we're paying these men," he said, "so don't mention it to him. I think they'll be able to stretch the wire by Wednesday or Thursday."

"They?"

"I think we need to go back with the girls on Tuesday," he said. "Ethan will be back on his feet soon, and we'll be leaving them in good shape."

"I know the kids need to get back, but I thought we ought to stay at least until the end of the week," she said. "I don't know when we'll get to see them again."

"We'll talk about it later," said Matthew, standing and offering his hand to his wife. "Come on, I think they're ready for me to say the blessing."

After everyone ate their fill, Faith brought out the birthday cake for Caitlin. She screeched with delight and loudly proclaimed that she thought everyone had forgotten about her birthday since no one had mentioned it all that day. She discreetly found Finn's face in the crowd and his smile told her that he knew exactly what this day meant for them, but they had agreed earlier to wait until the school holiday was over before they broke the news to everyone.

The fellowship continued throughout the afternoon. When K. James suggested they divide up teams and play a game of baseball, Mac brought out his Christmas presents: a baseball and a bat. They walked off a diamond shape in the yard, using burlap bags weighted down with corn and folded in half for the bases.

The kids decided to take on the adults, so Joseph volunteered to coach the children's team since he couldn't play. And since he was the only one who had actually seen a baseball game played, he went over the rules with everyone on how to play. The men and children were somewhat familiar with the sport, but the women hadn't a clue.

"You do what with that stick?" asked Mercy.

"It's called a bat, honey," said Jimmy.

"I think I'm too old for this," said France. "I'd better go sit on the porch with Julia."

"But we need you or the kids will outnumber us," said George.

"All right, I'll play... just as long as I don't have to hit or catch or anything," she said.

"Me, too!" said Mercy.

"That sounds like a good idea, France," said Allie.

"But that's the object of the game!" said George.

"We're sunk," said Matt.

The kids beat the adults seventeen to eight, and Joseph claimed they only got those points because his team felt sorry for the old folks. But Matt, Justin, and Jimmy each hit the ball over the pasture fence, which brought in most of the runs. After his homerun, Jimmy caught up to Mercy running around the bases, and when she slowed to a walk coming around third base, he impatiently picked her up and threw her over his shoulder to carry her across home base.

The women didn't like how hard the ball was to catch bare-handed, so Allie solved that by holding out her apron to catch it that way. Faith ran to the house to get several more aprons for her team and refused to share them with the younger girls. Matt even donned one after blistering his hand trying to catch a hard hit.

Julia's cheeks were sore from laughing—she couldn't remember the last time she had laughed that much. She made a mental note to order a baseball and bat for her grandchildren back in Grace—it seemed to be such a fun game for young and old alike.

Everyone visited with each other and grazed at the food table throughout the afternoon, and the time came all too quickly for the Samuels to load up and head back to town. Mercy told France they would come in a little early on Tuesday to visit some more before they caught the stage for Waco.

Joseph went home with his parents, but left the posthole digging tool with Finn to use since he was allowed to stay to help the Taylors with the fence building the following day. Faith said she would fix him a pallet next to Matt's in the front room close to the fireplace. He caught Caitlin's eye after everyone left, and they volunteered to take care of the chores in the barn.

Jimmy stood and offered to help with the horses.

"We can handle it just fine—you just rest your weary bones, Uncle Jimmy," said Caitlin. "I know we wore you out playing baseball."

"You want a rematch?" he taunted her.

"No, thanks—I was just kidding," she said. "We'll be back in a little while."

The evening air had cooled down quickly, so they put on their coats. Finn grabbed the milk pail and Caitlin picked up the slop bucket before they headed out the door.

They heard Ethan comment to Faith, "Those two have really stepped up and taken care of things around here."

Faith nodded, but noticed that Caitlin missed saying her usual words of parting.

But Caitlin had other things on her mind.

Once they got to the barn, Finn told her to feed the livestock while he did the milking. After he finished, he set the pail of milk on the corn bin and pulled Caitlin into his arms.

"Happy birthday, Katie," he said.

"I think this was the best birthday I've ever had. It was perfect."

"I thought we'd never get some time to ourselves."

"I know—I could hardly eat or play that game for thinking about you. But you really showed up your brothers. I think you scored most of the points."

"I was trying to impress you," he said, kissing the side of her head. "Did I?"

Caitlin looked up and nodded.

"You sure looked pretty in church today. In fact, you still do. It's not often that I see you doing chores in a dress."

"I can still be a lady when I want to."

"I've kind of gotten used to seeing you in trousers," he said. "You're the prettiest posthole digger I know."

Caitlin giggled. "That's not such a great compliment since I'm the only girl posthole digger you know. I'm glad we're waiting until after the break to tell everyone about us. It's going to be hard to be away from you, though."

"Yeah, I'm trying not to think about that."

"Well, we still have a week together," she said. "Let's make the most of it. Do you remember what you told me would happen after I turned twelve?"

"No, was it something important?" he teased, looking her in the eyes before he glanced at her lips.

"Well, if you don't remember, then it must not have been that important to you," she said with a sigh as she turned around to head back to the house.

"I'm kiddin', Katie," he said, laughing as he grabbed her arm and pulled her back to him, "It's been hard to think of anything else."

"Sure you don't want to wait?" she said, suddenly feeling nervous.

"I can't wait any more," he whispered breathlessly, leaning forward to kiss her on the lips.

Caitlin didn't have time to close her mouth, much less her eyes as Finn kissed her for the first time. All she could think of was that her mouth was open—she hadn't protected her innocence. When Finn pulled back, Caitlin's hand flew to her mouth.

"I wasn't ready!" she said.

"Ready for what?"

"I didn't close my mouth," she whispered and paused for a moment. "But I don't feel any different."

Finn looked questioningly at her before he recalled their conversation on the way to town the day before.

"I don't know who told you what it means to become a woman, but it's not about the kissing," he said.

"It isn't?"

Finn shook his head, no.

"That's a relief. Then can we try it again? I can't remember what it felt like."

Finn grinned as he leaned down to softly kiss Caitlin on the lips.

She stood there stiff as a statue.

"You can kiss me back," he said.

"But I don't know how."

"Feel my lips."

Caitlin started to lift up her hand.

"No—with *your* lips... like this." He cupped her face with his hands and tilted her head. Then he leaned down again and came within a hair's breadth to her lips and stopped, waiting for her to respond.

She placed her hands on his chest and leaned into him, touching her lips to his, softly and tentatively. Something in her midriff fluttered with the sensation of connecting with Finn in such an intimate way.

"Oh," she said with eyes wide as she pulled back from him. "Did you feel that?"

Finn nodded.

"Are you sure this has nothing to do with me becoming a woman?"

Finn nodded again.

"Good, then we can do this as much as you want to." She lifted her chin and shut her eyes, poised for the next kiss.

Finn chuckled. "No, we can't, and we definitely can't let your daddy find out about this or he'll wring my neck for sure. And you'll have to help me be patient. I'm going to have trouble keeping you at arm's length from now on."

"Then kiss me goodnight, and we'll go back to the house," said Caitlin.

So Finn obliged in a most satisfying way.

Chapter 43

The entire Taylor family, minus Julia and Ethan, joined Finn and Caitlin working on the new windmill pasture fence early Monday morning. Jimmy rode over and met the crew of men ready to start work on the fence that would run alongside the road to town. He had them measuring and digging postholes from the existing pasture fence about two hundred yards from the ranch's entrance gate. Jimmy figured the Taylor crew would reach the road by the end of the day and would be able to start stringing the wire from the old property marker post on Tuesday. He determined that the crew of townsmen would have the holes dug and posts set by Wednesday and could pick up and help with stringing the wire.

The Johnson men from the ranch to the south would begin work on Tuesday on their stretch from the marker post west to just beyond Pecan Bayou. Ethan and Caitlin would start helping them in a few days. Ethan asked George if he could spare Finn for one more week of work after the Christmas break was over. Faith offered to tutor him at the ranch during that time so he wouldn't get behind in his studies. Caitlin felt like that would be the best birthday present of all if Finn's parents agreed to it. But that meant postponing their announcement further, which was fine since it meant they would have another week together.

Julia and Matthew reached a compromise Monday night. Matthew would go home with Matt, Justin, Allie, and Mercy on Tuesday. Julia and Jimmy would stay until Saturday, which would allow Jimmy to oversee the completion of the fence.

But Julia and Jimmy knew it also gave them some time alone with Faith to break the news of her true relationship with her brother.

Between the hard work to be completed in a short amount of time and most of the Taylors leaving on Tuesday, Wednesday night had come before Julia and Jimmy were able to find time alone with Faith. She had gone upstairs to put the little ones to bed, and Ethan had insisted on going to the barn to help Finn and Caitlin with the chores. They didn't seem too happy about him joining them, but Faith assumed they were concerned about Ethan's health and assured them that he was strong enough to handle it.

Julia thought something wasn't quite right with that assumption, but let the thought pass when she realized the moment had come to talk to Faith. She finished drying the dishes and hung the dish towels on the front of the stove to dry as Faith came down the stairs. Jimmy caught his mother's eye, and she nodded her head.

"Sis, can you come sit down for a moment?" he said, pulling out a chair for her. "Mother and I need to talk to you about something."

Faith raised her eyebrows as she looked from her brother to her mother. "Sounds serious," she said. "Is something wrong?"

"No, honey," said Julia, sitting down to face her. She turned to Jimmy. "I'm not sure how to even start this conversation."

"Let me," he said, sitting down beside his sister and taking her hand. "Faith, I'm your brother."

Faith grinned. "I know, silly."

"Good heavens, son," said Julia, taking over. "That's not the place to start. Sweetheart, something happened the day Jimmy and I were shot. I was confused... I guess the shock of the injury did something to my mind, and I began to re-live what happened the day Nantan was killed."

"Daddy told me that people said you were speaking the Apache language after y'all were shot," said Faith. "He didn't understand why."

"I didn't know he knew—we never talked about it," said Julia. "But it was so odd—I understood what people were saying when they spoke to me, but I didn't realize they couldn't understand me. I didn't even recognize Mercy when she came up to Jimmy lying in the street. I thought he was Nantan at that moment. And I thought little Jack was Jimmy."

"Oh, Mother, I wish I'd been there to help you that day. Were you in much pain?"

Julia shook her head, no.

"Yes, she was," said Jimmy.

"No more than you," said Julia.

"And what made it worse was that she started having nightmares about her past," said Jimmy.

"But losing Nantan was a good thing, right?" said Faith. "He did nothing but hurt you."

"No, honey. That's what we wanted to talk to you about. Nantan was wrong in kidnapping Justin and me, but he wasn't as bad a man as I let everyone believe."

Faith looked confused. "I don't understand. Why are you telling me this now? And what does this have to do with me? I don't even remember him."

"I'm sorry I haven't told you this before, Faith, but we had to go on after Matthew brought us back to Grace. I had to make a new life for you and Jimmy. Your mother died…"

"And you took care of me," said Faith. "You're the only mother I've ever known, and Daddy's the only father I've ever known. I've wondered occasionally about the couple who gave me life, but I've never dwelt on it. Is that what you're concerned about?"

Julia turned away, overcome with emotion.

"What she's trying to tell you is that she was protecting your relationship with our father by not revealing who your real parents were," said Jimmy, "especially your father."

"My father?" said Faith. "What are you saying?"

"Nantan was your father, too," said Jimmy, pausing for her to grasp the significance of the news.

"What?" she whispered.

"Nantan was your father," said Jimmy, "*and* mine."

Faith swallowed, and her lips trembled as she spoke. "Does this mean…"

"I'm your brother—your blood brother," he said. "We have the same father."

Faith's eyes shut and her face crinkled up as she let the thought sink in. *Her brother?! Jimmy was her true brother?*

She let out a sob as she fell into her brother's arms. Jimmy's cool expression melted as he gave in to the emotions he had kept pent up for weeks now.

Julia stood quietly and grabbed a shawl before slipping out the door. She wanted to give them some time alone, but she also wanted to tell Ethan and Caitlin the news so they wouldn't be alarmed seeing Faith crying when they came back to the house.

After a bit, Faith let go of Jimmy's neck and reached up and wiped her runny nose. She shuddered at the end of a good long cry.

Jimmy exhaled. "I can breathe now."

She leaned back and looked at her brother.

"I knew there was a deeper connection between us," she said, ignoring the jest. "I just felt it."

She turned around to face her mother and saw she was gone.

"I'm sure she's talking to Ethan and Caitlin."

Faith thought for a moment. "Who was my mother?" she asked.

"Her name was Dark Moon," he said. "Nantan's sister-in-law. She became his wife after his first wife and son were killed."

"What happened to her?"

"She died in a fall when you were only two months old," he said. "Mother nursed both of us from then on. I was a month or two older than you."

"How long have you known?" she asked, and then answered herself. "Oh yeah, since the shooting. But why didn't Mother tell us before that?"

"She didn't want Father to know that you were Nantan's child, too. She didn't want to jeopardize your relationship with him."

"Oh. Do you really think it would have?"

"It caused problems between him and me for years, remember?"

Faith nodded slowly, remembering.

"And now she's afraid you're going to be angry with her for not telling you before now."

Faith shook her head. "She's my mother—I know she was only looking out for me. But it feels like a dream to hear this now. I'm so afraid I'm going to wake up, and it won't be true."

"I've always been your brother, blood or no, so that hasn't changed."

"Yes, but it means so much more to know this," she said, and then caught her breath. "And Nah-kay is really my grandmother, too! I wonder why she never let on."

"What would she say? She's never known that *you* didn't know you were Nantan's daughter. Has she ever treated you as anything other than a granddaughter?"

Faith shook her head and smiled with the realization.

At that moment, the door opened and Ethan's head tentatively peeked around the door frame.

Faith waved him in, and Caitlin and Finn followed. Faith walked over and hugged her husband.

"Are you all right?" he asked, looking over his wife at Jimmy.

"I'm giddy at the moment," she said. "I'm still trying to grasp the fact that Jimmy and I are actually brother and sister."

"I'm not surprised," Caitlin piped up, squeezing between them and hugging her mother. "Y'all are too much alike."

"Where's Meemaw?" Faith asked quietly.

"Sitting on the porch," Caitlin whispered back.

Faith started for the door.

"It's cold out there, honey... here," said Ethan, slipping out of his coat and wrapping it around Faith.

She gave him a grateful smile before grabbing a lantern and walking outside. The chilly air slapped her in the face, and she let out a groan of discomfort and pulled the coat more tightly around her. Julia sat in one of the rocking chairs. Faith could see that she had been crying, too. She hung the lantern on a hook and pulled a chair around to face her mother.

"I love you, Momma," she said, covering her mother's hands with her own. "That's never going to change."

Julia's face crumpled as the tears began to flow again. "I'm so sorry, honey."

"Sorry for what?" said Faith. "I know this must have been hard for you to relive those painful memories, and I know you were protecting me by hiding my true identity. But I'm so glad you decided to tell me and Jimmy. This is the best gift you could ever give us to know that we're truly brother and sister."

"I was so afraid you would be angry at me."

"I can't begin to comprehend what you went through taking care of Justin and two babies out there away from civilization. And you didn't have to take me with you when Daddy found us, but you did."

"After your mother passed, I thought of you as my own," said Julia. "I could never leave you."

Faith nodded. "Jimmy told me that you nursed me from the time I was two months old."

Julia smiled. "You were an easy baby to raise. Your brother was another story."

"I can imagine," said Faith. "It's cold out here—let's go inside."

"Don't you want to know about your father?" asked Julia.

Faith paused as tears filled her eyes. "I know my father very well, Mother. I know he loves me and he'd move heaven and earth for me if need be, and he did that this past week. I'll never forget seeing my brothers ride up to the porch that day, and then realizing Daddy had come to help, too. I'll never forget how that made me feel to know they cared that much—and that you and Mercy and Allie came all this way to help, too. It still overwhelms me. As for the man who was responsible for bringing me into this world, I'm grateful that he's given me a brother, and for now that's all I need to know."

"Your father must never know."

"He won't," said Faith, standing and helping Julia to her feet. "Now come inside. You know, I thought it was odd that you chose to stay longer when Daddy went back to Grace. I understand now. But what reason did you give him for staying longer?"

"I told him that you still needed your mother, and that was enough for him."

Chapter 44

On Thursday morning, Ethan insisted on riding in the wagon to examine the fence. Everyone held their breath as they approached the windmill. The barbed wire was strung from the marker to the water alley to the windmill tank and back to the original fence line and as far east as the eye could see.

"I can't believe y'all were able to get all of this done!" Ethan said, pleased to see the progress on the fence.

"Everybody's worked really hard this past week," said Jimmy, walking his horse up beside the wagon. "And I was telling you about Caitlin and Finn figuring out a way to stop the fence cutters…"

"What in tarnations is that?" Ethan interrupted him as he shielded his eyes to get a better look at the fenced-in alley leading up to the windmill.

Caitlin thought his breath looked something like smoke coming from a dragon. His face was turning red, too. She slunk down further in the back of the wagon. Ethan climbed down from the wagon seat and limped up to the tank.

"It's a water alley, Ethan," said Jimmy. "Caitlin came up with the idea and we all think it's pretty ingenious. And we haven't had any fence-cutting since the kids put the sign up."

"What sign?"

"A sign that offers to share the water."

"Cows can't read," said Ethan. "That's the stupidest thing I've ever heard. We need to close that gap. This is our land and our water and no law is forcing us to share it."

"But, Daddy…" said Caitlin.

"There's no *but, Daddy* about it, Katie. We've already talked about this, and it's settled. We're not sharing our water with anyone. I paid for the

217

drilling of this well and the windmill sitting above it—none of the free-grazers offered to share that expense with me. They're taking advantage of us. Why should we treat them any differently than they're treating us?"

"Because the Bible tells us to," said Caitlin. "We're Christians, Daddy. Momma says we don't act like the rest of the world."

That stopped Ethan in his tracks for a moment, but then he still didn't back down. He turned his back to everyone.

"She's got a point there, Ethan," said Jimmy. "We haven't had one incident of them tearing up the fence since this water alley has been laid out."

Ethan turned around and limped back to the wagon. "If I need your advice, Jimmy, I'll ask for it. But until then, I'd appreciate you keeping your opinions to yourself."

Jimmy's mouth dropped open. His conscience told him to let it go, but his anger wouldn't let him.

"So our coming to help you with the fence this week means nothing to you? Well, then we did it for Faith, who, by the way, is the reason you have this dang fence and this land and this windmill, if you've already forgotten. Tell me, Ethan, what exactly have you brought to the table? Or are you a free-grazer yourself, but in this case, with my sister's money?"

Jimmy had gone too far with his words, and he immediately regretted it. "I'm sorry, Ethan. You know I...I didn't mean that."

Ethan said nothing as he struggled to climb back on the wagon seat, but Caitlin could see he was angry—angrier than she had ever seen. It horrified her to see two of the people she loved the most in the world fighting, and over something she had started. She jumped off the back of the wagon and shouted, "I'm sorry!" and turned and ran towards the house sobbing.

Finn glared at Jimmy and Ethan before stepping off the wagon and going after Caitlin.

Ethan started to turn the wagon around. Jimmy reached out and pulled the reins to keep the horses from going anywhere.

"Get out of my way, Jimmy," said Ethan angrily.

"Dang it, Ethan! I'm sorry I said that. I'm just tired, that's all. I swear I didn't mean it. You're the best thing that's ever happened to my sister. I just let my temper get the best of me again. Forgive me, brother. I'm going to go apologize to Katie and Finn, too. Faith will never forgive me for hurting you. Please... let's make this right before we go back. I won't be able to face my sister and mother if we don't."

Ethan glared at Jimmy and his face skewed up before he dropped his head. "You're right."

"I know. I'm an idiot," said Jimmy.

"No, you're right," he said dejectedly. "I've brought absolutely nothing to this marriage. And I'm so scared I'm going to lose everything if I don't keep a tight rein on it all."

"What are you talking about?"

Ethan ran his hand across his mouth. "I've never had anything before—I don't know if I'm smart enough to be running this ranch—to make a life for my family out here. I had no idea something as insignificant as a little knife wound could almost take us down. We would've lost all our cattle if it weren't for you Taylors. And I don't know if this fence would've ever been finished if y'all hadn't come. You seem to know exactly what to do, and I've been pretty worthless the past couple of weeks..."

"For good reason," said Jimmy. "I've been pretty worthless for most of my life. I'm still trying to make up for that. But I have to give my father credit for knowing what to do. This was his idea; I probably would've made things worse. But I've worked with you, Ethan, and you've got what it takes to make a go of this ranch. You're not afraid of hard work. You've been preparing for this for years. You stand up for yourself and you've defended this ranch and your family. You've already made good improvements and have solid plans for raising more cattle and expanding your operations. Everyone suffers through a drought, but your ranch is in better shape than most around here because of what you've done. And as for bringing nothing to the table, you've brought plenty. I couldn't have asked for a better partner for my sister than you. And then there's that remarkable daughter of yours, who tends to act a lot like her father."

The corner of Ethan's mouth turned up as he looked over at the water alley. "That is pretty smart. And Katie thought of it?"

Jimmy nodded. "And Finn helped design it."

"And she's right," he said with a sigh. "We're not supposed to act like the world. *Give and it shall be given unto you.* That's definitely not the world's way, but I know it works. I've been so afraid of failing my family and losing everything that it's turned me into a selfish old miser. I let my doubts and insecurity overshadow my faith."

He took a deep breath and looked around. "And you're sure this is the reason they've stopped bothering the fence?"

"The kids didn't tell you because they didn't want you to worry while you were laid up, but they had more incidents of night riders tearing up the fence line until they put in the water alley and the sign. Then it stopped."

"Let's go find the kids," said Ethan. "I have an apology to make, too."

Chapter 45

That evening, Caitlin snuggled up closer to her grandmother in bed.

"It's getting colder," she said. "I'm happy to be back in my own bed, but I guess it'd be awfully chilly if I was by myself. I'm glad you're still here, Meemaw."

Julia smiled in the dark. "You think this is cold? Where I grew up in Illinois, we'd have to break a layer of ice in the water bucket in the mornings just to make coffee."

"Really?"

"And the snow would pile up so high at times, we couldn't even get out of the house."

"How'd you milk your cow?"

"We didn't have to," said Julia. "Her milk would be frozen solid until we could thaw out her udders in the spring."

"Really?!"

Julia chuckled. "No, Miss Gullible, I'm just teasing you. My father made sure our livestock was in the barn. We had a huge barn with lots of storage for feed. And it was a great place to play."

"Do you ever miss your family in Illinois?"

"Yes."

"Have you ever gone back to visit them since you came to Texas?"

"Once—my brother John and I went back for a visit. I was glad and sad at the same time."

"Why?"

"I was so happy to see my parents and my sisters and brothers, but when we left, I was afraid it would be the last time I'd ever see them. I think I bawled off and on all the way back to Texas."

"Was it the last time you saw them?"

Caitlin could feel her grandmother nod.

"Both of my parents have passed away since then, and I lost two of my other brothers within a month's time five years ago."

"But you'll see them again in heaven, right?"

"Yes; they were believers. I'm sure I will, and that's such a comfort to me."

"What about your sisters?"

"We still write each other occasionally. Life keeps us so busy, though, it's hard to make time to keep up."

"I'm glad you make time for us," said Caitlin.

"Me, too. I know your mother asked you earlier, and you told her nothing, but what really happened this morning?"

"I'm not supposed to tell."

"Oh. Is everything all right now?"

"Uh-huh."

"Good."

Caitlin waited for her grandmother to press her.

But that didn't happen.

"Well, I'm not supposed to tell you what was actually said, but I can say that Daddy and Uncle Jimmy had words, and I was afraid it was my fault, but they apologized to each other and to me for upsetting me, and everything's all right now."

"Was it about your water alley?"

"Uh-huh, but Daddy likes the idea now, so we're going to keep it. You won't say anything about it, will you?"

"I won't."

"Daddy doesn't like surprises, and I think we kind of hurt his feelings by not asking him, so from now on when I have an idea, I'm going to run it by him first."

"I'm glad you learned something from it," said Julia. "Did you know that some people go through life making the same mistakes over and over again, never learning from them?"

"That's sad."

"They blame their mistakes on everyone and everything around them except for themselves, so they never recognize that the problem needs to be fixed in here…" said Julia, touching Caitlin's forehead, "or here." She touched her chest and felt something hard. "What's that?"

Caitlin's hand flew to her heart locket. "Just a locket I wear."

"That reminds me, I haven't seen your racing pin yet."

"I'll show it to you tomorrow."

"I'm so proud of you, Katie, in more ways than just outrunning the boys," said Julia. "Sweet dreams, honey."

"Love you, Meemaw."

"Love you more."

Early Friday morning, Ethan said that the crew from town would finish stringing the barbed wire on the fence alongside the main road, and that Jimmy would stay with them and keep them on task. Ethan told Finn and Caitlin they could go work with the Johnsons on the south fence line.

"Why can't we just let them do it themselves, Dad?" said Caitlin. "I'm tired of digging postholes."

"Good neighbors share the expense of a fence," said Ethan. "We'll be using it, too, so we need to do our part. Take the wagon around the barn and load some more posts; we're responsible for providing half of the posts in that stretch of fence up to Pecan Bayou. It's shorter and won't take nearly as long as the other fence. Those Johnson boys will waste no time getting it up so it'll be finished before you know it, Katie. Then you can rest."

"Come in for lunch, kids," said Faith. "I'll have a hot meal for you."

"Come on, Caitlin" said Finn, grabbing her arm. "We can do this."

She let him pull her out the door.

"Love y'all," she said over her shoulder.

"Love you more!" a chorus responded behind her.

Faith did the laundry a day early so Julia and Jimmy would have clean clothes to pack for the trip home. Julia stayed inside and mended some pants while keeping an eye on Sam and the roast cooking. The laundry involved heavy lifting, and her shoulder still pained her to lift with it. But cooking was no problem.

Everyone came in around noon for roast beef with carrots and potatoes, and thick slices of buttered oatmeal bread. Julia told Caitlin that it was an old family recipe from her Aunt Tillie in Illinois. Julia had also made two pies with pecans gathered on the ranch.

Ethan decided he could go back with Jimmy and help oversee the last of the wire stretching. He assured Faith he wouldn't overdo it, and winked at Caitlin when he turned to walk out the door with hardly a limp at all.

"Love you, Dad!" she said, relieved to see her father acting more like his old self. "Come on, Finn. The faster we get going, the faster we'll finish."

Julia walked up the stairs with a stack of freshly ironed clothes and placed them on Caitlin's bed. She reached underneath it and grabbed her bag and set it beside the clothes to start packing. When she opened the door to the chiffarobe, she saw Caitlin's cigar box again and realized she still hadn't seen her granddaughter's racing pin yet. She pulled it down and looked again at the lid cluttered with buttons and bits of brightly colored ribbon.

She scooted her bag over and sat on the bed as she opened the lid. There it was—right on top of everything—how had she missed it before? The medal was simply a tarnished winged foot pinned to a wide loop of ribbon. Julia smiled as she imagined Caitlin leaving the boys in her dust. Directly underneath the pin sat the slice of cedar. She picked it up again and sniffed it and read again the carved letters in the heart and on the back. With a start, it dawned on her that the letters were phonetic and not the actual initials of names.

"Oh my," she said aloud, realizing she was trespassing on a secret. She placed the piece of cedar and the pin back in the box and stood to return it to the shelf in the chiffarobe.

"Mother!" Faith called out from the stairway.

Julia jumped at the sound and dropped the box and the contents on the floor.

"Are you all right?"

"Yes, I'm fine! I'll be right there," she said as she started to gather up the scattered treasures.

"No need—I just wanted to let you know I've put the girls down for their naps on my bed, and I'll be in the cellar with Sam."

"It's too cold down there for that baby," said Julia, standing up and stepping out of the room as she shut the door behind her. She would pick up the rest of the spilled items later. "Let me rock him to sleep while you're down there."

Julia hurried down the stairs and settled in the rocker beside the warm fire so Faith could hand her Sam. He squirmed for a bit, telling her, "I be up," which actually meant he wanted down. Then he told her, "I be back," which worked for the first few times at the dinner table until everyone figured out he had no intentions of coming back once he got down.

"Sorry, Sam," she said. "You need to rest, too, honey."

Sam fussed a bit longer, but Julia was firm.

"You're too smart for your own good. Rest here with Meemaw for just a little while."

She began to softly hum a tune, and Sam eventually laid his head on her chest. Julia shut her eyes, trying to burn into her memory how it felt to hold him. It would have to last her for a long time. She didn't know when she would see Faith and her family again. She opened her eyes to see if Sam was asleep yet.

His eyes were still wide open.

Julia almost chuckled aloud. She didn't mind, though. That just meant she could rock and hold him a while longer. She hummed another tune and watched his eyes get heavier and heavier until he finally went to sleep.

Faith came through the pantry closet under the stairs and smiled at her mother.

"Finally!" she whispered as she came over to take him from Julia's arms. "He fights sleep more than any child I've ever been around."

"Your brother was the same way. I think he was afraid he'd miss something."

Julia stood and stretched as Faith carried Sam to her bedroom. She came back, telling her mother she would be working in the cellar a while longer, so Julia returned to Caitlin's room to finish packing.

She opened the door and saw the remaining treasures scattered on the floor, so she knelt down to pick them up.

But her heart stopped when she saw the white feather.

"Oh, Lord, no," she said. "Please, Father, not this."

She stood and backed out of Caitlin's room. She ran downstairs and out the door, forgetting the cold and the ache in her shoulder. She ran around the house and down the road toward the windmill pasture.

Chapter 46

C aitlin stood beside the wagon. "I can't believe we're quitting early."

"Well, the Johnsons are," said Finn, waving to the men leaving in their wagon. "Do you want to stay a little longer?"

"Are you kidding? I'm so tired I can hardly see straight. Let's go back and work in the barn or something. I'm sure we can find something less back-breaking to do."

"All right. Get in the wagon—I'll load the tools."

Caitlin climbed up in the seat and looked back at Finn. He threw the tamping tool and a can on the back of the wagon and walked back toward the fence line to get the pickax and shovel.

Caitlin grabbed the reins and started the horses forward. Finn looked up and saw her grinning mischievously at him as the wagon started to leave him.

"Hey! Cut it out, Katie!" he shouted over his shoulder as he walked up to the tools. He picked them up and started jogging back.

"Catch me if you can!" shouted Caitlin as she laughed and slapped the ends of the reins on the horses' rumps. The wagon jolted forward as the horses began to take off in a run. The wagon was off the pasture road, and she didn't realize how rough the ride would be back towards the windmill. She grabbed the seat to keep from falling, but dropped one of the reins in the process.

She could hear Finn shouting behind her, so she pulled on the single rein to try to stop the horses. But all that did was turn the horses severely to the left back towards the pasture instead of the road. She turned around and saw Finn running after her, but the horses were too fast for him.

Caitlin began to panic. She didn't know whether to jump or to try to reach the other rein to stop them before the wagon overturned. In a split second, she chose the latter. She had done this before; she could do it again, her mind told her. But she pushed the thought out of her head that Finn was holding her that first time.

She held onto the single rein and grabbed the arm of the seat and leaned out as far as she could to reach the loose rein...

Finn screamed in terror as he saw Caitlin fall forward behind the horses as the wagon lurched over some obstacle. The horses kept running, unaware that no one was driving them.

A crumpled form lay in their wake.

Finn reached Caitlin in a matter of seconds and feared the worst. She was facing him, but her lower body was turned at an odd angle.

"Katie?!" he sobbed, falling down beside her. "Are you all right? Oh, dear God. Please let her be all right."

But he knew she wasn't.

Surely this was a bad dream, he thought. This couldn't be happening. He looked around, unsure of what he was supposed to do. Should he go for help? Should he try to carry her back to the house? He was afraid to touch her, though.

She moaned.

"Katie?" he cried. "Can you hear me?"

"Yes," she said the word as she exhaled, but her eyes remained shut.

"I don't know what to do," Finn sobbed.

"I'm sorry," she whispered.

"Don't talk; I'll go for help."

"Don't... leave me..."

"But I need to..."

"Please don't leave me..."

"Lord, help us!" he said, holding her hand.

"Finn!!" someone shouted behind him.

Finn looked around to see Mrs. Taylor running towards him. He began to sob.

"What happened?" Julia asked, trying to catch her breath.

"She fell from the wagon."

"Caitlin, I'm here, honey," she said, going down on her knees beside her granddaughter. "Where's the wagon, Finn?"

Finn pointed the direction the horses had run.

"Go find it and bring it back. I'll stay with Katie."

Finn took off running as fast as he could.

"Meemaw?"

"I'm right here, sweetie," said Julia, trying to keep her composure. She gently brushed Caitlin's hair out of her face and then grasped her hand. "What happened, honey?"

"I fell off the wagon," she said weakly.

"Where was Finn?"

"It wasn't his fault," she said, trying to open her eyes. "I took off without him and lost a rein. I fell when I reached for it."

"Sometimes we do silly things when we're in love."

Caitlin's eyes turned toward her. "You know?"

Julia nodded and smiled as the tears spilled from her eyes. "I saw your racing pin, and I saw the heart he carved for you."

"He's so smart." She grimaced when she tried to turn her head.

"Are you in pain, honey? Can I help you in any way?"

"I think I knocked my noggin on something, but nothin' else hurts," she said. "I can just hear Daddy now—boy, am I gonna be in trouble."

"No, you won't."

"I'm cold, Meemaw. Would you warm my hands?"

Julia looked down at the hand she had been holding and realized Caitlin couldn't feel it. She pulled her skirt and petticoats from underneath her and tucked them around her granddaughter.

"Tell Mom and Dad I'm sorry."

"You have nothing to be sorry about," said Julia, and under her breath she pleaded, *Lord, don't let her die! She's only begun to live.*

"I'm tired," she said, closing her eyes. "Would you mind if I rested for a moment?"

"No, honey, you rest. Meemaw will be right here."

She leaned down and kissed her cheek.

"Love you," Caitlin whispered.

"Love you more," said Julia.

And with a soft sigh, she was still.

"Katie?! Katie, honey?!" Julia patted her cheek.

No response.

She laid her ear on her chest and heard only silence.

"Dear God, no!!" she screamed. "Katie!! Come back! Please, Lord, don't let her go! Take me instead! Please..."

227

Chapter 47

The church was filled to over-flowing on Saturday afternoon. The whole town was in shock with the news. The pastor said many comforting words, and George Samuel even shared a few stories about Caitlin, including the fact that she had outrun all the boys in primary school last year. But that's not what everyone remembered about the funeral.

Finn had disappeared after they brought Caitlin to town Friday evening. No one had seen him since, although K. James and R. James had spent hours looking for him. But even the pianist stopped playing at the end of the sermon when Finn walked up the aisle to the front of the church and stopped beside the open casket. He looked haggard and lost. France put a hanky to her mouth to keep from sobbing aloud. Folks could have heard a pin drop when he reached in the casket for a moment and then leaned down and kissed Caitlin right on the lips in front of God and everyone. Then he walked back down the aisle and out of the church.

The preacher announced that the burial would be a private service at the Murray Ranch and thanked everyone for attending. The deacons ushered each row of mourners past the coffin so everyone could pay their last respects to Caitlin Murray and her family. When only the Samuel and Murray families remained to say their goodbyes, Emma and Zane were inconsolable when they saw the heart necklace around Caitlin's neck that Finn had uncovered for all to see.

The Samuels took the younger Murray children outside to give Ethan and Faith some time with Caitlin. Julia and Jimmy started to leave, too, but Faith asked them to stay. They all clung to each other and wept more tears as they looked at Caitlin.

"I don't want to close this casket," said Ethan, sobbing. "I can't put her in the ground."

"But you know she's not there anymore, Ethan," said Jimmy.

Faith turned to her mother. "I have to believe in the sovereignty of God right now, or we're not going to survive this, Mother."

"I asked God to take me instead," said Julia, "but it must have been Katie's time."

"It's just not fair," said Faith. "She's too young to be taken from us. And I still don't understand how you knew something had happened to her."

"I didn't know it was Katie until I found her in the pasture," said Julia. "I just knew something was wrong."

"But how did you know to go?"

"I saw the white feather in her treasure box. God has used that sign several times in my life when I needed him the most. But in this case, I've just felt a heaviness in my heart for several weeks."

"Why didn't God let us in on that? Why didn't he let us say goodbye to her and tell her we loved her?" said Ethan, choking on his words.

"But she wouldn't have told you goodbye, Ethan," said Julia. "Didn't she quit saying that word years ago?"

Faith nodded. "She always said, *love you*. Think about it, Ethan. She left nothing unsaid to us, sweetheart. And we always responded back with…"

"Love you more," he said.

"And you know we'll see her again," said Julia.

Ethan sighed. "That's what everyone's been telling me, and I know that, but it's not what I want to hear right now. I don't know if I can wait that long. I miss her so badly already."

"We all do," said Faith. "Our lives won't be the same without her."

"You all won't forget her, will you?" Ethan asked Jimmy and Julia. "It's important to me that she won't be forgotten."

Jimmy embraced his brother-in-law. "We'll never forget Katie. I promise."

He and Faith leaned down and kissed their daughter's face for the last time in this world.

"Love you, Katie," said Ethan as he and Faith slowly closed the lid to the coffin. They walked clinging to each other down the aisle and out of the church as Jimmy and Julia supported them arm in arm at their sides.

George and France had volunteered the use of Mercy's wagon to carry Caitlin back to the ranch, and Faith and Ethan smiled through their tears when they saw that their dear friends had usurped the funeral hearse driver's role and insisted on driving the wagon themselves. The rest of the Samuel children followed behind in borrowed buggies.

As the funeral procession passed through Brownwood, Faith was touched to see most of the townsfolk had stopped to line the streets in respect for the Murrays and their loss. As they rode slowly by the new jail, Faith saw fingers clinging to the bars on a high window. Then a face slowly rose up beside the hands. She was shocked to see it was Bear. His eyes met hers, but he lost his grip and disappeared from sight. Faith glanced at Jimmy and Ethan in the front seat to see if they had seen him, too, and was relieved that they hadn't.

Ethan insisted on stopping by Albert Beights' house on the way out of town. Jimmy pulled the buggy to a stop, and the funeral procession stopped behind them.

"Ethan?"

"This won't take long," he said as he climbed out of the buggy and walked up to the house.

"What does he think he's doing?" said Faith. "This isn't the time to do business."

"He must have a good reason, sis," said Jimmy, turning around.

Faith looked at her brother's face and nodded, and then turned to her mother. "I noticed something back in the town square."

"What's that, honey?"

"I tried to acknowledge folks for stopping to show their respect; that really touched my heart. But when I caught their eye, most women looked away weeping. But then there were some who didn't look away. They were crying, too, but they didn't look away from me."

"Did you know these women?"

Faith nodded.

"Tell me about the ones that didn't look away."

Faith thought for a moment. "Dorris Marsh and Leslie Terry and…" her eyes widened. "They know, Momma. They know what we're going through. Dorris lost her husband and two sons in the war. And Leslie lost several children with the consumption a few years ago." She paused. "And I probably looked away from her at her children's funerals because it hurt too bad to even imagine what she was going through. But I know now."

Julia put her arm around her daughter. "Maybe it would help to talk to them some day."

Faith leaned on her mother and said, "And I won't look away next time."

Ethan came from behind the Beights' house and climbed into the buggy.

"Why did you stop at Albert's house today? Surely not that post-hole thing," said Faith, fussing at her husband.

"It was important, Faith," he said.

They buried Caitlin on a rise above Pecan Bayou. A huge oak tree shaded the area. Ethan told everyone that he had picked this place out for him and Faith's final resting place.

"But I never expected one of our children would be here before we would," he said, as the tears came again.

Faith put her arms around him, as she had done dozens of times since yesterday.

Ethan regained his composure to say he wanted to put a pretty iron fence around this area and a family monument at least as big as George's. He wiped his eyes as he smiled through his tears.

"I'm not going to tell you how tall mine is," said George, patting him on the back. "But as for putting in the fence, I'm sure Finn would be glad to help you."

But France wasn't so sure. Finn didn't even come back to the ranch for the graveside service.

"Yeah, Finn and I have some talking to do," said Ethan. "Where is he, by the way?"

"Ethan, now isn't the time," said Faith quietly.

"We haven't seen him since the church," said France. "He's too upset."

"Well, tell him I want to talk to him when you see him," said Ethan. "I don't blame him for what happened. It was just a senseless accident. But I still want to talk to him."

George nodded.

On Sunday, the Murrays stayed home from church. Julia took over the cooking and watching the children to let Faith rest. She didn't come out of the bedroom until after the noon meal, and she was still in her nightgown. Julia offered to fix her a plate, but Faith said she just wanted some water. She drank several cupfuls and turned around and went back to bed.

Ethan busied himself around the barn and asked Jimmy if he would go get the sign Caitlin had painted and posted at the water alley. He said he would and wondered if Ethan had changed his mind about making the water available. After Jimmy brought it back to the barn, Ethan painted another line to the sign, which now read:

Free Water
Thanks to Caitlin Murray

"I want folks to know that this was Katie's idea," he said. "And I know cows can't read, but people pass that way occasionally, and I just think it's fitting to let them know who's responsible for that water alley."

"Good idea."

Julia made a pallet by piling several quilts on the floor by the raised hearth for the girls to lie down for their naps. She sat in the rocker and wrestled Sam for a few minutes until he finally went to sleep. Then she laid him beside the girls and covered him.

She walked upstairs to Caitlin's door and paused. She couldn't sleep in that room the past two nights without Katie in her arms. She put her hand on the door and leaned her forehead against it and wept again.

Baby girl, do you know just how much you are loved? Do you know just how much you will be missed?

Julia's mind told her that time would eventually heal this family, but at that moment her heart told her this was more than she and her family could bear. How could she help Faith and Ethan get through this when her own heart felt such despair?

Lord, your Word says that the things that happen to us aren't new and different—I know everyone experiences the loss of loved ones at one time or other. You tell us we can trust You—that we can let You bear our burdens, and I'm so thankful for that because, Lord, this is a huge one. I'm admitting to You, Father, that we're not going to get through the loss of Katie without You.

Give me wisdom in helping Faith and Ethan. Comfort our hearts here and the hearts of my family in Grace who have yet to hear of this tragedy. Show me what to do. Give me the courage to do the difficult things, Lord... like opening this door.

I ask all of this in Jesus' name.

Julia took a deep breath and opened the door. The sense of loss almost knocked her down as she stepped into the room.

Lord, help me.

Chapter 48

The room was cold. Julia walked over and sat down on the bed. She picked up Caitlin's feather pillow and put it to her face and wept some more.

When she thought she couldn't cry another tear, she looked around the room. The box of Caitlin's treasures sat opened on the dresser. She noticed some of the rocks were still scattered on the floor, so she got down on her hands and knees and started to pick them up. She smiled when she recalled the treasure hunting walks they'd had.

"Momma!?"

Julia looked up to see Faith standing in the doorway crying. But she still showed concern about her mother.

"Are you all right? Did you fall?" asked Faith.

"No, sweetie, I was just picking up Katie's rocks," said Julia as the tears came again.

Faith went to the floor and wrapped her arms around her mother. They began to talk through their tears.

"I was remembering good things, though," said Julia, wiping her nose. "Katie loved to collect rocks—I can't believe your house isn't filled up with them."

Faith chuckled. "It would've been a long time ago if I hadn't gotten rid of them. She'd walk in the front door with a skirt full, and I'd gradually chunk them out the back door when she wasn't looking. No telling how many of the same rocks kept finding their way back in the house."

"I didn't know if I could come back in here," said Julia. "I had to ask God to help me."

"I know—I've avoided it, too," said Faith, looking around. "But now that I'm in here, I feel such love in this room. It's all right if we keep it the way it is for a while, isn't it? I don't want to forget anything. I'm so afraid I'm going to forget something about her, and that's all I have left of her now. It breaks my heart to think that Cele and Ella and Sam won't remember their sister after a while."

She clung to her mother as she cried.

Julia brushed the hair away from her daughter's eyes and continued to run her fingers through her long, straight hair.

"That feels good," whispered Faith as she shut her eyes. "I knew grief hurts the heart, but I didn't know it made everything else hurt, too. I feel like somebody's taken a stick and beaten me. And I'm so tired. It sapped all my strength just to walk up the stairs."

Julia could see the pain etched in her daughter's face, and her eyelids were swollen from crying. Julia's heart ached for her.

An idea came to mind.

"How 'bout we start writing down our memories of Katie—our experiences with her, the funny things she did, what she was like through each of our eyes. Then we'll have something to go back to and remind ourselves, and to share with Cele and Ella and Sam."

Faith nodded her head. "Ethan would like that, too."

"It's chilly up here," said Julia, shivering.

"Cold? And this comes from someone who used to have to break the ice in the water bucket just to make coffee when she lived up north?"

Julia smiled. "I told Katie that very story a couple of nights ago."

"I'm going to write down that memory about you."

"Let's go downstairs where it's warm," said Julia. "You can get your brush and let me brush your hair for you like I used to do."

Faith smiled wearily and nodded. "I'd like that."

She stood and helped her mother stand. They walked out the door and Julia started to close it behind her.

"Leave it open now, Momma," said Faith. "Ethan's going to have to face it eventually."

But Ethan refused to go upstairs at all the next few days. He wouldn't even allow himself to look at the stairwell. He coped by staying as busy as possible from sun-up to sundown. His goal each day was to work so hard that he would be exhausted by the time his head hit the pillow, and sleep would overtake him before the anguish came.

On Monday, Faith told her mother that she needed to be on the stage the following afternoon.

"We'll be fine, Momma. I appreciate you being here, but I know you and Jimmy need to be home. You've been away from Grace too long."

"I'll go home with your father."

"But he doesn't even know what happened yet."

"He'll find out tomorrow, honey. Jimmy went to the stage office Saturday and canceled my ticket and sent a letter in my place. And you know your father will be back on the next stage."

"So you'll be here another week?"

Julia nodded. She could see that Faith was visibly relieved.

"I'm sorry to be putting you out."

"You're not putting me out—this is where I need to be right now."

On Thursday, Ethan and Jimmy went to town to pick up some supplies, including a new branding iron made by Mr. Beights. On Friday, they rounded up the cattle and brought them into the horse trap, and on Saturday morning, three of the Samuel boys and their father George came out to help Ethan and Jimmy with the branding. Finn was invited, too, but he declined. Joseph had already left for Waco on the mid-week stage to start the new term at Baylor on Monday. He told his parents he planned to transfer to Texas A.M.C. in the fall. He had also drawn the design for the posthole digger that he would include with the patent application he would mail soon.

George and Ethan added more wood on the fire heating the brand. They watched Jimmy showing the boys how to rope a calf.

"That's some brand, Ethan. Don't think there's another one like it in the country."

"Katie wanted a heart with an M in the middle of it," he said. "But I told her I didn't want my bulls and steers running around with hearts on their rumps."

"It's obvious you had a change of heart, I see."

Ethan smiled wryly at the jab. "Actually, Finn designed this brand."

"Really?"

"For Katie. He carved it for her."

George wasn't sure how to respond to that.

"Did you know he was sweet on her?" Ethan asked.

"No, I didn't."

"I wonder why they hid it from us. I've been wanting to talk to him, but he's avoiding us."

"He's still hurting, Ethan."

"Katie was too young to have a beau. He should've let her be."

"Finn would never disrespect Caitlin—and I think he blames himself for what happened, although it was clearly a senseless accident."

"I don't know why she took off in that wagon without him," said Ethan.

"They were just being kids."

"I keep telling myself that maybe if I'd been there, it wouldn't have happened... or if I'd taught her better..."

"Don't torture yourself with that, Ethan—it's not going to change anything except drive you crazy."

"I know... and I don't blame Finn, or maybe I do in some way... I don't mean to. Finn's a good kid... I'm just angry at what happened, and I'm missing Katie so bad at times I don't think I can make it."

George put his hand on Ethan's shoulder.

"It's only been a week, Ethan. Give yourself some time."

"But little things like this seem to help," he said, picking up the heart-shaped branding iron with the letters KT in the middle. He pressed it against an old board, watching the wood begin to smoke beneath the hot iron. "Love Katie," he read aloud. "It's another way for me to remember her by."

"Do you want me to tell Finn?"

Ethan shook his head, no. "I'll show him when he's ready to talk to me."

Chapter 49

B ut after four more weeks, Finn continued to steer clear of Ethan and Faith, even to the point he wouldn't come home after church when the Murrays came for Sunday dinner.

"Ethan tried to talk to Finn after church again today, but he just ducked his head and walked away from him," said Faith, drying the last pan. She hung the damp towel on the back of a chair. "Is he ever going to be able to face us?"

"I'm worried about him," said France. "I know he's still hurting, but he won't talk to us about it. We've even forced him to sit down and listen to us, but it's like there's a wall between us. We don't know how to help him, and he doesn't seem to know how to get past this."

"I'm not sure we're doing much better," said Faith. "Sam was trying to jump the other night, and the best he could do was lift up one leg and prance around in a circle. He looked so funny, I laughed out loud at him, but Ethan frowned at me like I'd done something terrible. The girls are so sad, but I think they're responding more to the way we're acting rather than mourning Caitlin. I miss her terribly, France, but when is it all right to start living again? It's not fair to Ella and Cele and Sam to live in such despair."

"It's not disrespecting Caitlin's memory to laugh, honey," said France. "God can give us peace and joy even in the midst of difficult circumstances. You concentrate on raising those babies with joy and laughter. There will always be a hole in your heart, and moments of grief and sadness are still ahead of you, but for their sake don't let it consume you. Ethan will come around eventually."

"What are you going to do about Finn?"

"I don't know."

"Hopefully he'll come around, too."

France sighed and nodded. "I'm glad your mother was able to stay with you longer."

Faith nodded. "I don't know what I would've done without her that first week. I can hardly remember the first few days. I felt so tired—like every bone in my body was exhausted. Just getting out of bed seemed to take everything out of me. And if wasn't for my babies, I'd probably still be in bed."

"Your mother's a strong woman," said France. "She's lived through some tough times, too, hasn't she."

Faith nodded. "And Jimmy, too."

"Your brother loves you very much, Faith. I know it hurt him to lose Caitlin, but I think it hurt him just as much to see how badly you were hurting."

Tears pooled in Faith's eyes. "I've been wanting to tell you this for a while, but the time wasn't right," she whispered. She looked around. "But I can't tell you in here."

"Come outside," said France out loud. "I want you to see those fancy new chickens George got in a trade."

The two women grabbed their shawls and stepped out the back door to walk towards the barn.

"Where are the chickens?" said Faith.

"I just said that as an excuse for us to go outside. Now what did you want to tell me?"

"When Momma was here, she told me that Jimmy and I had the same father—Nantan Lupan."

"What?!"

"Jimmy's *really* my brother," said Faith, smiling.

"He is? And you just found out? Why didn't your mother tell you before now?"

"Long story, but in a nutshell, she was protecting me. My father had such a hard time accepting Jimmy since he was the son of the man that kidnapped Julia and Justin. Momma was afraid Dad would be resentful of me, too, if he knew I was Nantan's daughter."

"And she's been carrying that secret all these years? What made her admit it now?"

"I think she would've carried it to her grave if she and Jimmy hadn't been shot that day in Waco," said Faith. "The shock of it took her back to the day Nantan was killed. She relived that nightmare again, but this time she thought Jimmy was Nantan. Daddy told me on his first visit that Momma was speaking Apache that day on the street. No one understood what she was saying, but Jimmy recognized it."

"Bless her heart—that must have been terrifying for her," said France. "How's your father handling the news?"

"He doesn't know, and he can never know," said Faith. "It would break his heart if it ever got back to him, so could you please keep this to yourself?"

"Your secret's safe with me. And Jimmy's your true brother? You know, now that I think about it, I'm not surprised. You and he are so close." France hugged her. "I'm so glad for you, honey."

"I just had to tell someone," said Faith.

Three men on horseback passed in front of the house heading toward the town square. At first they all looked toward the two women standing beside the fence.

"Keep your eyes straight ahead," one of the men ordered sternly.

But the man in the middle refused to turn his head. He kept staring at the women... at Faith.

France heard a sharp intake of breath from Faith.

"What's the matter?" she asked. "Who's that?"

But Faith kept quiet until the horses passed by.

"Bear," she finally said. "He was the rustler who threw Joseph out of the wagon that day. And he was the one Finn knocked out of the wagon with the shovel."

"Oh, my," said France. "So that was Bear. He's huge! I didn't know what he looked like since George wouldn't let me go to the trial."

"Ethan forbade me to go, too, but even if he'd let me, I probably wouldn't have gone. I didn't recognize the other two men—they must have come to take him to prison. Ethan said the judge sentenced the younger boys to some hard work in their communities, but Bear got prison time—nine years."

"He didn't look too happy. I hope he doesn't know that Finn lives here. And maybe he didn't recognize you."

"He knew me," said Faith.

"Where do you think they're taking him?"

"We first heard it'd be Huntsville, but then the State opened up a new penitentiary last year in Rusk, and it's a bit closer."

"I hope he changes his ways before he gets out. He can still make something of his life. Nine years isn't so long for a young fellow."

"He's an angry man," said Faith. "And anger can destroy a person. It almost destroyed my brother."

"But then God got a hold of him," said France, smiling.

"With Allie's help. But it almost cost him his life."

France's smile faded as she looked back at the house. "Please keep praying for Finn. It breaks my heart that I can't seem to help him."

Sunday, 3rd of May, 1884

Dearest Mercy & Jimmy,

We enjoyed your last letter so much, Mercy. I hope to see your precious children some day, but until then, keep writing us about them. I can picture each of them in my mind. I laughed out loud when I read about you finding Jack asleep on the porch curled up with your dogs and having to check him for fleas.

It sounds like you all are healthy and happy. We are for the most part, but George and I are at wit's end about Finn. We have given him a respectable time to grieve over Caitlin, but I don't think the boy has shed a tear since the day of the accident. He keeps his grief bottled up so tight I'm afraid he may explode one day. And it's affecting his schooling. He's gotten into fights and has been sent home three times now. We also heard from several irate parents that he's acted presumptuous toward their daughters at the dances, and that's not the Finn we know. George thinks his grief has turned to anger, and I'm afraid we're losing our boy over this.

We've been praying for wisdom and continue to covet your prayers for Finn, but we also have a huge request of you. Would it be possible for him to go to Grace and work for you this summer? He thinks the world of you, Jimmy, and maybe a change of scenery and your influence could turn him around. He's still a hard worker and you wouldn't have to pay him anything. We'd be glad to send money, and you could pay his wages with that so he could feel like he's accomplished something worthwhile.

We look forward to your response.

Yours very sincerely,
France & George Samuel

Chapter 50

Jimmy stood on the boardwalk watching the stagecoach pull up to the hotel in Waco. He turned away from the cloud of dust chasing the stage and overtaking it as soon as the horses stopped. Jimmy turned back around and watched the driver climb down and open the door. He wondered if Finn had actually made it to Waco. Jimmy remembered a time in his own life when he tried to run away from his misery and problems. But they managed to follow him.

A businessman in a derby hat stepped off the stage. Jimmy knew Finn was dealing with something he didn't know how to fix. An older couple exited the stage. And like the Samuels, Jimmy didn't know if he could help him either. In his mind he asked God again for wisdom in dealing with Finn.

The top of a cowboy hat appeared at the door as a tall, lanky young man looked down to step off the stage. He looked up and caught Jimmy's eye, and the corner of his mouth turned up.

The boy looked too old to be the Finn he knew.

"Finn?"

The other corner matched it to make a semi-circle on the boy's face, but the smile didn't extend to his eyes. They looked tired.

Jimmy walked over and grabbed him in a bear hug.

"You can't be Finn Samuel!"

Finn nodded.

"Good grief, how could you have grown that much in only five months, kid?" He stood almost eye-to-eye to the boy.

"Momma says she can't keep me in pants," he said. "As soon as she gets a pair made, she says I've already outgrown them."

"But you're only twelve!" teased Jimmy.

241

"I'm fifteen," he said defensively.

"Where does the time go? Come on—let's get your stuff and head to Grace. Do you need anything before we leave?"

Finn shook his head, so they found his bag and followed Jimmy over to a couple of horses tied at the side of the hotel.

"I figured after three days in that rattle box, you'd like a horse between your legs for a while," said Jimmy. "I was hoping you didn't have a trunk with you. That could've posed a problem."

"I'm glad we're riding; I haven't done much of that lately." Finn looked at the horses. "Well, hello, Brave. Haven't seen you in a while."

Finn patted Jimmy's horse before stopping in front of the horse he would ride. "This mare's an unusual color."

"She's called a *grulla*," he said as he tied Finn's bag to the back of the saddle. "Someone told me it means 'crane' in Spanish."

"Yeah, like one of those blue cranes."

"You don't see very many horses that color, though. I'm lucky to have her." He mounted Brave. "She's made a good horse."

"Did you raise her yourself?" asked Finn, following suit.

They started their horses down the street heading west out of town.

"Nah, but I've been training her. This is the horse that got me and my mother shot."

"You're kiddin' me," said Finn. "She's worth that much?"

"No, it was just a lack of communication between a father who sold the horse to me and his son who thought I'd stolen the horse."

"Oh, yeah. I forgot what happened."

"Well, she's going to be your horse this summer. I think you're going to like working with her."

"She rides easy—unlike Boomer. He was so rough, he'd make my teeth clatter."

At the edge of town, they loped their horses in silence for a while as Finn took in the scenery.

"Pretty country," he said when they slowed to a walk. "Back home, Brown County is living up to its name."

"You should see McLennan County after a rain. She doesn't have her best face on right now. The drought's really taking its toll around here, too. But it's in better shape than your stompin' ground."

"What do you want me to do for you this summer?" asked Finn. "Mother said you really needed my help."

Jimmy smiled when he realized how France had talked Finn into coming.

"What?!"

"I tried not to sound so desperate in my letter, but you know your mother," said Jimmy, covering his tracks. "She can read a situation better than anybody I know."

"I know what you mean," said Finn, nodding his head in agreement.

"We're fixin' to work cattle, and I heard you had some experience with that."

"I was a line rider last summer, but I didn't get to do much brandin' or cuttin,' but I can learn. I have to tell you, though, that I don't build fences anymore."

"We've already fenced our land. But there may be times when you'll have to repair a fence, though. Will that be a problem for you?"

Finn worked his jaw as he thought for a moment. "Well, repairing an existing fence and building a new one is two different things. I can fix a fence."

"Glad to hear it. And speaking of fences, did Joseph get the patent on the post-hole digger y'all designed?"

Finn shook his head. "He got a letter from the patent office informing him that a dozen or so men have already applied for patents on similar designs. We thought we'd come up with something nobody else had thought of, but we were wrong."

"Sorry to hear that, but it was a good idea. I hope he keeps designing things."

"He's transferring to Texas A.M.C. in the fall and plans to do just that."

"Good for him."

"Will I have to wrangle the horses every morning?"

"What do you mean?"

"When I was at the line camp, I was the youngest cowboy there, so it was my job to get up at four every morning and bring all the horses up," said Finn. "It was pitch dark and you couldn't see, so they put a bell on the lead horse so I could hear where they were in the horse trap and could go right to 'em. But that old horse got smart after a while and learned to stand still so the bell wouldn't clang, and I'd have to wander all over that pasture before I found 'em."

"Horses are smart," said Jimmy, laughing. "But you won't have to do that here. The horses will come to the barn when they hear me whistling."

Finn's mouth dropped open. "You taught them to come when you called them?"

Jimmy nodded.

"Then can I sleep until five?"

"Sure—we can all sleep until five."

Tonight was Finn's tenth night at Grace. He shared little Jack's bedroom with him, and the boy couldn't have been happier. He had heard about Finn and all the rest of the Samuels in Brownwood for as long as he could remember. And it didn't take long for him to start idolizing the older boy and imitating everything he did.

Finn smiled to see Pony asleep in bed with his old felt hat still on his head. He walked over and took it off and hung it on the bedpost. Then he raised the window sash a little higher in the hopes of coaxing more of a breeze into the room. He sat down on his side of the bed and pulled his boots off. He stripped down to his bare skin and slipped on the nightshirt Mercy had provided for him. At home he slept in nothing during the hot summer months, but that wouldn't be proper as a guest. The thought had occurred to him earlier that if there was a fire, he wouldn't have time to dress, and he didn't want to face that embarrassment.

He glanced at Pony before he blew out the lamp. He realized he was only a little older than Pony when he first met Jimmy. And it didn't take any time at all before he thought Jimmy had hung the moon.

Finn had never seen Jimmy and Mercy's children, but for some reason he felt right at home with them. When it dawned on him that Faith and Ethan's children were about the same age, a wave of longing and sadness drifted over him as he remembered the time spent on the Murray ranch. His thoughts drifted back to Caitlin, and he immediately shook the memories out of his mind and buried them again.

Finn doubted that Jimmy actually needed him as much as his mother said he did. He suspected that his parents had asked Jimmy to straighten him out, but Jimmy had said nary a word about Caitlin since he arrived. Finn had made up his mind to ignore him, too, if Jimmy tried to talk to him about the accident. He had decided that going to Grace was worth the chance that Jimmy might try to fix him because everywhere he looked in Brownwood seemed to remind him of Caitlin—his own house, their barn, their school, their church, Widow Turner's porch, Dr. Hood's house, the Murrays... He thought if he avoided all of that, it wouldn't hurt so badly. He was determined to leave the pain in Brownwood. Out of sight, out of mind, he told himself. Everything would be better in Grace.

His parents had told him that Caitlin's death wasn't his fault and that Ethan and Faith didn't blame him. His mind knew that, but his heart felt otherwise. He beat himself up on a regular basis about it.

At a couple of dances back in Brownwood, he had tried to dull the pain with his friends and their illicitly sequestered bottle of spirits, but that proved to cause more problems—most of which he had no memory of. But he learned later through humiliating confrontations with his parents and angry fathers that alcohol tended to make him overly forward with the girls. He apologized profusely for his bad behavior, but he felt even more remorse that he couldn't remember what he had done or if he had even enjoyed it. He decided from then on that he was finished with alcohol. If he was going to get in trouble for kissing a girl, he for sure wanted to remember it.

She stood there before him, all wide-eyed and innocent. He had waited so long for that moment, and then it felt like he was kissing a post. But he knew she had never been kissed and would need some learning.

"Touch my lips," he told her, and she did.

He felt her hands like fire on his chest and his arms felt the post soften as she leaned into him.

Finn awoke with a start and tried to get his bearings. He lay there breathing as hard as if he had run a race. The impact of her loss slammed into him anew as he remembered again that she was gone.

Katie was gone.

He threw back the bed sheet and pulled the nightshirt over his head. He dressed quickly, but carried his boots so he could creep downstairs as quietly as possible. The door creaked as he slipped outside and sat down on the edge of the porch to put his boots on. Then he headed to the barn.

He lit a lamp and grabbed a rope off a hook and began throwing a loop at a post. Over and over again he threw it until his shirt was damp with sweat.

Jimmy had heard Finn stirring earlier and left him alone. But when he hadn't come back in over an hour, he got worried and decided he had better check on him. He stepped outside and saw the light in the barn. He walked quietly through the cool of the night and stopped at the door.

"Finn?"

The boy jumped at the voice. "I didn't mean to wake you."

"What are you doing?"

"Practicing." He threw another loop and caught the post, pulling it tight.

"You're getting pretty good with that rope."

"Yep." Finn walked over, loosened it and started rolling it up to throw another loop.

Jimmy watched him for a moment.

"You all right?"

"Yep." He threw another loop and missed this time.

"You coming back to bed soon?"

"Yep." He started rolling the rope up to throw another loop.

"We're going to gather the cattle across the river and work the calves tomorrow," said Jimmy, pausing, "and…"

Here it comes. Finn nodded his head and turned away from him. *Here comes the talk.*

"… I'll see you at breakfast."

He turned to see Jimmy walking out of the barn.

Chapter 51

Finn was tired the next morning, but he wasn't about to show it. He threw himself into the work, trying to out-ride and out-work all the Taylors—men and boys alike. He would convince them that his coming here wasn't a case of pity or correcting a wayward boy.

At one point Finn insisted on branding the next calf and attempted to take the branding iron away from Matt's son William. His older brother Tres stepped in and jerked the hot iron away from Finn, burning his left wrist just above the leather glove. Finn let out a noise that sounded like an angry growl and tackled Tres. They rolled around kicking up dust until Jimmy and Matt pulled them apart.

"What in the heck do you think you're doing, Tres?" Matt yelled at his fourteen year old son. "That's no way to treat a friend!"

"Well, he's not acting like a friend!" said Tres. "He's trying to take over everything around here."

"I was just trying to help," said Finn, "but he burned me with the branding iron!"

"I didn't mean to! He took it away from Will, and I just took it back from him."

Jimmy walked Finn away from the vicinity of the fire and turned Finn's hand up to look at the underside of his wrist. The burn was already making a blister.

"Let's go up to the big house, and Mother can put some ointment on it," he said, turning toward his horse.

"But we're not finished here," said Finn, refusing to move.

Jimmy turned around and looked the young man in the face. His pale blue eyes had a fierce look about them.

"Yes, we are," he said slowly and firmly.

Finn had never seen Jimmy angry like that, so he started walking quickly toward his horse. Tres stepped in front of him, and Finn bowed up, ready to defend himself.

But Tres's face showed remorse.

"I'm sorry, Finn. I didn't mean to burn you."

Finn's shoulders slumped. "No—I shouldn't have grabbed it in the first place. I thought I was helping, but I guess I wasn't."

He turned to William. "Sorry, Will."

William nodded and put the iron in the fire again.

"We'll be back after while," Jimmy said to the others.

Jimmy and Finn rode up to the back of Matthew Taylor's house. They found Julia in the kitchen with Vestal.

"Finn accidentally burned his wrist with the branding iron," Jimmy told the women. "Can you doctor it while I go sharpen my knife?"

He started up the stairs.

"He probably misplaced his whetstone again," said Julia. "But he always knows where he can find his father's. Matthew has a certain place for everything. Sit down here, Finn, and let's take a look at your arm."

Finn took off his hat, sat down, and held out his arm. Vestal pulled off his glove and rolled up the sleeve to reveal an ugly burn. He winced when she pressed a damp cloth on it to try to clean it.

"Looks like you've been branded, too. Guess you belong to us now."

Finn couldn't help but grin.

"I have some clean cloths in the wash house we can use to bind his wrist," Vestal said. "I'll be right back."

"Didn't Jimmy show you which end of the branding iron to hold?" Julia teased.

Finn nodded, but his face turned red. He hoped he wouldn't have to confess to what really happened.

He watched her place a thick, green piece of aloe vera on the table and hold it down with her withered hand so she could use her right hand to peel back the skin with a knife. He looked away from the deformed hand, thinking it rude to stare.

Julia noticed his reaction.

"It's all right to look," she said. "It doesn't bother me anymore."

Finn looked at her face before looking at her hand again. "Katie told me an Indian did that to you."

Julia nodded.

"Do you hate him for what he did?"

Julia shook her head, no. "I've learned that anger and bitterness can eat away at you like a disease. You have to focus on the good in life and not the bad."

"Were you scared when you lived with the Indians?"

"At times—especially in the beginning when I didn't know what would happen to me and Justin. But I learned to depend on God to help us get through it."

She held up the oozing leaf, and Finn looked away.

"This is going to hurt, but it'll make it better." She lightly brushed the ointment onto the burn.

He didn't even flinch this time when she touched it. And when he spoke, it was barely a whisper... as if he were afraid to hear the words himself.

"But why did God let it happen?"

"I don't know, Finn. But I can tell you this: I wouldn't have Jimmy and Faith today if I hadn't been kidnapped. And if that was the only way to get them, I would do it again in a heartbeat."

"But something good doesn't always come from something bad happening," he said.

Julia realized he was talking about Caitlin's accident. She sat down beside him.

"There's a verse in the Bible that I quote when I'm going through a tough time in my life," she said. "It says, *and we know that all things work together for good to them that love God, to them who are the called according to his purpose.* God can turn ashes into beauty if we'll let him. He's done that many times in my life, but I've had to let go and trust Him."

"He could've saved her," he said. "Why didn't he?"

"Finn, there have been times of loss in my life that were so unbearable that all I could do was cry out to God and hang onto Him for dear life, because I wasn't going to survive otherwise. I was almost killed the day my hand was crushed, but that wasn't as devastating to me as seeing Jimmy shot or losing my precious Katie. I have no explanation for those circumstances except that we live in a fallen world with a fallen humanity. We make mistakes. Tragedies happen. We experience loss. We fail. And those things will destroy us if we can't rise above the pain. And all of us experience these things at one time or other in our lives."

Finn touched his chest. "I feel like my heart's been torn out of my chest."

"I know how you felt about her, honey. I saw the heart you carved for her."

His chest started to constrict. "You figured it out?"

Julia nodded.

"Did you know she could outrun every boy in her school?" he asked, trying to catch his breath.

Julia nodded as her heart broke for him.

Finn swallowed hard, grabbing at any humorous thought about her to try to maintain control. "Did you know she made the worst coffee?"

Julia smiled and shook her head as the tears spilled from her eyes. She put her arm around him.

"She was so pretty," he choked on the words, "even in boys' pants."

Finn suddenly realized his grief had surfaced, raw and exposed. He stood up to get away from Julia, to get away from this conversation. But she stood with him and wouldn't let go. He backed up against the wall, looking like a trapped animal.

"No, Finn," she said, holding on even tighter. "We're going to get through this together."

He slid down the wall covering his face as he sobbed, ashamed for her to see the tears pouring from his eyes uncontrollably.

Julia held him until he quieted. She had no idea how long they sat on the floor. She finally looked up and saw Jimmy sitting in the stairwell and realized he had been listening and grieving along with them.

Julia began to rub Finn's back.

"I'm so tired of hurting," he said.

"I know."

"All this time I thought I had to be strong; that if I let go and let myself feel the pain, it would destroy me. But I'm too tired to fight it anymore."

"You don't have to fight it, Finn. It's too big of a burden for you to have to carry, honey. You have to give it to God."

Finn nodded. "I've heard that before, but I don't know how."

"Just ask Him to carry it for you—to carry you, too, if need be."

"All right." Finn took a deep breath and whispered three words: "*Help me, God.*"

He looked at Julia. "Will that work?"

Julia smiled and nodded her head. "He knows what you're asking. Now let me ask you this. Would you rather have not known and loved Katie just to avoid going through this pain?"

Finn was quiet for a moment and then shook his head. "No, I'm glad I knew her. I'm glad I loved her."

"Then that's what you focus on, sweetheart. Be grateful that you had the chance to know her and love her—that the time you had together was worth what you're going through now, even as painful as it is. Katie was worth knowing and loving."

"I hadn't thought about it that way."

"And you know Jesus, don't you?"

Finn nodded.

"So you know we'll see her again some day."

He stood up and helped Julia stand. "Everybody's told me that since it happened, but I missed her so much that it just made me angry to hear it."

"It'll be a comfort to you some day, though," said Julia. "Trust me. You just haven't allowed yourself to grieve."

"Wonder what's taking Jimmy so long?" said Finn, looking toward the stairs.

Julia looked, too, but Jimmy had disappeared.

Vestal came in the door wiping her nose on one of the cloths she had in her hands. She wrapped a clean cloth around Finn's wrist, acting oblivious to what had just taken place in the kitchen. But Julia knew she must have been standing on the porch listening.

Jimmy came stomping down the stairs at that moment and told Finn they had cattle to tend to. He headed out the back door.

"Thanks for takin' care of my wound," he said to the two women. Finn donned his hat and glanced at Julia. "It feels much better now."

They watched him walk out the door and strike a trot across the porch to follow Jimmy.

Vestal reached over and touched Julia's withered hand.

"For a long time, Julia, I honestly couldn't tell you how anything good could've come from this withered hand of yours," she said. "But this isn't the first time I've seen God use it to help someone."

Chapter 52

Three days had passed since Finn and Tres wrestled over the branding iron.

"What's happened to him?" Matt asked Jimmy.

They watched Finn actually laughing at a not-so-funny joke Will had told.

"Mother," said Jimmy.

"That explains it."

"I thought France was sending Finn over here for me to help him, but every time I thought I ought to try and talk to him, my mind went blank. So I just shut up."

"I think that must've been God's doing," said Matt, grinning. "Maybe you'd do more harm than good."

Jimmy slapped his hat at him. "Thanks, brother."

"Nah, I think he just wasn't ready to listen. But he's been watching you, Jimmy. Don't underestimate your influence on him."

"He's starting to act like the old Finn I know. The boy's going to make something of himself, Matt. He knows how to work hard, and he's got a good head on his shoulders. This grief over Caitlin blindsided him for a while, but he's starting to see his way again."

"I hope Sis and Ethan can get through this."

"They will, Matt, with God's help… and time. And when it's time for Finn to go back to Brownwood, I think I'll go back with him to see how they're doing."

Friday, August 22nd, 1884

Faith hung the last bed sheet on the line and let the breeze blow the damp cloth into her face. She breathed in the cool, clean air. She glanced at the house and wondered if hanging wet clothes in the open windows of her house would cool it off, too. She looked up at the sky. No cloud in sight. Again. The drought still hung on. She wondered how long they could hang on.

Ethan had come in for the noon meal and left again to ride the fence line and check the windmills. Faith thought he seemed to look for reasons to stay away from the house. Her workdays were hard and monotonous. If it weren't for going to town one Saturday a month and most Sundays, Faith thought she would lose her mind.

She walked back into the quiet house. The children were napping. She looked at the basket of green beans and squash on the table. The only reason she had a garden crop this year was that she used a wheel barrow to haul water from the windmill tank by the barn every other day. Her cellar was filling up in spite of the drought.

After staring at them long and hard, Faith decided those beans weren't going to snap themselves, so she picked up the basket and walked toward the open front door where she knew there would be some shade for a little while longer.

She stopped in her tracks when she saw the shadow of a big man appear on the front porch.

She dropped the basket when she saw Bear fill the door frame.

Saturday, August 23rd, 1884

Jimmy rode his horse up to the Samuels' barn just after sunset. Finn rode the grulla mare right up to the back porch of his home and patted her neck before he hollered out to the house. He climbed out of the saddle as his mother hit the kitchen door at a run. She ran down the steps and threw her arms around her son's neck.

"You're already here!!" said France. "We didn't expect to see you until Tuesday on the stage."

"You're choking me, Mother," Finn felt obligated to say, but he loved how she loved on him.

George and the rest of his family piled out of the house and gathered around him.

France finally let go of him so his father could shake his hand. Finn let his younger brother Mac hold the reins of his horse while he greeted the rest of his brothers and sisters.

"You look good, Finn," France said to him and then turned to her husband. "I think he's gotten even taller, George! And I think he's put on some weight, too." She pinched his gut.

"It's muscle, Momma," said Finn.

"Well, come into the house so we can get a better look at you," she insisted.

"I have to put up my horse first."

"Your horse?!"

"Yeah, isn't she a beaut?" he said, stepping back so everyone could see her. "She's called a grulla because of her color. Jimmy gave her to me for helping him this summer."

"You mean you rode this horse all the way back to Brownwood by yourself?!" said France, getting her dander up. "What in the world was Jimmy thinking?!"

"I was thinking he could handle it just fine," said Jimmy, who had walked up behind her. "Hello, Samuels."

After another round of screams and hugs, France and the girls escorted Jimmy and George into the house. Finn's three brothers hovered around him like gnats and followed him to the barn to watch him put up his horse and to question him about his summer in Grace.

George and Jimmy went to the dining table to sit and visit while France added some wood to the cook stove so they could heat up the stew left over from supper to feed the hungry travelers. The cornbread was long gone, but there were still some cold biscuits from breakfast. Zane took two bowls from the cupboard, and Emma poured two glasses of milk.

Finn and his brothers came in just as France was filling the bowls at the stove. The others went on to the dining room, but Finn grabbed a spoon and stood beside his mother eyeing the stew.

France thought he looked something akin to a vulture at that moment. "You hungry, sweetie?"

"I'm starving," he said, grabbing a bowl from her and digging into it as he stood there.

"Well, did you leave your manners in the barn, too?" she scolded him. "I still need to heat up the biscuits."

"Nah, they're good cold," he said, grabbing three with his big right hand.

France noticed how rusty-looking it was.

"Did you remember to wash up, son?"

Finn stopped in mid-bite. "Dang," he said under his breath. He set the bowl down, stuffed a biscuit in his mouth and walked over to the sink to pump water into the basin bowl.

George and Jimmy chuckled as they listened to France's scolding.

"And what about you, Jimmy?!" Her voice drifted in from the kitchen like an unwelcome yellow jacket.

The grin faded as he looked down at his own grimy hands.

"Dang," said Jimmy under his breath. He scooted his chair away from the table and walked sheepishly into the kitchen to stand in line behind Finn.

France couldn't help but laugh. She and daughter Jenna carried the food to the table and everyone gathered around to visit with Jimmy and Finn.

After a good two hours of talking and laughter, France sent the kids off to bed. They groaned for their parents' benefit, but France knew they would probably kidnap Finn and sneak him upstairs to Zane and Emma's room to talk some more. And that was all right with her. Finn was finally home, and as much as her children fussed and fought with each other, they loved each other even more.

But she and George were anxious to talk to Jimmy alone.

Jimmy asked how Joseph was, and George told him he was doing fine and that he had left for College Station at the end of June, hoping to find a job and earn some money before the fall term started.

"That's an unusual-looking horse you gave Finn," said France.

"Would you believe she's the horse my mother and I were shot over?"

"Oh my," said France. "And you're letting her go?"

"She's made a good cow horse, but Mercy says she gets sad every time she sees her because it reminds her of that day. The grulla's bred, though, and I'd like to pick up the foal after its weaned, if that's all right with y'all."

"Sure, Jimmy, but you know you didn't have to give Finn a horse," said George. "We told you we would pay his wages."

Jimmy shook his head. "Finn earned that horse this summer. He's a quick learner, and he pulled his weight and more. I'd hire him full time if he was available. You oughta be proud of him."

"We are, and we appreciate you bringing him home."

"My pleasure; and I thought I ought to check on my sister and Ethan, too. It's been seven months since I was here."

"Finn seems like his old self, thank the Lord," said France. "How'd you do it?"

"All I did was work him hard. My mother was doctoring his arm one day and—"

"What happened to his arm?"

"France, let him talk," said George.

255

"He just singed it on the branding iron—it's fine now, although he's got a nice scar to impress the girls—"

"What?!"

George reached over and patted his wife's hand, and she hushed while Jimmy continued.

"And Finn saw Momma's bad hand and asked her about it and before too long, the conversation shifted to Caitlin. Finn must've cried a bucket of tears before it was over."

"Ah, my poor baby," said France. "I should've been there for him."

"No, Finn was in good hands," said George. "God answered our prayers how He saw fit, and we just need to be grateful for it."

"He still may have to work through a few things," said Jimmy. "He told me he won't dig another posthole. He and Katie dug so many together, I guess it's still too hard for him deal with that."

"Why didn't y'all stop by Ethan's today and come on in to church with them tomorrow?" asked France. "That would've saved you ten miles of riding today."

"I felt like that needed to be Finn's decision, not mine," said Jimmy. "Let's see how it goes tomorrow."

Chapter 53

Jimmy went to church with the Samuels Sunday morning. He waited outside under a shade tree for his sister and Ethan, looking forward to seeing the shock on his sister's face when she saw him. He stayed out there ten minutes into the worship service, but they didn't come. He finally went inside.

"Maybe one of the kids is sick," whispered France to him.

Jimmy nodded, trying to hide his disappointment. "I'll leave right after the service."

After church Jimmy said his goodbyes to the Samuel family, saying he would head back to Grace from the ranch in a day or two. He was surprised when Finn asked if he could ride out there with him. Jimmy acted nonchalant about it, but France had to turn away to hide her tears.

"I'll be back later," Finn told his parents.

When Jimmy and Finn came up to the entrance to the Murray's ranch, Finn climbed off his horse to open the gate. He stood there for a moment and took a deep breath and let it out slowly.

Jimmy could see the struggle in his face.

"I know this is hard for you, but you're doing the right thing."

Finn nodded and swallowed. He pulled off his hat and mopped his brow with his shirt sleeve before opening the gate for Jimmy to walk the horses through. Finn mounted his horse, and they walked slowly down the road toward the ranch house.

When they came to the curve in the road, a big bull lay under the shade of a scrubby tree.

"The old boy doesn't look half-bad for a drought," said Jimmy. "I helped Ethan brand them before I left the last time. Go take a look." Jimmy knew Finn hadn't seen the brand yet.

Finn walked his horse up closer so the bull would get up. When he recognized the brand, he leaned his head back and chuckled, wiping a few stray tears that slipped down his dusty face.

"What do you think about that, Finn?"

"I don't believe it," he answered. "Katie designed a heart brand with an 'M' in the middle of it, but Ethan told her his bulls and steers wouldn't be caught dead running around the countryside with hearts on their rumps."

"Ethan said you were the one that designed this one."

Finn smiled. "I never would've thought he'd turn that into a brand, but maybe that means he's forgiven me."

"Of course he has."

"And Katie got her way after all."

"Come on, let's go to the house."

"Would you mind going on ahead? I need to go visit her first."

"You want me to go with you?"

Finn shook his head. "Tell Ethan and Faith I'll be along shortly."

Jimmy watched him take off in a lope towards the south windmill pasture.

Finn passed a scrubby stand of trees and saw the big tree that Ethan had pointed out to him before Christmas where the family plot would be. He could see the back of a man digging a hole with a shovel. He could see more piles of dirt where several other holes had been dug.

What's Ethan doing? He asked himself.

Finn rode his horse up close and dismounted, tying his horse to a sturdy shrub. He took a deep breath before turning around to face Ethan. The man straightened up to his full height and turned around, but it wasn't Ethan. This man was way too big to be Ethan.

Finn's heart caught in his throat when he recognized him.

But this time Bear was holding the shovel, not Finn.

Jimmy rode into the Murrays' barn and dismounted. He started to unsaddle his horse, but decided he needed to go visit Caitlin's grave, too… after he got some food in him. He led Brave to the water trough and let him drink and then tied the reins to a post.

He walked across the dusty yard toward the house. It was quiet, but then he realized it was well after the noon meal, and the children were probably napping. Maybe Ethan and Faith were taking advantage of their day of rest, too, he thought. He could use a good nap himself.

He stepped onto the porch and up to the door. He started to knock, but then he was afraid he might wake up the little ones. He turned the doorknob and stepped inside, waiting to let his eyes get used to the dim light.

He could smell whatever Faith had cooked for lunch and realized how hungry he was. He walked quietly across the room to the cook stove to scrounge around for something to eat.

But he froze when he heard the click of a cocked gun behind him.

"Put your hands where I can see 'em," a low voice demanded from the bedroom door.

Jimmy immediately raised his arms. "Ethan? Is that you?" he said, slowly turning his head.

"Jimmy?! What do you think you're doing sneaking in here like that?! I could've shot you!!" said Ethan, stepping into the room.

"I was hungry, and I didn't want to wake you up!"

Faith almost ran over her husband getting to her brother.

The look on her face didn't disappoint him. He laughed as he caught her.

"What are you doing here?" she asked, putting her hands on his face, not quite believing her eyes. And she couldn't keep from smiling; it felt like sunshine had walked into the house.

"I brought Finn home. Now what's there to eat around here?"

"Sit down, and I'll fix you something," said Faith. "You want it hot or cold?"

"Cold's quicker."

"Fix us some coffee, too," said Ethan, pulling up a chair.

"I didn't mean to disturb your nap," said Jimmy, sitting down across the table from him.

"We slept long enough."

"What's the news from Grace? How's everybody doing?" asked Faith.

"They're all fine, and they said to tell you hello and that you're still in their hearts and that they love you and all that stuff," said Jimmy. "I think that was everything I was supposed to tell you."

"Such a compassionate messenger," said Faith, setting a plate of food in front of him.

"Thanks," he said as he dug in. "You got some bread?"

"Your stomach rules you," she said. "I hope you remember what happened to Esau giving away his birthright for a meal."

"Yeah, and oh, I forgot—I have letters to you from Mother and Mercy," he said, "but they're in my saddlebag."

"Jimmy!" said Faith exasperatedly. But she was elated to have her brother here. The mood of their house had completely changed in a matter of minutes.

"How's Finn doing?" she asked. "We've been so worried about him."

"He'll be all right, although he told me he's through with fence building."

"That's understandable," said Ethan. "I've been struggling with that myself."

"I wonder when he'll be ready to talk to us again," she said.

"Sooner than you realize. He came with me today."

"Out here?" said Ethan. "He's actually here?"

Jimmy nodded. "He's been blaming himself all this time for the accident, even though we've told him it wasn't his fault. But he was afraid you blamed him, too, and he feels like he let you down."

"Oh, Finn," Ethan said under his breath, looking down and shaking his head. "We've all been whipping ourselves over this for too long now, and Katie would never have wanted that." He looked up at Jimmy. "Is he in the barn? I want to go talk to him."

"He'll be here shortly—he told me he wanted to go see Caitlin first," said Jimmy.

Faith's eyes widened as she looked at her husband. "Oh, Ethan," she said as she remembered. "Finn's running right into Bear."

Chapter 54

Jimmy couldn't believe what he just heard. "Bear?! That cattle rustler's here?"

Ethan stood up and told Jimmy to come with him—that he would explain on the way. They ran out the door towards the barn.

"Did he break out of prison? What's that thief doing here?"

"A few weeks after they'd taken Bear to Rusk, he ended up saving the warden's life somehow. The warden just happened to be good friends of the governor, so Bear got pardoned last month and headed home."

"Why did he come here? Did he threaten you? Did he bother Faith?"

"No, although he scared her to death when he walked up on the porch yesterday." Ethan stepped into the horse pen to get Crazy Ears. "He says he just wanted to offer his condolences for our loss. I guess he heard about what happened to Katie while he was in the Brownwood jail. My wife must've made quite an impression on him the day y'all caught him."

"Yeah, I fussed at her for talking to him."

"Well, he told Faith that they had a library at that prison and a chaplain and even classes for prisoners to get an education, although he was only there about five months," Ethan explained as he saddled his horse. "He swore he's a changed man and wanted to make up for the trouble he caused since he didn't serve his full term. I figured it was just another one of those jailhouse conversions so he could get out earlier; either that or he just wanted an excuse to see my wife. But I have to admit he's nothin' like I remember him. He asked if he could do any work for us. I didn't want him to ride the fence because part of me doesn't completely trust him around our cattle yet, but Faith insisted we find something for him to do to help him clear his conscience. I'd bought some fancy wrought iron fencing a couple of months

261

ago to put around our plot. But I just haven't had the heart to start the job, much less finish it, so Faith suggested that Bear do that for us."

Ethan finished saddling Crazy, tightened the cinch and pulled the left stirrup down in place before he mounted the horse. Jimmy was already at the barn door with Brave chomping at the bit. The horse sensed that something was up, and he knew they were fixing to go somewhere fast.

"Bear's been over there working on that fence for us, and I honestly don't know if he's changed enough to forgive Finn for knocking him out of the wagon that day, or if he'd just whup the boy on sight. I don't know if he'll be too happy to see you, either, Jim."

"We'd better get there quick because Finn wasn't wasting any time getting over there himself," said Jimmy as he lit out of the barn, leaving Ethan in his wake. He lifted up a prayer for Finn's safety.

In a matter of minutes, Jimmy pulled up in a dry wash about a hundred yards away from the gravesite to let Ethan catch up to him.

"Now you let me handle this," Ethan said sternly, hoping to avoid a fight.

"Ethan, if he's hurt Finn in any way, I'm gonna have to hurt him back," said Jimmy.

They dismounted and stayed out of sight as they made their way towards the big oak tree. About fifty yards out, Ethan put a hand in front of Jimmy to stop him. The scene before Ethan was more than he could take, and he turned around to hide his tears.

But Jimmy kept looking, not quite believing what he saw.

Bear and Finn stood there working side-by-side… putting up that fence for Caitlin.

"Now, if that ain't a miracle, I don't know what is," Jimmy said quietly as he started to walk forward.

But Ethan stopped him again.

"Leave 'em be," he whispered, "and let 'em come back to the house when they're finished."

Jimmy nodded, and they both stood there for a moment longer watching Finn and Bear work together.

Ethan realized that much more than a fence was being built.

"She did it again, Jimmy," said Ethan thoughtfully.

"What's that?"

"Katie reconciled another conflict for us, didn't she," said Ethan as he turned to go. "Faith isn't gonna believe this."

"Yeah, she will." Then under his breath he whispered, "Thank you, Lord."

Chapter 55

Waco, September 22, 1884

Julia knew it was close to getting up time as she drifted in and out of sleep. She felt something crawl into bed beside her, and smiled when she recognized Caitlin snuggling up close. Julia wrapped her arms around her and hugged her tight, and asked if they were going rock hunting together later. Caitlyn leaned back and smiled apologetically as she shook her head, no.

With a jolt, Julia remembered why. She began to weep as she held on tight to her granddaughter.

"We miss you so much, little girl," said Julia. "It's been so hard for us."

"I'm all right, Meemaw," said Caitlin, "and I'm happy, so I don't want y'all to be sad. And you know what?"

"What?"

"My mother's beautiful. She reminds me of you, but younger like Mercy."

Julia smiled questioningly, but then realized Caitlin was referring to her deceased mother. "I hope to meet her someday."

"But don't tell Momma," said Caitlin. "I don't want to hurt her feelings."

"Faith will understand, and she'd be happy for you."

"And there's something else I need to show you." She stood up and pulled Julia out of bed.

Caitlin led her out of the room, down the stairs and out the back of the house. They walked past the barn and down the road toward the river. They held onto each other as they climbed down the steep embankment and past the big rock overlooking the swimming hole. Caitlin stopped at the river's

264

edge. The drought had drawn the water down so shallow that a little child could wade across at that point.

Caitlin stepped into the river and when Julia started to follow, she stopped her.

"You can't come with me now, Meemaw."

"Then why did you bring me here?" Julia asked.

Caitlin turned and looked across the river. Julia's eyes followed her gaze, and she gasped when she saw a man standing there. The tears began to fall as she recognized him.

Nantan Lupan raised his hand and smiled.

Julia looked beyond him to see a young woman and a little boy. Her eyes widened when she realized who they were, and her right hand went to her mouth to stop the sobs that threatened to overtake her.

"I thought you'd be happy," said Caitlin, touching her arm with concern.

Julia smiled through her tears. "I am, sweetie. I just didn't expect to see them."

She looked across at Nantan and slowly raised her hand in greeting.

He didn't say anything, but somehow she knew he was asking her something.

"Yes," she whispered, nodding her head. "Yes!" she said aloud.

Then suddenly, Caitlin was standing beside him on the other side.

"Love you, Meemaw!" she said as they turned to leave.

"No, Katie! Please don't go!" Julia said as she stepped into the river to follow.

But immediately Julia found herself back in bed, sobbing. She buried her face in her pillow to keep from waking Matthew. She came up for air after a moment and realized that her husband wasn't in bed. He had already risen and left the room.

Julia took a deep breath and let it out slowly. She thought about her dream and how real it seemed to her. She shut her eyes and remembered talking to Caitlin and how it felt to hold her. Then she remembered the river… and Nantan.

Julia sat straight up in bed. She had to talk to Nah-kay. She dressed quickly and wrote a short note saying where she would be and left it on the night table. She didn't dare leave without telling someone, not after the heartbreak of her and Justin's disappearance all those years ago. But that didn't mean she couldn't slip out the front of the house to avoid seeing anyone.

The sun hadn't risen yet, but she could see the road clearly in the gray light before dawn as she walked down toward the river. She enjoyed the cool of the morning, knowing that it would soon be replaced with the scorching heat of the day in a few short hours.

Just before she reached the path that led down to the big rock, Julia turned left and walked adjacent to the river towards a small, one-room house built on the rise above the spring where Nah-kay's teepee had previously sat.

She smiled when she saw the smoke drifting up from the old woman's fire out front. She figured Nah-kay must have been around seventy years old, and yet Julia knew no one at any age who worked harder than Nah-kay.

"Ah! Jew-ya!" said Nah-kay, stepping out from the house. "'Mornin'!"

"Good morning, to you, Nah-kay," Julia said, returning the greeting. "How are you, my friend?" She walked over and hugged her.

"Good!"

"Can we talk?" Julia asked, touching her lips.

"Hungry?" Nah-kay pointed to a bowl of cornmeal batter.

Julia shook her head, no. "Talk. Words—speak?"

Nah-kay nodded her head and walked over to the fire and sat down on a blanket. She motioned for Julia to come sit down beside her.

"I really need Jimmy here," said Julia. "I don't think I can make you understand what I need to talk to you about."

Castro stepped out of the house, and he nodded to Julia when she spoke to him. Nah-kay said something to him, and he left immediately, walking toward Jimmy's house, which was less than a half a mile away.

Julia looked at Nah-kay. "You understood me?"

"Castro get Jimmy," she said, setting an iron skillet on the fire and placing the bowl of cornmeal batter between them. "Good corn …crop. Hungry?" she asked again.

Julia smiled and nodded as she scooped up some cornmeal to form into a patty.

A little while later, Jimmy came running up to the two women.

"Are you all right, Momma?" he asked, trying to catch his breath.

"Yes, sweetie. I didn't mean to alarm you. What did Castro tell you?"

"He said you'd been crying. What's wrong?"

Julia's hands went to her eyes. "How did he know that? Do I look like I've been crying?" she asked Nah-kay. "Are my eyes puffy?"

Nah-kay just smiled and held out a couple of corn cakes to Jimmy. "Hungry?"

He grabbed them and sat down beside her. "Thanks, Grandma."

After his sixth corn cake, he reached for another, but Julia lightly slapped his hand.

"Leave some for Castro. And I still don't understand how he knew I'd been crying."

Nah-kay reached over and patted her thigh.

"Oh," said Julia, looking at Nah-kay. "I should've known. No one can put anything past you."

"Castro said you needed me," said Jimmy. "What's the matter?"

"I need to talk to Nah-kay. I need to ask her about Nantan Lupan— about the day he died."

Nah-kay perked up at the mention of her son.

Jimmy had made an effort over the past nine years to learn his grandmother's language. In return, Nah-kay had made an effort to learn a little English. Julia remembered some of the Apache language, but she wasn't sure how to bring up the difficult subject of her son's death.

Nah-kay said something to Jimmy.

"She said that was the first time she's heard you mention his name since she's lived here," he told his mother.

"I guess it is."

"Why now?" Jimmy asked.

"I had a dream, and it seemed so real."

"Tell me about it."

"It was early this morning," she said. "Caitlin climbed into bed with me. It seemed so real. I can still feel myself holding her."

"That must've been hard."

"It felt so normal, so good... until I remembered," said Julia. "Then she told me she had something to show me, and she took me to the river. I was shocked to see Nantan standing on the other side, and behind him were his wife and little boy."

"Oh, mother..."

Tears welled in her eyes again. "I didn't realize it until now, but that's where he first saw your brother and me before he took us. But this time Nantan smiled—he seemed happy. He didn't say anything, but I felt like he was asking my forgiveness."

"It was just a dream, Mother, why do you want to talk to Nah-kay about it?"

"But if my mind was creating the dream, why did it take me by surprise? Why didn't I know he was going to be in it?" said Julia. "Caitlin turned to go with him... like they were together. How would she know about him?"

"Your thoughts and memories put them together, not Caitlin."

"But what if it wasn't just a dream," said Julia. "Nantan knew he wouldn't live to see you grow up. How did he know that?"

"He probably knew your husband would track him down eventually. I certainly would have if he had taken my wife and son."

"Nantan yelled something just before he was shot—I don't know what he said; everything was so chaotic," said Julia. "Ask Nah-kay if she remembers what he said."

Jimmy asked her if she heard what Nantan said before he died.

Nah-kay shook her head, no.

Julia was disappointed. She thought she would learn something that would ease her mind—something that would explain her dream.

"Tell her I'm sorry for what happened to Nantan Lupan," said Julia. "I never had the chance to tell her before we left, and I haven't let myself think about it since she came to live with us."

"He was your kidnapper, Mother!" said Jimmy.

"He was her son and your father. He lived his life the only way he knew how."

Nah-kay spoke up. "Nantan no God."

"What?" Julia asked.

Nah-kay looked at Jimmy. "Nantan see God?" she said questioningly as she groped for the right words.

"You mean, Nantan knew God? He believed in God?" asked Jimmy.

Nah-kay nodded and began to hum.

Julia smiled and then started humming the tune to *Amazing Grace* along with her.

"All right, tell me what's going on," Jimmy said to them both.

Nah-kay said something in her language.

Jimmy turned to his mother. "She said he told her he believed because he saw God in you."

"He did?" said Julia in little more than a whisper, overwhelmed with the news. Then she leaned over and hugged Nah-kay.

"All this time, and I never knew for sure," said Julia. She turned to her son. "Do you realize you're going to meet your father some day?"

Jimmy smiled.

"But don't tell your father," she said.

"Now that would confuse most folks," he said. "But I know what you're saying, Momma."

Castro came walking up to the campfire and sat down as Nah-kay handed him some corncakes. Jimmy patted him on the back as he stood up.

"I left you a few," he told the old man.

"Thanks to me!" said Julia, lifting her right hand to her son.

He helped her to her feet. "Well, let me walk you home."

"No, I can get home just fine. I appreciate you coming over here to help me talk to Nah-kay. I can't tell you what it means for me to learn this about your father. Please make her understand that."

Jimmy talked to his grandmother for a moment, and then he and his mother said their goodbyes to Nah-kay and Castro and started walking their separate ways.

Julia stopped and turned around. "On second thought, Jimmy, I would love for you to walk me home."

He trotted up beside her and she took his arm.

"I know now that all the hardship we went through those six years wasn't in vain, if that makes any sense," she said. "Sometimes difficult things happen in life that we never get to understand why, and we just have to trust God during those times. But in this case I'm so grateful He allowed me to see that something good came out of something bad."

"Like me and Faith."

Julia chuckled and nodded. "Especially you and Faith."

They walked alongside the riverbank until they came to the rise over the big rock.

Julia paused for a moment, recalling her dream as she looked across the river.

"He's at peace now, Momma. And I think you're right—Katie's bound to be with him. He happens to be one of her grandfathers, you know."

"I hadn't thought about that, but you're right!"

They stood there for a moment looking across the river.

"Love you, Katie," Julia whispered.

She shut her eyes, and a smile spread across her face when she heard her voice whisper back, "*Love you more.*"

Author's Note

I love the happily ever after stories, but life isn't necessarily that way. One of the sources for this story was fictional—going back to Julia Taylor's original kidnapping, which eventually involved the death of her kidnapper, Nantan Lupan. I didn't know this character well enough to regret his demise since he had caused so much heartache for the Taylor family. But as I started writing the story, I discovered his life was worth saving, too, and mourned his passing. I also knew that a main character—someone I had become very attached to—would die in this story. I haven't lost someone that close to me in real life, and just trying to imagine that kind of loss in order to write the story was so difficult. But that is nothing compared to those who have experienced that loss firsthand.

The seed for that storyline was planted when my cousins, Rick and Terri Beights, lost their son Cliff in a tragic accident in 2006. In August of 2007, I was sixty pages away from finishing *Torn Asunder* when another cousin (and Rick's sister) Marsha and her husband Bruce Dockery lost their son Brad in another heartbreaking accident. He had only been married a few months.

My mother called me after the second funeral and said that Rick had told her that he had asked God for a sign to let him know that Cliff was okay and in His care. Somehow before my mother told me what that sign was, I knew what she was going to say... a white feather.

I had used the symbol of the white feather three times in this fictional story, so I believe that Rick's experience with a white feather was no coincidence. I wasn't quite sure what God was doing, so I set the story aside for four months to make sure I should continue this storyline. I eventually felt a peace about it so I began writing again around Christmas and finished the book soon after.

I asked Rick in a letter if I could share his story, and he said, *"Part of the healing process for me is to talk about Cliff and let others know how special he was to Terri and me. It has been almost two years, and it still seems like last week.*

"The day I received a sign from God was a day like almost every day since we lost Cliff. We were sad and depressed and missing him terribly. That day was his birthday, and the emotions were much stronger. Sometime in the morning I had gone outside to be alone to cry and pray. For grief this strong, prayer and God's help is the only thing that can help you. As I was praying, memories of Cliff were running through my mind. I

remembered the things he thought were amusing, his sense of humor, his love of Texas Tech and college life. I remembered the movies he liked so I prayed to God to send me a feather like on Forrest Gump, just to know Cliff was okay and in His care. We were going to the cemetery later in the day, and I needed God to give me strength. During the day I looked for my feather around the house, in the yard, watching the sky. When we got to the cemetery I looked all over for my sign, but there was still nothing. Just before we left, we stood over the grave and prayed. When I opened my eyes, the first thing I saw through my tears was a small, white feather. I had my reassurance that Cliff was in God's hands."

Both Cliff and Brad were exceptional young men. Both were taken early in their lives. Both knew and loved the Lord, and their families know they will see them again, but their hearts will grieve their loss for the rest of their lives.

God uses friends and family to be there for those hurting. We shouldn't look away and avoid those who have experienced loss. We all will walk in those same shoes some day. And like Caitlin in the story, we should leave nothing unsaid between us and our loved ones. What we share at funerals should be a retelling of what's already been said.

Death is the most difficult tearing asunder in life, but this story touches on several other ways that can also rend the heart, including geographical distance, illness, financial burdens, anger, and broken relationships. But the good news is that God is the great healer of hearts and restorer of relationships if we'll let go and let Him do his work in our lives.

Although God used a unique sign in Rick's life, we need to be aware that God treats us as individuals and works in unique ways. With some He may speak in a roaring wind; with others it may be a still, small voice, or any one of countless other ways including… a white feather. And if God knows even when a sparrow falls, think of how much more He knows and values each of us. Realizing that kind of love for us by what He allowed his Son to go through on the cross to reconcile mankind to Himself continues to astound me.

As Ira Stanphill wrote in one of my parents' favorite songs:
Many things about tomorrow, I don't seem to understand.
But I know who holds tomorrow, and I know who holds my hand.

And that's what I hang onto.

dvc

Printed in the United States
139256LV00002B/6/P

9 780978 793784